THE ASSET

A LANCE SPECTOR THRILLER
BOOK 1

SAUL HERZOG

AUTHORCONTACT

1

S ofia Ivanova looked out over the vast tundra with a feeling of foreboding. In those parts, the locals had a saying—the better the vehicle, the farther you had to walk back when it failed. The permafrost was unforgiving at the best of times. Now that it was thawing, it was downright treacherous.

She was at the head of a convoy of eight Russian-made, all-terrain six-wheelers. They'd been plowing through the endless Siberian waste in a straight line due east for six days.

Seven of the vehicles carried fuel, supplies, and laboratory equipment. The eighth held the tools and parts necessary to equip the entire convoy with heavy-duty caterpillar tracks. That hadn't been necessary, yet.

Just a few years ago, this ground was frozen solid and had been for thousands of years. That was changing.

She leaned her forehead against the window.

The president had called her personally the night before they set out. It was meant as a show of support, but it only added to her unease. No one, whatever they said, wanted a call from the Kremlin. She felt like Frodo under the eye of Sauron.

"Our tundra's warming at twice the rate of North America's," he'd said to her.

She was well aware of the fact. It seemed climate change was one more war in which Russia would have to fight as the underdog.

As head of the Permafrost Pathogen Institute, a secret laboratory headquartered in the military-industrial compound in Yekaterinburg, she was to be one of the Motherland's secret weapons on this new front—a wildcard that would level the playing field.

"My little Katyusha," the president had called her.

She hadn't known what to say to that.

"What is it our American friends say?" the president asked. "When life treats you like shit, drink lemonade?"

That wasn't exactly right, but she got the point.

"Are the sat phones still working?" she asked Vasily.

"Sofia, relax," he said.

Vasily Ustinov was her second in command at the institute, though he didn't look it. He wasn't the type who lived in his lab coat, nor did he sport the brown-corduroy-with-elbow-patch look other senior government scientists were so fond of.

He'd grown up in the Caucasus and had an unruly mane of black hair and an even more unruly beard. It made him look like a cross between Che Guevara and Jack Sparrow. He gave the impression of knowing his way around a Kalashnikov. Traveling with him to a climate conference in Sweden a few years earlier had been a lesson in airport security profiling.

Despite all that, he was the best anthrax specialist the country had produced in a generation.

"We're sixteen hundred miles from the nearest airfield," Sofia said.

"And if anything goes wrong, they'll come right for us. We're their top priority."

She clenched her jaw.

The truth was, it wasn't the remoteness that bothered her. It was the nature of the mission. No one became a doctor because they wanted to kill people.

She and Vasily were in the front vehicle, and behind them were four more scientists from the institute, along with twelve armed soldiers who'd been assigned as their security detail. She had no idea what the soldiers were supposed to be protecting them from. Neither did they, it seemed.

"They're watching us," Vasily said when he first saw them. "Making sure we don't do anything... *unpatriotic*."

Sofia knew he was right.

From Yakutsk, they'd been ferried north along the Lena River on a military barge, the hull of which could withstand impact with ice three feet thick. That was reassuring. For someone in charge of daring scientific expeditions, Sofia was surprisingly timid around open water. And the Lena was vast even by Siberian standards. Over five miles wide at places, it was unspanned by any bridge. The barge took them north as far as the Vilyuy tributary, where Sofia was glad to plant her feet on the solid, shaley beach of the river's east bank.

They were deep in the territory of the Sakha Republic, one of twenty-two republics recognized within the Russian Federation. It covered more than a million square miles, about a third the size of the contiguous United States, and in all that space, there was only a single city, Yakutsk, which battled with Norilsk for the title of coldest on earth.

The terrain was continuous permafrost, land that, unlike the rest of Eurasia, hadn't thawed at the end of the last ice age. For centuries, trappers and explorers had been finding the remains of strange, long-extinct creatures there. In the thawing ground, they found perfectly preserved steppe ponies, mammoths larger than any living land animal, and wooly rhinos with horns over a yard long.

Sofia squinted through the windshield and imagined a herd of mammoths lumbering across the ice. On the remote islands of the Laptev, the enormous creatures had survived until surprisingly recent times. Long after druids built Stonehenge, and all the major pyramids had been completed in Egypt, mammoths were still roaming Wrangel Island far to the north.

"What I wouldn't do for a hot shower," Vasily said.

Sofia nodded. "And a real bed."

They'd been gaining altitude at an almost imperceptible rate since leaving the river. The effort of it kept the engines straining, and the sound and vibration added to her fatigue.

"What's he doing now?" Vasily said, looking in the rearview mirror.

Sofia turned back. Petrov, the commander of the military escort, was flashing them from the vehicle behind.

Vasily stopped, and Sofia opened her door. Apart from the idling engines, she doubted there was a sound other than the wind for a thousand miles. That kind of isolation was a force all its own. It pressed against her.

When she was a child, her parents took her on a cruise through the Black Sea. At night, when they were out of sight of land, she terrified herself by imagining jumping off the ship and being left alone in the water. Who knew what lurked in those depths?

The tundra gave her the same feeling. Alone in her tent

at night, she had nightmares of the convoy leaving without her. No matter how cold it got, she had to get out of her sleeping bag and make sure the rest of the tents were still there.

"Doctor Ivanova," Petrov called through the comms.

"What is it?"

"We're at the geotag. This is my marker."

She jumped down from the vehicle, and her boots sank six inches into slush. This was the moment she'd been waiting for. She reached into the vehicle and pulled out her backpack. Inside was an envelope bearing the seal of the president.

She carried it to Petrov.

"What's this?"

"What does it look like?"

His eyes widened when he saw the seal. He opened it and read the orders. Sofia already knew what they said. The scientists were to go on alone.

"We'll set up camp here," Petrov said, "and wait for you."

"Very good," Sofia said.

He climbed back into his vehicle and returned with a polymer gun case. He put it on the hood of his vehicle and opened the latch. Inside were six government-issue side-arms.

"What do we need these for?" Sofia said.

"Protection."

"Protection from what?"

Petrov shrugged. "Monsters?" he said.

Sofia rolled her eyes and grabbed the case. She signaled the four other scientists to follow her, and they trudged together to the lead vehicle.

"This is it," she told them. "This is what we trained for."

Vasily opened a special storage compartment containing

hazmat gear, and they suited up. Then they went back to their own vehicles and fired up the engines, covering the last part of the journey without the soldiers.

When Sofia saw the massive rib cages sticking out of the snow, the sight took her breath away. They looked like the hulls of sunken boats.

"It's a graveyard," Vasily said.

Sofia's heart raced. The satellite imagery from the military had been given to them almost a year before, and they'd had to wait for what seemed like forever before the conditions were right for an attempt.

She'd initially suggested flying in by chopper, but the generals were against it. "We can't take that risk," Major General Anton Yevchenko had said. "If there's any contamination, I don't want it flying back to Yakutsk on a chopper. I want a slow, overland convoy."

What he'd meant was that if Sofia and her crew didn't contain the samples properly, he wanted them to die alone on the tundra and any risk of contamination with them. She couldn't blame him. At these temperatures, anthrax spores could lie dormant for thousands of years. If there really were some primordial strain of the bacillus among these carcasses, as the herds of dead reindeer in the satellite imagery suggested, there was every reason to be afraid.

What no one else on the team knew, and what was making her so uneasy, was the president's suggestion, which had initially come from some madman at the GRU lab in Moscow, that the carcasses might also harbor an ancient virus strain.

Finding a previously unknown anthrax bacterium could be the beginning of a formidable new Russian bioweapons program. That was the official purpose of their mission and something that made Sofia uneasy, to begin with. But what really made her lose sleep at night, what made her wake up soaked in sweat, what made her consider taking some sort of drastic action, was the last-minute call from the president.

"Tell no one," he'd said.

"But, sir. A virus. It would be communicable. It would jump from person to person without any way of stopping it. There's no way we could ever use it on the battlefield."

"You leave those details to the generals," the president said. "I don't need to remind you what's at stake."

"No, sir."

"Let the team search for the anthrax. But you, Sofia, you're the secret weapon. I want you to search for a virus."

"A virus requires a host, sir. There's no way one would survive out here all these centuries."

"Just run the tests, doctor. When it comes to this thawing ice, anything is possible."

As the next vehicle crested the rise, the voice of her lab technician came loudly over the comms.

"An entire herd," he said excitedly.

There were hundreds of them.

"We could reconstruct the entire genome from this," Vasily said.

Sofia nodded grimly. She would have liked nothing more, but this was a military expedition.

"Everyone, double-check your suits," she said. "They won't let us back on the barge if there's even a hint of contamination."

As they neared the site, the bones of the mammoths rose higher and higher. Shifting, thawing permafrost deep below had pushed them to the surface after millennia of perfect preservation.

Vasily brought the vehicle to a halt a hundred yards from the closest carcass, and the others pulled up next to him. Everyone looked out in awe. The sun shone obliquely through the site, casting macabre shadows of the rib cages and tusks as flurries of snow whipped around them like dust devils.

A primordial graveyard.

Harboring primordial germs.

To a microbiologist, it was hard to imagine a more terrifying sight.

2

———

A seven-foot-tall, three hundred pound beast of a man with muscles the size of Yukon potatoes and a neck as thick as a hubcap swung a wild punch.

The man he was aiming for took an easy step backward, out of range.

"You little bitch," the big man said.

The other man was nimble, fast on his feet. He wore a green army t-shirt and moved like someone who'd received more than his share of combat training. A pair of Ray-Ban sunglasses was clipped to the neck of his shirt, and he placed them on the bar for safekeeping.

"Lance," the bartender said, "don't do it."

Lance looked at the bartender for a second, then back at the big guy. "Come at me, buddy," he said, beckoning him with his hands. "Come at me."

"I'm going to make you wish you'd never been born," the big man said, lunging forward.

Lance dodged.

"Please, Lance," the bartender said.

Lance turned to him and said, "Watch those sunglasses."

The big man swung again. Lance sidestepped, then pushed him in the direction his momentum was already taking him. He slammed face-first into the bar, sending bottles of Budweiser crashing to the floor.

"That's enough!" the bartender yelled.

Lance shrugged as the big man got back to his feet and took another lunge at him. At the same moment, one of his companions swung a pool cue at Lance's head.

Lance caught the cue and pulled it toward him. The swinger held on and came with it. Lance hit him in the face and stepped back in time to avoid the big guy.

"Lance, come on," the bartender pled. "Who do you think's got to pay for all this?"

"I didn't start it," Lance said, as the big man came at him again, this time knocking over a table and sending more drinks flying.

"The hell you didn't."

"All I did was talk to her," Lance said. He glanced at the girl for the first time since the fight started. She looked like she always did. He knew because he'd been watching her for weeks, driving by her house, following her into bars. She'd noticed him, might even have known who he was, but they never spoke.

She was wearing fishnet stockings that went all the way to her ass and leather boots that looked like they'd come from a BDSM fetish site. On her wrist was a tattoo of a red spearhead with a black dagger and the word 'Airborne' above it.

"You walked right up to her and told her to come with you," the big man said. "Right in front of my face."

"Calm down," Lance said, but he wasn't calming anybody.

"Calm down?" the big guy said.

"All I did was ask how she was doing."

The big guy couldn't believe it. No one stood up to him, not even the cops. He controlled the drug traffic at Roosville, Chief Mountain, and a few other small border crossings. People knew not to mess with him.

"And what gave you the idea to go and do that?" he said.

Lance wasn't sure what to say. He looked at the girl, then back at the big guy. He turned to the bartender for support, but he wasn't offering any. "Look at her," Lance said.

He said it to the room, to the bartender and the guys in flannel shirts and Timberlands by the pool table. He said it to the girl. The words didn't sound right, but he didn't know how else to put it.

It was the girl who replied. She took the gum from her mouth and said, "*What* did you say?"

Her voice was harsh. Just listening to it put the taste of an ashtray in Lance's mouth. He looked her over, head to toe, then at the rest of the guys in the bar. "This can't be right," he said.

"*What*," the girl said pointedly, "can't be right?"

Lance shrugged. "Any of it."

"Any of *what*?"

Lance shook his head, but the girl was insistent.

"No," she said. "You got something to say to me, have the guts to say it to my face."

"All right," Lance said. He made a motion with his hand like a hammer going up and down. "You look like you suck dick for meth."

The girl's eyes narrowed. She was pretty, beautiful even, but her lifestyle was catching up to her. There were bruises around her eyes, faded, but they'd been bad a week earlier. The big guy was roughing her up.

Lance remembered the first photo of her he'd seen. She

couldn't have been more than four or five, happy as could be, sitting on her daddy's knee.

"You don't need to be with these guys," he said.

The girl rolled her eyes. "Who are you to say what I need?"

The men she was with were older than her. Lance pegged them at about forty. They wore matching jackets with the emblem of their two-bit gang on the backs. Lance knew they moved drugs south from Canada. Chinese fentanyl. They sometimes moved Chinese women too, set them up in brothels and massage parlors across northern Montana.

That was what they'd do to her too. Handjobs for lumberjacks and ranchers. Maybe some extras if it was payday. She sure was dressed the part, with the dominatrix boots and skimpy leather skirt.

But the looks wouldn't last. The life in her eyes wouldn't last. These men would hurt her in ways that would never heal. Not her body. Not her soul. Six more months and the spark would be gone from her eyes—six years, and even they wouldn't have a use for her.

"You're coming with me, Sam," he said to the girl.

Her eyes flashed. She hadn't expected him to use her name. She wanted to know how he knew it.

"Sam?" the big guy said.

They had their own name for her. Lance knew what that was too. Candy.

"Come on," Lance said. "It's time to go."

"With *you*?" she said incredulously. "Mister, I don't even know who you are."

He kept her gaze. He didn't want to lose her. "You know who I am, Sam."

She looked back. He knew she knew. There was no one

else he could be. No one else was coming for her. Ever. This was it. This was the cavalry.

She looked from Lance to the big guy, then to the big guy's friend lying on the floor with his hand on his nose, a river of blood flowing from it. "Knock his teeth out," she said.

The big man charged like a bull. Lance ducked, letting him drive his fist straight into the brick wall. He yelped in pain. Lance grabbed his wrist and bent it back until he felt the snap.

He wanted to kill the man. The thought of it flashed through his mind. It would be so simple—nothing more than a quick yank of the neck.

"That's enough, Lance," the bartender said.

Lance let go of the man. He fell to the floor, clutching his wrist in agony. His buddy lay next to him, so much blood coming from his face that he was going pallid.

The girl just stood there, watching it all, speechless.

Lance looked at the bartender apologetically.

"I don't want to hear it," the bartender said.

Lance turned to the girl. "You're coming with me," he said.

"Uh-uh," she said, shaking her head.

The big guy tried to get up, and Lance raised his foot and brought it down on his face. The man collapsed, unconscious.

The other guy made to move, and Lance said, "You want to join him?"

The man shook his head, and Lance turned away. Then, thinking better of it, he swung back and kicked him in the face too.

The bartender spoke again. "Lance, get the hell out of here before I call the cops."

Lance reached into his pocket and put enough cash on

the bar to cover the damage. Then he picked up his sunglasses and clipped them back on the neck of his shirt.

He looked at the bartender, who was wearing an ACLU t-shirt from a campaign a few years back protesting the death penalty. "I thought you liberals all had bleeding hearts," he said.

"You're a dead man, Lance. I don't care where you served. These guys will gun you down like a dog in the street."

Lance looked down at the two unconscious bodies. They didn't look like they'd be causing him trouble any time soon. "I guess I'll take my chances." Then he turned to the girl. "I don't care if I have to carry you. You're coming with me."

3

Sam got into Lance's pickup without a word.

He climbed in next to her and cracked the window. He had a pack of cigarettes on the dashboard and lit one. He offered them to Sam, but she ignored him.

He fired up the engine. It was a cold night, and he turned the heat on full. Ice covered the windshield, and he grabbed the scraper and got back out.

When he returned, Sam was smoking one of his cigarettes.

They pulled out of the parking lot and headed north. There was a McDonald's, and he asked if she was hungry, but she didn't answer.

This was her town. Beulah, Montana.

Lance had been coming for a few weeks, keeping tabs on her, getting to know her life. She'd been easy to find. She spent her time in bars, pool halls, sleeping in until four in the afternoon in a cheap apartment with her scumbag boyfriend.

Lance had seen her getting high in the parking lot

behind the drugstore. He'd seen her running out of the apartment at four in the morning with blood on her face. He'd seen her twist an ankle on a dance floor wearing seven-inch stilettos.

He kept his distance but saw everything.

They passed the motel Lance sometimes stayed at and crossed the bridge over the Kootenay River. The road from her town to his wove through a steep mountain pass next to the river. Dense forest covered the slopes on both sides. An hour tops, and they'd be at his place unless the snow caused a road closure. It looked like the first big storm of the season.

"Can I ask where you're taking me?" Sam said about ten minutes out of town.

Lance really wasn't sure what he was going to do with her. All he knew—what he'd decided without speaking to anyone or even considering asking Sam her view on the matter—was that she was headed down a bad path.

Drugs.

Prostitution.

Crime.

He knew how it would end.

"I told..." Lance began before stopping himself short.

"You told *what*?"

Lance took a long draw from his cigarette and threw the butt out the window.

Sam did the same, then leaned back in her seat. "You're kidnapping me," she said.

Lance shook his head. "That's a bit dramatic, don't you think?"

"Then let me out of this truck."

"Here? In this weather?"

"So I'm not free to leave?"

"Not here."

"That's kidnapping."

He shook his head again.

They drove another few minutes, and she said, "So that's it? No explanation? No discussion. You're just going to clam up?"

Lance cleared his throat. "I guess you already know who I am," he said.

"Know who you *are*? I never met you in my life."

"You saw me outside your apartment."

She didn't say anything.

"And in the bars where you and your idiot boyfriend hung out."

"I saw some creepy dude dressed like what's-his-face from Top Gun."

"Tom Cruise."

"No, not Tom Cruise. The other guy."

"Iceman?"

"Yeah."

"Oh, *come* on."

"What?"

"*Iceman*?" He looked at her like she'd just told him the earth was flat.

"You don't like Iceman?" she said, and he could tell from the look on her face she was taunting him.

He drove on, taking the curves faster, letting the truck swerve.

"Calm down," she said.

"I am calm."

"You sure hate Val Kilmer."

Lance shook his head. He slowed down a little and said, "You never said anything to your boyfriend about me."

"I didn't want to give him another reason to mess me up."

The snow got heavier. The road might have been closed behind them. "Lucky we got out of town when we did," Lance said.

At the top of the pass, about halfway between the two towns, was a gas station and motel.

"Maybe we should stop," Sam said.

Lance had been thinking the same thing, but her saying it made him reconsider. "We'll press on."

She looked out the window at the brightly lit restaurant. It was late, maybe ten. He figured she was getting hungry.

"Press on where?" she said.

He didn't answer.

"Let me guess," she said. "You've got a soundproof room in your basement. You're going to keep me there."

"I'm not going to do that."

"Like that movie. Come in and rape me whenever you're in the mood?"

"I'm not going to rape you."

"You better not."

"I'm not," Lance said.

"Yeah, well," she said, pulling her skirt as far over her thighs as it would go.

The heat was on, but she was cold. Lance undid his seat belt and took off his jacket. "Take this," he said.

She put it over her legs.

When they saw the glow of the town in the valley below, he felt her relax.

"I knew your daddy," he said.

She didn't say anything to that.

They drove into town and pulled up to a diner on the main drag. Sam followed him inside, and they took a booth by the window where they could see the road. The snowplows were out in force.

Sam sat there, looking so ferocious Lance made a mental note of where her fork and knife were.

"I suppose you're thinking I had no right to do what I did," he said.

She shook her head. She was upset. Him talking wasn't helping.

"I met you once," he said.

"I don't want to hear this."

"At the funeral."

She gritted her teeth. "Stop talking."

A waitress came over. Lance knew her. Marlene.

"We'll have the special and coffee, sweetie," he said. When she looked at Sam, he said, "The both of us."

Marlene sensed the mood and left them alone. She came back a minute later with two cups of coffee and some sugar and creamers.

Lance took a sip. He wasn't good at this sort of thing. He didn't spend enough time with women. He was rusty.

"I told him I'd look out for you," he said.

Sam pursed her lips. She inhaled deeply. She looked like she might start hyperventilating.

"I'm sorry," Lance said.

She said nothing. She was more upset than he'd pictured her being. He supposed he should have known.

She had a mug of coffee in her hands. She'd put a decent amount of cream in it, but it could still scald. "The funeral was seven years ago," she said.

He nodded.

"Seven *years*."

"I know."

"Stop saying you know. You don't know shit. If you wanted to step in, that was the time. Now you're... you're too late."

Sam's father had left to go serve in the army. He'd come back in a pine box with a flag draped over it. That was all the closure she ever got.

Lance knew that was the time he should have come. It would have been messy. There would have been tears. But he could have done something for her then. For her mother.

The mother was dead too now. A car accident. She'd taken so many pills beforehand the doctor thought it may have been on purpose. She took a father of three out with her. No wonder she was messed up.

"Why now?" she said.

Lance didn't have an answer to that. He'd been adrift. He'd been drinking too much and screwing around too much. He couldn't sleep at night.

"I wanted to keep my promise," he said. It was the wrong thing to say. He knew it as soon as the words left his mouth.

"*You*," Sam said, "wanted to keep *your* promise?"

"I checked in and saw you needed help."

"I needed help? Give me a break! You're the one with survivor's guilt. You feel bad because you're alive, and good men like my father are dead. You feel guilty, you son of a bitch, and you want to feel better about yourself."

Lance looked at her. He felt like she could see right through him.

"You want to be able to sleep at night," she went on, "so you come interfering in my life, where you have no business."

"Those guys you were with," he said, "they were bad news."

"Oh, thanks for the tip, Sherlock. You got a team of detectives working round the clock on that? What gave it away?"

"I just want to help."

"And what a fine job you've done. How am I supposed to go back now? You know what they'll do to me when they find me?"

"I'll take care of that."

"Well, everything's fine then, isn't it? I'll quit worrying because you'll take care of everything."

Lance didn't know what to say.

"Those guys will kill you," she said. "And then they'll mess me up real good too."

He took a sip of his coffee to avoid having to say something.

"Yeah," she said when she saw he had no answer. "Thought so."

The waitress returned with their food. Sam had lost her appetite. She sat, staring at Lance, never even looking at the plate. Lance had lost his appetite too but didn't know what to do other than eat.

"I thought I could help," he said.

"You kidnapped me, you psycho."

"I didn't kidnap you."

"You want to help? Go back to Iraq, you piece of shit. Do your job. Serve your country."

He looked down at his plate, shoveling the chili methodically into his mouth, not tasting it.

"Go back," she said again, louder. "Go back and fight, coward."

He put his fork down.

"Go be a real man and quit sitting here while men like my father take the bullets meant for you."

Then she did it. He'd seen it coming. She picked up her mug and threw the coffee in his face. He could have stopped it, but he didn't. He owed her that much.

4

Deweyville, Montana was a town of about a thousand people. It hadn't changed much since its founding by miners and frontiersmen in the eighteen hundreds. Visitors could be forgiven for thinking it was a resort, custom-built to look like an old mining town. It still had a hunting and trapping store, a tobacco store, and a massive wooden statue of a lumberjack in front of the court-house. The town's largest building was the old headquarters of the Farmers and Merchants Bank. It was such a fine example of the western commercial architecture style that it was on the national register of historic places. It was all pretty as a postcard, the kind of place people liked to think small towns were still like, nestled in a mountain valley nine miles south of the Canadian border.

Lance pulled his truck up outside a bar called The Eureka and got out. He was followed by Sam. She hadn't made a run for it yet, which he took as a positive sign.

The bar was fitted out like an old saloon, and when the bartender saw Lance, she smirked. Then she saw Sam and looked away.

It was a cold night, and there was a log fire burning. Lance warmed his hands by it before going to the bar. He pulled up a stool for Sam and sat next to her.

"Still snowing?" the bartender said. She was blonde, early twenties, looked like she could have been Sam's sister.

She was squarely in the bracket of too young for Lance. At thirty-eight, he should have been past hitting on girls like that. "What time you get off?" he said.

The bartender looked at Sam.

"Don't worry about her," Lance said. "She's my niece."

Sam rolled her eyes. "I'm not his niece."

"What are you then?" Lance said.

"I ain't your nothing."

"Well, she's not my date," Lance said to the bartender. "Don't go thinking that."

That was something Sam could agree with. "He's all yours," she said, holding her hands up like she'd rather put them on literally anything than Lance.

"Well, thanks, guys, really," the bartender said, "but I've got plans."

Lance shook his head. He'd been with her half a dozen times. She didn't have plans.

Apart from an old guy at the far end of the bar who might have been asleep, Lance and Sam were the only customers.

He looked at Sam. She wasn't impressed. She'd slept all night and most of the day. He'd offered her the bed, but she took the couch.

"Snow," he said. "You know what that means?"

"What does it mean?" Sam said.

"Hot toddy."

She shrugged.

Lance held up two fingers, and the bartender reached for the Jameson's.

"How about the Maker's?" Lance said.

She took the bottle of Kentucky bourbon from the shelf and broke the wax seal.

"I had a buddy in the army from Kentucky," Lance said.

The bartender nodded. She was used to his stories. Sam wasn't, but she knew what this was.

"You know it snows in Afghanistan?" he said.

"I did not know that," the bartender said.

"Everyone thinks it's hot as hell over there."

She put their drinks on the bar in front of them.

"Turns out, it's cold as a witch's tit."

He was addressing the bartender, but Sam knew the story was for her benefit.

"Me and my buddy, we were in mountains as big as the Rockies. I won't tell you the name of the place. You're not interested anyhow."

"Sure I am," the bartender said.

He smiled at her. "Anyway, all I wanted to say was my buddy was from Kentucky, and it was a night like this. We were in the snow, and we thought we had a real cold night ahead of us, and then, out of his pack comes this bottle of Maker's. If that don't make you love the stuff, I don't know what will."

Sam took a long sip of her drink, then turned to Lance and said, "What do you think you're doing?"

Lance shrugged.

"What's that supposed to mean?" she said.

"I don't know, honey."

"Seriously. What am I supposed to do with that?"

"Look," he said. "I don't know what to tell you. I was friends with your dad. I brought you here because of that."

"You know I can't go back, right? You know that's the only reason I'm still here?"

Lance nodded. He knew she was afraid of her ex. He'd beat the crap out of her if he showed up now. But old habits died hard. "It's not so bad here, is it?" he said.

"I don't know, Lance," she said, indicating the empty bar. "Buttfuck, Montana? You tell me."

Lance finished his drink and ordered two beers. "It's not so bad here," he said again, as much to himself as her.

Sam bit her lip. "You've lost your mind, haven't you? You're one of those guys who comes back all loopy. Too many grenades went off close to your head."

"Maybe," he said.

"Seriously. What did you think? That I'd come home with you and just settle in? Become your daughter?"

"No," he said.

"Then what, Lance? For God's sake, what were you thinking?"

He took a sip of his beer. "Why don't we just wait and see?" he said.

Sam sighed, but he could tell she was less angry than she'd been the night before.

"Just stay a few days," he said. "See how you like it. It's not like you've got anything to go back to."

"Thanks to you," she said.

Lance raised his bottle. "Thanks to me," he said.

She shook her head but clinked his bottle.

Two young guys came into the bar, and they couldn't have been better timed. They were right up her alley. Lance saw the way she looked at them. He wondered if things might work out after all.

The bartender went to serve them.

Lance turned to Sam and said, "You know, I nailed that chick."

Sam gave him a withering look. "Don't make me throw up."

5

Tatyana Aleksandrova didn't have the heart of a killer.

But she killed.

She didn't have the heart of a traitor.

But she did anything she had to.

She didn't have the heart of a zealot.

But she worked for the Main Directorate, Russia's CIA, still referred to by its Soviet moniker, the GRU. It was an organization that required blind faith as much as any religion ever had.

She'd sworn an oath to the 'Greatness of the Motherland'.

She had reasons to hate the Motherland, but she was too much of a pragmatist to do so. Hate was a luxury. As was love. If Tatyana believed in anything, it was austerity. Austerity of emotion. Austerity of hope. Austerity of despair. It was the only way she could live in a world that killed so frequently and so callously.

She grew up in the post-Soviet era, but in many ways, she was better suited to the world that existed before. She understood those times. She related to them and to the people who lived in them.

People who grew up in Communism understood things differently. They did the things that had to be done. Not because those things were necessary in and of themselves, but because if they were not done, there would be punishment.

They believed only in what they could see. Steel, coal, grain, railway lines, nuclear reactors, rockets. Those were things they could count on. Cold things. They offered nothing. They took more life than they gave.

But they were real, and only a madman or a liar would deny them.

She believed in the Akula-class submarine her father died on, suffocated when a freon leak sucked the oxygen out of his chamber.

Tatyana was in her mother's womb at the time.

She believed in Saint Petersburg Hospital Number 40, which refused to admit her mother because she didn't have the right paperwork. It was one of the largest hospitals on earth, and one of the most renowned. It had treated soldiers during the Russian Civil War. It was destroyed by the Germans during the Second World War and rebuilt larger and better. It was said to have treated a quarter of a million Soviet citizens by the time of the collapse.

Tatyana's mother was not one of them. A bureaucrat refused to admit her. She died a month later of tuberculosis in their two-room apartment. Tatyana didn't know it at the time, she was only four years old, but she later found out that tuberculosis had killed as many as one out of every seven people who'd ever lived.

That was until the cure was found. In 1943, streptomycin was discovered by doctors in the United States, and by the

1950s, it was being used to treat and cure tuberculosis all over the world. The UN listed it as one of the essential medicines every human on the planet should have access to.

The wholesale cost of a streptomycin treatment was thirty-eight cents.

That was what Tatyana believed in. A thirty-eight cent dose of streptomycin. She thought of it every time a cashier handed her a few coins.

She believed in the coldness of the world. The hardness of it. Being locked in that two-room apartment with her dead mother for six days, holding her hand, talking to her, telling her bedtime stories, opening and closing her eyes every morning and night—it made her believe in things other people were afraid to accept. That life was as hard as nature. That man was the cruelest animal of all.

Winston Churchill once called his rival a sheep in sheep's clothing. Tatyana knew all too well that many of them, beneath the layers of wool, really were wolves.

She wasn't a traitor. She was a realist.

She worked for the GRU not because she believed in it, not the dogma, not the philosophy, not the politics. Like her mother and grandmother before her, she was a pragmatist before all else. She had no other choice.

And for all the pomp and ceremony, the oaths and emblems and mottos, that was how her superiors liked it. They believed it made her predictable, tractable.

As her car approached the gates, the eight concrete floors of the Permafrost Pathogen Institute loomed above her imperiously.

The government had established the institute when thawing cattle burial grounds in Yakutsk began causing spikes in anthrax deaths that hadn't been seen in centuries. Traditionally, Siberians didn't burn butchered animal carcasses. Firewood was too valuable. Instead, they buried them in the permafrost, which until recently had been an effective means of disposal.

Now that the ground was thawing, spores that had been frozen for centuries were coming back to life.

Anthrax had always been a scourge in the region. They called it Siberian ulcer or Siberian plague. It caused painful black ulcers on the skin, fever, vomiting, bloody diarrhea, and eventually death.

During the Soviet era, it had been a favorite of bioweapons scientists. They tinkered with it, tailored it, developed new strains. A single gram of dried, aerosolized anthrax contained a trillion spores. There was no limit to the havoc it could wreak.

The scientists had two objectives when working on anthrax—increasing virulence and increasing antibiotics resistance. A number of bioweapons treaties, and a leak in 1979 from that very compound, hampered their progress.

But the work continued. Even after the collapse of the Soviet Union, it continued. Right up to the present day.

Now, they were finding that the ancient strains coming from the permafrost were more lethal than anything the labs could ever come up with.

An outbreak in the Yamal region two years earlier had been completely untreatable. A hundred percent mortality rate. The entire village—man, woman, child, dog, cat, rat, and farm animal—perished.

And the Kremlin took notice. They called it a gift from the Motherland.

Tatyana was there to meet the head of the institute, the leading researcher in the field of paleo-pathogens. Her name was Sofia Ivanova, and she'd made waves when she wrote a paper about some soldiers from the civil war who'd surfaced in the tundra with viable traces of smallpox and Spanish flu in their clothing. In her lab, she successfully reanimated the diseases, and in the process, accidentally killed a lab technician in the only known case of smallpox in Russia since the disease had been eradicated.

Under the illusion her job was curing disease, Sofia tried to publish her findings, but the GRU suppressed her article, seized her data, and made her an offer she couldn't refuse. She could run their new lab, or she and her team could sleep under blankets doused in smallpox. "The way the Americans did with the Indians," the general said.

Now she was working on weaponizing thousand-year-old strains of diseases that the world would be as powerless against as any Shawnee tribe ever was.

Tatyana went through the building's extensive security procedures and waited for Sofia in a small lobby that reminded her of her dentist's office.

When the doctor emerged, Tatyana was startled by how much weight she'd lost. The photos she'd seen of her were just six months old. This woman was a ghost of her former self.

"Agent Aleksandrova," Sofia said.

"Please, call me Tatyana."

"Very well."

"I got your message," Tatyana said, getting straight to the point. She knew she had to be careful. This meeting wasn't authorized. If anyone ever found out about it, they could both be killed.

Sofia hesitated. Tatyana could see she was terrified. "They sent us to dig up thousand-year-old carcasses from the ice," she said.

"And did you find what you were looking for?"

"We found pathogens. Ancient pathogens."

"Were they viable?"

Sofia said nothing.

Tatyana could only imagine what this was like for her. "You can trust me," she said.

Sofia looked at her. There were tears in her eyes.

"There's still hope," Tatyana said. "As long as people like you and I resist, there's still hope."

"I found what they wanted," Sofia said hesitantly.

"A weapon?"

"It really is what they asked for," Sofia said. "A biological Chernobyl. Unstoppable."

"I see," Tatyana said.

"Do you?"

Tatyana looked at the doctor closely. "You're losing your resolve, Sofia."

"It's not a small thing," Sofia said. "To unleash something like this. To be involved in something so..." Her voice trailed off.

"Destructive?" Tatyana said.

Sofia didn't seem to hear. She reached into her pocket and pulled out two small glass vials. To Tatyana, they looked like perfume samples from a department store.

"You know it's what ended the Soviet system," Sofia said.

"What is?"

"Chernobyl."

Tatyana shook her head. "Sofia, if you didn't accept this post, someone else would have."

"I know," Sofia said quietly.

"It had to be you. If it were anyone else, this never would have gotten out."

"I know," Sofia said again.

The two women looked at each other. Then Sofia opened a drawer in her desk and took out a small titanium case. She placed one of the vials inside it, snapped the clasps shut, and handed it to Tatyana.

"This isn't an anthrax bacillus," she said. "This is something else."

"Something else?"

"Something the president requested personally."

"What did he request?"

"Something transmissible. Something that would spread. Something that would never stop."

"I don't understand."

"A virus," Sofia said. "The president asked for a virus."

"I see."

"A virus more deadly than anything we've ever seen."

6

The US Consulate in Istanbul was a fortress on a hill. Attacks in 2008 and 2015 led to the implementation of some of the most stringent security measures of any diplomatic building on earth. The compound's outer perimeter extended seamlessly from the rocky cliffs overlooking the Bosphorus in a sheer wall of stone a hundred feet high. Multispectral cameras and motion sensors scanned the approaching slopes for intruders. Four companies of marines were stationed inside the compound, and round-the-clock satellite surveillance was fed to the control room in the basement.

There was zero chance of getting in undetected.

The closest anyone could hope to get was the massive security post on Kaplicalar Street, a structure that looked more like the fortified entrance to a medieval castle than anything built in modern times. The main gate was guarded by a fifty-foot-high tower, beyond which was a steep, rocky slope leading to the main consulate building.

The entire compound looked like it had been designed to withstand a military assault.

And it had.

Directly across the street from the entrance was the Café Americano, an upscale establishment serving cappuccinos and lattes that tasted more like traditional Turkish coffee than the names suggested. Not that it stopped the consulate employees from frequenting the place. A brief glance around their offices revealed dozens of the café's distinctive white and yellow take-out cups.

On a drizzly afternoon in December, a taxicab pulled up in front of the café, and Tatyana stepped out wearing a pair of oversized sunglasses, an Audrey Hepburn-style silk scarf in her hair, and a knee-length black coat.

She entered the café and ordered an espresso in English, speaking with a slight accent. She waited at the counter, paid in cash, and took a seat by the window. She searched her purse for her phone before remembering she hadn't brought it.

She tapped her spoon against her cup and kept looking at her watch. There was a manila envelope in front of her that she flipped incessantly on the table, reading and rereading the name on the front.

Lance Spector
    US Army SFOD-D
    Syria
    Hand Deliver

She looked at her watch. Forty-five minutes had passed, and she was running out of time. Any longer, and her absence would be noticed.

She got up and asked the proprietor, an overweight,

overworked bearded man in his fifties with a coffee stain on the front of his skin-tight shirt, to call her a cab. She returned to her seat, and when she saw the cab, she got up and left.

She'd left the envelope on the table.

7

S ofia glanced nervously at Vasily and prayed he didn't do anything stupid.

Before them stood Major General Yevchenko, his uniform bristling with enough ornaments for a Victory Day parade. From what Sofia had seen, he was a man used to being disliked. His men called him the Kaiser because of his mustache, and it was no compliment.

He'd come to the institute with three other officers. They arrived unannounced in an armored cavalcade. The expressions on their faces said it wasn't a social call.

"What can we do for you, Major General?" Sofia said.

She was standing behind her desk as if it would somehow protect her. Next to her was Vasily, his temper simmering below the surface. He'd had his share of run-ins with the army. Growing up where he had made it unavoidable.

Technically the institute was a civilian facility. No one wanted international inspectors coming around waving their treaty provisions, but everyone in the room knew who called the shots.

The fact they were located within the electrified fence of a military compound said it all. It was in that very compound that the USSR's most notorious bioweapons facility, Biopreparat, had operated during the Cold War. The fact was an open secret. The Moscow bureau chief of *The Wall Street Journal* broke the story decades ago. The KGB later got to him—he disappeared without a trace—but they were too late. The word was out, and the world knew about Biopreparat and the work it did. They knew what the Soviet government had been up to.

"I'm sure you can guess why we've come," Yevchenko said.

It was always the same song and dance. The military bigwigs loved nothing better than playing games, showing who was boss.

"Why don't you give us a clue?" Vasily said.

Sofia's heart pounded. He was feeling punchy. She could hear it in his voice. Yevchenko would jump at any excuse to get rid of him.

"I'm sorry," Yevchenko said. "I haven't met your second in command."

"Of course," Sofia said. "Major General Yevchenko, this is Doctor Vasily Ustinov."

"You look familiar," Yevchenko said.

Sofia held her breath. Vasily's record was problematic, to say the least. It seemed he'd taken part in every campus demonstration there was while at university. It had all been thoroughly investigated during the vetting process, but there was always a risk it would come back to bite them on the ass.

"Doesn't he look familiar?" Yevchenko said, turning to his officers.

Sofia stole a glance at Vasily.

"You ever been on TV?" Yevchenko said.

Vasily didn't respond.

"Yeah," Yevchenko said. "I know you. You're that fighter. You beat Conor McGregor."

The officers began to laugh.

"Very funny," Vasily said.

"Khabib," Yevchenko said, grinning. He was very pleased with himself. "Khabib Nurmagomedov. The face, not the hair. Do you see it?" he said to his officers.

The officers nodded, pretending to be amused.

Sofia had no clue what they were talking about, but it seemed the tension was lifting. "How about some tea?" she said, nodding to her secretary.

The general and his men took seats, and Sofia breathed a sigh of relief.

"I'd like to see you in a papakha," Yevchenko said.

Vasily let out a brief chuckle.

"The sideburns," Yevchenko added.

Sofia shook her head. She knew what a papakha was—the hat worn by shepherds in Vasily's region—but she wasn't getting the joke. "Am I missing something?" she said.

"He's teasing me," Vasily said.

"I see," she said, looking from him to Yevchenko.

"He's all right," Yevchenko said. "I read his file. He's lucky he's from Dagestan and not Chechnya."

Sofia's secretary brought in a tray of tea, and Sofia began to pour.

"So," Yevchenko said, adding sugar to his cup, "*Sibirskaya yazva*. What have we got?"

Sofia and Vasily sat down. *Sibirskaya yazva*, Siberian ulcer. It was the traditional name for anthrax. This was the moment Sofia had been dreading since the first day the GRU approached her.

"I guess we all thought those years were behind us," she said.

Yevchenko smiled. "Some things never change."

She nodded.

"I trust your team is progressing on schedule."

"Well," Sofia said, "I think what we've achieved will speak for itself."

"The bacillus from the mammoths?"

"Yes, sir. The bacillus."

"And it's ready for delivery?"

"Delivery, sir?"

"We're not just here to talk science, doctor. We're here for a weapon."

"Yes, of course, sir. But...."

"*But* nothing, Sofia. The General Staff has ordered me to begin production."

Sofia always knew this day would come. The General Staff wanted a weapon, and a weapon meant production. If they were to arm warheads, create stockpiles, equip units, it required product. A lot of product. Until now, she could sleep at night telling herself she was only a researcher, that her findings could be used as much to protect against disease as to cause it. Once they started production, that myth would be over. They would be creating a form of the bacillus that had only one purpose—Killing.

On an industrial scale.

"Is that wise, sir?" she said.

"Wise?" Yevchenko said, shaking his head. "You know what I think is wise?"

Sofia said nothing.

"Following orders."

"But production, sir?"

"The order for production comes from the top,"

Yevchenko said, nodding toward the mandatory photo of the president on the wall.

Sofia felt the strength drain from her body. Fighting the military was the most exhausting thing she'd ever done in her life. It was like trying to hold back a glacier. It moved slowly, but the weight of it could reshape continents.

"Preparing for production will take time," she said.

"You let us worry about that."

"What do you mean?"

"The military is going to take over."

That was not good news. Making a weapon was one thing. Making it badly, in a poorly run military facility, was about the only thing she could think of that was worse. "Production like this is very complicated, sir."

"I'm not here to debate with you," Yevchenko said. "Production will begin at a military facility. There's nothing more to be said about it."

"What quantities are we talking?"

"We're talking tons," Yevchenko said.

She felt the blood drain from her face. "Tons?"

"Tons."

"Sir, that's impossible."

"Nothing is impossible, my dear." A lecherous smile crossed his face that she tried to ignore.

"Sir, this strain, I don't think you understand."

"I understand perfectly."

"This is more deadly than anything the Fifteenth Directorate has ever worked with."

Yevchenko smiled. "Orders are orders."

"Rushing this into production is asking for disaster."

"There will be no disaster. The facilities necessary, the tanks, the vats, they're already under construction."

"It's not just tanks and vats, sir. It's filters. It's safeguards. It's procedures."

"We have it all under control."

Sofia felt a shudder run down her spine. This wasn't just some tactical point she was trying to make. Lives were at stake. A lot of lives.

"Where?" she said.

"Chkalovskaya industrial area."

"Chkalovskaya. Sir, that's inside the city."

"Everything's being built to the highest standard. You have nothing to worry about."

"But sir, respectfully. This bacillus, once it's aerosolized, the number of spores—if even a single gram...."

Yevchenko stood. "Enough. Need I remind you what's at stake for you personally? For your team?"

Vasily was getting restless. She put a hand on his arm to stop him from speaking.

"This is madness," she said.

"That may be," Yevchenko said. "But what the Kremlin wants, the Kremlin gets. Now don't make this any more difficult than it has to be. Is the bacillus ready for delivery?"

Sofia looked at Vasily, then back at Yevchenko.

"We've come a very long way," Yevchenko said. "It would be a terrible shame to go back to Moscow empty-handed." He turned to his officers. "Terrible shame," he repeated, grinning.

Sofia looked at them. She knew what this was. The life of every person working at the institute was in her hands. "I can have the lab prepare it now," she said.

Yevchenko nodded to his men, and Sofia turned to Vasily. "Do as they say," she said. "Take them to the lab and make sure the sample is secured properly. The last thing any of us wants is a leak on these fine officers' flight back to Moscow." It was her turn to look smug.

The officers went with Vasily, leaving Sofia and Yevchenko alone in the office. Yevchenko went to the door and locked it. Sofia took a deep breath. She knew her ordeal wasn't over. It was just beginning.

"Now that we're alone," he said, "perhaps you'd like to give me an update on your little side project."

"The virus?" Sofia said, her heart pounding in her chest.

"The virus," Yevchenko said.

"Sir, this goes beyond the dangers of the bacillus."

"I'm aware of that, doctor."

"Anthrax is a bacteria," she said. "It's extremely deadly, but it's not contagious. If it's spread on a battlefield, it will kill only the soldiers on that battlefield."

"And if it's poured over a city," Yevchenko said, "it will kill only the inhabitants of that city."

Sofia had to take in a deep breath just to calm herself. She thought she was going to throw up. "We'd never do that, would we?" she said.

"Have you no faith in your own government, Sofia?"

She looked into his gray eyes. For a moment, she wasn't sure if he was actually being sincere.

Then she said, "Anthrax won't spread, sir. It will kill the target it's used against, and then it will stop."

"I'm aware of that," Yevchenko said.

"But a virus is different," she said. "A virus spreads like dye in water. It spreads from person to person exponentially. Once it's unleashed, you can't control where it goes."

"I know what a virus is, doctor. And I can assure you the president would not have asked for one if it was not what he wanted."

"A virus has no legitimate military purpose," she said.

"Why don't you leave military matters to the experts?"

"The Geneva Convention, sir."

"Are you suggesting what I think you're suggesting?" Yevchenko said, his smug grin changing to a snarl.

"Sir, I'm only saying that a virus spreads. A virus like the one you've requested, it's unstoppable. It will spread and spread, and we'll have no ability to control it. Like a genie, sir. Once it's out of the bottle, it will never go back in."

"Why don't you just tell me if you managed to isolate it," he said.

Sofia shook her head. She couldn't say the words.

"Sofia," he said, "did you do it, or did you not?"

She remained silent. She'd always been good at reading people. She thought about the GRU agent, Tatyana Aleksandrova. Everything depended on her now. Sofia knew next to nothing about her. A single meeting months ago. Just a hunch. A feeling. And now, she was the only hope.

Yevchenko stepped forward and slammed his hand on the table, yanking her from her thoughts.

"I did it, sir."

He smiled luxuriantly. The news seemed almost to arouse him sexually. "And it's effective?"

"Effective, sir?"

"Effective, Sofia. Virulent. Lethal."

"Lethal?"

"Doctor," he said, drawing his gun, "I'm here on orders from the President of the Federation. Don't mistake my calm demeanor. I'll order the death of every person at this facility if you don't give me what I want. I'll go after your families, your children, your parents. I'll go after your dogs if it brings me closer to my goal."

"Sir," she said, swallowing, "this is like nothing we've

ever seen. Ebola, Marburg, plague, Q fever, Junin, glanders, even smallpox. They all pale in comparison."

"So you've done it? You've given him what he asked for?"

"I have a deliverable, sir. Yes."

"A virus?"

"Taken from the same mammoths as the anthrax."

"And it's stable?"

"It's a nuclear bomb," she said. "It should be destroyed immediately."

Yevchenko smiled. "Now, now. Let's leave that for the president to decide."

Sofia had a safe under her desk, and she bent down to unlock it. "I trust I don't have to tell you how sensitive this is?"

"This isn't my first rodeo, dear."

"This vial," she said, holding it up for him to see, "contains possibly the most virulent substance ever seen. Certainly the most dangerous thing ever to come out of a Russian lab."

"I would expect nothing less," Yevchenko said.

"The number of people it could kill, it's unthinkable, sir. It would be easier to count the survivors."

"Yes, yes," he said impatiently.

"Under no circumstances should the vial be tampered with." She placed it inside a sealed titanium transportation case. "Under no circumstances should this case be opened. You must deliver it intact to Directorate scientists in Moscow."

"I'll be careful with your little package, doctor."

Sofia held it out to him, but as he took it, her fingers refused to let go.

"You don't trust me?" he said.

"When it comes to something like this," she said, "I trust no one."

"Well, surely you can trust the President of the Motherland."

Sofia looked at him wryly. "If we can't trust him, who can we trust?"

L aurel Everlane was good at her job. It was her entire world. At thirty, getting recruited into the CIA's Special Operations Group was the singular achievement of her life. She'd given up everything to be there—friendships, romantic relationships, the chance to start a family. She'd given up who she was, her very identity.

And this was the payoff, this corner section of the sixth floor of the CIA's new headquarters building at Langley.

The space was considered prime real estate. Its large windows overlooked a leafy section of the Potomac River and the George Washington Memorial Parkway.

She sat in a glass-walled conference room, her papers and pen arranged neatly in front of her, and gazed across the office.

He was late. He was always late.

The Group was small but punched above its weight in terms of authority and access. The bigwigs in congress rarely said no to them. Its field agents, known officially as Paramilitary Operatives but within the Group as Assets, were secretly acknowledged to be the most elite units in the nation. They were recruited exclusively from Navy's SEAL Team Six, Air Force's 24th Special Tactics Squadron, Marine Corps' MARSOC, and Army's Delta Force. It was a team that actually did something, struck at the enemy, hit them where it hurt, and that was what Laurel liked about it.

She was a girl with an ax to grind.

When she was sixteen, she'd appeared in a music video for a local rapper dressed in a bikini and holding a machine gun. At her insistence, the video ended up including footage of her shooting the gun at targets with the faces of all the men on the Bush Administration's card deck of most wanted terrorists.

She meant business.

She grew up in Dale County, Alabama, within sight of Fort Rucker. She'd been an only child, and her mother died during childbirth. Her father died when she was fourteen. He was an army colonel, killed at Camp Qargha in Kabul when a soldier in the Afghan National Army shot him in the back during an inspection tour.

Laurel didn't attend the funeral. She now lived less than fifteen minutes from his grave at Arlington Cemetery but never visited.

She had issues with the old man. There was a wound there. But also a need. A need to prove herself. A need to show the world it couldn't shoot her father in the back and get away with it. Not on her watch.

After high school, she attended Harvard on full scholarship, moving on to Yale after graduation to specialize in psychiatry. She could have gone anywhere from there. She could have earned a million dollars a year at a fancy specialist clinic. But she chose the army.

She spent four years in military hospitals treating posttraumatic stress disorder and combat trauma before going overseas.

It was there that Roth found her. He saw her treat a soldier in the back of a Chinook helicopter. The soldier had just seen his entire squad blown up, and Laurel handled him like a horse whisperer with a wild stallion.

Levi Roth was a man who knew it when he saw it, and when he saw her with that soldier, he took notice.

When she saw him, she thought anyone who wore a tailored Tom Ford suit and horse-bit loafers around Fallujah was out of his mind. But she had to admit, there was an allure to him—a mystique. He was not a young man, but he moved like one. He spoke like one. She had the impression that if some drunk soldier in a bar picked a fight with him, he'd hold his own. Soldiers on the base called him the Rabbi because of his beard, but there were also rumors he was the only person in the CIA with a weekly face-to-face with the president.

That got Laurel's attention.

She remembered standing in front of his desk at their first meeting, his secretary handing her a plastic cup of ice water.

"Are you ready to be all you can be?" he said.

The meeting was a blur now, but she remembered learning that the operatives under Roth's command were the most valuable assets the nation possessed, and that he wanted her as handler for one of them.

She wondered now if she was still the person he'd seen on that helicopter. She looked at her reflection in the glass conference table and wondered, if he asked her now, would she still say yes?

He offered her the job of handler without saying what it entailed, and she accepted.

She later learned what an Asset was, and that her job was to keep one of them on task, to make sure he achieved his objectives, came back after missions, and didn't go off the deep end in the lulls between assignments.

And it was the lulls they worried about. Those were the times when alcohol, drugs, and sex threatened to overtake the men who had nothing, and no one, to lose. By the time a new Asset completed his first few missions, his handler was the only person he could speak to. She was the one who knew what he'd done. The risks. The dangers. The sacrifices he'd made. The sins he'd committed.

She heard him.

She saw him for who he was.

She cared.

Or at least it was her job to appear that way.

Assets were a special breed, and they required a special breed to handle them.

She rechecked her watch, then got up and made herself a cup of dark roast from the machine in the corner.

She didn't regret her decision. She was glad that she was where she was. It offered her the opportunity to do something real with her life. Something important. But she'd be lying if she said it had worked out exactly the way she'd imagined.

She had her own office. She had access to vast resources within the Group, including a staff of specialists who provided planning support. She had her own budget.

She'd done everything Roth asked of her, including deleting her civil record and legally changing her name and identity. She'd cut ties to everyone she knew.

She'd built her own network of properties, apartments, vehicles, weapon stashes, safe deposit boxes, and bank accounts around the world. She'd traveled to dozens of countries to cultivate contacts in foreign spy organizations and embassies. She'd recruited her own informants in the US Military, State Department, and Intelligence Community.

She'd been there two years.

She was ready for action.

She was locked and loaded.

There was only one problem. She had no Asset. She had no one to activate. Her slot was empty.

Something had gone wrong with her predecessor. She'd been compromised. And she was gone now. *Retired.* The term was ambiguous. Laurel knew it probably meant she was dead, but there was a sliver of doubt that allowed her to fool herself into thinking it might be something else.

Every Asset had a codename. They were named after the cars the handlers had owned when the Group was first created.

Paramilitary Operative Codenames
1. Mustang
2. Rebel
3. Camaro
4. Hornet
Special Operations Group Database

Laurel's was slot number one. Mustang.

She sat back in her chair and sipped her coffee. Roth supposedly had something important to tell her, but he was so late now, even by his own standards, that she was beginning to give up hope of him ever showing. She wasn't even sure he was in the building.

Then she saw his office door open. *Finally*, she thought, but it wasn't Roth who left the office. It was Mansfield. Harry Mansfield was the NSA Director, and as far as Laurel could tell, his job was to make Roth's life as difficult as possible. Their arguments were legendary.

The first time she met Mansfield was at a meeting at the White House, and right in front of the president, Roth threw a cup of water in Mansfield's face.

If they'd been at it tonight, she doubted Roth would be in any mood for their meeting.

She looked at her watch. If she left now, she could be home by eight. She began to gather her things and then noticed something was going on out in the office. There was a commotion among the specialists.

One of them stood to get people's attention. Then another.

Laurel went to the door.

A third specialist rose from his computer. "Comms are down," he said.

Laurel hurried to her desk and opened the Keyhole Satellite Relay on her computer. Usually, she could zoom in on any spot on the globe and get a live view. She could direct the orbiting cameras directly from her desk. It was the most complex communications system she had access to, and if it was glitchy, it was a good barometer of wider issues across the network.

The relay was completely offline. She'd never seen that before.

She opened her camera monitors.

Part of her job was to prepare resources that were likely to be of use when she was finally assigned an Asset. To that end, she'd placed cameras in the offices and homes of some of her informants and targets. The cameras were on a completely separate network from the satellite relay. They were down too.

The fluorescent light above her head flickered. Across the office, the lights went out, one by one.

Everyone went silent. The government had invested billions of dollars in the Group's resources. They had backup upon backup, servers, generators, ventilation systems—you name it. They should have been completely immune to the vagaries of telecom and utility outages.

On the sixth floor of the CIA building, the comms were never down.

The power was never out.

She could have heard a pin drop.

And then, as suddenly as they'd stopped, the fans of the air conditioners hummed back to life. There was an audible sigh of relief from the office. The computers began to reboot. The lights came back on.

Looks on faces were puzzled, bemused even.

"What was that?" one of the specialists said.

"The raptors just slipped out of their pen," another said.

Laurel checked the satellite relay. It was back up.

9

L aurel had trouble sleeping that night. She groaned when her five a.m. alarm went off. She stumbled into the bathroom and popped three extra-strength Tylenol before getting in the shower and letting the warm water coax her to full consciousness.

Something had been off about the night before. The glitch. It was unnerving. She should have been able to put it from her mind—Roth had ordered a full security audit, which she supposed would be the end of the matter—but still, it niggled at her.

She needed coffee. On her kitchen counter was the fanciest espresso machine money could buy, copper with brass accents. She made herself a strong americano, then sat at the counter and stirred stevia into it absently. She turned on the TV and let the news anchors drone on a while. Her attention shifted to the goldfish bowl by the coffee machine. Her goldfish was dead. *Again.* She flushed it down the toilet, then left the apartment.

CIA headquarters was in a leafy suburb outside the city. It would have been a nice place to live, but Laurel refused to get an apartment there. Instead, she paid twice as much to live in a loft on U Street in downtown DC. It was lively, with dozens of nearby restaurants and bars. It let her escape the world of federal bureaucracy she inhabited for work, but it meant leaving early to avoid traffic.

She'd dressed hurriedly, without makeup. She could put that on in the car. It was parked a block away, and she bought more coffee at a Starbucks on her way to it.

At Langley, she hurried through security and went straight to the conference room she'd been in the night before. Her meeting with Roth had been bumped. She was ten minutes late, but he would be later. He wasn't on time as a matter of principle. He was a man so aware of his own importance he'd ordered the Cadillac Escalade used for his transportation to be fitted with the same protective measures the Crown Prince of Saudi Arabia used. The upgrades included a bombproof undercarriage, bulletproof windows, and a specially built, supercharged seven liter V8 Corvette engine capable of horsepowers in excess of 700. It could get the massive vehicle from zero to sixty in less than four seconds.

Laurel forgave his quirks. He was a master at what he did. He got results, and at the end of the day, that was what they were all there for. She didn't care that he ruffled feathers. The world had bigger problems.

She made her third coffee of the morning, black with sweetener, and Roth's, just black.

Levi Roth was in charge of the most sensitive, high-value operations of the CIA's entire portfolio. His status rivaled that of the CIA Director, the Defense Intelligence Agency Director, and the National Security Advisor. Not only did he have direct access to the president, but unlike his rivals, he also had full operational autonomy.

He didn't report to anyone. He didn't answer to anyone.

And everyone, whether they liked him or not, recognized what he brought to the table. He hand-selected his Assets based on combat performance, and sent them to a facility at Camp Peary, Virginia, where they went through a grueling program he'd designed personally. If the rumors were true, it killed as many candidates as it graduated.

No one but Roth and the Assets knew for sure what the entire program entailed—each instructor knew only their own portion of the curriculum—but it certainly covered advanced aspects of modern weaponry, explosives, foreign and domestic firearms, hand-to-hand combat, tactical driving, escape skills, surreptitious entry, vehicle hot-wiring, extreme survival, wilderness training, field medical training, tactical communications, cyber skills, and tracking.

Roth took pride in the fact that all past Assets had received the highest valor awards the CIA had to offer—the Distinguished Intelligence Cross and the Intelligence Star. Not that the honors did them any good. They were awarded posthumously, in a secret ceremony attended only by Roth, Mansfield, the Director, and the President.

The Assets never officially existed. There was no star for any of them on the Agency's memorial wall. Roth was required, by Act of Congress, to maintain complete deniability in relation to all their activities. That secrecy was pursued to an extreme degree. If anything went wrong, anything at all—if their identity was compromised in any way—they were immediately disavowed. And in the Group, disavowal didn't just mean you lost your job, your 401k, the gold watch on retirement.

When an Asset was compromised, Roth was authorized by secret presidential memorandum to issue a kill order. And he did it. He knew better than to leave loose ends.

When an Asset outlived his usefulness, Roth, like the angel of death, came for him.

So when he entered the conference room, stepped up behind Laurel, and lightly patted her ass with an open palm saying, "Good morning, Vietnam," in an atrociously bad imitation of Robin Williams, she accepted it as part of the natural order of things.

In Langley, more often than not, she was the only woman in the room. It wasn't easy living in a boy's club, it wasn't *fun*, as some of her colleagues liked to imagine, but she was enough of a realist to recognize the potential advantage in it. In a place where everyone was constantly taking out their opponent, sex could be a tool—a weapon. There was a lot to be gained, *if* she played her cards right.

"You want one of these?" she said, holding up the coffee she'd poured for him.

"Sure," he said, taking a seat at the table. He flicked a switch, instantly clouding the glass walls of the room, and opened his laptop.

Laurel sat across from him and looked up at the screen on the wall. "What have we got?" she asked.

On the screen was a photo of a manilla envelope. A label was printed on the front.

    Lance Spector
       US Army SFOD-D
       Syria
       Hand Deliver

"Lance," she gasped. She'd never met the man but knew his name as well as she knew her own.

"The one and only," Roth said.

"He's in Syria?"

"No, he's not."

"But he's back in play?"

Roth spread his hands. "That will be up to you."

Laurel shook her head. She couldn't believe it. She'd been waiting two years for this moment. Finally, it had come.

She'd been briefed so many times on Lance's psyche profile, his training record, his tactical resumé, his service record with Delta Force, that she could have recited all of it from memory.

In one sense, she knew him as well as a person ever could know another. And yet, she didn't know him at all. His personality, his character, the events that led to her recruitment as his handler, were blanketed in fog. The records were utterly silent, redacted, deleted by Roth. Where Lance had been for the past two years, why he'd gone off the grid, what he'd been doing, and what had happened between him and his previous handler, were all questions that were shrouded in mystery.

Laurel had tried to pierce the veil. She'd tried everything she could think of to piece together an idea of Lance, of who he was, and most importantly, of where he was. But there was nothing. Anywhere.

Other than the pictures.

Roth had given her hundreds of images of Lance's previous handler. She knew what that woman looked like down to the minutest detail. But other than that, she knew nothing at all.

She had an idea in her mind, of course. She'd formed an image of Lance based on what she knew about Assets in general. But it was just that—an imagined picture, a fantasy.

The man she imagined led a solitary life. Assets didn't just operate alone in the field, out of contact with the military and the rest of the CIA, but even stateside, when they were off the clock, they were legally required to maintain secrecy to such an extent that family life was impossible.

Part of Roth's selection process was to identify candidates who were unmarried, had no children, and no close living relatives. Their mental well-being was closely monitored, and the Group's medical program included more psychological and psychiatric assessments than physical evaluations.

The whole thing seemed like a recipe for disaster.

But it worked and had done since the end of the Cold War when the Group was established by Roth to deal with the ever-widening range of asymmetric threats faced by the world's sole remaining superpower.

"You know I always had him slated to be your guy," Roth said.

Laurel looked at him incredulously. "Are you kidding me?" she said. "Look at me, Levi."

"Of course," he said, shaking his head.

"I mean...."

"Of course," he said again.

"We were ready to go," she said, her voice unintentionally rising. "We were locked and loaded. I was in that hotel room in Berlin in a pair of blood-red Louboutins and a lace dress. Remember?"

"Of course I remember."

"You pulled the plug at the very last minute."

"Something wasn't right."

"Well, you sure took your time making up your mind."

"I did what I had to do."

"You couldn't have thought of that before you..." she stammered, raising her hand to her face in a helpless gesture. She couldn't say it.

"I know it was... *disappointing*," he said.

She looked at him scornfully. "Disappointing? Do you know what I went through?"

Roth nodded. He let out a long sigh as he looked at her. "You're so beautiful," he said.

"Don't," she snapped. "Don't you dare, Levi Roth."

He nodded. Retreated. Tried another approach. "At its heart," he said, "this is a game of instincts."

"Of course it's a game of instincts."

"One wrong move, one wrong... anything," he said, grasping for the right word.

"And people die," Laurel said.

"Yes, they do. All too easily."

"I know that," Laurel said.

"And you know about your predecessor."

"Only what you've told me."

"Then you know how badly it can go."

She shrugged. She was under no illusions. The game they played was dangerous. She'd accepted that a long time ago. "So we want to bring him back into play?" she said.

"We want to try."

"Why?"

"Because he was the best Asset I ever had."

"If he was so good, why did you pull the plug?"

"I had no choice."

"Something he did?"

Roth shrugged. "More like something he was about to do."

"He'd become unreliable?"

"Unreliable's not the right word."

"Damaged goods?"

"Something like that," Roth said. "Yes. *Damaged* goods."

"And now you want him back because of that envelope?"

Roth said nothing. There was more to it, but she knew she wouldn't get it out of him.

She looked at the screen. An envelope. It wasn't much.

"We're going to pay him a visit, you and I," Roth said.

"What?"

He nodded. "He's been laying low under an assumed identity out in the sticks."

"He's in the US?"

Roth nodded.

"He's been right here this entire time?"

"I'm sorry," he said. "I know you were...."

"Were what?" she said. "What was I?"

"A lot was asked of you."

She shook her head. That was possibly the biggest understatement she'd ever heard in her life.

10

Their flight was supposed to be direct to Missoula, but the first major snow of the season had them redirected. That meant the Lincoln Navigator they'd reserved from Hertz wasn't waiting at the airport, and they had to make do with a Hyundai Accent.

"This isn't going to cut it," Laurel said to the Hertz employee who showed them the vehicle.

"It's the only car they have," Roth said.

"This can't be all there is," she said.

"Whatever they assigned you at the desk," the kid said. He couldn't have been out of school more than a year and didn't look like he'd dealt with too many people like Laurel in his customer service career.

"Are those even winter tires?" she said.

"All our vehicles are safe for winter driving."

"Really?"

"Yes ma'am, it's company policy."

She rolled her eyes at Roth. "Company policy," she muttered.

The kid looked at them blankly.

"Wait here," Roth said.

Laurel waited with the kid in his heated cubicle, and when Roth returned, he had the keys to a Chevy Impala.

"Better?" he said when they were inside the car.

"Barely," she said.

The drive should have been four hours, but because of the weather, it would be more like six.

Roth had taken the driver's seat and adjusted the position. It looked like he was going to try and make the most of the situation. He tuned the radio to the local NPR station. "What about some snacks for the road?" he said.

Laurel didn't give him an answer. She put on her headphones and tried to sleep. When she woke, they were past Whitefish, and Roth finally admitted they should have waited for the military aircraft she'd requisitioned before leaving Langley. That would have flown them straight to Malmstrom, and the Air Force would have gotten them to Deweyville from there.

"I just hate those planes," Roth said.

"You know we're crawling through this snow because you wanted a hostess?" Laurel said. They'd flown business class, and there was no question the civilian flight was more comfortable.

"I didn't see you complaining when you were watching your TV show."

"Movie."

"Ah yes, Adam Sandler. And they say the golden age of cinema is dead."

Around Stryker, the snow got so heavy they had to pull over.

"Sure is beautiful country," Roth said as they sipped

lukewarm coffee in a gas station, but it had been dark so long Laurel wasn't sure he was even fooling himself.

It was after midnight when they finally got to Deweyville. Their hotel was an EconoLodge—a modest, ninety-nine dollar-a-night place on the main drag that had the only vacancies in town.

"You're in room 309," the girl at check-in said, and Laurel thought she would physically strangle someone if anything else went wrong that day.

"Room?" she said.

"Yes, ma'am."

"We booked *two rooms*."

"We only have one," the girl said as if that ended the conversation.

"But we booked two. I have the thing right here. The confirmation."

"Well, with the snowstorm and all, we had to make a few accommodations."

"Accommodations?"

"Yes, ma'am."

"What does that mean?"

"We were flooded with last-minute requests."

"And you decided not to hold our booking?"

"Well, technically, we only hold bookings until ten p.m. It's after midnight."

"Our flight was diverted."

"If you'd called ahead...."

"Called ahead? We've been in the middle of nowhere for six hours. We didn't have signal. We're lucky we made it at all."

The girl looked to Roth for help.

"Come on, Laurel. It will be all right."

Laurel gave up. "Fine," she said, picking up her bag. "Are

there two beds at least?"

The girl typed on her computer, and Laurel already knew by how long it was taking that the answer was no.

"Forget it," she said.

"I'll take a cot," Roth said.

"We're out of cots," the girl said.

"The couch, then?"

The girl said nothing.

"Come on, Laurel," Roth said, reaching to help her with her bag. "We'll make do."

"I've got it," Laurel snapped, yanking the bag from him.

Apart from only having one bed, the room wasn't that bad. It was basic but had a coffee machine, a TV, and a clean bathroom with hot water.

"There's no couch," Roth said.

Laurel threw her bag on the bed. "Surprise, surprise."

"I'll take the floor."

Laurel shook her head. "I'll take the floor," she said. She slumped onto the bed and picked up the TV remote. She liked home improvement shows, people flipping houses, redecorating kitchens. She found something familiar and turned down the sound. "I'll tell you one thing," she said. "This Lance Spector better be worth the trip."

Roth shrugged. He had his suitcase open and was taking a leather toiletry pouch from it. It looked like something her grandfather would have packed. The sight of it, the domesticity, made her stomach turn.

"I guess that depends," Roth said. He hadn't told her much in the briefing. That wasn't unusual, but in this case, it didn't seem there was much more he could have told her.

A low-level embassy staffer in Istanbul had been handed an envelope at a local coffee shop. The owner of the coffee shop said a woman with dark hair had left it. Whoever the woman was, she was no novice. She'd known exactly where the embassy's security cameras were, as well as local police CCTV cameras, and managed to avoid being picked up by any of them. She arrived by cab and asked the owner to call her another cab when she left. The driver she'd come with couldn't be tracked down. The one that picked her up only took her a few blocks, letting her out at a nearby bus stop, again unmonitored by CCTV. After that, she disappeared.

The café owner said she never once removed her sunglasses or scarf. Apart from her hair color, the only identifying information he'd been able to provide was that she was slim, of average height, and ordered in English. He got the impression she was Russian, there were always a lot of Russians in Istanbul, but it wasn't anything more than a hunch.

The woman had apparently known that an envelope left at that café would find its way into the embassy.

As it happened, the staffer handed it in at the front gate, where it was scanned and opened by security as per protocol.

The envelope contained a printed note.

"I will only speak to Lance Spector."

There was a return address on the back for a mailbox service in Manhattan. Roth had it checked out. Against regulations, no ID had been taken for the box rental, and payment had been accepted in cash. The name used on the rental form was Reggie White.

"Did we track him down?" Laurel said.

"Who?"

"Reggie White?"

Roth chuckled. "I think it's a fake name, sweetie. Reggie White was a big player for the Eagles."

It had also contained a small titanium case, something clinical with a biohazard label on it.

The envelope and its contents were flagged by security, and the titanium case was put in a secure locker.

An embassy bulletin was sent to Delta Force at Fort Bragg informing them of the note, and they forwarded it to Langley. Within hours, the bulletin was on Roth's desk. He immediately had the CIA field office in Istanbul pick up the titanium case, and they sent it to a government lab in Germany for analysis.

Roth had managed to brief Laurel on everything to do with the envelope while refraining from giving her the slightest clue on what to expect about Lance Spector.

She'd pulled Spector's file before leaving Langley to see if it had been updated. It was as sparse as the day she'd first read it. The suppressed civilian record. The sanitized army record. His Group file with the Delta Force recruitment code and training record. Roth hadn't been kidding when he said Spector was good. He had the best training scores she'd ever seen. But that was where the file ended. It was as if Spector had disappeared after training.

Whatever he'd done for the Group, and whatever had led to his leaving, had been wiped.

From his birth certificate, she knew he was thirty-eight. His birth name had been erased, but he was born in Montana, which was where he'd been since Roth froze his status two years ago. He had no living family, no kids, never married.

The thing that stuck out about it all was Roth's treatment of him. The old man had stuck his neck out. That was weird.

He wasn't one for sentimentality. Spector should have been terminated when his status was frozen. The rules were black and white. And ruthless.

No one simply got to check out.

She could see from the file Roth had taken pains not to make a final ruling on Spector's status. It was purposely kept in limbo.

"So," Laurel said, "when are you going to tell me why you've got such a hard-on for this guy?"

"Hard-on?"

"Yeah," she said, holding her fist in front of her groin. "Hard-on."

Roth made to say something, then stopped himself.

She raised an eyebrow. He really had no explanation.

"His name pops up, and we fly halfway across the country in a snowstorm," Laurel said. "If this were any other Asset, you'd have sent a bullet, not a welcome wagon."

"He's a good soldier, Laurel."

"They're all good soldiers."

"He's different."

"No one's different."

Roth looked at her. "You don't really think that."

She shook her head. She wasn't that cynical. Not yet.

But the Assets were all as near flawless as soldiers could be. Laurel couldn't imagine what made Spector different enough to warrant special treatment. He had a good training record, sure, but so what? They all did.

They were, by design, one-man wrecking balls. They received no support, no supplies, no government preapproval or political cover for their mission. They entered the arena alone, carried out their objective alone, and watched their own back. If something went wrong, no one came to their rescue. If anyone from the government did come, it wasn't to offer assistance.

"You'll meet him tomorrow," Roth said.

"And then I'll see for myself?"

"I don't know that you will."

"It's all instinct, right?"

Roth shrugged.

"Let me ask you this," she said. "If he's so good, why did you cut him loose in the first place?" She couldn't help being curious. She'd made serious sacrifices to be this man's handler, and he was still little more than a ghost to her. "I mean, on paper, he's perfect."

"There was more to it."

"What more?"

"I had the file altered."

"You're hiding something."

"I didn't say that."

"But there was a red flag."

Roth shrugged.

"He's a nut?" Laurel said.

"No."

"He went off the deep end?"

"No."

"You altered the file. Something wasn't good."

"He's not a nut."

"You stuck your neck out for him."

Roth raised his hands. "Fine," he said.

Laurel sighed. "All I'm saying," she said, "is that if my life's about to be tied to this guy, and there's a red flag, something big enough for you to put him on ice for two years, I think I should know what it is, don't you?"

Roth was no idiot. Sure, he spent too much on clothes and had a fondness for women of a certain type, women young enough to be his daughter, but he also had his finger on the pulse of the nation's security in ways other people could never imagine. He was the man behind the secret assassinations, the targeted drone strikes. He was the puppet master pulling the strings. He decided who lived and who died. He kept the enemies of the world's most powerful government awake at night.

Sometimes, when Laurel looked at him, she saw everything that was wrong with the world—the privileged, pompous, domineering relic of a bygone era, a man so used to taking what he wanted that he no longer remembered what it was like not to have it. He'd never struggled to make his rent. He wasn't ogled from head to toe when he walked into a room. He certainly didn't have the hand of someone forty years his senior squeezing his ass.

But every once in a while, Laurel saw something in him that made her reassess. A man didn't find himself in Levi Roth's position by accident. He knew what he was doing. People in the know trusted him. The Pentagon and the CIA each had dedicated dark money budgets set up solely to ensure he got whatever he asked for—tens of millions of dollars in numbered bank accounts around the world. No auditor would ever ask him to account for those funds. No oversight whatsoever would ever be exercised. He was given the jobs no one else wanted, the things too dangerous, too toxic, not to contaminate whoever was sent in to deal with them. He'd been granted powers that would cause a political scandal on the scale of Watergate if they ever came to light. And everyone in the security apparatus, from the president down, knew that the weight of the world was on his shoulders.

Others would have buckled under the pressure.

Many of his operations were known to no one on earth but himself.

An objective might originate in a congressional subcommittee or a high-level Pentagon briefing. It might be mentioned quietly over brandy in the Oval Office, or on a golf course, or in the private dining room of an expensive restaurant. Sometimes, it was something Roth came up with all on his own.

In any case, there was never any paper trail. Nothing was explicit. Nothing was authorized. Roth's missions took shape like eels emerging from mud. Their form was the form he gave them. They were his golems. He worked on them quietly, taking his time, sometimes years, nurturing them like personal grudges. Some took so long that the person who'd initially mentioned the objective no longer remembered doing so. Often they'd retired, or died, or been removed from office.

But Roth remembered. He took them on. He made them his own. And when no one expected it, boom. A bomb went off. Or a drone struck. Or an assassin walked into a room and killed every man, woman, and child in it.

Nothing could be traced back to Washington. The president and the men in the big offices could sleep soundly. An enemy was dead, a threat was neutralized, and it was truly deniable. No one but Roth knew the entire story.

Laurel looked at him, and for a moment, she felt as if she was looking at her own future. A life of solitude, of loneliness, of quiet, faceless killing.

Roth cleared his throat. "Spector is an assassin," he said. "He's received more training on that art than anyone else on earth. More even than his own government is aware of."

"Okay," Laurel said.

"He's killed a lot of people for this country. Even before I found him, the body count was piling up. After I recruited him, it only grew."

Laurel nodded.

"There's a lot of blood on his hands."

"I understand."

"I mean, you could fill a graveyard."

"I get it," Laurel said, growing impatient. "He likes it too much," she said. "Got too much of a taste for it."

"No," Roth said.

"What then?"

"A man like him. You know what makes him different?"

Laurel wanted to shake it out of him. "Tell me," she said.

"The perfect killer. You know what makes him stand out?"

"Come on," Laurel said, exasperated. "Spit it out."

"It's knowing when not to pull the trigger."

She leaned back, surprised. That wasn't what she'd expected. "I see," she said.

Roth had taken some dental floss from his leather pouch and was in the process of wrapping it around his fingers.

"That doesn't sound like what we do," she said.

"It's not," Roth said.

"You don't like it."

"When you're in our line of work," he said, "someone not pulling the trigger is the scariest thing in the world."

"Even if they're right?"

Roth shook his head. "They're never right."

Laurel wasn't sure what to make of that. All she knew was that she was not going to stay there and watch Roth floss his teeth, getting bits of food all over the bed. "I think I'm going to go out for a bit," she said.

"Out where?"

"A drink. I saw a bar on the way in."

"Good idea," Roth said. "I'll join you."

Laurel shook her head. "No."

"No?"

"No offense, boss, but charming as your company is, I think I could use a little break."

11

The Yaroslavsky Train Terminal in Central Moscow had the distinction of being mile zero of the longest railway line on earth. The fact was commemorated by a small, concrete marker just outside the station with moss on its north side and a barely legible 'o' carved into its west face. The marker was placed in 1916 by a young engineer from Petrograd named Myasnikov, who personally oversaw the placement of every single marker along the ten thousand kilometer route. Myasnikov died in 1937 in a Siberian gulag, within sight of marker 3,434. His crime had been to suggest *improvements* to a later route drawn on a map by Stalin himself with pencil and ruler.

A passenger on the Trans-Siberian could get on a train in Moscow and pass Myasnikov's markers at a rate of one per minute for seven days, finally disembarking at the Pacific coast in Vladivostok, or Beijing, or even Pyongyang if they had the paperwork.

Marker 1816, the only one located on a bridge, marked the spot where the train left Europe for Asia. The bridge spanned the Iset River. The peaks of the Urals were visible in the distance. Across the river rose the Soviet-era buildings of the city of Yekaterinburg.

It was there, in 1723, that Peter the Great ordered the construction of a massive iron-making plant that would eventually become one of the largest metallurgical facilities ever built.

It was there also, in July 1918, that Tsar Nicholas II, with his wife and children, was executed by the Bolsheviks. The site of the execution—or massacre, depending on one's viewpoint—was the Ipatiev House. In 1977, at the order of the Politburo and to prevent it from becoming a symbol of revolution to future generations, local party chiefs oversaw the complete demolition of the house. Even the foundations were dug out of the ground.

The city's streets were laid out on a sprawling grid exhibiting some of the Soviet Union's most historically significant, if unattractive, constructivist architecture. The mile upon mile of uniform, concrete buildings appeared soulless even to the men who built them. One of the more distinctive neighborhoods, known as the Chekist town, was built in the 1930s to house the hundreds of members of the NKVD based in the city. Rumors still circulated of underground interrogation rooms and torture chambers that the secret police used to terrorize the population.

It was in this neighborhood, in the city's Infectious Disease Center, a few blocks from the train station, that Doctor Olga Abramova ran from her ward to make an urgent phone call. The number she dialed was for a line inside the secretive government institute located in the military compound south of the city center.

Sofia Ivanova was in her lab when the orderly came to get her.

"Doctor, you have a call. Very urgent."

She followed him to the main office and picked up the phone. It was rare she got a call through the switchboard. It usually signaled something official, a dreaded Moscow call.

"This is Doctor Ivanova," she said.

"My patients are dying," Olga said in her distinctive Irkutsk accent. Olga had grown up in a small village south of Lake Baikal, close to the Mongolian border. She had a way of speaking that some people found unsophisticated.

Sofia had always thought it charming. "Excuse me?" she said.

Sofia was the daughter of a prestigious doctor in Moscow and had gone to all the best schools. Her youth had been about as different from Olga's as was possible. She spoke English, German, and French fluently and had a way of making her Russian sound so soft and elegant that people in industrial Yekaterinburg sometimes mistook her for a foreigner.

She and Olga had studied together. They'd worked together before Sofia was plucked into military service and given the directorship of the institute. They'd been friends and remained so.

"Pneumonia," Olga said. She was agitated. "Something like that. We've had nine now."

"Olga," Sofia said. "Slow down. What on earth are you talking about?"

"Something's not right," Olga said. "Nine dead on this shift."

"What?" Sofia said.

Sofia had never told Olga what exactly she did at the institute, only that it was classified government work, but of course, Olga had her suspicions.

"Nine," Olga said again, and Sofia felt a wave of panic flood over her. She leaned on the counter to steady herself.

She glanced around the office. It was the nerve center of the institute, the place where all the calls came in, and the researchers did their paperwork. Everything looked perfectly normal. One of the administrators had had a birthday, and there were balloons by her chair. There was an open box on her desk with a half-eaten medovik cake in it.

Sofia told the orderly to grab her a pen and paper. "Nine fatalities?" she said.

"In two hours," Olga said.

"Symptoms?"

"Fever," Olga said, "headache, cough, chest pain." She was speaking very quickly.

"When did the symptoms start?"

"All nine women woke up feeling perfectly normal this morning," Olga said.

Sofia scribbled down the notes. "Women?"

"All of them."

It was in the air, Sofia thought. "What did they have in common, Olga?"

"Oh my god," Olga said. There was something going on in the background, some commotion. "They're bringing more now."

There was a click, like the receiver had been dropped, and Sofia heard Olga talking to someone else, her voice muffled. Then she was gone. The line wasn't dead, she could still hear sounds in the background, but Olga had left the phone.

"I've got to go to Infectious Diseases," Sofia said to the orderly, hanging up the phone and grabbing her coat.

She hurried to the elevator and threw on her coat. Outside, the snow swarmed around her. It seemed early in the year for the temperature to be so low. She got to her car and fifteen minutes later was at the east entrance of Olga's building.

She double-parked in an ambulance bay, and before she was even out of the car, she saw a woman coming out of the hospital. The woman wore the light pink uniform of the Empress Catherine textile factory. Sofia knew the uniform well. She passed the workers every day. The factory was located in Chkalovskaya, just south of Yevchenko's proposed production facility.

The woman hurried down the steps and stopped. She reached for the rail to hold herself up and began coughing. Then she fell to the ground.

Sofia ran to her. The woman couldn't breathe. Sofia looked around frantically for help but didn't dare leave. The woman gasped for air, and Sofia helped her to her feet. "Come on. Let's get you back inside."

The woman leaned on Sofia, but they only made it a few steps before falling.

When they hit the ground, Sofia's head smacked painfully against the ice. She got back up but felt dizzy as she tried to lift the woman. She was too heavy. Looking around desperately, Sofia cried for help.

A security guard came out of the hospital. "What's the matter?"

"She's not breathing."

"I'll get a stretcher," he said.

Sofia didn't know what to do. The woman was dying, and against all her better judgment, all her years of training, she did the one thing she knew might save her. She administered CPR.

She leaned the woman's head back, pinched her nose, put her mouth over hers, and breathed into her lungs. She did it over and over, interspersed with chest compressions, counting the time between movements.

By the time the guard returned, the woman was dead.

Sofia helped him get her on the stretcher, and they carried her into the hospital.

Inside, she saw why no one else had come to their assistance. It was complete chaos. People were on chairs in the waiting area, on the ground, in the examination rooms. There were women everywhere, dressed in the same pink uniform.

Sofia stopped a nurse in the corridor. "What's happening?"

"They just keep coming."

"From the Empress factory?"

"Yes. They can't breathe. They've been poisoned."

Another woman burst out of an examination room, and the nurse ran to her, catching her as she collapsed.

The nurse looked at Sofia desperately. "What should I do?" she cried. "They're dying. They're all dying."

12

L aurel found a bar that looked like it had come off the set of a Sergio Leone movie. Inside was a man talking to the bartender and another at the far end, his head on the counter.

"Is he asleep?" she said to the bartender.

The bartender nodded.

It didn't look very promising, but the thought of going back to Roth convinced her to give it more of a chance than she ordinarily would.

The other man was settling his bill, and Laurel got on a seat a few down from him.

When she looked at him, she nearly fell off the stool. It was him—the Asset.

He glanced her way and noticed her staring. "You look like you just saw a ghost," he said.

Lance Spector, in the flesh. She couldn't believe it.

Her mind ran over what she knew of him. Not nearly enough. Delta Force. Training at the farm. Everything had been so redacted.

"They don't make them like you, where I come from," she said.

That was always her fallback. Her go-to strategy. Flirtation. There was no quicker way to get a man to let down his guard.

"And where's that?" he said.

"Dale County, Alabama."

Laurel was comfortable around men. Where she came from, a girl had no choice. Looks-wise, she was a regular Homecoming Queen, with blonde hair billowing over her shoulders and blue eyes like two sapphires. Men had been underestimating her for her entire life—starting with Daddy.

He'd been a soldier, an officer, a hero, but also one mean drunk. He'd taught her the first and arguably most important thing she'd ever learned—trust no one. The lesson served her well in the Alabama state foster care system. It also served her in the CIA. The two had more in common than they should have.

Laurel learned early to hide weakness. Feelings stayed under the surface, invisible. No one should ever know what you were thinking. And they sure as shit shouldn't see you coming.

When you strike, strike once, and strike hard.

When you shoot, shoot to kill. Don't ever let anyone come back at you.

All of which was to say, she knew how to handle herself. And she knew how to handle men.

Lance nodded. "I know Alabama."

"I bet you do."

She leaned on the bar to give him a better view of *her* assets. She wanted his attention. He'd been about to leave the bar and she needed him to stay.

He sat back down and ordered a refill. "And whatever my friend's having," he said.

The bartender gave him some attitude. "Isn't your niece waiting?"

Lance looked toward the door. "Wait here," he said, then went outside with his keys.

Laurel and the bartender eyed each other like cats about to fight. Two women, one man, thirty minutes to last call.

Lance came back and sat two stools closer to Laurel than he'd been before. There was only one empty seat between them now.

Laurel gave the bartender a look that said, 'any other objections, bitch?'

She had nothing.

"What are you drinking?" Lance said, oblivious to the tension.

"Vodka soda," Laurel said.

The bartender poured the drink, and Lance said, "You know Fort Rucker?"

Laurel nodded.

"I know that place," he said.

"Not like I do," Laurel said. She threw her hair back. As with any predator, it was always good to let them see the neck.

She knew exactly what she was doing. It came naturally to her—the slow walk down a path that led to only one place.

She figured if she was going to be his handler, now was as good a time to start as any. A handler wasn't required to sleep with her Asset. In fact, technically, there was a rule against it somewhere in the handbook. But Laurel was no fool. She knew how the world worked. There'd been a time when the handlers were men, back when Langley was a boy's club, and they were still naming Assets after muscle cars. Those days were over. Assets were expensive, their job was intense, and the government had yet to come up with a better way of blowing off steam than the one nature provided.

She knew she was playing with fire. She wasn't his handler yet, and might never be. Roth might be pissed. Lance might know more than he was letting on. She really didn't have enough information.

But right then, she had a bigger worry. If she didn't somehow get herself between Lance's sheets, she'd be sharing a room with Roth. And that was not happening.

She had no doubt—zero, nada—that if she went back to room 309 of the Deweyville EconoLodge, Roth's hands would find their way onto her body. He wouldn't be able to help himself, whatever his intentions.

She knew men.

And that wasn't even the worst thing about it. Because if she said no to him, he'd stop. She knew that. He wouldn't like it, it would make things awkward between them, but he'd stop and never bring it up again.

No. The thing she hated was that she might not say no. She might let him have his way. As much as she knew men, she knew herself better. And she wasn't in the habit of lying to herself. If she went back to that bed, she'd go through with it, let it happen, and then she'd torture herself afterward. She'd hate herself.

She had daddy issues up the wazoo. She'd slept with so many older men that the Dale County Retirement Home probably had a wing named after her. And she didn't like that. She didn't like thinking about it. It made her feel dirty.

All she knew was that if she was getting screwed either

way, it might as well be by Lance. At least that way, there was something in it for her.

Lance was better looking than she'd expected. In their line of work, there was an advantage to being able to disappear in a crowd. Any woman would spot Lance a mile away. And she'd remember him. He had a Clint Eastwood ruggedness about him, like he knew he was attractive but gained nothing from it. He wore high-waisted Lee jeans and a checkered shirt. His jacket was aviator-style, tan leather with a fleece lining. He was tall, muscular. The way he moved, she'd have been able to tell he was ex-military even if she didn't already know it.

"You from around here?" she said.

"Born and raised."

"What's that like?"

"Not so bad."

"You get used to this cold?"

"Sure, you do."

The bartender came back over. Lance was the only man in the place who actually had a pulse, and she wasn't ready to let him go. "He's been to all sorts of cold places, haven't you, Lance?"

Lance smiled.

"Do tell," Laurel said.

"I've been here and there."

"Don't be modest, Lance," the bartender said.

Laurel hoped she didn't sound like that when she flirted.

Lance looked at the bartender, then at Laurel. "She doesn't want to hear it," he said.

"Sure, she does," the bartender said.

"You can't leave me hanging now," Laurel said.

Lance sighed. "I guess I was telling my friend here I was in the army."

"He said he was in mountains as cold as the Rockies," the bartender said.

Laurel looked at him. She was surprised he was willing to speak about his past at all. "Where were those?" Laurel said.

Lance looked at her, and his face was more open than she'd expected. More honest. "They were in Afghanistan," he said.

Laurel was all ears. She wanted him to talk. She'd come all this way. She wanted to see what the fuss was about. "I imagine there's a lot of dangerous men over there," she said.

Seduction was all about suggestion. The way she formed her words, the way she shaped her lips, the angle at which she presented her body. If she showed him that he could have her, that he was going to get what he wanted, he'd give away more of himself than he intended. It was a biological quid pro quo.

"Not so dangerous," he said.

"Not so dangerous? Isn't that the home of the Taliban?"

"So they say," Lance said.

"You don't think they're there?"

"Oh, they're there. No denying that."

"But you don't think they're dangerous?"

"No more dangerous than men anywhere."

Laurel wasn't so sure. A large part of her life had been spent thinking about the man who'd killed her father. To her, that was what Afghanistan stood for.

"There's a lot of dead soldiers would say otherwise," she said.

"Anywhere in the world you dig," Lance said, "you'll find the bones of dead soldiers. Anywhere at all."

Laurel thought a second. "More in some places than others," she said.

Lance shrugged. "I suppose that's true."

"Although," Laurel said, "what would I know? I've never been there."

That wasn't true. She'd been to Afghanistan, Iraq, Syria, Yemen, everywhere. She'd seen more war than anybody.

"Men—" Lance said, then stopped. He thought and said, "You travel to a dangerous place, you'll find the men there are no more dangerous than the men in any other place."

"*Any* other place?"

Lance nodded.

"Like where?" she said.

He shrugged. "Boise, Kansas City, Wichita."

"Wichita?"

"For example."

"You're saying men in Raqqa are no more dangerous than men in Wichita?"

"Well," Lance said, "there's a fight going on in Raqqa."

"But?"

"But the men themselves, they're no more dangerous."

Laurel looked skeptical. "Really?"

"Really," he said.

"So if I go to a bar in Raqqa...?" she said.

"There are no bars in Raqqa," Lance said.

"Right, but I mean, if I met a man there, you're telling me there's no difference between him and some random guy I meet in a bar in Wichita on a Saturday night?"

"Look at it this way," Lance said. "Someone from Wichita can get on a plane and be in Raqqa in less than a day. Does that make him more dangerous when he steps off the plane? Or someone in Raqqa can be in Wichita. All it takes is a plane ride."

"And a visa, thankfully."

"And a visa," Lance said.

It was Laurel's turn to shrug. "So you're saying...?"

"I don't know. I'm just drunk."

"No, you're making *some* sense."

"Well, that's something I don't hear every day."

"It's interesting."

Lance shrugged. "Maybe I'm smarter than I look," he said.

Laurel laughed.

"Smarts aren't even my best skill," he added.

"Oh, really?" she said. "And you say men aren't dangerous."

He shrugged. "Present company excluded."

"I'd like to see some proof of that," she said. She had him. It was too easy, like taking candy from a baby. And she knew he'd be a monster in the bedroom. She could tell by the way he held himself. She was in for a wild night.

But there was no hurry.

The longer it took, the sweeter the prize.

"So just for the record," she said playfully, "you don't think men anywhere are dangerous?"

Lance smiled. "What is with this chick?" he said to the bartender.

"I'm sure I wouldn't know," the bartender said.

Lance missed the attitude. "People think the world is full of dangerous men," he said.

"But not you?"

"Men aren't so dangerous. They're predictable. They follow orders. If you give them a weapon and tell them to fire, they'll fire."

"That sounds dangerous."

"It isn't."

It was time for her to move in for the kill. The poor

sucker. There he was, talking about men, when the real danger, as usual, was coming from a woman.

She put her hand next to his on the bar. He turned to her and let his knee touch hers. Contact. All she had to do now was reel him in.

She was about to lean in and whisper something in his ear. Something naughty. She'd brush her lips against his ear as she whispered it. Something truly dangerous.

But just then, the door of the bar burst open.

Some blonde, dressed like a prostitute, burst in. She was crying.

13

L ance looked wistfully at Laurel. The resemblance was uncanny. It was almost unfair of Roth. Where had he found this woman?

"Lance!" Sam cried from across the bar.

He sighed. It almost hurt to pull his attention away from Laurel.

Sam's mascara was all over her face. Her shirt was torn. Her lip was bleeding.

"That didn't take long," he said to Laurel.

Laurel was looking at Sam. "You don't seem too concerned," she said.

"Believe me," he said, getting to his feet, "I'm very concerned."

Laurel watched him walk toward the girl. "That's his niece?" she said to the bartender.

The bartender rolled her eyes. "Lady," she said, "I don't know who that girl is."

"What happened?" Lance said when he reached Sam.

She was frantic. Her hands were shaking. "They were waiting for me."

"At my place?"

"Yes."

Lance raised an eyebrow. "Wonder how they found you."

She looked away. "They must have followed us."

Lance smiled. "In that snowstorm? Incredible."

Sam looked at him. He made note of her tells. She was a good liar, but no one was perfect. She spoke too fast, tried to move things along too rapidly. For all the trouble she caused, she was a conflict-avoider.

Attention, yes.

Drama, yes.

Real trouble, no.

A big guy like the ex—and Lance already thought of him as the ex—would have an ego to repair. That was why he was there. But that was fixable.

The complicated part was Sam. Why was she calling a man she knew would beat her? And what would it take to make her stop?

He had some idea.

In about sixty seconds, the ex would come through the door. And he'd be armed.

"Go back there," he said to Sam, sending her to the bar where Laurel and the bartender were waiting.

"What are you going to do?"

"I'm going to make sure you don't call him again."

Sam hesitated, then said, "He has a gun."

"A gun don't mean much if he doesn't know how to use it," Lance said.

He went out the door into the cold night. There was a white Range Rover on the street with tinted windows, engine running, its blue headlights shining in his face. The wind brought a flurry of snow from the mountains, and Lance raised his hand in front of his eyes.

Someone was getting out of the passenger side of the Range Rover. Lance strode over and kicked the door shut before they got out. Then he held one fist in the other and heaved his elbow through the window.

The ex was inside, shattered glass all over him, his one wrist in a cast. His massive hulk filled the seat like he was a grown man sitting in a toy car. He had a Sig Sauer 9mm pistol in his good hand. Next to him was the friend with the broken nose.

The ex swung the gun, and Lance knocked it from his hand and grabbed it.

"Hello, fellas," he said. "Fancy seeing you here."

He grabbed the ex by the back of the head and slammed his face into the dashboard. The other guy reached for something under his seat, and Lance said, "Uh-uh."

The guy paused, then went for it anyway. Lance shot him in the thigh with the 9mm.

The man cried out.

"Reach for it again," Lance said.

The man looked at him, then at his thigh. "You shot me!" he cried.

Lance pulled the ex up by the hair and said, "So what brings you fellas to town?"

The ex shook his head.

"I ought to warn you," Lance said, "the sheriff's department is all the way in Libby. We just don't have the tax base here for a force of our own."

The ex raised his hands. "Mister," he said.

"Mister?" Lance said.

"You don't know who you're messing with," the ex said.

Lance scoffed. "*I* don't know? *Me*? You come to *my* town," he said. "*My* house. You point a gun in *my* face."

"Mister," the ex said again, and Lance slammed his face against the dash even harder.

The friend made to reach under his seat again, and Lance pointed the 9mm at him. "Go ahead," he said.

The man raised his hands.

"Keep them on the wheel," Lance said.

Lance pulled the ex's head up again and said, "Hardly seems fair he's the one who got the bullet. It's your show, after all."

"No," the ex cried as Lance reached into the car and pressed the gun against his leg.

"Here?" Lance said.

"Don't," the ex cried as Lance pulled the trigger.

The ex cried out in pain and grabbed his leg.

"Now, fellas," Lance said. "What say I get in the back seat, tell you to drive somewhere nice and quiet, and then kill the both of you?"

The other guy shook his head, but the ex said, "You're the one's going to die."

Lance made a 'tut-tut' sound and unceremoniously shot him in the other thigh. "Look what you made me do now," he said.

The ex screamed in pain.

Lance shook his head. This was a situation he was all too familiar with. Either he kept things simple and killed these two pricks, or he let them go and then had to worry about what they chose to do with their good fortune.

He checked if the back door was open and got in. He reached under the driver's seat and fished out another gun. It was a Rohm .22 revolver.

"I guess the simplest thing for us to do is go for that drive," he said. "Get this sorted once and for all."

"Please," the friend said, shaking his head, "this ain't my fight."

"Oh, I don't know about that," Lance said. "I can see where you're coming from, it being his girl and all, but this is twice I've seen you now. You've got a stake in it, one way or another."

The ex spoke. "You don't have to kill the two of us."

"Oh!" Lance said. "Look at this. A man of honor."

"Fuck you."

"If you have to die, he has to die," Lance said. "You know that."

"Why?" the driver stammered.

"You're a witness, Einstein. Think about it. I'm not going to shoot him, then drop you off like it's the end of a prom date."

"I'll never say a word," the driver said. "I swear to god, I won't."

The ex looked at him.

"Fair-weather friends," Lance said to the ex.

The ex scoffed.

"Besides," Lance said, "letting him off just doesn't feel right, does it?"

The friend was about to mount another protest when Lance tapped him on the arm conspiratorially. "Tell me honestly," he said. "You ever screw around with the girl?"

"What?" he said.

"You heard me."

"Fuck this," the ex said.

"Hold on," Lance said. "I want an answer."

The friend didn't know what to say.

"I knew it," Lance said. "You sly bastard. You just had to have a taste, didn't you?" Lance glanced at the ex. Weighed his reaction. Nothing. "You're not surprised," he said. "The two of you together? You dirty bastards."

"Fuck this," the ex said again.

"You dirty bastards," Lance said again. "She's barely old enough to drink in a bar. You know that?"

The ex knew it was over. He was shaking his head.

"Tell me why I don't put a bullet in each of your heads right now?" Lance said. He asked the question, and he meant it. He was looking for a reason not to kill them, and he was having a hard time finding one. Them dead made Sam safer. It made the world safer. And it had the added advantage of being convenient. There were a million places along the border he could throw the bodies. No one would come looking.

"That girl's not as innocent as you think," the ex said. "She asked for everything we gave her."

"I never said she was innocent," Lance said.

"Then why all this trouble?"

Lance raised his hands like he had no explanation. Like they were asking why he threw a bad pass in a football game.

"This is crazy," the friend said.

"Look," Lance said. "I'm going to tell you straight up why I'm here. That girl's daddy took a bullet that was meant for me. The only thing he ever asked in return was that I look out for his kid."

"Well, keep her then," the friend said. "Like we give a shit."

"I don't know," Lance said. "I don't want you guys saying something just because you think it's what I want to hear."

"We mean it," the ex said. "You won't hear from us again."

Lance sighed. "Yeah, but I let you fellas go, and honest as

you're being right now, a bit of time passes, and you get to thinking, and you change your minds. And then you come back, and we have to go through this all over again."

"We won't come back," the ex said.

"Better safe than sorry," Lance said.

There was a long silence in which no one said anything. Snow had covered the car. They couldn't see out the windshield. Apart from the broken window, they were completely cocooned. The night was deathly silent.

The friend whimpered. The ex was more stoic. That was probably why Sam chose him. Less of a pussy.

Lance had made up his mind. He knew men like this. If he wanted to look out for Sam, they had to die. It was harsh, but no one ever said life was easy. "That's enough chitchat," he said. "Come on. Let's go."

"No," the friend begged.

"Come on, buddy. Take it like a man," Lance said.

"I can't die," he blabbered.

And then Sam's voice. "Lance."

He looked up. She was looking in through the broken window. Lance had two guns in his hands, and the two men were covered in blood. "What is this?" she gasped.

"They know where I live," Lance said. "Now I have no choice. I've got to kill them."

"Kill them?"

"This isn't a game," Lance said.

"You don't have to kill them," she said.

"As long as they're out there, you're not safe."

"I called them," Sam said, starting to cry. "It's my fault they're here."

"You let us go, you'll never hear from us again," the ex said.

Lance let out a long sigh. "I don't know," he said.

"You have my word," the ex said.

"Your word?"

"Yes, sir."

"And I can count on that?"

"Yes, sir."

"I can take that to the bank?"

"Yes, sir."

Lance sounded skeptical. "And your word?" he said to the friend.

"For the love of God, yes," the friend said.

He looked out the window at Sam. The bartender and Laurel were there too. They were all staring at him like he was the psychopath.

"And you're going to stop calling them?" he said to Sam.

"Yes," she said, tears falling over her face.

"I'm sorry," Lance said, "but I don't buy it."

"What?" Sam said.

"They've got to die. If they live, they're going to come for you again."

"No," she cried.

"Come on, fellas. Let's go."

"No," Sam cried again. "Lance. You can't do this."

Lance looked at her for a long time. Then he said, "I'm going to regret this."

"You've got to let them go," the bartender said.

All three women looked at him, their eyes wide like they couldn't believe what they were seeing.

He sighed and leaned forward. "I ever see either of you around that girl again, and you're going to wish you were never born."

14

When Laurel got back to the hotel room, Roth wasn't there. She was too tired to figure out where he'd gone and climbed into the bed, as far to one side as she could get. She was out before her head hit the pillow.

When she woke, he was in the room, dressed, with coffee. Light came in through a gap in the curtains.

"What time is it?" she said.

"Eight."

"I slept in."

"You had a long day," he said, handing her a cup of coffee.

"Where were you last night?" she said.

"I couldn't sleep, so I worked."

"All night?"

"I fell asleep in an easy chair in the lobby."

She looked at him a few seconds—a gentleman after all.

He ruined it by saying, "I'll have to molest you some other time."

She took a sip of her coffee.

"Anything interesting happen last night?" he said.

Laurel shook her head. "You were out there, weren't you?"

"I'm still a spy."

She smiled. "You tell me what you saw then, spy."

"I saw the same thing I've been seeing from Lance Spector since the day I met him."

"And what's that?"

"A loose cannon."

"He handled the situation," she said.

"Handled the situation? He nearly killed two men."

"They had it coming."

"It was a mess."

"No, really. That girl's the daughter of someone in his old unit."

"I know who the girl is."

"It shows loyalty," Laurel said.

Roth shook his head. "You let him charm you," he said.

She looked at him, then away.

Roth finished his coffee. "I'll let you have some privacy," he said. "Meet me in the breakfast room when you're ready. There's a buffet."

After he left, Laurel had a long, hot shower. She used the hairdryer to clear the steam from the mirror and then stood staring at herself, seeing what Lance saw. It felt like someone else was looking back at her.

It had been cold in DC but nothing compared to the mountains. She'd packed the down jacket she usually brought skiing. It was nowhere near as warm as it should have been for what she paid for it, but she grabbed it before leaving the room.

She went downstairs and found Roth doing the *New York Times* crossword. He was doing pretty well for a Thursday.

They got a table, more coffee, and Laurel had toast with marmalade. Roth made his own waffles with batter scooped from a messy plastic bucket and then drowned them in fake syrup. He had another plate solely for sausage.

"How's the diet going?" she said.

"What are you, a doctor now?"

"Yes, actually."

He forked a sausage and put it whole into his mouth.

"So," Laurel said, "what's the plan?"

Roth ran his tongue over his teeth. "I need to go back to the room and floss before we go."

"Go where?"

"To visit Lance."

She waited for him in the lobby, and they walked out to the car together. They drove out of town into the mountains, and when they got to Lance's place, Laurel's eyes widened.

"Not what you expected?" Roth said.

She shook her head.

The house was stunning, perched on an outcrop of rock high above a steep, forested valley. It was built from hand-hewn logs, and she could tell a lot of labor had gone into it. "It's beautiful," she said.

"Built it himself," Roth said, and she was surprised to hear a trace of pride in his voice.

The second level opened onto a balcony, and she could only imagine the view from up there.

"His truck's here," she said. "Want me to go knock?"

"No need," Roth said, nodding toward the balcony.

There was a man stepping onto it from inside the house, looking very comfortable in a plush bathrobe and matching white slippers. He had a lit cigar in one hand and a shotgun in the other.

"Levi Roth," he called out. "You better get off my property before I shoot you off."

Roth looked at Laurel. "Don't worry," he said. "I've got this under control."

"I can see that," she said.

Roth looked up at Lance. "We're just here to talk."

Lance pumped the shotgun and aimed it at Roth. "Nothing would give me more pleasure than filling your ass with lead, Levi."

"There's no need for that, Lance."

"I'll tell you what there's a need for."

"Maybe if you invited us in to talk, rather than standing out here looking like Hugh Hefner...."

Lance aimed above them and fired into the sky.

"What the hell?" Roth said.

Laurel stepped forward. "Maybe you should let me try," she said.

"Be my guest."

"Lance," she said. "We're just here to talk."

"I don't give a rat's ass why you're here."

She looked at Roth uncertainly.

"He's an animal," Roth muttered. "Always has been."

"What happened between you?"

"Long story," Roth said.

She looked up at Lance. "Hey," she said, "I don't know what the history is here."

"That's right," Lance called out. "You don't."

"We just want to talk, Lance. We've come a long way."

Lance looked at her for a minute.

"Please, Lance," she added.

He sighed and lowered the gun. "He's lucky he brought you."

"I know he is," she said, looking at Roth, then back at Lance. "So, we can come in?"

Lance didn't answer. He went back into the house. Roth shrugged.

"I'm going in," she said. "You can wait out here if you like."

She climbed the steps to the porch, and Roth followed. She swung open the heavy wooden door. It led to a surprisingly spacious room. A vaulted ceiling rose comfortably above them and to one side was a stone fireplace with a log fire burning in it. There was an old velvet sofa in front of the fire. On it was a pile of blankets that Laurel realized covered the girl from the bar. To the other side, a wall made of glass looked out over a dramatic stretch of mountain, its cliffs falling precipitously to the valley floor.

"Is that an eagle?" Laurel said, pointing out the window.

"Yes, it is," Lance said from the staircase.

Laurel turned to him. He was a sight to behold. She was beginning to regret failing to seal the deal the night before. She'd had him in the bag. It was a done deal. Then that girl showed up and pissed all over the parade.

Lance went to the stove and put a pot on for coffee. Laurel and Roth looked at each other, uncertain if he was going to draw another gun on them.

"Still black?" Lance said to Roth. Roth nodded, and Lance poured him a cup. "And you?"

"Black with sugar," Laurel said. "Or sweetener if you have it."

He slid sugar and a spoon her way and poured himself a cup. Then they sat, and everyone stared at each other. Laurel couldn't help noticing the view of his chest through the loosely tied robe.

"It turned out beautifully," Roth said, indicating the house.

Lance looked at him. "I ain't ready for small talk with you."

Laurel wondered what could have happened between them. There was clearly a lot more history there than what she'd been let in on.

She looked at Roth, but his face remained blank.

"We came to talk business," Roth said, then added, "in private," nodding toward the pile of blankets on the sofa.

Lance shook his head. "I'm not a businessman anymore, Levi. You know that."

"Come on, Lance. You were born to it."

"People change."

"Not you," Roth said.

Both men spoke through gritted teeth. Laurel could hear the tension in their voices.

"Is he still flossing his teeth during meetings?" Lance said.

She nodded.

"I hear there was a little kerfuffle last night," Roth said, changing the subject.

"Kerfuffle," Lance said with a slight shrug. "I suppose you could call it that."

"Three gunshots," Roth said.

Lance held out his hands like he'd been caught in the cookie jar. "You got me, Roth. Unpredictable as ever."

Laurel watched Roth. He shifted uncomfortably. He couldn't control what Lance said in front of her, and it was making him nervous.

"It appears that way," Roth said.

"Which begs the question," Lance said, "if I haven't

changed—and I assure you, Levi, I haven't—then what are you doing here?"

Laurel looked back and forth between them. Whatever they'd been to each other, one thing was clear—it wasn't recorded in the file.

"I don't think we should continue this conversation until we have more privacy," Roth said.

"What conversation? This is just a visit from an old friend, right?"

"And a new friend," Laurel said.

Lance looked at her and their eyes locked. It was the first time that morning he'd given her his full attention, and it sent a thrill through her. "And a new friend," he added. "And might I say, what a charmer she is."

Roth said nothing.

"No, really," Lance said. "You couldn't have found someone more perfect for me, Levi. Bravo."

"What's he talking about?" Laurel said.

"He's just trying to get under your skin."

"Am I?"

"Yes," Roth said.

"Has she seen the pictures, Levi? I swear I don't know how you do it."

"What is this?" Laurel said.

"Show her, Levi."

Laurel felt her blood rise. "Show me what?"

Roth sighed. "This is a waste of time."

"The hell it is," Laurel said. "I want to know what he's talking about."

"Sweetie," Lance said, "you got a sister?"

"What is this?"

"I'm not continuing this conversation here," Roth said.

"Lance, we're at the EconoLodge for another few hours. If you want to talk, find us there."

"I didn't mean to upset you, boss," Lance said.

"Go fuck yourself," Roth said as he stood.

He made for the door, and Laurel said, "Roth, wait," but he didn't slow down.

When he slammed the door, the girl, Sam, woke up. She stretched and looked around the room. When her eyes adjusted, she saw Laurel.

"Oh," she said. "Sorry."

"Don't worry," Laurel said. "I was just leaving."

"I hope I didn't interrupt anything."

"You didn't," Laurel said.

Lance got to his feet. He seemed to have enjoyed getting Roth's hackles up. "You don't have to leave just because he did," he said.

"What was all that?" Laurel said.

"You'll have to ask him."

"I will."

"Is that coffee?" the girl said.

Laurel almost rolled her eyes. Whatever the relationship was between the two of them, she knew a girl like Sam wouldn't be content sleeping on the couch for long. Laurel stood.

"Really," Lance said, "stay. He'll get over it."

"Unlike you, he's still my boss," she said and gathered her things. On her way to the door, Sam gave her a breezy goodbye, and Laurel, for some reason, found herself slamming the door even harder than Roth had.

Roth was sitting in the car outside, and when Laurel got to it, he grinned at her. "You're more flushed than I am," he said.

"Don't talk to me," she said as she got in.

He seemed pretty pleased with himself for someone who'd just lost his temper. He sat there like an idiot, watching her put on her seatbelt.

"What?" she said. "Drive."

"We're not going anywhere."

"What do you mean?"

"You wanted to be his handler, right?"

"What are you talking about?"

"Sweetheart, this is the job you signed up for."

Laurel took a deep breath. She looked at him, still with that stupid grin on his face. "Oh, come on. You want me to go back in there?"

"No, I want you to come back to the hotel with me and watch some more home improvement shows while I finish the crossword."

"This is unbelievable," she said, unbuckling her seatbelt.

"This is the job, honey."

"It's a waste of time, is what it is. He wanted to shoot us the second he saw you. "

"But he let us in, didn't he?"

"He let me in."

"Yes, he did, and he'll take the bait. Mark my words."

"Bait?"

Roth smiled. "Bait, sweetheart."

15

"You like omelets?" Lance said.

Sam was leaning languidly over the back of the sofa, the shape of her nipples clearly visible through the thin t-shirt she'd slept in.

Then the front door opened, and it was Laurel, back for more. She looked just as flustered as when she'd stormed out two minutes earlier.

"Come on in," Lance said. "Roth leaving without you?"

"He's going to wait at the hotel."

"And you're back to convince me to come with you."

"You know how this works better than I do."

Lance wondered what she'd been told, how many of the blanks she'd been able to fill in, and how much of a shock she was still in for.

"How about some more coffee?" he said.

Laurel followed him back to the kitchen and sat down. He poured three fresh cups and brought one to Sam. When he reached her, he said, "You ever have a roommate?"

"I can take a hint," she said.

"Raincheck on the omelet?"

"Whatever," she said, and he averted his eyes as she got out from under the blankets in the flimsy t-shirt and a skimpy lace thong.

She pulled on her things, and Lance said, "Take my truck into town and buy yourself some clothes."

"Okay," she said.

"There's a credit card in the glove box. The PIN is 1963."

"I don't need your money."

He knew that wasn't true. "Well, if you need gas or something," he said, "1963. The year of the Kennedy assassination."

"The Kennedy what?"

Lance looked at her.

"I'm kidding," she said.

She left with the keys, and Lance prayed she'd buy herself something decent. If he'd been sleeping with her, that would be one thing, but he wasn't, and the thongs and nipples were killing him.

He went back to the counter and sat next to Laurel. He let himself look at her again and had to admit Roth truly had outdone himself.

"Where on earth did he find you?" he said.

Laurel shifted uncomfortably. "How about I ask a few questions?"

Lance raised his hands apologetically. "I beg your pardon," he said. "Ask away."

"What happened between you and Roth?" she said.

"What happened between us? You're not asking the right question."

"And what's the right question?"

"The right question," he said, "is where do you fit into all this?"

"What do you mean, where do I fit in?"

"Why did he get you to step in as my handler?"

"He wanted me for the job," she said, betraying the first crack of doubt in her smooth exterior.

"I'm sure he did," Lance said. "But why?"

"I have the skill set—the background. I'm a psychiatrist."

"Really?"

"Yes."

"And have you always looked like this?"

"What does that mean?"

"This," Lance said, waving his hand in front of her. "This face. This hair."

Laurel leaned back. "You better tell me what you're talking about, or I'm going to walk out of here."

Lance got up. "Wait here," he said.

He went upstairs to the safe. He'd installed it himself, built it right into the stone of the chimney stack. He turned the combination dial and pulled open the thick steel door.

Inside were passports, guns and ammo, cash in various currencies, and a folder of documents. He pulled out the folder and rifled through it until he found what he was looking for.

He went back downstairs, holding an eight-by-twelve-inch black and white photograph. It was a photo he'd taken. He'd developed it himself in a field lab on old Ilford paper. On it was a woman. She was naked, lying on her back, looking at the camera provocatively.

He handed it to Laurel, and when she saw it, her eyes widened. She looked up.

"Yup," Lance said.

"What is this?"

"You never knew?"

"I don't even know what I'm looking at."

Lance sighed. He wasn't sure what to believe, but he

wouldn't have put it past Roth to pull something like this on both of them. "Her name was Clarice," he said.

"Was?"

"She's dead."

"And she was your...?"

"She was my handler," he said before the silence had time to hang.

Laurel nodded.

Lance looked away. Roth was more messed up than he'd given him credit for.

Laurel cleared her throat. Lance knew this couldn't have been easy for her. No one wanted to find out they were a dead woman's replacement. She sipped her coffee, and Lance poured her a glass of water. "Thank you," she said and drained it in one go.

"I'm sorry to be the one telling you this," he said.

"It's not your fault," she said, and she looked at him for so long, so intently, that he was forced to break eye contact first.

"When," Laurel said, clearing her throat again, "when did she die?"

Lance sighed. This wasn't something he liked to talk about. "I'm guessing right about the time Roth went and found you."

She nodded. He watched her. He could see the truth percolating through her mind. "It can't be a coincidence, can it?" she said. She was angry. He couldn't blame her. She was only now beginning to see things as they actually were.

And it would only get worse. This was the tip of the iceberg.

Working with Roth, things were never how they seemed.

Lance shrugged. "They didn't make you get plastic surgery, did they?"

"What? Of course not."

"And you don't have a sister?"

"Not that I know of."

"Then you've never seen this woman before?"

"Never in my life."

They both looked at the photo for a few seconds. Laurel stared. Lance felt sorry for her.

"You could be sisters," he said.

"Yes," she said.

"I think it's fair to say you were recruited for more than your technical abilities."

She nodded.

"That's not to say you're not good at what you do," he said.

"Please," she said. "You don't have to sugarcoat this."

"They wouldn't hire you if you couldn't do the job."

"The job?" she said, biting her lip.

"It's not what it seems," he said.

"You know what Roth said to me when I went out to the car?"

"What?"

"That I was bait."

Lance nodded. "He knows what he's doing."

"Does he?" she said, and she looked so vulnerable in that moment. So like Clarice.

He took a deep breath. Whatever he felt, he owed it to this woman to keep his cool. "He does," Lance said. "We're talking, aren't we?"

"Did you know last night when you saw me at the bar?"

"Why do you think I loaded the shotgun?"

Laurel nodded. She went to the sink and refilled her water glass.

"How did Roth recruit you?" Lance said.

"I was in Iraq with the 82nd Airborne."

"And he just ran into you?"

He watched her cast her mind back. He felt for her. He knew that was what Roth intended, but he couldn't help it.

Laurel saw everything differently now. In the blink of an eye, everything she'd thought she'd been, everything she'd thought she was doing with her life, had changed. Whatever she thought she knew would have to be filtered through the prism of this new piece of information. She'd been chosen as bait. She'd been chosen because she looked uncannily like someone else.

Someone he'd been in love with.

"Can I ask you a question?" she said.

"All right," Lance said, pouring himself more coffee.

"Roth's not exactly on a first-name basis with the other Assets."

"As far as you know," Lance said.

"Yes," she said, and he could see she had a whole new respect for Roth's ability to deceive her.

Lance let out a deep sigh. "Look," he said, "Roth has a job to do. And it's not always the job we think it is."

"I see that," Laurel said.

"Doing his job... don't take it personally, but to do his job well, sometimes it means lying to us."

"I'm not in kindergarten," Laurel said. "I get that."

Lance shrugged. "Well then, whatever he's told you, whatever he's said about this mission, about me, about your role...."

"I know," Laurel said. "Don't trust it."

"You ever seen the movie, *The Departed*?" Lance said.

"I've seen it."

"You remember what Mark Wahlberg said about the feds?"

She smiled. "'Keep them in the dark and feed them shit'."

"That's what Roth does with us."

Laurel nodded. "I guess I always knew that."

"You just didn't see it hitting so close to home."

"No, I didn't."

"The thing about it," Lance said, "is that to do this job, you have to take every word Roth says as gospel."

"Even though half of it is lies," Laurel said.

Lance nodded. "More than half. And you have to eat it all. You have to swallow and not ask yourself what's true and what's not. To do this job, you have to tell yourself that as far as you're concerned, the truth and the bullshit taste the same."

"Swallow and don't ask questions."

"That's the job."

"Reminds me of a few other jobs."

"Yes, it does," Lance said.

Laurel threw her hands up. "Screw it," she said. "This is nothing I didn't already know."

"If you can accept it," Lance said, "if you can really get down with it, you'll sleep better at night."

"And I'll do my job better."

"Sure," he said.

Laurel went to the window. "Do you suppose he knew we'd talk like this?" she said.

"Sure he did," Lance said. "He orchestrated it."

"Then we're playing right into his hand."

"Well," Lance said, "to be honest, he probably thought we'd be upstairs by now."

Laurel looked at him.

Lance took a step toward her, and another, and she raised her hands like she thought he was about to throw a stray cat in her face. "Come on, Lance."

"Sorry."

"I just found out I was hired because I look like your ex."

"Sorry."

"I mean...."

"I said, I'm sorry."

"What do you think I am?"

"I know. I know."

She took a breath.

"You seemed game last night," he said.

"I didn't know my whole life was a lie then, did I?"

Lance shook his head. "I'm sorry," he said again.

"Give me some time to let it sink in."

He nodded. He sat back down, and they stared out the window in silence for a minute. Some birds were circling in the sky.

"Those birds are going to kill something," Laurel said.

"Look at you, all maudlin."

"I can't believe I was hired because I look like your ex."

"Ex-handler," he said.

"Come on."

He sighed.

"You had a thing with her," Laurel said.

"I did."

"And something happened."

"Something always happens."

"And Roth was involved."

"Yes, he was," Lance said, and the way he said it made it clear there was more to the story.

"Was she ever here?" Laurel said.

"What do you care?"

"I'm curious."

"Try not to get hung up on her."

"Just tell me."

Lance sighed. "Fine. Obsess."

"Cut me some slack. I'm practically her twin. I just want to know."

"She was never here. I came back after she died."

"Was that before or after Roth hired me?"

"I don't know when Roth hired you."

"Two years and four months ago."

Lance did the math. "It was a little before that."

"Why did you come back?"

"Because I needed to get my head straight."

"So he gave you time?"

"Yes."

"And you've been on the books this whole time?"

"I guess so."

"He could have ordered you killed."

"I know."

Laurel shook her head. "You guys," she said.

"Laurel, believe me when I say you don't know the half of it."

"Do I want to know?"

He fixed her in his gaze. "No," he said, "you do not."

16

S ofia had to stop.

She went to a sink and scrubbed her hands. She didn't realize she was crying until Olga shook her.

"Sofia. Sofia."

"Please," she cried.

"Wash your face, Sofia. You're covered in blood."

Sofia washed, and Olga brought her through some doors to a private area. For the first time since she arrived, Sofia felt like she could breathe.

The emergency room was armageddon. The victims kept pouring in. First, they'd come from the textile factory. Young women in pink uniforms, their hair tied up in nets, coughing blood, choking, clawing at their necks. Then from the surrounding areas—children in school uniforms, little girls in navy blue jumpers and white blouses, boys in matching gray shorts and blazers. Then shoppers from the Pokrovsky department store. And finally, residents from the massive apartment blocks south of the textile factory.

"Sit down," Olga said. "Have you had any water?"

There was a bench under the window, and they sat next to each other.

The patients presented as if suffering from severe pneumonia—high fevers, coughing, vomiting. But pneumonia didn't strike like this. The people kept coming, and they kept dying. They were dying within minutes of exposure. That wasn't pneumonia.

Sofia knew what it was. But she didn't dare say it.

The casualties would keep coming. They'd continue for days. The death toll would be horrible, but it would be the other side of it that got really ugly.

The politics. The cover-up.

It had happened before.

And even as the bodies continued to pile up, that was the battle Sofia was steeling herself to fight.

The bodies were piling up faster and faster. They lay in gurneys in the corridors where they'd been left by orderlies. They lay in the waiting room, scattered among the living. She'd seen one body in an elevator doorway, the doors opening and shutting on it over and over.

A nurse entered. "Doctor Abramova," she said. "There's something you need to see."

Olga and Sofia turned to look out the window. The parking lot was chaos, with ambulances and cars everywhere. Some had been abandoned, their doors open and hazard lights flashing. One had crashed into a concrete pillar of the receiving bay. There was blood on the windshield.

But what the nurse wanted to show them was in the sky.

"It's the army," Sofia said.

At least four helicopters swarmed above them.

"They don't look friendly," Olga said.

"No, they don't."

Then they saw soldiers marching down the street from a fleet of troop transports.

"They're locking us down," Sofia said.

Olga nodded.

Both women had worked in infectious diseases. They knew the protocols. Even for the most virulent outbreak, this was a very fast response on the part of the military. Sofia realized Yevchenko must have had the forces at the ready.

The soldiers formed a cordon around the hospital. They were letting traffic in, but Sofia doubted they'd let it back out so easily. They were setting up a quarantine.

The sight of the soldiers alone would spread panic. They were in white hazmat suits with gas masks that made them look like something out of a horror movie. Sofia knew they'd be authorized to shoot to kill. Their Kalashnikovs were loaded with live ammunition.

"How many have died?" Sofia said.

Olga shook her head.

"Olga," Sofia said. "I need to call the institute. How many casualties?"

"I don't know."

"Two hundred? Four?"

"Four," Olga said.

"And no signs of transmission?"

"No."

"No hospital staff are sick?"

"None, so far as I know."

There was a clunky old phone on the wall next to the notice board, and Sofia picked it up and dialed Vasily's number back at the institute.

"Sofia," he said when he picked up, his voice frantic. "I've been trying to get hold of you for hours. What's going on?"

"I was going to ask you that," she said.

"Yevchenko was here. They've locked us down," he said. "No one's allowed to leave."

"There's been an exposure," Sofia said.

"What have you seen?"

"Hundreds have come in, Vasily. It's a nightmare."

"How is that possible?"

"They've been coming from the textile factory."

"What?"

"Yes."

"The Empress Catherine?"

"Yes."

"That's right in the middle of the southern industrial district."

"I know."

"The production facility."

"I know, Vasily."

"But the facility, it's not operational. It's just a bunch of empty tanks and vats."

"They must have started production without telling us."

"How could they do that?"

"I don't know," Sofia said, shaking her head. "I don't understand how they could be so reckless."

"They started from the sample we gave them?"

"It's the only way."

"That's madness."

"I know."

"What are they using for containment?"

"I don't know."

"It's criminal. Those military techs don't know the first thing about what they're doing. They don't have a clue what they're dealing with."

"I know, Vasily."

"They're asking for disaster."

"I've got to speak to Yevchenko," Sofia said.

"He was here," Vasily said.

She heard him put down the phone, followed by arguing. He must have been in the main office. She could picture it—the staff all there, soldiers guarding the doors, making sure no one left.

Vasily came back on the line. "He's not here. He's left."

"Where is he?"

"The governor's office. You'll have to try there."

Sofia dialed the governor's office, and a middle-aged woman's voice answered. Sofia said, "I need to speak to Major General Yevchenko."

"That's not this desk," the woman said. "You need to call Chkalovsky desk."

"No," Sofia said, her voice rising. "My name is Sofia Ivanova. Head of the Permafrost Pathogen Institute in Sverdlovsk Military Compound Number 19. I need to speak to Major General Yevchenko immediately. It's an emergency."

"It's impossible," the woman said.

"Listen to me," Sofia said. "I've got bodies piling up. Women from the factory. Children. Unless I speak to Yevchenko immediately, it's going to get worse."

There was a pause. Sofia knew there were two ways this could go. The woman on the other end of the line had decades of training. Today, Sofia was asking her to make an exception. To bend a rule.

"Sofia Ivanova," Sofia said into the phone. She kept her voice as calm as possible. "I'm at the Infectious Disease Center. Soldiers are here. It's very important. I have authorization."

There was a click, a long pause, and then Yevchenko's voice. "Hello?"

"You son of a bitch," Sofia said.

"Sofia, you don't know what you're talking about."

"You son of a bitch, Yevchenko."

"I'm going to hang up this phone."

"Hazmat suits? Kalashnikovs? That's just the beginning, isn't it?"

"I'm following procedure."

"This thing isn't contagious. It's a leak from your facility."

"I'm following orders, Sofia."

"This is the bacillus, Yevchenko. Not the virus. The quarantine is unnecessary."

"Do I need to remind you who you're speaking to?"

"Yevchenko! This is on you. This blood is on your hands. You never should have started production."

"Who told you we started production?"

"*Please.*"

"You better be careful what you say next," Yevchenko said, but Sofia was past caring.

"Locking down the hospital? That's going to end in bloodshed too."

"Sofia, this is an open line."

"I don't care."

"Someone's listening, Sofia."

"Let them listen. Let them hear this. You idiots did this, and these deaths are just the beginning. We're going to see the whole nine yards. The cleaning trucks with the chlorine. The livestock culls. The pyres of corpses burning. This is all on you."

Yevchenko let out a laugh. "Listen to yourself," he said. "Tying your own noose."

"Someone ought to hang you," Sofia said.

"You're the one who created this," Yevchenko said. "This came from your lab, Sofia. The most deadly substance ever produced."

"You gave me no choice."

"But you outdid yourself, didn't you? One picogram, Sofia? One picogram? You know how small that is?"

"That's why I begged you not to start production."

"It's a trillionth of a gram, Sofia."

"You shut up, Yevchenko. You shut up."

"Seven times more toxic than polonium, my dear. No one told you to do all that."

"You told me to harvest the pathogen, and that's what I did."

"This thing will silence entire cities," Yevchenko said, sounding almost giddy at the prospect. "It was inevitable it would lead to an accident."

"And what are you doing to contain it?"

"Whatever I have to, my dear."

"I'm going to kill you, Yevchenko."

"You did this, Sofia. You did this. And if your virus is anywhere near as deadly as this—"

"You better destroy that virus, Yevchenko."

"Or what, Sofia? Or what?"

17

———

Laurel and Lance went to the EconoLodge by taxi. They didn't say much until Laurel broke the silence.

"How's this going to turn out?" she said.

"What do you mean?"

"You know why we're here."

He shrugged. "You haven't told me much."

"But it's obvious there's a reason. Roth's got something in mind."

"There's a mission," Lance said. "There's always a mission. Some new crisis in the making."

"And are you going to say yes?"

He looked at her. She knew he saw the other woman now. Clarice. A woman he'd loved.

There was power in that. Maybe she'd write a paper on it one day.

"It depends on what he says," Lance said.

"But you know what he'll say. You said so yourself. A new crisis. Life or death. He wouldn't have come all this way if he didn't need your help. Yada yada."

Lance looked at her. He said, "I truly doubt there's anything Roth could say that would make me come back."

She sighed. They were almost at the hotel. She already knew how the meeting would go. A photo of an envelope wasn't going to change his mind. Whatever had happened in their past, it wasn't about to be undone by one piece of mail. Unless Roth had something very big up his sleeve, the only way they were going to get Lance back was if *she* did something to change his mind.

They got to the hotel. Roth was waiting in the room. He'd set up some basic signal blocking measures—the device was on the bedside table, its red light blinking.

"I see you're ready to talk business," Lance said as Roth shut the curtains.

Laurel turned on the bedside lamps for extra light. It gave the room a mysterious feel.

"Coffee?" Roth said.

They shook their heads.

"Right down to business then," Roth said.

No one objected, and he began opening his briefcase.

"Before we start," Lance said, "I think you should know, Levi, that nothing's changed for me."

"In what sense?" Roth said.

"Since I left."

Roth nodded. "All right. I hear you. I didn't expect you to forget what went down."

"And I haven't."

"But time heals all wounds," Roth said.

"Not this wound."

Roth nodded again, like he was hearing Lance's objection, but continued rooting in the briefcase all the same. When he found the file, he pulled it out and held it on his lap.

"What I'm saying," Lance said, "is I don't see that we have a whole lot to talk about. What you did, there's no forgiving that. And there's no forgetting."

"Why don't you hear me out?" Roth said.

"Why bother? I can see how thin that file is. We both know there's nothing in it that will change anything."

Roth was agitated. He knew that was true. Laurel could see he had no ace up his sleeve. Just the envelope. "Will you at least hear us out?" he said.

"As long as you don't tell me anything classified," Lance said. "If you've got any state secrets in there, things that will create complications if I'm told about them, I'd rather not know."

"When have you ever been to a meeting like this and not exchanged sensitive information?"

"Come on, Levi. We both know this is a charade. You're not going to change my mind, and even if you did, you know as well as I do you don't want me back."

Laurel could see it playing out. Any minute, Roth would lose his patience and blow it. He and Lance had too much history. She was going to lose Lance before they'd even told him why they were there, and she was damned if she'd waited two years for that to happen.

She got up, took the file from Roth, and pulled out the photo. "Laurel," Roth said.

"I didn't come here to watch you two measure dicks," she said.

He threw up his hands. "Fine. You tell him."

She handed the photo to Lance. "That envelope was handed in to the US Consulate in Istanbul," she said. "As you can see, it's addressed to you."

"All right," Lance said, taking the photo from her.

"Any idea who would want to speak to you?" Roth said.

Lance shrugged.

Laurel showed him the next photo. The typed note.

"I will only speak to Lance Spector."

"Please tell me there's more than this?" Lance said.

"No idea who it's from?" Roth said.

Lance looked at the envelope. "Do you?"

"Someone who knew you were in Delta Force," Laurel said.

"I can see you didn't hire her only for the looks."

Laurel threw her hands up.

"Come on, Lance," Roth said.

"I was kidding."

"There's no need for that."

"I said I was sorry," Lance said. "Man, who knew you two were so sensitive?"

"We need to make progress on this," Roth said.

Laurel nodded. She couldn't take another two years of being sidelined. "What about the titanium case?" she said, looking at Roth.

Roth nodded.

"There was a small titanium case in the envelope," she said. She had no idea what it contained, but she assumed Roth had sent it to a lab. That had to be the reason they were there. The analysis had found something. She turned to Roth. "Did we get a lab report?"

"Yes, we did."

Laurel and Lance waited.

"If I talk about this," Roth said, "we're veering into sensitive territory."

"All right," Lance said. "I don't want to hear it."

"I do," Laurel said.

Roth shook his head. "This is a waste of time."

She flicked through the file and found the report. "The case contained a vial," she said. "The vial contained a virus. Completely unknown. V-2, they've called it." There were some stats, and she went through them. "Virulence is off the chart," she said. "I've never seen anything like it."

"That's lethality," Roth said to Lance.

"I know what virulence is."

"It's not exactly the same as lethality," Laurel said, "but drug resistance is off the chart too." She went down the list of antibiotics it had been tested against. "My god. It's unstoppable."

"Every single med they tested," Roth said.

"What's the estimated lethality?" Lance said.

"Without treatment?" Roth said. "Very high."

"How high?"

"There's no way of knowing."

"And with treatment?"

"Weren't you listening? There is no treatment."

"That can't be right."

"It's right."

"What about virality?" Lance said.

Laurel flipped through the report. "The Ro—" she said.

"Ro is the number of people one infected person can spread the virus to," Roth said to Lance.

"Will you stop explaining everything to me?"

"This thing is armageddon," Laurel said.

"The Ro is twenty-five," Roth said.

"Where did this come from?" Laurel said.

Roth shrugged. "We don't know yet."

Lance cleared his throat. "Russia."

"He speaks," Roth said.

"You know as well as I do this thing is Russian."

Roth nodded. "I'd like to get some confirmation. Trace it to a specific lab. To a specific scientist. Find out what we're really dealing with."

"You think that would lead us to an antidote?" Laurel said.

"If one exists," Roth said.

"One had better exist," she said, "because if these numbers are correct, this thing is a ticking time bomb. It's unstoppable. It will wipe out everything it touches."

"So that's what this is about?" Lance said. "A new Russian bioweapon?"

"You're saying that like it's nothing serious," Laurel said.

"Oh, it's serious," Lance said. "I get that. You're the doctor, Laurel, but those numbers suggest whatever lab came up with it has finally figured out what Russian micro-biologists have been trying to figure out for the best part of a century."

"Which is?"

"They've found their biological super weapon. Something that will stop NATO in its tracks. Get us to back off and let them rule their sphere without interference, once and for all."

"This is far more than a deterrent," Roth said. "This is a holocaust. A holocaust in a bottle. I've been told a single person carrying this virus steps off a plane, and we have five hundred cases in twenty-four hours."

"Good luck containing an outbreak like that," Lance said.

"Excuse me?" Laurel said.

"Look, sweetie, it's been real nice meeting you. And Roth, you've really outdone yourself with this one. She looks so much like the real thing I'd be hard-pressed to tell them apart. But I don't work for you anymore. And I haven't forgotten what you did."

"Maybe I'm not making myself clear," Roth said.

"Oh, you've made yourself perfectly clear."

Roth was losing his temper. "How long are you going to hold one mistake against me, Lance?"

"One mistake? Oh, please. You're lucky you're still breathing. I swear that on my life. The number of times I've pictured blowing your brains out."

Roth slammed his fist on the table. "You shut up and listen," he said.

Laurel was taken aback. She'd never seen Roth like this before. His face was red, and his voice was loud enough that someone out in the corridor would be able to hear him.

"I don't work for you, Levi."

"Don't you even care that this thing is going to kill people?"

"It's dangerous," Lance said, "but they won't use it. They can't."

"Why not?"

"Because there'd be no way of controlling it."

"What if they don't want to control it?" Roth said.

Lance said nothing. He took a step toward the door.

"That's right. Walk away. Like you always do," Roth said.

"What did you say?"

Laurel stepped between them. It looked like it was taking all the willpower Lance had not to knock Roth's lights out.

"Fuck you, Levi."

Roth stood up and stared back at him defiantly. "Fuck me? Look at you. Standing there like this has nothing to do with you. But this thing arrived with your name on it, Lance."

"I don't have to listen to this."

"The most virulent thing we've ever seen, and your name's right on the bottle."

Laurel put her hand on Lance's chest to hold him back.

"Sit down," she said. "Hear us out."

He looked at her, then back at Roth.

"Just sit down," she said again.

He didn't sit, but he took a breath. "You really have no idea who sent this?" he said.

"That's why we need you," Roth said. "To find whoever sent it. And talk to them."

Lance shook his head. "It could be from anyone. I already told you it's Russian. For all we know, it's a trap. Did you think of that?"

"Of course I thought of that."

Lance started putting on his coat. That was it. Roth was going to let him walk out.

"No," Laurel said.

"Laurel..." Roth said.

"I'm not going to let him just leave."

She wanted him. She wanted to be his handler. She wanted to get him back in play. She hadn't joined the CIA to sit on her hands.

"This vial is a warning," she said.

"I don't care," Lance said.

"It's going to lead to deaths."

"Then find out who made it and stop them," Lance said.

"You know what's going to happen," she said.

"It's the same thing that always happens," Lance said. "It's the way of the world. War, war, war. Death, death, death. It never changes. And I'm done fighting it."

Laurel shook her head. "Are you really going to pretend you don't give a shit?"

"Come on, Laurel," Roth said. "Let him go."

"No," Laurel said. "Whoever sent that vial wants to talk to him. They're offering to talk to him. And only him."

"I don't know who they are," Lance said.

"You don't know who they are? So what? They're offering, and people are going to die. This thing ever gets out, it will be game over."

"I'm sorry," Lance said, making for the door again.

Laurel raised her voice. "No," she cried.

He turned and looked back at her.

"Don't go," she said. "Please." He was still holding the papers she'd given him. She knew what she was doing. He was looking at her and seeing Clarice. "Don't leave."

18

T atyana flew back to Moscow on a Challenger 605 that was cleared to land at Khodynka Aerodrome. The airport was closed, the land had been sold to property developers, but the GRU still made use of the concrete, 1400-meter-long runway because air traffic control was too scared to order them not to. Located seven kilometers from Red Square and literally steps from GRU headquarters, it was too convenient not to use.

Tatyana was the only passenger on the flight. She stepped out of the plane into the frigid cold of a Moscow morning and searched for the car.

The Military Intelligence Directorate screwed up a lot of things. It got its agents killed at an alarming rate. It practically forced western governments to issue wave after wave of sanctions on the beleaguered Russian economy. It spent more resources trying to hack the World Anti-Doping Agency than it did protecting domestic financial systems.

But there was always a car. Always black. Always with blacked-out windows. And despite everything that might have happened between the two nations politically, it was always German. Today it was a BMW.

The GRU headquarters, a massive edifice that contained as much concrete as four Olympic stadiums, was referred to by its occupants as the Aquarium.

Tatyana was dropped outside despite her request to be taken home first and began the arduous process of passing through the layers of security, getting into the rickety elevator, and making her way to the office of her boss, Igor Aralov.

Igor's office was located on the northwest corner of the eighth floor and overlooked the field in Khodynka, where, on the 30th of May 1896, the last Emperor of Russia, Nicholas II, had been crowned. On that day, half a million people gathered for the festivities. When word spread that gifts were being handed out, the crowd got out of control. The resulting stampede led to over thirteen hundred people being crushed to death. The gift that caused the stampede was one bread roll, one piece of sausage, one pretzel, and one gingerbread cookie per person. Despite the tragedy, the bodies were cleared, the festivities continued, and the Tsar and his wife appeared before a jubilant crowd at the central pavilion as planned. The night of the coronation, after learning the full extent of the tragedy, the royal couple attended a celebratory ball at the French embassy. The feelings of the French ambassador trumped those of the Russian people.

Visitors to Igor's office had to pass an enormous oil painting of the event. It hung in the anteroom, which was also decorated with a red carpet and an imposing antique desk.

At the desk sat Igor's secretary, Agniya Bunina. There were many things to be scared of at GRU headquarters, and for Tatyana, this woman was among the foremost. In her late sixties, she had snow-white hair, a mole shaped like a fly above her mouth, and eyeglasses Tatyana was sure were made of real ivory.

"He's expecting me," Tatyana said.

Agniya looked up at her over the rims of her glasses. "Agent Aleksandrova," she said. "Welcome home."

Tatyana eyed her cautiously. Agniya wasn't normally one for pleasantries. "Thank you," she said.

Behind Agniya were two armed guards, standing at attention, their eyes glazed over as perfectly as if made of wax.

"Take a seat," Agniya said.

Tatyana was tired, she badly wanted to get home to her apartment and run a bath, but she knew that the slightest hint of impatience would only make the wait longer.

She sat down and waited. Agniya completely ignored her, working fastidiously on her computer.

After ten minutes, Agniya got up from her chair and entered Igor's office. It was only then that Tatyana allowed herself to think the worst. Her little excursion in Istanbul had been discovered. Or the missing vial had been reported. Or someone on the American side let something leak.

Agniya came out of the office and looked at Tatyana. "The director will see you now," she said.

Tatyana smiled meekly and went into the office.

"My darling," Igor said, "I'm so sorry to have you dragged from the plane."

Calling her 'darling' was no accident. He did it with all his Widows. It was a point of pride, like there was a relationship there that went beyond the merely professional. Igor was one of those men who saw his agents as his own personal property, his pets, and to a large extent, he was correct. He'd created them. He'd recruited them. He ran them. They owed everything to him. 'Widow' was his term. It started out as 'Black Widow' and got whittled down.

"Worse has happened," Tatyana said.

"Quite so," he agreed. He had an unlit cigar in his hand and rolled it between his thumb and forefinger. Tatyana set herself the challenge of getting the meeting over with before he lit it.

"I sent a full report from Istanbul," she said.

"Yes, yes," Igor said, uninterested.

He ran his tongue over his ripe lips. They were so red one could be forgiven for thinking he was wearing makeup. But Igor was a man who steered clear of adornment of any kind. He knew instinctively that it drew attention to a body no one wanted their attention drawn to. Not other men at the banyas and steam baths he frequented. Not the women whose company he paid so handsomely for at the strip clubs off the Garden Ring. And certainly not Tatyana.

He picked up a gold-plated cigar lighter from his desk and lit the thing. Blue smoke billowed from it. "I'm afraid there's been a development in Yekaterinburg," he said.

"Yevchenko?"

"Yes."

"He started production."

"Yes, he did."

"The idiot."

"He was following orders."

"His Directorate doesn't know the first thing about working with microbes. It should have been left to the scientist at the institute. What's her name?"

"Dr. Sofia Ivanova."

"Yes," Tatyana said. "That's why we have her, isn't it?

That's why we gave her the institute? So that things could be done correctly?"

"Well, they weren't."

"Why not?"

"There are some questions about Ivanova and her team. Questions about their reliability. Their *patriotism*."

"Patriotism?" Tatyana said. This wasn't good. If the doctor was drawing suspicion, it wouldn't be long before that suspicion spread to Tatyana herself. She needed to warn Sofia of the danger. "They never wanted to develop bioweapons," she said.

Igor looked at her. "Well, they should put those feelings aside in defense of the Motherland, wouldn't you say?"

"Of course," Tatyana said, remembering who she was speaking to.

"NATO has been boxing us in for two decades. We're surrounded by a ring of advanced missile systems. We need new weapons."

"But taking production out of the scientists' hands. That was a mistake. Now we have casualties to deal with."

"Yes, we do."

"And a cover-up."

"That is correct."

"How many?"

"So far, four," Igor said.

"Four," Tatyana said. It was tragic but acceptable, she supposed. Inevitable, even. When you were dealing with something this dangerous, people died.

"Hundred," Igor continued.

"Hundred?"

"Four hundred," Igor said again.

"Four hundred deaths?" Tatyana gasped.

Igor nodded. "At least."

Tatyana was standing by the door. Distance was something she tried to maintain in that office. There was a reason the Directorate insisted Igor's secretary be a woman in her sixties. He'd screwed the daughters of so many generals that it eventually caught up with him. They hadn't been able to strike him directly—his position afforded him certain protections—but they'd succeeded in getting the old battle-ax assigned permanently to his office. Of course, he'd screwed her too, but no one seemed to care about that.

Tatyana stepped closer to the desk and sat on the ornate wooden chair. She felt numb. "How did this happen?"

Igor licked his lips again. "We're looking into it."

"Was there an attack?"

"No. Just an accident."

"An accident? Four hundred people, Igor."

"Like Reactor Four."

In the Aquarium, all accidents were compared to the one accident that could never be forgotten. Chernobyl Reactor Number Four. The accident that brought down the entire communist system.

"But four hundred? It can't be. Are you sure?"

"There's no doubt."

"We never knew it was this lethal, did we?"

"The scientists had an idea," Igor said, "but Yevchenko never fucking listened."

19

Ramstein Air Base was located southwest of Frankfurt, about halfway between Mainz and the French border, and was as large as a city. Over fifty thousand American service members were stationed there, along with their families, support staff, and civilian and military contractors. All told, the base had a population roughly equal to that of Savannah, Georgia.

The site was initially selected by Hitler's Luftwaffe when a new autobahn bridge collapsed in 1940. It was discovered that the swampy land was unsuitable for a bridge of that size, rendering a large new section of highway on the far side unusable.

The Luftwaffe used the abandoned stretch of road as a runway, and it was taken over as such by the advancing American forces during the final months of the war.

After the Second World War, the surrounding land became the largest single-spot construction site in the world, with the American military employing over a quarter-million European laborers to drain thousands of acres of swampland.

Because of its vast size, the base was frequently used for operations the American government wanted to keep secret or off domestic soil.

During the 1950s, it was used to house NATO's underground combat operations center, a 37,000 square foot control room from which a full air war could have been waged against the Soviet Union. The bunker's massive switchboard, complete with eighty teletype machines, was capable of coordinating in real-time with the Pentagon, NATO Supreme Headquarters, and dozens of strategic air bases around the globe.

In 2015, it emerged that the base was being used as a massive drone control center, with hundreds of pilots remotely piloting drones over Pakistan, Yemen, Afghanistan, and Somalia. The German government was furious, claiming that their territory was being used to circumvent American constitutional restraints that would have made the strikes illegal if conducted from the US.

In the same year, a Serbian tabloid newspaper reported that the base was being used to funnel massive quantities of illegal weapons to Syrian rebels. Again, the German government was caught off guard, and while the operation was a clear violation of German arms laws, there was nothing they could do about it because their investigators weren't permitted to enter the base without American authorization.

Another thing the Germans didn't know was that the base housed an advanced CIA laboratory specializing in the analysis of substances deemed too dangerous to bring back to the continental United States.

The vial from Istanbul fit this bill, and it was there that the analysis Roth ordered had been carried out. A team of four technicians worked overtime on the report, calculating virulence by infecting rats with such minute amounts of the substance that doses were measured in Daltons, or twelfths of the mass of a carbon-12 atom. The technicians worked in an underground, lead-lined lab using state-of-the-art containment practices and protective clothing made to a higher specification than NASA had commissioned for its manned spaceflight missions.

The head of the lab, a man named McKinsey, arrived at work before dawn. He liked the winter, and walked to work across a forested portion of the base in snowshoes that had been sent by his mother from her home in Baudette, Minnesota. He was surprised when he arrived at the security perimeter to find that the shutdown routines from the night before hadn't been run correctly. He called the lead technician, Thomson, but there was no answer on his cell. He tried his house, and Thomson's wife said he'd never come home the night before.

As employees of the CIA with top-level clearance, the technicians at the lab were subject to a rigorous security regime. If any of them left the base, the head of the lab was immediately informed. McKinsey checked the email on his phone, but there was nothing from the base notification service.

It wasn't like Thomson not to be available. He was a steady man, reliable, but everyone had their moments.

When he called Prout, Rutherford, and Aston, the other three technicians, and none of them picked up, McKinsey realized he had a real problem.

This was a severe protocol breach, and he was required to pass it up the line to base command. But before he did, he went down to the lab to make sure he wasn't over-reacting. The lab had an airlock procedure that would have required him to suit up before entering, but it also had video cameras connected to screens in a control room that gave him a clear view of what was going on inside.

He went to the control room and scanned the cameras.

The lab was empty.

Then his eye stopped on something unusual. It was a shoe. Someone was lying on the ground.

20

Novouralsk was a closed city about fifty miles from Yekaterinburg. When it was founded during the Second World War, it was known simply as Sverdlovsk-44. Mail was sent to Sverdlovsk, where the 44 postcode designated it as military.

No one who lived in the city was allowed to divulge its existence to outsiders. Residents were severely restricted and were prohibited from traveling abroad or communicating with the outside world. The city appeared on no road signs or railway timetables. In order to travel there, special papers from the KGB were required.

Its existence was not admitted by the Russian government until 1994, when satellite imagery made a mockery of attempts to keep a city of a hundred thousand secret any longer. Although its existence was no longer denied, the city remained enclosed in a security perimeter that was watched by armed guards in towers.

Sofia Ivanova sat motionless in the back of a military helicopter as it landed. Wind whipped down from the Urals so ferociously that the entire chopper swayed over the helipad.

When they'd taken her from the hospital, they never said where they were going. Four soldiers simply appeared in full hazmat gear, pointing assault rifles at her. She could still see the red laser dots when she shut her eyes. She'd known they would come, and had forced Olga to hide before they arrived. "Someone needs to stay to treat these people," she'd said when Olga objected.

The soldiers brought her to the roof, where the Mil Mi-24 waited, engines running.

It flew so low that Sofia felt like she could reach out and touch the tops of the trees. In the frozen forest, they sparkled in the moonlight like glass ornaments.

From the chopper, she was brought into an aircraft hangar. It was as cold inside as outside, and she wasn't dressed for it. She was still in her medical scrubs. If they'd believed the outbreak was contagious, they never would have transported her like that.

Powerful overhead lights lit the hangar, and she could see it was in the process of becoming a staging area for whatever was going on in Yekaterinburg. Soldiers and federal officers of the MVD police ran about, assembling equipment and weapons for airlift into the city.

Amid the chaos, standing serenely as if immune to it all, was an elegant woman with dark hair, a knee-length coat, and a silk scarf. Sofia recognized Tatyana instantly.

Tatyana strode toward her and said, "Dr. Ivanova, thank you for coming."

"I had no choice," Sofia said. "I was brought at gunpoint."

Tatyana nodded and led her to the back of the hangar. Passing crates of military equipment, they climbed a metal staircase to an office overlooking the hangar floor. Tatyana held the door, and Sofia hurried inside. She was relieved to see an electric heater in the office and went straight to it.

"I'll get them to bring you something warmer to wear," Tatyana said.

Sofia held her hands to the heater as Tatyana made a call on her cell. "I'm with the doctor," she said. "She needs warm clothing."

"Thank you," Sofia said when she hung up.

"I'm sorry you were brought by force," Tatyana said. "The military gets skittish in these situations."

"As they should," Sofia said.

Tatyana nodded.

The two stood and looked at each other for a few seconds, sizing each other up.

It was Sofia who spoke first. "What did you do with the virus?" she said.

Tatyana's expression changed to one of alarm. "Don't talk about that here," she hissed. "They could be listening."

"I need to know."

"They'll kill us both."

"I have to know what you did with it," Sofia said, holding her ground.

Tatyana went to the door and made sure no one was standing outside. "I got it out of the country," she said.

"To the Americans?"

Tatyana nodded. "If it's as bad as you say, then they need to have a chance to defend themselves."

"I agree," Sofia said. She felt a sense of relief knowing that someone other than Yevchenko and his cronies knew about the virus. If the Americans knew, they would be formulating a response. They would be coming up with a plan to get it out of the GRU's hands—to destroy it. They had to.

Tatyana cleared her throat. "Regarding the bacillus," she said, "I know you're not going to believe me, but we're on the same side."

Sofia looked out the window to where the soldiers were gearing up for a full-scale containment operation. "I'm sorry, but I highly doubt that," she said.

"I can't do anything about the military response," Tatyana said, following her gaze.

"They're going to kill people," Sofia said.

"People are already dying."

"Because of them. Because of their ineptitude."

Tatyana shook her head. "I'm not here to argue with you, doctor."

"Well," Sofia said, "maybe you could tell me why you're here."

"I'm here to warn you."

"Warn me about what?"

"They're getting suspicious. Why do you think they took production out of your hands?"

"Because I would have insisted on doing it safely."

"They see the world differently than you do," Tatyana said.

"You can say that again."

"I'm just saying, be careful. For your own sake. For your team's sake."

"It's a bit late for that, wouldn't you say?"

Tatyana sighed. Sofia looked at her. She didn't want to argue.

"I also need your assessment of the outbreak," Tatyana said.

"Outbreak?"

"Or whatever you want to call it."

"I'd prefer to call it a leak."

"All right," Tatyana said. "In here, just you and me, you can call it whatever you like."

"They won't be able to hide the truth," Sofia said.

"That's exactly what they're going to do."

"Everyone knows about Biopreparat here," Sofia said. "They've grown up with the stories. There have been leaks in the past."

"I'm aware," Tatyana said.

"Then you know that if the government simply admitted what was happening instead of orchestrating a cover-up, a lot of lives would be spared."

Tatyana nodded. "If you're looking for openness today, I'm sorry to be the one to disappoint you."

There was a knock on the door. Tatyana opened it, and a soldier came in with a military parka. "Thank you," Tatyana said and handed it to Sofia.

Sofia put it on.

They waited for the soldier to leave.

There was a seat, and Tatyana indicated for Sofia to take it. Tatyana sat across from her.

Sofia liked to think of herself as a good judge of character, but when she looked at Tatyana, she wasn't sure what she saw. Tatyana seemed to know emotion was a waste of time, and she did not give the impression she was someone who wasted time.

"I'm a doctor," Sofia said. "I don't know what role you have here, but I presume it's not the same as mine."

"My role is to protect the interests of the state," Tatyana said.

Sofia nodded.

"That's not so different from yours," Tatyana said.

"My role is to save lives."

Tatyana shook her head. "I'm sorry, doctor. I think we both know that's not true. In a different world, maybe. But not in this one."

Something in Sofia rose up, some well of emotion. She knew Tatyana was right. She was no longer a doctor. She was a bioweapons scientist. She was the scientist who'd created this pathogen. And that truth made her want to scream.

"You know they threatened me," she said, "threatened my whole team."

"That's how things work sometimes."

"They threatened to give us smallpox."

"I'm sorry," Tatyana said.

"I never would have done this if I'd had a choice."

"We all work at gunpoint," Tatyana said.

Sofia looked at her and realized it was true. Neither of them wanted this. Neither of them wanted the world to be this way. They didn't want to see school children clawing at their necks, struggling to breathe, while scientists worked on creating diseases rather than curing them.

"What do you want from me?" Sofia said. "Why have you brought me here?"

"I'd settle for an antidote," Tatyana said.

"To the bacillus?"

"Yes."

Sofia shook her head. "There is no antidote," she said.

"I don't see how denying an antidote helps the situation. At the very least, we need it to inoculate our own troops on the battlefield."

"I'm not denying it, Tatyana. We don't have one."

Tatyana took a moment to process this information. It was the first time Sofia had seen her flinch. "Hundreds have died already," she said. She spoke more quietly now, almost in a whisper.

"I know that," Sofia said.

Tatyana shook her head. "How can you create a weapon and not have an antidote?"

"Tatyana," Sofia said, "this is nothing. This is a sideshow. Compared to the damage the virus will cause if it gets out, this bacillus is a drop in the ocean."

Sofia watched Tatyana's reaction. It seemed she was only now truly realizing what it was they were up against.

"Last time we met," Sofia said, "I told you that this was a biological Chernobyl. I was lying. The truth is, the virus in that vial, if it gets out, it's not Chernobyl we'll be looking at. It's Armageddon. It's the End Days."

21

———

Tatyana's flight to New York went via Helsinki. Her plane was delayed because of snow, and she decided to use the relative safety of the terminal to make a phone call. Once inside the US, the risk of being followed by her own side increased significantly. Despite the passing of three decades, the GRU never lost its Cold War fear of defections. It was well known within the agency that more GRU agents were killed in the US by their own side than by the CIA.

Before making the call, she went to the washroom. She'd purposely allowed her phone battery to die on the plane. She had a charger in her bag and now crushed the connector under the heel of her shoe. The transit terminal in Helsinki was a known GRU transfer point, and there was no room for error.

The payphones were located next to a huge wall of glass overlooking the runway, and she'd heard of agents being watched there from inside planes. It wasn't ideal, but there was nowhere she was safe from the GRU's watchful eye. She may have been a good girl. Obedient. She never complained, never asked for anything, and never said no to her bosses, no matter the request. But she knew there were no guarantees. They watched everyone. And they would be watching her.

She went to the newsstand and browsed the magazines. She grabbed a new charger, a bottle of water, and some potato chips. Every move she made was calculated. She did nothing that could be used against her. Every action had an explanation. If it was all eventually to be analyzed under the cold microscope of paranoia, she would be ready.

She paid for the things and found a seat near the payphones. She opened the charger and plugged her phone into an outlet by her seat. Then she got up and threw the packaging and the old charger into the trash.

There was a bank of payphones nearby and she went to them, keeping her back to the window. She looked at every passenger and airport staff member within sight.

She had a Hermes scarf in her hair, and she took it off and held it casually in her hand. When she dialed, she let it drape over the number pad. An automated voice from the phone company asked for payment at a high international rate, and she fed it a twenty Euro bill.

The number she dialed was a Manhattan business called Village Mail Service. It was a twenty-four-hour place that handled UPS and DHL packages, provided copy services, and took passport photos. She'd selected it because it had no security cameras, accepted cash, and was too small for anyone there to watch her unnoticed.

It was owned by an Indian family, and Tatyana's contact was the son, Ayaan. She'd introduced herself to him by asking about his Eagles jersey, which he wore every day, and then by bribing him with season tickets to the Giants.

"You're in New York," she'd said to him one afternoon. "It's time to prove your loyalty."

"Village Mail?" she said into the phone.

"That's us."

"I need to speak to Ayaan."

"Who's this?"

"His mother."

"Funny."

"Is he there?"

"You should be a comedian."

She sighed. "Who's this?" she said.

"His cousin, Raj."

"Well, when's he in, Raj?"

"Not until tonight."

She hung up, and a torrent of change fell noisily into the tray under the phone. She fed it back into the machine and dialed Ayaan's cell. He'd better pick up, she thought. She'd invested a lot into him, and she expected to be repaid with interest.

"Hello?"

"Ayaan?"

"Yes."

"It's me."

His voice dropped a tone. "Where have you been?"

"What's wrong?"

"It's been weeks."

"I've been in Russia."

"The police were here."

He was panicked. She needed to calm him down. "About the mailbox?"

"Yes."

"What did they say?"

"They wanted to know who rented it."

"You didn't tell them, did you?"

"Of course not, but I've got family here. Immigration issues. I can't afford trouble."

"Don't worry, Ayaan. You've done nothing wrong. They've got nothing on you."

"They wanted to know why I accepted cash. Why no ID was provided."

"It's not a big deal."

"There are rules about it. The federal mail."

"Have they been back?"

"No."

"See?"

He took a breath.

"Look, I'm going to be in town," she said. "I want to see you."

"When?"

"Tonight."

"Where?"

She could practically hear him salivating. "I don't know yet. I still have to get a hotel."

As far as Ayaan was concerned, she was a Russian litera-ture professor who attended conferences in the city and liked to get naughty while she was there. She'd told him she was married, which was why everything was always on the down-low.

She'd offered him no real explanation for why she needed the mailbox but let him suspect it had something to do with Russian academia, government restrictions, the chance of a job offer from an American university.

He hadn't expected the police.

Not that it mattered. She'd be done with him soon.

"My father is angry at me for accepting cash," Ayaan said. "He thinks I'm stealing from him."

"Is the box still empty?"

"Yes."

"Did the police do anything with it?"

A slight pause, then he said, "No, nothing."

"Don't lie to me, Ayaan."

"I'm not the one who's been lying."

He was done. He was scared. Meeting him now would be risky. She'd get what she needed and cut him loose. "Just tell me what they did," she said.

"They're watching the box with a camera."

She nodded. Lance was watching. It made her breathe a little easier.

"I've got to go, but watch that box. If anyone comes, anyone at all, I need to know."

She hung up and scanned the terminal. No one.

She fed the remaining change back into the phone and called her operator in Moscow. The devil was in the details. If Igor ever asked why she'd used a payphone in Helsinki, this was the reason.

The operator answered, and Tatyana identified herself. "Proceed," the operator said.

"Tell the boss my flight's been delayed in Finland," she said.

22

L aurel and Roth were in the back of the Escalade on their way from the airport when Roth got a call from the head of the lab at Ramstein. He put it on speaker.

"Sir, there's been a leak. All four technicians are dead," McKinsey said.

"Listen to me," Roth said. "Seal the lab. Under no circumstances is anyone to go in there. You've seen the numbers on this virus."

"Yes, I have, sir."

"Just stay there, and wait by the phone. I've got to figure out what we're going to do."

Roth hung up and looked at Laurel. She said, "Sir, you need to shut down the base."

"It's one of the largest in the world," Roth said. "They run half of Europe out of that place."

"Call the president, sir. Do it now. If this thing gets out," she said, tapping her briefcase, which contained the virus analysis, "it's going to be on us."

Roth nodded. He called the president immediately. They

had to wait a few minutes while the operator handled the authorization, then the president's voice came on the line.

"Mr. President," Roth said, "we have a situation."

"That doesn't sound good."

"We need to lock down Ramstein Air Base."

"That's impossible."

"I'm sorry, sir. This is a Level Five threat."

"Roth, come on."

"I'm serious, sir."

"You better be deadly serious. Level Five is an existential threat."

"I assure you this is justified, sir."

The president was silent for a few seconds. "You got everything under control, Roth?"

"Yes, I do, sir. Shutting down the base is a precautionary measure. But it's something that has to be done. No one can be allowed in or out. No one at all."

"The Germans are going to be all over my ass," the president said.

"I'm sorry, sir."

"All right," the president said. "I'll make the order. But I need you to come in and explain what's going on."

"I'll be right there, sir."

Roth hung up and called the Pentagon. He made sure the order to shut down the base was being passed on immediately, and he asked to speak to the base commander in person. They connected him, and he told the commander that in addition to locking down the base, he wanted a protective cordon placed around the CIA lab. "No one and nothing gets in or out," he said.

The base commander assured him the cordon would be set up, and then Roth called back McKinsey at the lab.

"How you doing, son?" Roth said.

"I'm all right, sir."

"I've had the base commander set up a protective cordon around the lab. I'm afraid you're not going to be allowed out for a while."

"I understand, sir."

"I want you to start sending everything you have to the Center for Disease Control in Atlanta."

"I'll get started right away."

"Digital data only," Roth said. "Under no circumstances are you to unseal that lab. I understand you have the best containment at that facility."

"Yes, we do, sir."

"So send the data to Atlanta, and keep that lab sealed."

"I understand, sir."

Laurel looked out the window at the passing traffic. She allowed herself to imagine, just for a second, what would happen if a virus like this got on the loose. Then she shook the thought from her head.

"You keep the containment intact," Roth said. "Do not attempt to recover the bodies of the technicians. I'm sorry, but this virus can't be allowed to get out. You're on lockdown, son. You hear me?"

"Loud and clear, sir."

Roth hung up the phone.

"The man's a professional," he said to Laurel as if trying to reassure her. "He understands how dangerous this is."

"You think we locked things down quickly enough?"

Roth looked at her, and she saw the moment of terror as he thought what it would mean if they hadn't. "I think so," he said. "That lab's the only place that opened the vial. It's completely sealed."

"You'd better be certain," Laurel said.

Roth picked up the phone and called back the Pentagon.

"I need the base commander again," he said. They connected him, and Roth said, "When the CDC has all the data it needs, I want you to destroy that lab."

"What about the scientist?" the base commander said.

Roth had been looking at Laurel, but he looked away. He picked up the phone to take it off speaker. "Him too," Roth said. "Nothing comes out of there. Not a lab rat, not a computer, not the scientist. It's all got to be burned down."

He hung up and stared out the window.

"Sir," Laurel said, "has it crossed your mind that if our scientists had a leak, even with the best procedures in the world, how much greater the risk is at a Russian lab?"

Roth nodded but didn't say anything. He was silent for the rest of the ride into the city.

When they finally pulled up outside Laurel's apartment, she looked at him. She felt sorry for him. He looked like he'd aged ten years in the time it took them to drive home from the airport.

"Good night, boss," she said, getting out of the car.

"Get some sleep," he said.

She looked back. "I wish we got Lance."

"We gave it our best shot."

Laurel wanted to say something else, something comforting, but she couldn't think of anything.

Geopolitics was a giant chess game to Roth, and this envelope, the vial, the message for Spector, changed everything. His job, the job of the entire CIA, was above all else to preserve the status quo. This virus altered the position of every piece on the board. It threatened the entire game. Ever since 1949, when Stalin successfully tested his own version of the twenty-kiloton Fat Man, the global chessboard, to a mind like Roth's, had changed not at all.

Now, it had been upended in a single stroke.

"We've still got the mailbox," Laurel said.

Roth nodded. "Look into it in the morning," he said through the window of the car as it pulled away.

Laurel saw the world differently than Roth. To her, it wasn't a chessboard. It was personal. And she intended to look into the mailbox lead very closely.

She waited for Roth's car to round the corner then began walking, not to her apartment but to the closest metro station. She caught the metro to Union Station and bought a ticket to New York on the last train of the night.

She got a little sleep on the train, maybe an hour or two, and was in Penn Station by midnight. From there, she caught a cab to Bleecker and Tenth in the Village.

She stepped from the cab into the chilly New York night. It felt good to be in the city.

She pulled her phone from her pocket and called Langley, where she was connected to one of the specialists on night duty.

"It's Laurel."

"What can I do for you?"

"Do you have contact with the surveillance detail on the mailbox?"

"Sure, why?"

"I'm a block away. Tell them I'm paying a visit."

The phone clicked, and when the specialist came back, he said, "There's a gray van across the street from the store."

Laurel was walking in that direction and could see the van. "Are they expecting me?"

"Yeah, they see you."

The back door of the van opened, and Laurel got in. "Gentlemen," she said.

One of them pulled the door shut behind her, and she was immediately overcome by the smell. Three men, cramped in a confined space on eight-hour stints, eating as much takeout as they wanted.

"You Everlane?"

"Yes, I am."

"This your stakeout?" The guy asking the questions was sitting up front. The other two were in the back with Laurel.

"Roth's," she said.

"What's he hoping to find? Because we ain't seen a peep."

They had a camera inside the store feeding them a live view of the mailbox. Someone had drawn a circle around it with a sharpie right on the monitor.

"That the one we're watching?"

"I can see why they like you," the guy said.

Laurel sat back. She took a pack of cigarettes from her coat pocket, and the guy up front said, "Oh hell, lady. You've got to be kidding."

Laurel smiled. "I thought it would mask the body odor."

"That's musk," he said.

Laurel looked at him.

He said, "Hey, you want to sit here all night? Let's see how you smell at the end of it."

"Well," she said, "I guess I can take a hint." She wrote her number on one of the takeout containers. "Call me if anything happens. I'll be close by."

"You don't want to wait with us?" one of the guys in the back said. He was wearing an Oakland A's ball cap.

"I don't know," she said. "I feel like I'm cramping your friend's style."

They'd been cooped up so long they were going stir crazy. "We could crack a window," he said to the guy up front.

"Let her smoke," the third guy said.

"Fine," the guy up front said.

She leaned back and lit her cigarette, blowing the smoke toward the tiny crack in the window. She looked out at the mail store.

Whoever had sent them the message had been careful. They knew enough to leave the envelope where it would find its way into the consulate. They knew how to avoid the CCTV cameras. Whoever they were, they were sending a warning, and they'd risked their life to do it.

It had to mean a deal. A defection. She knew Lance had been right about it being a Russian.

Russia had the bioweapons labs. They contravened every treaty they ever signed. They sent agents to places like Istanbul and New York and gave them reason to want to defect.

"I'd bet dollars to donuts we're waiting for a Russian," she said.

The guys nodded.

"I bet it's a woman," the guy in the A's cap said.

"What tells you that?" Laurel said.

"Stakeouts like this are all we do. You get a feel for them."

"A feel?"

"Yeah, like the location. Lots of people around. Nothing too secluded. Women don't go in for secluded meets."

"Unless they have to," the guy in the front said.

"Right," Laurel said.

The danger to a defector always came from their own side. The GRU had more assets operating on the east coast of the US than anywhere else on earth. The White House, the UN, the embassies, Wall Street, K Street, Capitol Hill— there was a concentration of power there that was simply unmatched. Nothing in London, Berlin, or Tokyo compared.

When Russians defected, this was where they did it.

The land of the free. The home of the brave.

But there was more to this. Someone was telling them something. Why ask for Lance? They must have known he was more than just another Delta Force operator. And why this mailbox, this location? They had to know it was being watched.

This mailbox wasn't an accident. And the surveillance team in a van outside wasn't an accident either.

Laurel worked through what she knew for certain. What she knew and what the person who'd sent the message knew.

They'd know that if anyone came to check the mail, they'd be tailed by the CIA. The store was so small that there was literally no chance of sneaking in unnoticed. A locker at Grand Central would have been better for that. For an anonymous message, a phone number or email address would have sufficed. Or better yet, an encrypted messaging service.

"Why are we here?" she said.

"Roth gave us the address."

"No," she said. "Why this place specifically? Why would anyone want to meet at a place like this?"

"They're scared," the third guy said. "And not of us. If they gave this location to our guys, it's because they want us to be here."

"We've got a Russian defector on our hands," Laurel said.

"A female Russian defector," the guy in front said.

"I'll give her some diplomatic immunity," the third guy said, smirking.

The others laughed.

"One minute in this van, and she'd wish she was in the *Gulag*," Laurel said.

The guy in the A's cap asked Laurel for a cigarette.

"You too now?" the guy in front said.

The man shrugged and lit the cigarette. "I'll tell you one thing," he said. "Whoever owns that mailbox wants to know exactly who's delivering her mail."

Laurel nodded.

She called Roth's cell. It was redirected to his operator. "I need to talk to him," Laurel said.

"He's with the president," the operator said.

"I know."

The operator sighed. "You're sure it can't wait?"

"It really can't."

The operator put her on hold, and then Roth's voice came on. "Laurel! What is it?"

"Sorry, boss."

"Everything okay?"

"I'm in New York with the surveillance team."

He cleared his throat. "I had a feeling you weren't ready to let this one go."

"I want him, boss."

"I bet you do."

"As an Asset."

"Of course. They spot anything yet?"

"No, and they're not going to."

"Well, they might as well keep waiting."

"No, I mean the message we got. This mailbox."

"What about it?"

"That's the thing. They're never going to come."

"Then why give it to us?"

"I'm right outside. It's a tiny store. There's no way of accessing it without being seen."

"Right."

"It's a hole in a wall, boss. Someone's got to stick their hand through first."

"And hope the person on the other side doesn't cut it off?" Roth said.

"Exactly."

"So you're saying they're not going to stick their hand through first."

"Would you?"

23

Being an agent of the Main Directorate came with perks. They might not compensate entirely for the downsides, but Tatyana knew enough about life to enjoy them while they lasted.

A first-class transatlantic flight. A fully reclinable bed. A flute of champagne on landing. She took it all and would have taken more if it was offered. As far as she was concerned, she'd earned it.

The Russian government had taken everything from her, and she was under no illusions they'd eventually come for her life too. She wasn't bitter about it. As a young, single woman in Moscow, she was screwed anyway.

Her allegiance was to herself.

"Lie to them," her grandmother told her. "Lie to your husband, to your boss, to the government. All of them. But never lie to yourself."

Tatyana took the lesson to heart.

And whatever she did for the GRU, regardless of what she thought of it, regardless of whether she found it palatable or not, she never lied to herself. She never once told herself she was doing it for her country.

Her grandmother also told her that she could do anything, anything at all, so long as she didn't work for free.

And working for the GRU paid. You just had to know how to work it. Like so many things in life, it could screw you but also get you off. It kept her in the things she'd grown accustomed to, things she valued not for what they were but because of what they stood for. And what they stood for was that she'd beaten the odds.

She wore Chanel, Dior, Prada, Hermes. When she got off the plane, she was in Saint Laurent ankle boots and a matching alligator-skin purse. She was a classics girl. She didn't go in for the brashness of Gucci or the flamboyance of Louis Vuitton. She liked the things that had stood the test of time.

If it meant she had to sleep with the occasional diplomat, or shoot a politician, or strangle someone with a length of wire, she'd learned long ago that she could stomach that.

They paid, so she worked.

At least she had a modicum of control over her life. It was a life of her own making. She'd taken each step that led to where she was now. She'd brought herself to this place.

Sometimes she didn't sleep at night. Sometimes she woke drenched in a cold sweat, so terrified she didn't dare move until the sun came up. Sometimes she went so many days without keeping food down that the doctors had to put her on an IV.

But it was a job.

She passed through immigration at JFK with doctored documents and made her way to the taxis in front of the terminal.

"Your bag, madam?" the driver said.

"Don't bang it," she said. She got into the backseat and checked her phone.

"Where to?"

"The Four Seasons."

"It's between Park and Madison, right?"

The driver was Russian. She could tell from the accent. "Yes," she said in Russian.

"What street?"

"Fifty-eighth."

They got out of the airport, and he said, "Nice place."

"The airport?"

"No, the Four Seasons."

She nodded. It was a nice place, one of her favorites. They called that stretch of the street Billionaire's Row. Rooms started at a thousand a night. There was a penthouse suite, the third most expensive in the world according to the hotel's website, that was over sixty thousand.

According to Agency legend, it was in that very suite that the Russian and Chinese presidents had met to discuss their new joint strategy. It was there they'd formulated the policy that set the future course of the GRU, and which would see Russia and China oppose American hegemony on every front, in every theater.

If America was a mighty bison, Russia and China were the wolves nipping at its heels, letting it tire under its own lumbering weight until it faltered and they could get it by the throat.

It all served to give the hotel a special place in GRU lore, which was evinced by the fact that they charged more nights there to their expense accounts than any other hotel in the world.

The driver was eager to talk, but Tatyana stopped

answering his questions. She was thinking about the operation.

She needed to make contact with Spector and speak to him personally and make sure he understood the seriousness of the virus. It had been easy to manipulate Igor into sending her to New York. There was a Canadian trade negotiator who she'd said was worth targeting. The target was real. He'd been to Ukraine multiple times, and his profile was rising on the GRU's exhaustive list of people around the world worth pursuing. He was currently ranked 4,893rd. Not exactly a top priority, but enough to be plausible. Everyone was talking about Ukraine. The target was outside his home country. He was rated as corruptible. Why not hit him?

It was a mission that would attract little attention in Moscow.

Even still, she knew the risk she was taking. Tatyana was a good agent with a clean record, but there was a defection-risk profile for agents like her. She was an unmarried female under thirty with no children, no living relatives, and few reasons to miss Moscow if it should ever transpire that she couldn't go back.

That was the reason they paid so well. The Russians realized long ago, after an embarrassing number of defections, that if they wanted to send young women overseas to seduce foreigners, they had to give them a lifestyle they wouldn't willingly throw away. At a time when Russian GDP per capita was under eight thousand dollars, Igor's budget per widow was three million. Line items for specific operations were in addition.

Tatyana traveled with GRU credit cards and could buy whatever she wanted. As long as she kept coming home after assignments, the faucet would keep flowing. And as long as everything she bought was chargeable to American

Express and didn't look like it would be useful to a person planning a life outside Russia, no one asked any questions.

That meant no real estate, no securities, no transferable assets, no savings. Just luxuries. Things of no use to a defector.

Which was fine by her. She was authorized to shop, and shop she did. It would have been suspicious if she didn't.

Besides, the boutiques in the Four Seasons lobby alone would put Moscow's luxury district to shame.

She got to the hotel and checked in under the same name as the passport she'd used to enter the country.

Widows generally traveled under one of two honeytrap covers. Either they were the young, disaffected trophy-wife of some rich oligarch, or they were a penniless translator toiling in a low-paying government job at the nearest Russian embassy. Either way, they were desperate for a savior, a foreign man who would whisk them away from their drab reality into the glamor and sparkle of the West.

That it worked at all was proof to Tatyana of how the world really operated. James Brown had it right all along. It was a man's world. And Tatyana had learned that men were driven by one thing. Not lust, not greed, not even the desire for power. The force that really made the world go round was the delicate, tender, all-too-easily-wounded snowflake that was the male ego. That was what brought nations to war, what brought soldiers to the battlefield, and what brought men to women's beds.

Either version of the cover story worked, but the top brass preferred the penniless translator version. It was cheaper, but it was also more effective. It turned out powerful men were significantly more turned on by a woman who was broke than one who already had every-thing material she could want. The trophy-wife was reserved for operations where access to the target required wealth or status to be plausible.

Like all government agencies, the GRU was a bureaucracy. And like all Russian bureaucracies, it was on a gargantuan scale. It lumbered like a T-34 tank. It was not nimble, or reactive, or innovative.

In Tatyana's university, students constantly debated whether Tolstoy or Stalin or Russia as a whole better resembled a hedgehog or a fox. The fox knew many things. The hedgehog knew only one thing but knew it well.

Tatyana asked the same question of intelligence agencies.

The CIA was a fox. MI5 was a fox.

The GRU was a hedgehog, and no matter how sophisticated its adversaries grew, no matter how large a technological gap they opened up, they would never be able to deny a simple fact the Russians had learned long ago.

That at their core, Westerners were not equipped for war.

They could never truly be warriors because, in their hearts, they still clung to the promise of peace. They lived their lives as if those Memorial Day barbecues, those Thanksgiving turkeys, those Christmas presents under the tree meant something. As if they were real and would go on forever. As if all those quaint, familiar comforts somehow protected them from the reality of the world. They were slaves to their delusions as much as any Soviet apparatchik.

And it led the GRU to focus intensely on the pursuit of *kompromat*. Because the men who led the West slept with their eyes closed. They slept like babies. They let their guard down. They were more afraid of a fight with their wives than the terrors their enemies might bring to their door.

Hence the lists, thousands of names long, of foreigners worth targeting.

Russia knew it couldn't win in the skies. It couldn't win on the oceans. It couldn't win in space. So it won in the bedroom, in the toilet, in the brothel.

Russia knew that no matter how advanced an army became, a photo of a general cock-deep in a Russian whore could stop him in his tracks as surely as the Siberian winter ever stopped Napoleon, and the Wehrmacht, and everyone else who'd ever thought they could march in and win.

24

Igor Aralov stood by his office window, blowing cigar smoke against the glass. They were building a new shopping mall outside, and the workers crawled around the site like ants.

From where he stood, he could see the newly built offices of KPMG, Ernst & Young, and Norton Rose. It wasn't enough that they'd won the Cold War. Now they'd come to build monuments on the ashes of the vanquished.

Even German firms were building dazzling new towers, glittering edifices taller than anything Moscow had ever seen. AEG, IG Farben, ThyssenKrupp, the very companies that had brought the Wehrmacht within sight of the Kremlin. Hitler hadn't been able to knock down the door by force, so the Duma did it for them.

Within a year, the last of the aerodrome, including the runway, would be gone.

The GRU itself was being rehoused in a modern building that would share services with the headquarters of a French defense company.

In fifty years, he doubted the country would exist at all. At least not in the form he'd spent his life defending.

He'd been a sniper in a previous life, and his Dragunov SVD rifle was still in its case beneath his desk. He had thirty-two confirmed kills with it. He thought now about taking it from its case and picking off a few construction workers, adding to his total. They were dismantling the country as surely as any foreign soldier ever had.

A knock on the door pulled him from the thought.

"I said I didn't want to be disturbed," he said irritably to his secretary.

"It's Timokhin," she said.

Igor turned. He looked at her for a second. Her face betrayed nothing. The spectacles, the mole on her cheek, the thin lips. She was as impervious to his suspicions as a stone. She took no joy in her life and allowed none in his.

And they'd assigned her to him permanently.

He'd never trusted her. She was too intelligent. Too quiet. And she'd pretended to orgasm when they slept together. No one did that without an agenda.

"Igor," she snapped.

"Bring him in," Igor said. "Bring him in. We must not keep such an important visitor waiting."

Her lip curled. She knew something. She left, and a moment later, a dark hulk appeared in the doorway.

"Mr. Director," Igor said, scuttling around the desk.

Timokhin had always been more bear than man. He didn't walk. He lumbered. As he entered the room, he ducked slightly.

Igor pulled out a chair for him.

"I'll stand," Timokhin said.

"A drink then? Or a cigar?"

"This will only take a minute."

"Of course," Igor said, backing away.

Timokhin looked around Igor's little kingdom like a landlord come down to the slum. The place was distasteful to him, unsanitary, disease-ridden. He stepped as if the carpet might soil his shoes.

"I see you got a view of the runway after all."

Igor nodded. He didn't know whether to sit or stand. He pulled out his chair but stood behind it.

"You're comfortable here," Timokhin said. His voice was a guttural grumble. Over-sized vocal cords, Igor imagined.

Timokhin's office was on the top floor, the lofty heights, with the *Spetsnaz* men and the sycophants. Igor hoped to join them one day, once he'd sufficiently demonstrated he'd sold his soul.

But until that day, Timokhin was a danger to him—a scorpion in the cradle, a ferret in the hutch.

Timokhin stood still, his eyes narrow.

Igor shifted his weight from one foot to the other. When he was a boy, he'd kept lizards as pets. The way Timokhin looked at him now was exactly how the basilisks looked at the mice at feeding time.

No one spoke for a time, but Igor could hear the heave and pull of Timokhin's breathing.

"I'll get to the point," Timokhin said.

"Please do."

"This concerns your operative in New York."

"New York?" Igor said as if he'd never heard of the place.

"Tatyana Aleksandrova," Timokhin said.

Igor's jaw clenched.

Timokhin continued, "I'm afraid her name's been brought up."

Igor felt his heart thump. Decades of practice had taught him to keep a steady hand. At moments like this, one had to show nothing, betray nothing. "I don't see why Tatyana Aleksandrova would be of concern to anyone," he said as evenly as he could.

Timokhin smiled. "Oh, but she is, Igor. She is. She's being watched by the highest level."

There was that look again—the lizard sizing up its prey.

The mice could never fight back. They could only freeze in the gaze of the predator. There was no terror on earth like that. When the lizards were young, he fed them baby mice that were so tiny, so helpless, that they hadn't even grown fur. Their eyes were closed. They didn't know what was happening to them. That bored him. It was when the lizards got older, and the mice were large enough to know what was happening that things got interesting.

Igor thought of that. He thought of what this was going to mean for Tatyana—the mouse, his mouse—and felt an overwhelming urge to attack Timokhin. He imagined flinging himself over the desk, his hands outstretched, clawed, ready to grip Timokhin's thick neck and jerk it back and forth until it snapped.

"You look like you need to sit down, my friend," Timokhin said.

Igor shook his head. "We're not friends, Fyodor."

"Come, Igor."

"What's your interest in Tatyana? The operation in New York is minor by anyone's standards."

"If it's so minor, you won't mind my incursion."

"I mind all incursions," Igor said.

"Igor," Timokhin said, observing him closely. "If I didn't know better, I'd say you had feelings for her."

Igor took a deep breath. "Even you know better than that."

"Do I?" Timokhin said, as softly as if soothing a child. "Do I really?"

"What's this about, Timokhin?"

"Fathers love their daughters, don't they?"

"You'd better start making sense, or I'll have the guards come in."

"They love all their daughters, but they have a special place in their heart for the slut of the litter."

Igor felt his blood boil.

"I'll be sorry to have to slit the slut's throat before getting to taste her other slit," Timokhin said.

Igor's mind went blank. The chair in front of him was solid oak, carved decades ago. He heaved it up and flung it across the table.

Timokhin didn't flinch. He raised a hand, just one, and caught it mid-flight.

"Igor, Igor, Igor," he said, putting the chair back on the ground with mock care. "It seems I've poked a tender spot."

"Fuck you, Timokhin."

"I had no idea she was so dear to you."

"I think you'd better leave," Igor said through gritted teeth.

Timokhin raised his hands. "Fine. I'll leave. I'll pursue this another way. Just remember, I came to you first, Igor. I came to tell you that your favorite slut betrayed you. And you sent me away."

He turned for the door. Igor indulged the fantasy of pulling out his pistol and shooting the man in the back. He pictured him stumble. A man his size would take more than one bullet to bring down. He would turn in time to see Igor pulling the trigger a second time. And a third. And a fourth. And a fifth. He wouldn't stop until the gun clicked empty.

Tatyana had betrayed him? How was that possible?

"Fyodor, wait," he said.

Timokhin smiled. He turned and looked at Igor again with that lurid, reptilian gaze.

"Tatyana would never betray me," Igor said.

"If you truly believe that, then we have nothing to talk about."

Igor could barely stand to look at the man. He was so pleased with himself. So content. So smug. "Why is it," Igor said, "that every time you look at me, I feel like Gregor Samsa?"

Timokhin smiled. "Who's Gregor Samsa?" he said.

25

S ofia looked down as the chopper descended. The entire hospital had been cordoned off. There were soldiers everywhere—on the roofs of the surrounding buildings, in vehicles on the streets, even in other choppers in the sky around them.

"This isn't going to end well," the pilot said through the comms.

She nodded. What the hell did the generals think they were doing? They'd cut off the hospital as if they thought they were containing a zombie apocalypse.

She'd told everyone at the staging area the same thing. The outbreak wasn't a virus. It wasn't going to spread. Contagion wasn't an issue.

The only one who'd listened was the woman, Tatyana, but she'd disappeared after their meeting and left her alone to explain the situation to the military boneheads who were in charge.

The only thing they'd been concerned about was sealing off the hospital and keeping everyone affected inside. It was like they heard the word 'anthrax', and their minds went blank. All they could think of was their jobs. The city had seen outbreaks before, and they'd always cost a lot of officers their jobs. If there was one thing the top brass was good at, it was protecting their own skins.

The chopper touched down on the rooftop helipad, and Sofia leaped out. She kept her head low and ran to the door, where two soldiers let her pass.

Once inside, she made her way to the ground floor of the hospital.

"Olga," she cried when she saw her.

Olga was standing by the window, looking out at the situation. "Sofia, where have you been?"

"The military is staging this operation from Novouralsk."

Olga grabbed her by the shoulders and pressed her tightly against her chest as if afraid she would disappear again. "I was so worried," she said.

Sofia looked out the window. "What's the situation?"

"Apart from the army surrounding us?"

"How fast are new cases coming in?"

"They've slowed," Olga said, "but they won't stop for days. You know that."

Sofia nodded. The fact they'd slowed was something. "They must have figured out the source of the leak," she said.

Olga looked at her cautiously. The two had never talked openly about what it was Sofia actually did inside the military compound. "Let's hope so," Olga said.

Outside the window, they could see soldiers running everywhere.

"If they've stemmed the leak," Olga said, "why are they still here? It looks to me like they think they have a virus outbreak on their hands."

"They don't know their asses from their elbows," Sofia said. "They're following orders, and right now, their orders are to keep us contained."

"They're creating a pressure cooker," Olga said.

Sofia nodded. For now, it seemed the people inside the hospital were willing to allow the quarantine. They understood the need for precautions. But tensions were high. Ambulances were still bringing in new patients. The hospital was getting more and more crowded. One wrong move, one trigger-happy recruit, and things would get ugly real fast.

And as Sofia looked out the window, she saw that the military was doing nothing to calm the situation. Men were in the process of setting up machine-gun posts on steel platforms right outside the fence. The guns all pointed inward.

It was already starting to make people nervous. There were groups forming in the parking lot, men standing around smoking cigarettes, eyeing the soldiers.

A huge tanker truck drove slowly toward the gate. It stopped, and four men in hazmat suits got out. The truck was equipped with two hoses and the men, like firefighters, worked in teams to uncoil them. Then they opened the valves and began spraying down the street in front of the hospital. The smell of chlorine wafted over the hospital immediately.

Chlorine was toxic in concentrations as low as eighteen parts per million. At eight hundred parts, it would kill fifty percent of people exposed to it. Sofia wondered what concentration the military was using and whether they were smart enough to ensure they didn't allow the concentrations to become dangerous.

She got her answer when they hosed down the hospital

gates, taking no precautions to protect the people in the parking lot or even their own men guarding the gates.

"We'd better get those people back inside," Olga said, looking out at the scene.

Sofia nodded. "The last thing we need is more poisonings."

The truck finished hosing the entryway and began driving along the street. The soldiers walked along next to it, spraying everything.

"A week from now, the trees will be dead," Olga said.

Sofia nodded. She turned to Olga. "So what now?"

Olga spread her hands helplessly. "Everyone exposed is dead," she said. "There's nothing to do but bring the bodies to the morgue."

"Are they being burned?"

"No, the military said to preserve them, but the morgue isn't equipped for so many bodies. They're just piling them up."

"If they want to perform autopsies, they'd better come soon," Sofia said. "I'll make a call."

Olga went to the samovar and poured two cups of tea. She handed one to Sofia. Neither of them had slept since the start of the outbreak, and they were close to exhaustion. "We should try to get some rest," Sofia said.

Olga nodded. "There's something I don't understand," she said.

"What?"

"If the outbreak came from the military's own compound, which we know it did...."

Sofia nodded. "Yes?"

"A leak?" Olga said.

"Right."

"I mean, they didn't do this on purpose. It's a leak from their own facility, and they know that."

Sofia nodded. She felt an overwhelming wave of guilt. This was the result of her work. She'd done this—or been a part of it. And now, people like Olga would have to figure out the solution.

"Then why are they locking down the hospital? We're not the source of the threat."

Sofia thought about that. There was a small chance of contamination from an exposed person. Spores in their body or on their clothing could still be active. But Olga was right. That risk was minuscule compared to the fact that their own facility had been spewing spores into the sky just a few miles away.

"They're covering their tracks. They're trying to make it look like this is a natural outbreak so that they can deny it's a bioweapon. We signed treaties saying we wouldn't do this. Saying we'd stop making new bioweapons."

"We need to get out of here," Olga said.

Sofia nodded. "But how? They've surrounded us with machine guns."

26

Tatyana leaned back on a velvet sofa. She was in one of the hotel's boutiques, and two girls fluttered around her.

"Maybe that one," she said, pointing to a black Chanel dress with jewels embroidered around the neckline.

One of the girls went to get it from the rail, while the other offered her a bottle of Perrier on a silver tray. Tatyana waved the water away. "No," she said. "Not that one. The one with the crystals."

The girl took the correct dress carefully from its hanger and held it up to the light. It sparkled exquisitely. "Oh," Tatyana moaned, "it's so beautiful."

"It is," the girl said. She was pretty. She had a pleasant demeanor. Tatyana wondered what it would be like to have a life like that—a life that was honest, that was safe.

Maybe if she'd been born in America instead of Russia, she'd be a girl like that. A girl who showed rich, foreign women dresses that cost more than she earned in a month.

"Would you like to try it on?" the girl said.

Tatyana was about to say yes when her phone rang.

It was her operator. "He wants to speak to you."

"I'll hold," Tatyana said.

She waited for the click and then Igor's voice. "Arrived?" he said.

"I'm at the hotel."

"How's the room?"

"I haven't been up yet."

Igor chuckled. "The boutiques?"

"You'd be suspicious if I didn't," she said.

He laughed again, and she thought he sounded very jolly. She could tell he was smoking a cigar. "Is everything okay?" she said.

"Of course. Why wouldn't it be?"

"You don't usually call for a chat while I'm shopping," she said.

"Quite," he said.

She rolled her eyes at the sales assistant and pretended to yawn. The assistant smiled.

Part of Tatyana's job was to constantly sell herself to Igor. There was no shortage of blonde girls in Moscow who would sleep with foreigners for a Chanel dress. The bosses knew it. The girls knew it. Stroking Igor's ego was something Tatyana was used to. She was good at it.

"Miss me?" she said.

Not only did she have to flirt with him, but she also had to convince him that he got more bang for his buck with her than any of the literally hundreds of other girls who wanted her job. That meant getting information out of the targets, information that could advance Igor's career or give him an edge over his adversaries. And all the while, she had to make him feel she was grateful to him—grateful for the privilege of having a job, for getting to wear nice things, for flying first class. Grateful like the money was his, like it came from his wallet personally.

In that sense, every Widow was a double agent before she ever left the Aquarium. She learned to play both sides from day one. She knew instinctively what men like Igor took years to figure out—that there was no difference between a Russian cock and an American one.

"Everyone's a whore," her grandmother told her on her sixteenth birthday. "The only thing you decide is what part of yourself you sell. Your brain. Your hands. Your pussy."

There was never any doubt which paid best.

"There's been a change of plan," Igor said.

"Oh?"

"You've got a new target."

"I see."

"Someone more valuable."

"You're sending me files?"

"Agniya's preparing them now."

Tatyana took a deep breath. She told herself this was nothing unusual. She'd manipulated Igor into sending her after a second-rate target. It wasn't surprising someone up the chain had decided to switch them out for someone better. "Is everything all right?" she said.

There was the slightest hesitation from Igor, and then, "Yes."

"You're sure?"

"Yes, it's just... this new target. I haven't had time to vet him personally."

"Well," she said, "if the order's from upstairs, I'm sure they've done their due diligence."

"You'll have to be careful."

"I always am," she said. She waited for him to say more, but he was uncharacteristically reticent. Something was distracting him. "Are you sure everything's okay?" she said again.

"It's okay. Just... you know."

"Upstairs?" she said.

"Just keep your wits about you."

"I will."

"I know I can count on you, Taniusha," he said, using the familiar form of her name. It showed affection. He'd never called her that before.

Then the line went dead. Tatyana looked at the phone to see if there was a problem with the call.

"Everything all right?" the sales assistant said.

Tatyana nodded absently. "Just..." she said, thinking. "Just work."

"Do you still want to see the dress?"

"Pack it up."

"You're taking it?"

"Yes, I am."

"It's four thousand dollars."

"That's fine," Tatyana said. She paid for the dress and went back out to the lobby. The concierge offered to help with her bag, but she brushed past him without speaking. In the elevator, she felt nauseous. All the travel was catching up with her. She needed rest.

When she got to her room, she could tell the advance team had already been there. Cameras would be hidden everywhere, even in the bathroom, which she always felt was gratuitous.

She flung the bag on the bed, went into the bathroom, and threw up.

Then she ran a hot bath and lay in it for half an hour. She felt better when she got out. She wrapped herself in a robe and lay on the bed. She had the files to read, but she needed a few minutes. She set a thirty-minute timer and shut her eyes.

27

Laurel felt the adrenaline. She'd gotten too used to working from a desk, putting the pieces in play from the safety of Langley. Actually being in the field was a rush.

She'd already told Roth he could call off the surveillance, and the van was just pulling away.

She walked into the mail store and looked around. It was nothing. Harmless. There was no one there but a kid in a Giants jersey playing on his phone, so bored he was almost comatose.

She looked for the camera the surveillance guys had installed and couldn't see it. They'd done well, getting it in place while the police gave the owner a hard time.

She wasn't sure how her defector was monitoring the mailbox, and she hoped she wouldn't have to wait too long for a response.

She browsed the store for a few minutes to maximize her chances of being seen.

"Can I help you?" the kid at the counter said.

"I'm looking for bubble wrap," she said.

"Packaging materials," he said, pointing to a shelf.

She pretended to take a look. The mailboxes were at the back. They were clearly visible from every part of the store.

"I know someone who has a mailing address at this store," she said to the kid.

He looked up at her. "We provide mail services," he said cautiously.

"She has a box."

"Yes, we rent boxes there at the back." She could tell he was suspicious. After what had happened with the police, he was under no illusions that this was an innocent inquiry.

"My friend rented hers without ID," Laurel said.

The kid looked toward the door. "Your friend?"

"Yeah."

"We require identification for all box rentals," he said, glancing around as if expecting another swarm of police to barge in. "It's our company policy."

"I see," Laurel said.

"Is there anything else I can help you with?" he said.

"I need to get a message to my friend," Laurel said.

The kid said nothing.

Laurel reached into her pocket and handed him a card. It was from a bar a few blocks away.

"What's this?"

"My friend wanted me to set her up with someone."

"What?"

"A date."

"With a guy?"

"Yeah."

The kid said nothing.

"He'll be at this bar tonight at midnight," Laurel said.

28

Lance looked at Sam sitting at the bar. She was beginning to look like she might fit in. She was wearing jeans and a warm sweater, and the dye in her hair faded a little every time she washed it.

"Two beers," he said to the bartender.

"I'll have a club soda," Sam said. She was playing with a pack of cigarettes in her hand, and she said to Lance, "How long are you going to string this out?"

"String what out?"

"You know what."

Lance shook his head. He knew what she was referring to, and he didn't like it. She'd caught the gist of Roth and Laurel's visit. Or at least, she thought she had.

"You don't know as much as you think you do," he said.

"I know as much as you knew when you barged into my life."

"And I was right, wasn't I?"

"About me?"

"Yes, about you."

"Maybe you were."

"You're better off here."

She shrugged. "I should have had a say in the matter."

"But it's working out, right?"

She nodded reluctantly. "It's working."

He could tell she'd be okay. His place was big enough for the two of them. She was a smart girl. A fresh start in a fresh town was all she needed. "You'll get a job, maybe go back to school."

"Let's start with a job," she said.

"See? I wasn't so wrong."

"We're not talking about me," she said. "We're talking about those two government people."

"You don't know who they were."

"I saw enough to know they wanted you back."

He nodded.

"But you're still sitting here in this bar with me, wasting time."

The bartender brought their drinks, and Lance smiled at her. She didn't smile back.

"How's this a waste of time?" he said.

"Letting other people fight your battles for you."

"They're not fighting my battles."

She shrugged.

Lance sighed.

"They've gone back to fight your fight while you sit here on your ass drinking with women half your age."

"What makes you think their fight had anything to do with me?"

"Come on," she said. "Why would the government come all the way out here if it had nothing to do with you?"

"It was a job offer, basically."

"When the military comes to you, when they come all the way to your door, that's not a job offer."

"Oh, no?"

She shook her head.

"What is it then?"

"It's a duty."

He took a sip of his beer and watched the pack of cigarettes in her hand as she deftly turned it over and over. "Since when are you such an expert?"

Sam shrugged. She took a sip of her drink. "I'm just saying."

Lance drained his beer and ordered another. He leaned back in his seat and looked around the bar. It was busier than the last time they were there. There were groups of people sitting at tables having a good time.

"This is life, Sam. Right here. This town. This is where I grew up. This is real life."

"For some people," she said.

"Maybe I want to be some people. Maybe I want to settle down. Find a woman. Start a family. Don't I get to do that?"

She shrugged.

"No, really," he said. "I filed my application to join the army when I was sixteen years old. I had to wait for them to accept me. I had to get a waiver."

"And look at you now," she said.

"I gave them everything, Sam."

"So now you want to start a family? Get a Labrador? A picket fence?"

"I don't know. I've never had a chance to figure that out."

"Come on."

"What's wrong with that?"

Sam shook her head. "I don't know, Lance. Nothing, I guess."

"You guess?"

"It just seems... I don't know, like a cop-out."

"A cop-out?"

"I mean, if you had a woman, maybe I'd believe it. But you're sitting here smiling at a bartender young enough to be your daughter. And she doesn't even like you. That doesn't look like you're planning on laying down roots."

"I was being polite."'

She took another sip.

"And how do you know she doesn't like me?"

Sam rolled her eyes. "What are you afraid of?" she said.

"Afraid?"

"You're afraid of something."

"I'm not afraid."

"Then why won't you go back?"

"Because I've seen the things they want from me. I've been down that road. I know where they want to send me. And I know what it leads to."

"You're a soldier," Sam said. "You shouldn't be thinking like that."

"How should I be thinking?"

"Look at yourself," she said. "You've been sitting in this bar every night since I got here. You've got more life left in you than this."

"What do you want from me?"

"I told you the first time I met you," she said. "Go back and fight for your country."

"You mean, go back and die for my country."

"If it comes to that. Better men than you have done it."

"Not on purpose," Lance said.

Sam shook her head. "No, I see it. Maybe I'm speaking out of line. I mean, I know I'm speaking out of line. But you're scared, Lance Spector. You're afraid of something. Something you saw over there rattled you. Now you're afraid to go back and face it."

"I never saw the point in dying over there when I could die perfectly well right here at home."

"They wouldn't have come if they didn't need you. They came. They asked. Whatever happens now is on you."

Lance let out a long sigh. Her words bothered him. He was used to people giving him their two cents. Everyone in the military knew what that was like. You came back, and people didn't understand. There'd been times in his life when he felt he couldn't walk into a bar without someone getting in his face. He'd learned a long time ago to tune it out.

People's opinions didn't matter. He knew that. The problem was, he felt he'd lost track of what *did* matter.

"I told you, I signed up as soon as I could," he said.

She nodded. "You told me."

"Well, the truth is, it wasn't because I wanted to fight for my country."

"You needed a job?"

"I needed to get out of here. The army was my ticket."

"I don't think they'd hold that against you. They basically say that much in the recruitment commercials."

"I know," he said. "And when I got out there, when I actually saw action, felt the heat of battle, saw the face of the enemy, I didn't fight for my country then either."

Sam looked at him.

"I fought to save my own skin. And I fought for the guy standing next to me. For the guys in my unit. We had each other's backs."

"I think that's normal," Sam said.

"It is," Lance said. "You fight for the man next to you. They tell us that too."

"So what's the problem?"

"The problem?"

"Why don't you go do that again?"

"Because all my friends are dead. There's no one left to fight for."

"All of them are dead?"

"Every last one of them."

Sam sighed. "I'm sorry."

Lance nodded.

"That's war, I guess."

"Sam," Lance said, and he put down his beer and looked at her. "War is something I understand. What I don't understand is all the other bullshit that comes with it."

"What are you saying?"

"It doesn't matter."

"No. I want to know."

"I can't get into it."

"Was that how my father died?"

"No, your father died taking a bullet for me. He saved my life."

"And that's why you came for me?"

Lance didn't say anything.

"Who were they?" Sam said. "Those two people who came?"

"That man you met. He and I were friends once. We've been through more shit together than you'd believe."

"But he let you down?"

"He did more than that."

"He hurt you, didn't he? Something personal."

Lance looked at her, then looked away.

Sam nodded. She finished her drink and stood up.

"You're not staying for another?"

"I'm going to call it a night," she said.

"All right."

"Just one last question," she said.

He looked at her.

"The woman. What about her? Isn't she your friend?"

"I barely know her."

"I saw the way you looked at her."

"How did I look at her?"

Sam hesitated, then said, "Like you wouldn't send her into war alone."

29

Tatyana woke to the alarm on her phone. She checked the time. It was an hour since she'd set it. She'd slept right through.

It took more willpower than usual for her to get up from the bed. She wanted nothing more than to close the curtains and call it a day. She hoped she wasn't coming down with something.

She opened the file system on her phone and checked to see what Igor had sent. The last-minute change of target was a minor snag. She was so used to these missions she barely looked at the research. Her job was to play dumb and drop her panties. In general, the less she knew, the better.

Her original target, the trade negotiator, had been a sixty-five-year-old Canadian. The new guy was a fifty-eight-year-old American. It made no difference to her. It wasn't a date. He was an advisor to a senator from Rhode Island. That definitely bumped him up the priority ladder. He'd been involved in negotiating the latest round of sanctions against Russia, which explained the top floor's interest.

There was nothing the top dogs hated more than sanctions. Even the country's most powerful oligarchs had seen their net worth and foreign holdings drop precipitously as a result. Combined with the recent drops in the price of oil, Russian billionaires were in for a rough Christmas.

The target's name was Sheldon Goldin, and he seemed a little puritanical for Tatyana's liking. Happily married for twenty-nine years, he was an ardent church-goer, attending Trinity Episcopal in Newport every Sunday morning. He had three daughters in their twenties, all in Ivy League schools, all dating eligible bachelors from prestigious families.

None of them would want to see Daddy getting his freak on.

Tatyana knew the value of a target like that. The GRU wanted him not just for the information he held directly but as a potential means of tapping the senator. Planting spyware, avoiding firewalls, hacking email servers—those were all things that got a lot easier when you had someone on the inside.

Not that any of that would be her job. She would make sure he got caught on camera with his pants down. What the top floor did with it was up to them.

She knew a lot of what she did got wasted. If a target resisted, if he called their bluff, there wasn't a whole lot they could do to him. They could send the footage to the man's wife or leak it to a local political opponent, but the GRU had to be careful not to overplay its hand. If people caught on that there was a concerted attack, they'd respond. They'd adapt. And *kompromat* would lose its effectiveness.

The trick was keeping people in the dark, making each target feel like he was the only one who'd been caught, making him feel isolated.

In most cases, just having the footage was enough. It

would never be leaked, never viewed. It would be stored on a server somewhere in Russia, along with similar footage on literally thousands of other men from countries all over the world. A diplomat in Estonia. A congressional staffer in DC. A trader on Wall Street. A journalist in London. All that footage added up to a massive arsenal of influence.

And once they got a target to do something small for them—tip them off on a story, or send the minutes of a meeting, even something that wasn't illegal, something of limited value, something in the public domain like the phone number of a judge—once they did anything, the GRU owned them. Because then, they hadn't just cheated on their wife, reprehensible as that was—they'd aided the enemy. They'd crossed the line. That was when you really had something. That was when you had the first step on a path that led all the way from law-abiding citizen to out-and-out treason.

That was the *kompromat* game, it was Tatyana's bread and butter, and it was what kept Russia in the top tier, even now, when its military budget had fallen to ninth in the world, barely above that of South Korea, and well below countries like France, Germany, and Britain. With its economy shrinking, its military faltering, its superpower status nothing more than a memory, *kompromat*, human intelligence, good old fashioned espionage, was what kept Russia on page one of the US President's Daily Brief, and had since the final days of Hitler, and Mussolini, and Emperor Hirohito.

Igor had sent photos. The target was balding, jowly. The bottom half of his face reminded Tatyana of the bullmastiff a neighbor in her building in Moscow owned. The animal drooled nonstop, left big globs on the carpet in the elevator.

The target's reported income in the previous year was

over two million dollars, mostly earned lobbying the state senate in Providence on behalf of Elmaria Mutual, Northern Citizen Bank, and other large financial companies with a significant presence in Rhode Island.

Despite his church attendance and apparently happy marriage, he'd been deemed corruptible by the GRU. Tatyana looked at that part of the report closest. It was the part that affected her. It said he'd traveled to Beijing six months earlier. It wasn't government work—it was for one of his private financial clients—and because he was on the GRU list, a junior member of the diplomatic staff at the Russian consulate in Beijing wrote up a report.

The Russian staffer ran into Goldin at a meeting at the Mandarin Oriental and afterward invited him to a strip club. At the club, Goldin threw around some money, got hideously drunk, and spent the night in one of the club's champagne suites. According to the report, those suites weren't cheap and weren't for the faint of heart. Whoever Goldin was on Sunday mornings in Newport, that wasn't who he was in the champagne suite.

Reports like this were the true contribution Igor had made to his country. They were the oxygen of his program. He'd spent decades traveling the world, meeting with Russian embassy officials and consular staff, impressing on them the importance of his list, the Black List as he called it, and sending them notifications anytime anyone important was scheduled to travel to their city.

If an embassy staffer met with someone on the list and filled out a simple report afterward, they got a thousand dollars. Even if nothing happened, even if the most important detail the report contained was how the target took his coffee, it was a thousand dollar minimum for the embassy official. And Igor always paid, always on time, no questions asked. It was something the staffers could rely on, and they filled out the reports diligently. If the report actually covered something interesting, something truly compromising, the price went up exponentially.

The report Tatyana was reading on Goldin had probably earned its author five thousand dollars. If there'd been photos of Goldin in the strip club, or video of him getting a lap dance or something, it might have been worth twenty. It wasn't a huge amount in the grand scheme of things, but more than enough to keep the keyboards clacking at Russian embassies around the world.

Tatyana knew there was scarcely a world leader left that Igor didn't have dirt on. Even the countries with female leaders. Everyone had a vice. Everyone had a skeleton in the closet.

Tatyana went into the bathroom to get ready. She looked at herself in the mirror. She knew she was attractive, although she didn't always feel it. She had the classic Russian physique that men the world over seemed to bend the rules for. Igor told her she had the face of an angel and the body of a stripper. It was probably a compliment. But sometimes, when she looked in the mirror, she couldn't help seeing her mother. And when she pictured her mother, she was always dead. Those days in the apartment, the lifeless eyes, the flesh slowly turning rancid. It came to her in dreams too, and then, she would wake up so drenched in sweat she would have to change the sheets.

She'd been trained in two principal means of attack. Either she would work a target hard, like a stripper behind on her rent, or she would capitalize on the babyface, put her hair in braids, wear knee-length socks and a schoolgirl skirt, and make the target feel like she needed his help. Neither approach was guaranteed to succeed, and she knew this mark could go either way.

Getting freaky at a private club in Beijing was one thing —a city like that could feel like another universe to a guy used to the pace of Newport or Providence. There was no guarantee he'd act with the same sense of abandon closer to home. Manhattan was a world of its own. It could put a spell on people, but Tatyana knew she would have to help it along.

She was used to that. That was what made her good at her job.

Her early targets had all been foreign embassy staffers stationed in Moscow. Those guys were deemed fair game for training purposes. No one really expected her to succeed. They were far from home, and Moscow had a healthy reputation for hedonism, but the staffers all had their guards up. They knew where they were. They knew the GRU was watching. Honing her skills in that difficult environment helped her develop the techniques she would use on Sheldon Goldin.

She put on the Chanel dress she'd purchased downstairs, some provocative black stilettos, and a Chanel purse. She tied her hair up, revealing as much of the dress's jeweled neckline as possible.

When she was ready, she went down to the lobby and ordered a martini. It would help loosen her up.

She'd also learned that men liked the smell of alcohol on a woman. It got their hopes up. And it helped explain what might otherwise seem like unusually forward behavior.

She sat at a table, and the waiter brought candied almonds with the drink. Her job now was to wait. Her operator would tell her the next move.

She sipped her drink and watched the other people in the bar. Hotels like this had a certain type of clientele. Ordinary expense accounts wouldn't cover it. These were people who owned things. Companies. Countries.

Her phone dinged, and she shut her eyes before looking at it.

This was it. Personal time was over. It was time to earn her keep.

But when she looked at the phone, it wasn't her operator, but Ayaan. She looked at her watch and then decided to answer. "What is it, Ayaan?"

"Someone was here. They asked for you."

"What do you mean, asked for me?"

"She said you asked her to introduce you to someone. A man. At a bar."

"She?"

"The woman."

"A woman said she'd introduce me to someone?"

"She was like you. Nice clothes. Walked like she had a stick up her ass."

"Who was she?"

"I don't know, but she said she knew someone who got a mailbox without ID and wanted to leave her a message."

"What exactly was the message?"

"It's a bar around the corner. The Horse's Head. Your date will be there at midnight."

"My date?"

"Take your own messages from now on."

"Ayaan," she said, but he hung up.

30

Igor stepped out of the elevator and tried to look relaxed. He liked to think he belonged on the top floor, but his heart was thumping in a way that said he didn't. Not yet. He'd been there, of course, for meetings, for assessments of his performance, but this was his first visit as an actual player.

An omen of things to come, he told himself.

Before him was a heavy wooden desk with a receptionist sitting at it. She was flanked by two guards, and behind her on the wall was a large portrait of the president. His mousy eyes followed Igor around the room.

"Director Aralov," the receptionist said. He noted her age, her attractiveness. No one worried up here about the girls getting diddled with.

The top floor had been designed by Stalin himself. Two floors had been combined into one, allowing for ceilings twice the usual height. It created a space like a ballroom or the lobby of a grand hotel, rather than the maze of dingy corridors Igor usually inhabited.

"I'm here to see—"

"Director Timokhin," the secretary said, finishing his sentence.

He nodded.

"If you'll follow me." She led him down a wide hallway with a white marble floor.

Igor ran his tongue over his lips as he followed the girl, her hips swaying left to right as if her skirt was cinched too tightly at the knee.

To say the hall was opulent was an understatement. Gold flagpoles extended from the walls, and inlaid wooden panels bearing the nation's coat of arms decorated each set of double doors. They passed about ten of these doors before the secretary came to a halt.

Igor straightened his jacket. He was carrying a bottle of Stolichnaya vodka, and he passed through the doors, holding it out in front of him like a schoolboy presenting a gift to his teacher.

He'd been expecting to enter Timokhin's office but found himself in yet another anteroom, with another desk and another secretary sitting at it.

"Director Aralov," the new secretary said, getting to her feet. Behind her were two more soldiers, two more flags, two more doors. To her left was an office full of women sitting at desks, typing furiously.

This secretary, even younger than the last, led him through the next set of doors where he finally found himself in Timokhin's presence.

Across a huge office, Timokhin was perched regally on a high-backed chair, a stunning vista visible behind him through the double-height windows.

"Sit, Igor, sit," Timokhin said.

This was the top floor. This was where real power lived.

Timokhin had gotten there by stabbing people in the

back. It was a well-trodden career path in the GRU, which made it all the more impressive that he'd made a name for himself at it. They called him Black Timokhin because of the number of his rivals who'd found their way to early graves.

He was dangerous. Even him knowing your name was dangerous.

Igor knew that. But the director was dangling a key to the top floor in front of Igor's nose, and that was something worth taking a risk for.

Igor placed the vodka on the table, and Timokhin produced two crystal glasses from a drawer. Igor filled them and said, "To the Motherland."

They knocked back their shots with a workman's efficiency, and Igor refilled them.

"So it's done?" Timokhin said.

"I gave her your target."

"She didn't ask questions?"

"She trusts me."

"Don't be stupid."

"I told her the new target came from the top floor."

"You old cretin," Timokhin said.

"Don't call me that."

"If you're going to do this job," Timokhin said, waving a hand to indicate the top floor office and all it entailed, "you have to accept what you are. Now drink up. You've earned it, selling your favorite slut down the river."

They drank and Igor refilled the glasses. "What will happen to her?" he said.

"As if you don't know."

Igor knew Tatyana was finished. A casualty of war. He'd accepted it. But what he wanted to know was how it had happened. "She did it to herself," he said.

"Of course she did, Igor. Of course she did."

"You mock me."

"You tell yourself what you have to. I want you to sleep well tonight."

Igor downed his shot and watched Timokhin do the same. He refilled the glasses. He'd seen Timokhin slip up once before. Just a small slip. They'd been at a function, a grand gala with the wives, and Timokhin got very drunk. In the men's room, standing in front of the urinals, Igor asked him about an operation, about a mole he was running, and Timokhin gave away that she was a woman. He'd looked across the urinals, cock in hand, and winked. A small thing, but enough.

It was a dangerous game, and Igor had no choice but to roll the dice. Tatyana may have been leaking to the Americans, but someone had found her out. Someone had reported her. And it had happened in Igor's house, under Igor's watch.

"Was it the American who betrayed her?" he said.

He knew it wasn't. She'd been betrayed by someone on their own side. Someone closer to home.

"Now, now, Igor," Timokhin said. "We're here to be friendly, not settle scores."

"I know," Igor said, forcing himself to smile. "It's just... let me confide something in you, Timokhin."

"Yes?" Timokhin said, leaning forward.

They knocked back another shot, and Igor refilled the glasses. "I'm not sure if you've heard the rumors."

"This building is full of rumors, Igor."

"Well, let me put it this way. You know I'm a man with red blood."

"I never doubted it," Timokhin said.

"I have..." he held out his hands, "appetites."

"Let me assure you," Timokhin said, "it would take a lot more than *appetites*, as you put it, to shock me."

"I'm glad to hear that," Igor said.

"I have stories that would shock a priest," Timokhin said.

Igor laughed.

"Really," Timokhin said.

"Then I can tell you," Igor said, "this slut, Tatyana."

"Yes?"

"She had a way of scratching my itch that will not be easy to replace."

"Igor, Igor, Igor," Timokhin said. "The first lesson of the top floor is that everyone can be replaced."

Igor knew he had to dangle something juicy if he was to get anywhere. "Not this," he said, eyeing Timokhin. "This was something very... *specific*."

"How so?"

"It's a niche thing," Igor said. "Not something your average whore would be willing to accommodate. Even for extra."

Timokhin was wondering what it could be that would give a whore pause. Igor knew he'd be interested. Even by Igor's standards, Timokhin was a deviant creep. This was right up his alley.

"She really is unique," Igor continued.

"You're sorry to see her go."

"Like you told me," Igor said, "all fathers have their favorites."

"You'll get over it."

"I'll tell you the truth," Igor said. "I'm wondering if it's avoidable."

Timokhin smiled. He liked this feeling of power. It was the reason he was where he was, sitting behind this desk on the top floor—and why he'd gone to hell and back to get there. He leaned in his chair. "Whatever is it that she does for you?" he said.

"Use your imagination," Igor said.

Timokhin smiled. He was beginning to smell a rat. "Why don't you tell me what you're really up to, Igor?"

"I want to bring her back."

"You can't be that naive," Timokhin said. "She's a traitor. It's beyond question. I don't care what she can do with her cunt."

"If she was speaking to the Americans," Igor said, "that's something we can use."

"*Disinformaciya?*"

"We could use her to feed them a crock of shit. We've done it before."

"We're already using her, Igor. We're drawing out her contact in the CIA. We're ready to pounce."

Igor brought the glass to his lips but paused. "She's so talented, Fyodor."

"She's a rat."

"She'll be your rat."

"She lied to you, Igor."

"We all lie in this place. Who knows what she was up to, or why? Maybe she was obeying someone else's orders."

"Your agent, Igor. Your slut. Taking orders from someone else?"

"Let's at least bring her back for questioning. Find out what's going on."

Timokhin drained his glass and slammed it sharply on the table. "Enough," he said. "This is nonsense. She sold us out. Now she's got to pay. You know the rules."

"Timokhin—"

"You're fishing, Igor, and I don't like it."

Igor refilled Timokhin's glass. "Very well," he said, raising his glass. "A final toast."

"Very well," Timokhin said.

"Only the good die young."

"The good die young," Timokhin said and drank.

Igor knew he needed to offer something of value now. He looked at Timokhin. "Tell your man she carries an old Browning pistol in her purse, chambered in a 9x19 millimeter round."

Timokhin nodded.

Igor had to be very careful with what came next. He was feeling the booze. Timokhin's guard was up. The wrong move could blow everything. "I know who was watching her," he said.

Timokhin laughed. "If you did, you wouldn't be up here plying me with vodka."

"It was the hag," Igor said.

Timokhin laughed. "You're guessing, Igor."

And that was it. As simple as that. Igor's secretary was no spring chicken, but she was far from the only hag he might have been referring to. For Timokhin to get the reference so quickly, that was the slip.

"I think," Igor said, wiping his brow, "that I've had too much to drink."

Timokhin's eyes were glazed. "You're a soldier, Igor," he said. "You're not paid to think."

Igor made to get to his feet. He had to steady himself on the chair. He was drunk.

"There's something I need to tell you," Timokhin said, pouring two more glasses.

"Very well."

"Sit," Timokhin said.

Igor slumped back into the chair.

"The reason I called you here," he said, "the reason I'm dangling the prospect of a top-floor office in front of you."

"Yes?" Igor said, a little too eagerly.

"We're going to war, Igor."

Igor watched him form the word. He said it with such relish, as if he was saying the name of a lover. "If that's true...."

"It is true. Straight from the top," he said, nodding to the portrait of the president on his desk. "We're done staring at the Americans across the curtain. We're finally going to war."

"Real war?"

"Real war, Igor. The war we've been waiting our whole lives to fight."

Igor reached for the bottle, almost knocking it over. It was Timokhin who caught it. "But we can't win," he said.

"We don't have to win," Timokhin said. "We only have to prove our loyalty."

"And how do we do that?" Igor said.

"By sacrificing our souls, Igor. By sacrificing our souls."

31

L ance pulled up to the departure terminal. Sam was sitting in the truck next to him, looking at him. "What?" he said.

"Nothing."

"Why are you looking at me like that?"

"I don't know."

"What difference does it make to you?"

"It doesn't. It just.... I don't know. It feels right."

"Feels right?"

"You're a soldier, Lance. You belong over there."

He let out a long sigh. He was still conflicted about the decision, but there was something about what Sam had said, about him letting Laurel go and fight his fight, that didn't sit right. He knew he couldn't let her go alone.

"So I can trust you to hold down the fort?" he said.

"Yes."

"You're sure?"

"I swear, Lance."

"Because it wasn't so long ago you were calling me a kidnapper."

"I was upset."

"You said I was going to lock you in the basement."

She shrugged.

He took the keys from the ignition and handed them to her. "A lot of things in life," he said, "end up not working out."

"You'll just have to trust me," Sam said.

"Don't mess up my truck."

"I won't."

"Or my place."

"I won't, Lance."

"And take care of yourself."

She looked at him. "I'll try."

He hoped that was true. If she managed to turn things around, that would be something he'd hold on to, something he'd be able to point to and say it had worked out, in a world where very few things ever did.

All the things he'd ever done, things that were supposed to make the world a better place, a safer place, the people he'd killed, the targets he'd taken out, the men he'd trained and led into battle. All the oaths he'd sworn, the allegiances he'd pledged, the god in whose name he'd fought. All of it had turned to dust. It had brought him nothing but loss and anguish and death.

He'd read something once. 'The tree that bears no fruit is fit for the fire'. That was how he felt about his own life.

But there was a part of him that refused to give up. He did his best not to listen to it, to keep it buried down at the bottom of his mind where he couldn't hear it, but it was there. And that was the part of him now that told him if things worked out for Sam, if she found some sort of peace in the world, that would be a fruit he'd be able to hold onto.

He'd packed a single bag, and it was on the seat behind

him. He grabbed it and got out. Sam came around the truck and hugged him tighter than he'd expected.

"You're going to miss me," he said.

"I'm not going to miss you."

"Sure you are."

He'd walked to the entrance of the terminal when she called out, "You come home now, you hear?"

He raised a hand but didn't turn back.

On the flight, he said a prayer for the first time in years. "Keep her safe."

When he landed at Dulles, he realized he hadn't been in the capital since Clarice's death.

So many people were dead. Everyone he'd ever cared about. His family, the people he'd grown up with, the men he'd trained with, the men he'd gone to war with.

Outside the arrivals terminal, he found a cab.

"Where you headed, buddy?"

It was late, and he didn't see the point in wasting any time. "You know Monroe's Diner in Foggy Bottom?" he said.

When Lance lived in DC, he'd had a practice of always eating breakfast at the same diner. If Roth or anyone else wanted to meet him, that was where it happened. He called the habit his own personal *Monroe Doctrine*.

As the cab got onto the highway and sped up, Lance leaned back in the seat and looked out the window. He had the card Roth had left, and he dialed the number on it. It went to voicemail. "Roth. I'm back. Call me when you get this. I'll be at Monroe's."

When the cab arrived at Foggy Bottom, he got out and entered the diner.

"Hello, stranger," the waitress said when he entered.

He looked at her. "I didn't think anyone would still recognize me," he said.

The girl blushed. "Where have you been?"

"Montana."

"So you're here for a visit?"

He nodded, and she showed him to the table that had been his regular spot. He didn't know the waitress's name, and she didn't know his.

He sat and looked around the diner. Nothing had changed—the same ketchup and mustard bottles on the tables, the same ceramic coffee mugs with the handles slightly lower than normal, the same plastic-coated napkins that repelled more grease than they absorbed.

"What'll it be?" the waitress said.

"You remember my usual?"

She smiled and left. A moment later, she came back with black coffee.

Everywhere Lance looked, the past came flooding back to him. The way Clarice flipped her hair out of her eyes, the way she looked away when he said something she especially liked, like she thought what he'd just said was too good to be true and that she might jinx it by looking at him.

Whatever they'd had sure as hell was jinxed.

She'd been his handler from day one, from the day he came out of training at the Farm, and when she died, he swore he was done for good.

32

S heldon Goldin sat in the back of a town car, looking out the window.

"We can't sit here all night," the driver said.

They were on Madison Avenue at Twenty-Fourth. Across the street was an upscale bar called The Beverly, the type of place where the waiters wore tuxedos, and the drinks came in crystal glasses.

"There's cars lined up behind me, boss."

Goldin glanced over his shoulder at the traffic. "Move when I tell you to move," he said.

The driver, a large man, sank into his seat like he was trying to hide. He winced each time a car behind them honked.

Goldin examined his fingernails—he'd had them manicured that afternoon—and put on a pair of leather gloves.

"There she is," he said.

Timokhin had sent pictures. The girl was a real piece of ass, the kind that practically begged to be used as a weapon. There were many ways to wage war. This creature, in her black dress and pearls and dangerously high stilettos, certainly was one. Just looking at her gave him the same thrill as the sight of a new piece of military hardware.

He bit his lip in anticipation of spending a night with her.

Russians killing Russians, that was how he justified himself. Not that he lost much sleep over it. He'd long ago sold his soul.

The first time Timokhin approached him, almost thirty years earlier, at a conference in Warsaw, Goldin had been employed by a big defense contractor. "I'm no traitor," he'd said to Timokhin.

"I understand that," Timokhin said in his gravelly voice. His accent was so thick he sounded like an actor in a low-budget Dracula movie. Even his laugh was like that, like that puppet on Sesame Street with the black cloak.

Since then, the two men had been through a lot together. Goldin's prospects as an assassin rose as Timokhin climbed the ranks of the GRU. Now, Goldin was as tried and true as anyone on the GRU's books.

Initially, his targets had all been Russian, which was what allowed him to tell himself he wasn't betraying his country. He was just doing dirty work for a foreign government.

Very dirty work. That paid very well.

Then, targets from NATO countries began showing up in his briefs. That gave Goldin the briefest pause, his atrophied conscience finally raising its head. But the pay increased correspondingly, and as always, Timokhin had the sense not to push the envelope too far too fast. He sent targets from Eastern Europe, Turkey, nationals of the most recent NATO additions, countries he knew Goldin wouldn't think of as real allies. It was years before Timokhin sent the first French, British, and Canadian targets.

And only after years of that did he graduate him to killing Americans.

Goldin had trained himself to carry out his jobs without thinking of any of that. He focused on the mission at hand and didn't worry whether or not it made him a traitor.

He lived a double life. When he was performing hits for the GRU, he lived the life of a playboy in an expensive New York apartment. The rest of the time, he lived in his childhood home with his mother in New Jersey, mowing her lawn on Saturday mornings, cooking her breakfast. In the psyche profile Timokhin had commissioned in Moscow, they said Goldin probably had a split personality.

This job was a classic—Russian on Russian.

Easy money. Plus, he was getting laid.

His target was a GRU agent. She'd done something to upset someone up the chain, broken a rule, or just found herself in the wrong place at the wrong time. Whatever it was, they wanted her dead, and that, as far as Goldin was concerned, was that.

Timokhin had sent the file a few hours earlier. The target, Tatyana Aleksandrova, was classed as highly dangerous.

She'd been told Goldin was a senatorial aide being targeted for *kompromat*. Goldin was no expert on the doings of senators and their aides, but it was a role he knew how to play. His job was to let her seduce him, make her think her mission was going well, then follow her after it was done.

She was expected to make unauthorized contact with someone in the city, someone on the American side. Timokhin needed to know who she was meeting. Goldin was to film the exchange. Then he was to kill her.

It was straightforward, but because of Tatyana's training, he'd have to be careful. She was as familiar with killing as he was and wouldn't think twice about it. She was trained to look for the slightest signs of incongruity. A single slip-up, and he'd be done for.

His advantage was that she had no reason to suspect him. She thought he was her target—a soft, dimwitted slob. Nothing he did in the bedroom would cause her to think otherwise.

His phone rang. It was Timokhin.

"Hey, asshole," he said to the driver. "Get out."

"What?"

"Get the fuck out of the car."

The driver unbuckled his seatbelt and got out of the car.

"Close the door, dipshit," Goldin said.

The driver closed the door and waited on the sidewalk.

They were still blocking the lane. Traffic wasn't heavy at this time, but that didn't stop every second car from honking.

"What is it?" Goldin said into the phone.

"She's arrived," Timokhin said.

"I saw her."

"You know how to do a Rhode Island accent?"

"Close enough," Goldin said. "She won't know the difference."

"She's smart, Sheldon."

"I'll be careful."

"She thinks you work for a senator."

"I read the file."

"Just be careful. This is... *important*. Sensitive. I need footage of the meeting."

"I got it, boss."

"We have to get confirmation of who she's meeting. That's critical."

"Any idea what to expect?"

"I just received more data. I'm sending you photos now. Male. American. Thirty-eight. Very dangerous. Used to be Delta Force."

"Delta Force?"

"Just film the meet. Don't approach them. He's extremely dangerous."

"The file said to kill her."

"Forget that. This new data changes everything. If her contact shows, just film them. Under no circumstances are you to approach. From what they sent, this guy is some sort of assassin."

"And what if the man doesn't show up?"

"He'll show. This meet is the only reason she's in New York. She's risked a lot to be there."

"All right."

"Let her do all the work. She'll be motivated."

"Oh, she'll work. Believe me."

A police cruiser pulled up behind him and flashed its lights.

"I've got to go, boss. We're blocking traffic here."

"She keeps a gun in her purse."

"I know. A Browning. I told you, I read the file."

33

When Tatyana entered the bar, heads turned. People made way.

She looked like Chanel paid her to wear the dress. And that was the point.

The hard part of her job wasn't tempting these men but giving them a reason to believe a woman like her would want them.

This jowly Goldin from Rhode Island wasn't an idiot. If a woman like her approached him in a place like this, he'd want to know the angle.

And she would give him one.

She took a seat at the bar.

"What's the most expensive red wine you have?" she said to the bartender.

He looked up at her. "By the glass?"

"Yes."

He thought for a second and said, "I've got a nice Bordeaux."

She nodded.

The restaurant was a good place to make a move. It had

plenty going on for this time of night. There were four single men at the bar, two couples, and a few people scattered around at tables. Everyone was done eating, and the atmosphere was relaxed.

She'd been told Goldin would be there, but she didn't see him.

She noticed two of the men at the bar looking at her. That was nothing unusual. An attractive woman drew attention. But this target was from the top floor, which meant there was a chance she was being observed. For now, that wasn't a concern. She was where she was supposed to be, doing what she was supposed to be doing. It was later when she went to meet Spector that she would have to be vigilant.

She glanced toward the door.

Bingo.

Sheldon Goldin. Fifty-eight. Father of three. Senator's office. Lobbyist. Providence, Rhode Island.

She'd have him in bed within the hour.

She waited to see where he sat and whether he was with anyone. Perfect. A table for two. No date. He ordered a drink.

Tatyana took a sip of her wine and picked up her phone. She spoke into it in English as if answering a call. "You can't do this to me," she said loudly.

Some people looked up, including Goldin. His drink arrived, something amber in a rocks glass, and he took a sip.

"I'll have nowhere to go," she cried into the phone. "I have no one here."

She was a good actor. She brought tears to her eyes and motioned for the bartender to bring her another glass of the Bordeaux. "You can't do this," she said again.

She put down the phone and looked around the bar. Every pair of eyes in the place was on her. She got off her seat awkwardly and made for the women's washroom. In the washroom, she messed her eye makeup a little to make it look like she'd been crying.

On her way back to the bar, she walked right by Goldin's table and knocked over his drink. "Oh my god," she cried.

She bent down to pick up the glass and cut her hand on it.

"Don't worry about that," Goldin said.

She looked up at him, bent over by his knees, and the view down the front of her dress got his attention instantly. "I'm so sorry, sir."

"A little help here," Goldin said to the hostess, who was already on her way.

"I'm so sorry," Tatyana said again, then started to cry.

"Please," Goldin said. "Don't cry. It's just a drink."

"I ruin everything," she said.

Goldin looked from her to the hostess, as if she might know how to handle this situation.

Tatyana stood up. Goldin tried to speak to her, but she went back to her seat. She gathered her coat and purse and asked the bartender for her bill. "Put the gentleman's scotch on it," she said.

Goldin heard her and came over. "That's not necessary," he said.

Tatyana knew she was moving fast, but it was working. If she could avoid drawing this out, she'd have more time to make her meet with Spector. She wasn't sure how long he'd wait for her at the bar in the Village.

"Please," she said to Goldin, tears still in her eyes. "Let me pay for your drink. I'm so mortified."

He acquiesced.

The bartender gave her the bill, and she whipped a credit card from her purse. She made a fuss of going through the options, added a handsome tip, and then purposely entered the wrong PIN.

"Let's try that again," the bartender said, re-entering the transaction.

"I'm so sorry," Tatyana said. "I really can't do anything right tonight. I should never have left the hotel."

She went through the payment process again, and again mistyped the PIN. She did it a third time, and the card got blocked by the issuer.

"I don't know what to say," she said, eyeing Goldin. "I can't pay this bill."

Goldin reached into his pocket and took out his wallet. "Please allow me," he said.

oldin was surprised by how fast Tatyana moved. She hadn't even bothered chatting him up. She just threw herself at him, got him to pay for her thirty-eight-dollar-a-glass wine, then pulled him out of the restaurant.

"You can't leave me," she said when they got outside.

It was scarcely fifteen minutes since he'd stepped into the bar, and he was beginning to worry they were moving too fast. Timokhin had specifically told him to stall.

"I should get back to my hotel," he said.

"We'll share a cab," she said. "I have no money. I need you."

"Where's your hotel?"

"Fifty-eighth street."

He got into the cab and tried to think of ways to slow her down, but by the time they got to the hotel, she had her hand in his pants and her tongue in his mouth. There was nothing he could do then but let nature take its course. That was what he was supposed to do anyway. It meant she'd be through with him sooner than planned, but the truth was, he couldn't have held back even if he'd wanted to.

She started in the car, then rushed him through the lobby of the hotel like they were lovers reunited after a long separation. She had the buckle of his belt open before they got out of the elevator. Within minutes of getting him into the hotel room, she was screwing his brains out.

She ran the gamut, made sure she made excellent tape for whoever was recording them, and when he was spent, grabbed a pack of Russian cigarettes from the bedside table and lit one.

Her body was slick with sweat.

He hadn't had a workout like that in a while. He wasn't a man of particularly ravenous appetites, and she'd coaxed three climaxes from him in less than an hour.

She was a worker. He'd grant her that much.

"You can't smoke in here," he said as she lit a cigarette.

She shrugged. "What do I care? My credit card's already been declined."

He smiled. "You're not afraid of what they'll say?"

"Believe me. I have bigger worries than the maître'd."

She got up and stood in front of the window. The sky silhouetted her body perfectly. Outside it had started to snow. The flakes floated by like ash. Her purse was on the sill in front of the window, and his mind went to the Browning. For the briefest of seconds, he wondered if she was going to reach for it.

She turned and looked out the window. "Have you ever been to Russia?" she said.

He got up and crossed the room. She didn't turn, and he pressed his body against her back. "Why do you ask?"

"I'm just curious."

"Never," he said. They stared out the window together,

and he wondered about her. "Do you get homesick?" he said.

She freed herself from him and went into the bathroom without answering. He waited until the door was locked, then rooted through her purse until he found her Browning semi-automatic pistol. He was surprised by it, by the age of it. It was from the Second World War. He withdrew the magazine, then removed the chambered bullet. He replaced the magazine with the one he'd brought, loaded with blanks.

When Tatyana returned, he was lying on the bed, his flaccid member on his lap in front of him like a worm. It wasn't flattering, but it served to distract her. She glanced at it and then away.

She'd fixed up her makeup. "I have to be somewhere," she said.

Goldin had to give her credit. She was a smooth operator. It had been scarcely an hour, and she was already done with him and moving on to the next item on her agenda. She had what she needed and saw no reason to keep up pretenses.

If he'd really been her target, ending things this abruptly might cause a little suspicion, but what did she care? The GRU had its *kompromat*. He'd learn soon enough what this had been about.

"What's the rush?" he said.

She was applying underarm deodorant. "I usually charge a thousand," she said.

Goldin laughed. "What?"

"A Russian never works for free," she said.

"I thought that was all you did."

She smiled thinly. "You thought wrong."

She was putting on her tights, and he said, "I don't have a thousand dollars."

She shrugged. "Then get it. You can leave it in an envelope with the concierge. Room 4546. A thousand. Plus tip."

"What is this?"

"What do you think it is?"

"In this country, we usually negotiate the price upfront."

"Well, you didn't seem in the mood for *negotiations* when you had your tongue down my throat," she said.

He couldn't believe it. She was a real piece of work. "What if I don't pay?" he said.

She smiled again. "Someone who works for a senator would never walk out on a bill like this."

"You slut," he said.

She fixed him in her gaze like a cat about to pounce on a mouse. "Don't make me angry, Sheldon. It won't go well for you."

He had to admit, he was impressed. It was effective. It would get him out of the room. It would piss him off but look legit. And it would give her an envelope of cash. Something Moscow didn't know about. If she did that enough times, she'd have a nice little nest egg. That had to be useful to someone in her position.

It also reminded him of something he'd heard about Stalin once.

"Is it true," he said, "that during the Stalin years, when the government killed someone, they sent the family a bill for the bullet?"

Tatyana looked at him for a second. "I thought you'd never been to Russia."

"I haven't."

She pursed her lips. He shouldn't have said anything. "It's a myth," she said.

"It doesn't feel like a myth."

"That was the Chinese."

"Really?"

"A bullet fee. The Chinese did it. And the Iranians."

"But not Stalin?"

"You want to know about Stalin? Here's some advice."

Goldin looked at her. She had an answer to everything.

"Stalin said, if you're afraid of wolves, keep out of the forest."

Goldin chuckled. He wasn't going to antagonize her. He needed her to feel like she was in control, that everything was going according to plan. He didn't want to give her any reason not to make her rendezvous.

"A thousand's kind of steep, don't you think?" he said as he got dressed.

"Don't be cheap," Tatyana said, holding the door for him. "You did pretty well for yourself tonight."

"You want me to leave the money with the concierge?"

"Cash. In an envelope. A thousand. Plus tip."

"Tip?" Goldin said.

She nodded and put her hand on his groin. "It's not my fault you have expensive taste," she said, closing the door in his face.

Goldin walked down the hallway. He knew she was watching him through the peephole. He made his way hesitantly to the elevator, looking back at the door twice as if conflicted about what had happened.

He entered the elevator, got out on the ground floor, made his way through the lobby, and got in one of the many cabs parked in front of the hotel.

He handed the driver a twenty and told him to wait.

The driver started the meter and sighed. "I ain't sitting here all night," he said. "Just so you know."

Goldin handed him another twenty and told him to shut up.

He watched the door of the hotel, gambling Tatyana would come out the same way they'd entered, and she did. She didn't get in a cab, though, which threw him.

She began walking. It was after midnight, and there were so few pedestrians she would have noticed anyone following her on foot.

She cut a distinctive figure in her dress, heels, and black trench, and Goldin sat tight until she turned at the end of the block.

"Drive," he said.

"Where to?"

"Just to the corner," he said, handing the driver another twenty.

The driver went as far as the intersection and stopped at the light. Goldin peered down the street. Tatyana was just getting into a cab, and Goldin told his driver to turn right.

"I'm in the wrong lane," he said.

"Do it," Goldin said, and the driver turned onto Park.

They followed Tatyana's cab as far as the West Village. They took a few detours and eventually stopped outside a bar called the Horse's Head.

"Stop here," Goldin said to his driver, keeping a distance of a few hundred yards. "We need to wait."

35

Tatyana was spooked. She knew something was wrong. She hadn't survived this long without developing a sixth sense.

She didn't know if he was with the Americans or her own side, but that asshole was following her. She was just glad she'd managed to get out of the hotel room without having to fight him. Goldin was in better shape than any senator's aide she'd ever met. She'd been more than close enough to tell. Fighting him off would not have been easy.

The entire night had been off. Too easy. He'd done everything she wanted. It should have taken her hours to talk a married man like that into bed. And a lot more alcohol.

The file said he went to church.

It didn't add up.

All she knew was that getting to this meeting with Spector just got a whole lot more urgent. Whoever Goldin was, he'd be easier to deal with once Spector was on the scene.

She looked behind her out the window. Goldin's cab was still there.

"Can we step on it?" she said to the driver.

One thing was certain—what she'd been told about Goldin was not true. Igor's file was wrong. The question was, did Igor know that? Did the top floor? Were they on to her, or was Goldin with the Americans?

She clenched her fists and took a deep breath. She wasn't thinking clearly.

Goldin had been heaving and panting on top of her, sweat on his forehead, the wiry hairs of his chest brushing her face when she realized something wasn't right. It came over her like a chill. The kiss of death, her grandmother would have called it.

She'd kept her cool, wrapped things up without letting him know anything was wrong, and got herself out of that room. That had been her first priority. She didn't want to have to face off with him in the room. He'd have flung her around like a rag doll.

She was armed with a pistol, chambered in a 9mm parabellum, but she didn't know anything about him. Everything she'd learned in her years as a spy told her never to get in a fight without all the facts. You needed to know your opponent. And you needed to have surprise on your side. Goldin was holding all the cards. All she knew about him was that he was circumcised. Not exactly the tactical edge she needed.

Goldin's cab driver certainly wasn't a pro. He did none of the things a trained driver would. That was something she could use.

"Turn right here," she said.

"Why?"

"I need to check something."

Her driver turned, and sure enough, Goldin's did the same. He even signaled his turns when her driver did.

"Okay," she said.

"What's okay?"

She thought about aborting. She could get dropped off somewhere crowded—the train station, maybe—and disappear. There was nothing Goldin could do to prevent that, not with the driver he had.

But this was her chance.

If she didn't meet Spector now, she didn't know if she ever would. She'd risked everything to get in contact with him. And if her cover was blown anyway, meeting Spector was the only thing that mattered. She had nowhere else to go.

She looked at her watch. She was already late. She prayed he was still there. He'd never given her the impression he was a particularly patient man.

"Lady?" the driver said. "Lady? You all right?"

"I'm fine," she said. "Just get me to that bar."

"It's up ahead."

She had to force herself not to think about what had gone wrong. There were too many permutations, and the situation at hand was more urgent. She had to get through the next few minutes, get to Spector, get this Goldin creep off her back, and then she could figure out how much shit she was in.

She'd brought this on herself. She'd known it would cost her. There would be a price, and she was ready to pay it.

She just wanted desperately for it to be worth the cost.

The cab pulled up outside the Horse's Head, and she peered out the back window. Goldin's cab was behind them at the last set of lights.

She looked around the street. It was all but deserted.

There were a few cars crossing at the intersections. There was a guy walking down the street, smoking a cigarette.

She reached into her purse and felt the reassuring steel of her pistol.

"I ain't got all night, lady," the cab driver said.

36

L aurel looked at her watch for the thousandth time. It was almost one a.m.

"Hey, lady, I've really got to get going," the bartender said. He'd already put up the seats, swept the floor, and was finishing his cash out. He'd agreed to let her wait while he closed, but her time was up.

"Just a few more minutes," she said.

"Lady, it's snowing outside, and I've got to get all the way across town."

"She's coming," she said. "I'm sure of it."

"I don't care. I've got to lock up. It's time to call it a night."

Laurel didn't know what to do. She'd been certain if she left the message at the mail store, someone would show.

"Fine," she said, grabbing her coat from the back of the stool.

She let the bartender usher her out, then offered him a cigarette to stall for time. He took it, and she lit it for him.

As he locked up, she said, "Any idea where I can get a cab at this time of night?"

"Just try the corner," he said as he went down the steps.

She watched him walk away, leaving deep footprints in the snow behind him.

The snow had really started to fall. It was piling up on the street, causing the cars to slow down and giving everything an eerie stillness. It reminded her of the town in Montana. She looked up and was fairly certain she could see a drone in the sky. It wouldn't have been unlike Roth to send one in when he pulled the surveillance team.

She saw a cab approaching and raised her hand. To her relief, it pulled over.

She hurried down the steps, reaching for the door, but it opened before she got to it.

"Oh," she said, surprised.

"Excuse me," a woman said, getting out.

Laurel stopped and looked at her. Her accent was Russian. She was wearing a long coat and expensive shoes that were going to get ruined in this weather.

Laurel leaned inside the cab and said to the driver, "Wait right here."

She turned to the woman, and immediately, the cab pulled away. "Come on," she yelled after it, but it did no good.

The woman ran up the steps to the door of the bar.

"It's locked," Laurel said.

The woman turned to her. "I was supposed to meet someone here," she said, panic on her face.

There was another cab down the street. It had stopped at the intersection, and the woman looked over her shoulder at it. Then she pulled at the door of the bar as if she didn't believe it was locked.

"What's the matter?" Laurel said.

"I was supposed to meet someone. A man. He said he'd be here."

"I'm here to meet you," Laurel said.

"What?"

"You sent the message. In Istanbul."

The woman's eyes widened. "Oh no," she said.

"What?"

"Where's Spector?"

"He's not here."

"I said only Spector," the woman said. She was scared. She looked again at the cab at the intersection, then at Laurel. "I'm being followed."

Laurel turned toward the cab. It was still idling ominously at the intersection. The street was completely deserted.

"We're not safe here," Laurel said.

"I should never have come."

They both looked at the cab. The back window opened, and someone reached out.

"What's he doing?" Laurel said.

"I think he's filming us."

Laurel nodded.

"Are you armed?"

"Yes," Laurel said. "You?"

The woman nodded.

They watched the cab. The man stopped filming, and the window went back up.

"What's he doing now?" Laurel said.

The woman was about to speak when a flash lit up the inside of the cab, and a split second later, the distinctive crack of a gunshot.

"Oh, shit!" the Russian woman said. She ran back down

the steps and took cover with Laurel behind a parked car. "He filmed us."

They drew their guns.

Laurel understood. "We have to stop him."

The back door of the cab opened, and a man stepped out.

"Who is he?" Laurel said.

The woman shook her head. "That's what I've been trying to figure out."

The man opened the front door of the cab and pulled the body of the driver out onto the street. Then he got into the driver's seat.

"Why kill the driver?" Laurel said.

The woman shook her head.

Laurel stood up and aimed her handgun. She couldn't see inside the cab but fired two shots straight through the windshield where the driver would have been. Then she fired two more at the front driver's side tire, hitting it twice.

The women looked at each other as the cab started to move. It came toward them slowly, at a walking pace.

Both of them had been trained for this. They knew the man in the cab was a professional. They knew their chances.

"Are you CIA?" the Russian woman said.

Laurel nodded.

The other woman spoke quickly, keeping her eye on the cab. "I'm GRU. Tatyana Aleksandrova. The man in the cab, I think Moscow sent him."

"How do you want to handle this?" Laurel said, reloading her gun.

"I can't run for shit in these shoes," Tatyana said.

Laurel nodded. "We'll take him here then. There's two of us."

"But he's got the vehicle," Tatyana said.

The cab was still fifty yards from them, rolling slowly through the snow, smoke billowing from its tailpipe. Laurel peered at it and noticed the driver's window opening.

"Do you think you hit him?" Tatyana said.

Laurel shrugged.

Along the street, just where the cab was passing, a man opened the door of a building and came out onto the step. "What's going on out here?" he shouted.

"Get down," Laurel yelled, but it was too late.

Two sharp cracks from the cab. The bullets struck the man in the torso and head, and he smacked against the wall of the building before hitting the ground.

"We've got to stop this guy," Laurel said.

"You go to the next car," Tatyana said. "Don't let him see you. When he's across from you, I'll stand up and draw his fire. You'll have a clear shot."

Laurel nodded. Keeping low, she ran to the next vehicle, a pickup truck, and took cover. The cab was still moving. She couldn't see the driver through the open window. He was crouched low, not really steering the car so much as keeping it straight while he prepared to shoot. Whoever he was, he knew what he was doing.

Laurel thought about shooting him through the door, but she'd be shooting blind, wasting ammo. Waiting was the better plan.

The seconds the cab took to reach her felt like an eternity. Her mind raced from thought to thought. The drone in the sky. This guy in the cab. The Russians were already on to them.

She waited. The cab inched closer. Finally, it was directly behind the truck. She looked to Tatyana and nodded. Then, gripping her gun, Tatyana rose.

A split second behind her, Laurel rose too.

Time compressed, and she no longer registered what was happening. There was supposed to be covering fire from Tatyana. That would distract the driver while Laurel got a line of sight and took him out.

But when she stood, there was no covering fire. And when she took aim, the man was already pointing his gun right at her.

Laurel pulled the trigger, and her shot hit home, smacking the man in the shoulder, but not before he got off two shots of his own, both of which hit her in the upper torso.

Everything went black.

37

W hen Tatyana stood, she could see Goldin through the open window of the cab. He was leaning back, his gun out in front of him, ready to fire.

She pulled the trigger, her gun flashed, and there was a report, but she knew instantly that the bullet was blank. She pulled the trigger three more times, but the entire clip was the same.

When she saw the CIA woman fall to the ground, she dropped her gun and ran.

Goldin, abandoning the cab, followed her on foot.

She pulled off her shoes and ran barefoot. The frigid snow felt like walking on shards of glass.

She glanced over her shoulder and saw Goldin lumbering after her. He'd been shot in the shoulder, and the wound was slowing him down.

The narrow streets were deserted. It wasn't until she reached Hudson that she saw any traffic. It was sparse, but there were cars making their way slowly through the snow.

She ran into the middle of the street and tried desperately to flag them down. Cars swerved around her and kept going.

She kept trying, and finally, a car stopped, and a man in a hoodie opened the door.

"What's the matter?" he said, and then bang, his head opened up as a bullet struck it.

Tatyana looked at the man for a second, stunned, half a skull where a face had just been.

She thought of pulling him out of the car. The keys were still in the ignition, and the engine was running, but another bullet clanged against the steel door, and she gave up the thought.

She continued running, losing her bearings, desperate to keep ahead of Goldin. Despite his wound, he was keeping up.

When an entrance to a subway station appeared ahead, she ran straight for it.

As she reached the top of the steps, a bullet struck the steel railing. She ran down the steps, leaping over the turnstile, and glanced desperately around the platform for help. The station was completely deserted.

A sign above the northbound track said a train was due in one minute.

She looked back the way she'd come. Goldin's silhouette was at the top of the stairs. He was leaning on the railing, almost spent. She knew he wouldn't be able to chase her much longer.

She glanced around and saw there was no exit from the station other than the steps she'd just descended.

The platform had thick pillars every twenty yards, and she thought she might be able to string out a chase until the train arrived. Or if she could draw Goldin slowly down along the platform, she might find a way to get around him and escape back up the steps.

She dashed to the first pillar and got behind it just as Goldin reached the bottom of the stairs.

"I know you're down here," he called out, his voice hoarse from the exertion. He saw that a train was approaching and made his way to the northbound side of the platform. "You can't hide forever," he said.

Tatyana regulated her breathing. All she had to do was stay out of his line of sight until the train got there. She could already feel the breeze that preceded it.

Staying very low, she peered around the pillar. Goldin was just five yards away, looking right at her.

She jerked back in time to dodge the bullet that smacked into the tiled column.

She ran for the next pillar as Goldin reloaded.

"It's all over, Tatyana."

"Then tell me who sent you," she said.

He laughed.

She ran to the next pillar and the next, staying out of sight.

He lumbered slowly after her, carefully checking each pillar to make sure she didn't get around him. She glanced back and saw him leaning against one of them, blood dripping onto the ground beneath him.

"Who found me out, Goldin?"

He didn't answer.

"You were the worst I ever had," she shouted over the noise of the oncoming train.

Goldin rounded the pillar he'd been leaning against, giving himself a clear view of the platform. If Tatyana tried to get on the train, he'd have a straight shot at her. He was less than twenty yards from her. She'd seen his aim. Even wounded, she knew he wouldn't miss.

His position cut her off from the train but also reduced his visibility of the other side of the platform. There was a slim chance of getting around behind him.

The time was now. The sound of the train already echoed down the tunnel.

"It was the secretary, wasn't it?" she said.

The moment she said the words, she backed around the pillar and crossed the platform. She had to be fast. The train would be screeching into the station in seconds, taking his attention for just a moment.

She ran to the next pillar, back in the direction of the steps, and then the next. The train came rushing into the station, and she peered around at Goldin. He was still watching where she'd been, his gun pointed, waiting for the train doors to open and her to dash for it.

Instead, she took a deep breath and made to cross behind him. If he turned to his right, she'd be passing right through his field of view, but she had no choice.

She ran, and at that moment, she realized it wasn't just the northbound train that was arriving, but a southbound one also.

Goldin heard it at the same moment she did. She knew, in that instant, that she'd made a mistake. Goldin turned instinctively to the right, raised his arm, and pulled the trigger.

The bullet hit Tatyana, and the force of it knocked her sideways into the path of the oncoming train.

38

W hen Lance got Roth's call, the sun was already beginning to rise. He'd been sitting at his table at Monroe's all night, drinking coffee and getting up to speed on the files Laurel had left with him.

"I'm in the city, Levi," he said.

"Lance," Roth said, his voice hoarse. "Something's happened."

"What do you mean?"

"You still at Monroe's?"

"Been here all night."

"You know the payphone outside?"

"If it's still there."

"It is. I'll call you on it in one minute."

Lance got the waitress's attention and told her he was going outside and would be right back.

When he reached the payphone, it was already ringing.

"It's me."

"Good. After our call, get rid of your phone, all your electronics. Get a burner and call me."

"You had a system breach?"

"I don't know what we had, but I'm flushing the lines."

Roth was head of the most elite group in the CIA. If he'd been breached, something major was going down.

"What's going on?"

"Laurel went to make contact with the Russian."

"When?"

"Last night."

"What did she get?"

Roth was agitated. Something wasn't right. "I got drone footage of the meet. Facial recognition has the contact as a GRU agent. One of Igor Aralov's in the Main Directorate."

"What's her name?"

"Tatyana Aleksandrova."

Lance was removing the sim card from his phone. He nearly dropped it when he heard Tatyana's name. He remembered her as clearly as if it had been just yesterday. They'd both been in the Syrian capital at the same time. There were Russians everywhere in Damascus back then, but Tatyana was different.

"I remember her, Levi. But it's not what you're thinking."

"And what am I thinking?"

"You're thinking I had a thing with her."

"I could care less what you had with her."

"Then what's bugging you?"

"She's dead is what's bugging me."

"What?"

"You heard me."

"How?"

"Shot in a subway station in New York."

"When?"

"A few hours ago."

"Is Laurel all right?"

There was the briefest pause, and then, "She was shot too."

Lance said nothing. He suddenly felt like the world was spinning out of control.

"Lance?" Roth said. "Lance?"

"So the Russians found out?"

"They must have."

"How did Laurel and Tatyana get caught in the open like that?"

"Something went wrong. We found Tatyana's handgun. It was loaded with blanks."

"A trap?"

"And they walked right into it."

"How is that possible?" Lance said. "They were pros, Roth. If the Russians were on to Tatyana, she would have known."

"She thought she was meeting you. We think that's why she didn't cut and run."

"Me?"

"Laurel told her you'd be there. That's why she went."

39

I gor sat motionless at his desk for a long time. He couldn't believe Tatyana was really dead.

She'd been so young.

The truth was, he'd always been fond of her. She wasn't like other women her age. She was more like the women of his generation.

She hadn't softened with the softening of history. She was still on a war footing. Stalin. Purges. Collectivization. Famines. Gulags. Police torture chambers. She'd known such things were real and that they could all come back in the blink of an eye.

His other agents didn't think that way. They didn't believe—not in their bones. They were like city folk who'd heard stories of bears and wolves in the forest but had never seen them. How could they fear things they'd never seen?

Tatyana did fear them. She believed in every monster she'd ever heard of. And she lived her life as if they were always there, right behind her, ready to pounce.

And now they had.

Igor wasn't like some of his colleagues who thought everything that came from America was decadent. He read American books and regarded their authors as highly as any of the Russian greats. It wasn't Tolstoy or Dostoevsky or Pushkin or Chekhov on the table next to his bed. It was an American.

"When the lambs is lost in the mountains, they is cry. Sometime come the mother. Sometime the wolf."

He remembered that line now. For Tatyana, it had always been the wolf that came. And someone would pay.

He picked up his phone and called the secure switchboard. It would provide after-the-fact authorization for what had just happened in New York and would protect him against any later charge that he'd turned on one of his own agents.

The switchboard was partially automated, and if nothing went wrong, his message would be recorded, stored, and no one would ever hear it. It was an insurance policy. If his loyalty was ever in question, he'd be able to refer to it and show that Timokhin had forced his hand.

A woman with a lifeless voice answered, and Igor said, "This is Igor Aralov with authorization from Director Fyodor Timokhin."

"Target Russian agency?" the woman said.

"Main Directorate," he said.

"Target Russian agent?"

"Tatyana Aleksandrova," he said, amazed at how easily the words came to him.

"Location?"

"Christopher Street Metro Station, New York."

"Confirmation of death?"

Igor cleared his throat. "Target shot and hit by oncoming train."

"Identity of assassin?"

"Classified."

"Please hold," the woman said.

The system would now allow him to leave a secure recording that would be categorized and saved according to the information he'd just provided.

There was a click, and then a recorded voice said, "Please record at the tone."

The tone sounded, and Igor suddenly found himself lost for words. "Igor Aralov," he said, even though it was unnecessary. "On orders from Director Timokhin, I allowed my agent, Tatyana Aleksandrova, to meet with a member of the CIA. Aleksandrova was leaking information to the Americans, and our purpose in allowing the meeting was to find out who on the American side she was meeting."

He waited. Nothing happened. There were no further prompts. Just a tape recorder somewhere deep in a vault beneath the city, listening to his confession.

Igor felt scattered. He wasn't sure of himself. He didn't know if what he'd said was enough to justify what he'd done to Tatyana. It certainly didn't feel that way.

"For the record," he added, "Tatyana Aleksandrova was killed for selling secrets and possibly defecting to the Americans."

He stopped talking. He was rambling now. His hands were shaking. He could barely hold the receiver. He didn't know if there was anything more to say. Technically, the recording was for his protection, an explanation of his actions leading to the death of one of his agents. But he didn't know where the recording was kept, how it was filed, or who might be listening.

He cleared his throat again and added one final sentence. "Leaked information related to bioweapons program at Sverdlovsk Military Compound 19."

He hung up the phone and sat back. He opened his top collar button and pulled the shirt from his skin. He was tacky with sweat. His hand was shaking.

He opened his humidor and took a King of Denmark cigar from the top shelf. It had been a gift from the president on his fiftieth birthday. As he cut it, he wasn't sure whether he was rewarding or compensating himself.

Igor knew there was more to this than Timokhin had let on. They were preparing for war. The bioweapon was part of that. But that wasn't the only angle Timokhin was working.

Igor had been sent Goldin's recording of the meeting between Tatyana and her American contact. The contact was a woman. They were still trying to find out who she worked for.

He couldn't believe Tatyana had allowed herself to be so exposed, even though she knew she was being followed. It was an inexplicable error in judgment, and it had cost her dearly. He watched the footage over and over, trying to make sense of it, but he couldn't.

He lit the cigar, and as he smoked it, he went to the window and imagined looking out on all the construction work from a window on the top floor. Tatyana was dead, and he was on his way up in the world. If he was to have any chance of survival up there, he had to know what was going on.

And Agniya was his only lead.

He reached inside his drawer and pulled out the PYa, or *Pistolet Yarygina*, his military-issue side-arm, and put it in the holster under his jacket. Then he sat back at his desk and pressed the button that called his secretary to the room. She opened the door.

"Come in, Agniya Bunina," he said, aware of the ominous undertone of using her full name. "Shut the door. Take a seat."

She eyed him suspiciously as she sat.

"It seems we've had a little slip-up," he said.

"How so?" she said, her voice flat, betraying nothing.

"Director Timokhin had one of my agents killed."

"I see."

"Tatyana Aleksandrova," he said.

"I see," she said again.

He was toying with her, trying to make her squirm. "It's regrettable," he said.

"You were close to her."

"Yes, I was close to her."

"I'm sorry, sir."

"If there are any more leaks from this office," he said, "I will be very upset."

She said nothing. She denied nothing. Confirmed nothing. Just sat there, looking at him blankly.

He dismissed her and leaned back in his chair, staring at where she'd been sitting.

That evening, he went into town. He spent a few hours at one of his favorite restaurants close to the Patriarshiye Ponds. It was an expensive place, and he got a table that allowed him to watch the traffic along Bolshaya Sadovaya. He dined alone and ordered Beluga vodka with his steak.

Afterward, he went to Agniya's apartment building. It

was even nicer than his own, overlooking the park. He waited for another resident to open the door and then went in. He took the stairs to the fifth floor and knocked.

He waited until he heard her approach then shot the lock with his pistol. He kicked open the door and saw the elderly woman standing there in shock. She really hadn't seen this coming.

Poor creature.

She was wearing slippers and a bathrobe and holding a paperback romance novel. Prokofiev was playing on a vinyl record player in the living room.

Igor dropped his gun and leaped at her, knocking her over. She was like paper. She fell on her back and hit the ground hard. Igor climbed up on top of her, his hands on her neck. He began to squeeze. She flailed wildly, her arms grasping for anything within reach. She managed to grab something, Igor didn't see what, and struck him on the side of the head with it.

The blow almost caused him to blackout, and he lost his grip on her. She scrambled away from him. He reached up to his temple. There was blood there.

Agniya was struggling frantically to get to her feet, and he grabbed her ankle. In a single motion, he pulled her back to the ground. She swung at him again. She was holding a heavy glass snow globe. Inside it was an ice skater.

He grabbed her wrist and forced her hand to the ground.

"Agniya," he said.

"You monster," she screamed, then, with her free hand, clawed him across the cheek with her long nails.

He grabbed her other wrist and pressed both her hands to the ground. Looking down at her, he remembered the night they'd screwed. It had been in a seedy motel close to the office. She'd been surprisingly lithe for a woman her age. Afterward, they showered together, and she'd washed him.

He thought of it often. He slept with so many women, women forty, sometimes a full fifty years younger than her, but it was her he thought of most. Even more than his memories of Tatyana. When he was alone in his bed, and there was nothing but his imagination to satisfy him, it was her he turned to.

"You betrayed me, Agniya," he said.

"I would never betray you, Igor."

"Tatyana was selling information to the Americans, and everyone knew but me."

"I had no choice, Igor. I swear it."

"How did they catch her?"

"They've been watching her for years."

"Who has?"

She said nothing.

"Who's been watching her?"

She struggled furiously.

"You're going to pay," he said.

She struggled again, and he squeezed her wrists so tightly he thought they might break.

"I have information," she gasped.

"What information?"

"Spare my life."

A sneer crossed his face. "It's too late for that, my dear."

Agniya spat at him. He moved up on her body so that he could pin her arms under his knees. She struggled helplessly. He put his hands on her throat. She was so frail, so vulnerable. He could have done anything to her.

"What's this information you speak of?" he said.

She struggled even more frantically as he began to press down on her throat.

"Give it to me, and I'll make this painless," he said.

ofia stood in the parking lot of the hospital, glancing this way and that frantically. The mood was turning fast. People had started shouting insults at the soldiers. Some were at the gates, demanding to be allowed out.

She could tell that at any moment, things were going to get out of hand. After twenty-four hours of lockdown, patience was turning to anger and panic.

The morgue, which was in a separate building across the parking lot, was full to capacity. People could see the orderlies outside it, wondering what to do with the bodies that kept coming. There was a blue tarp covering a mound outside the entrance, about six feet high, and it was obvious the sheet was covering corpses.

"What are they doing over there?" Sofia said.

The man next to her wore a green orderly uniform. "They're at capacity," he said.

"Tell them to start the furnace. They can't just keep piling up the bodies like that."

"It's cold enough," he said. "They won't turn."

Sofia shot daggers at him with her eyes, and he turned and hurried toward the morgue.

Two large trucks drove by, and Sofia was overwhelmed by the wave of chlorine that sprayed out of them. She fell into a fit of coughing, and Olga had to help her steady herself.

"They're using too much," she said when she caught her breath.

They'd been hosing down the streets with chlorine all day, and it was getting to the point where people's eyes were starting to sting.

Olga nodded. Both women had done everything they could to get the military to break the quarantine. They'd called health officials and military commanders, Sofia had called the institute to see if Vasily could do anything— they'd even called local news media. No one could do anything. The order to contain the hospital had come directly from Moscow. Short of a stampede, there was no way the guards were going to stand aside. And a stampede was something that was looking increasingly likely.

The soldiers, from inside their hazmat suits, were getting as antsy as the people. They'd been ordered to point their guns at their own people, and had even less idea of what was going on than those inside the hospital.

"Let us out!" a man in overalls shouted at the guards.

Inside the suit, the soldier couldn't speak back.

The man in overalls picked up a stone, about the size of an egg, and flung it at the soldiers. It hit one of the vehicles parked behind them and bounced off the windshield, leaving a large crack.

Some other men cheered him on.

"Let us out!" he shouted again, and this time his demand was backed by more voices.

"There's going to be a massacre," Sofia said. "We have to get these people back inside."

She pushed her way to the front of the crowd and grabbed the man in overalls. "Hey," she said, "you've got to calm down."

"Calm down?" he said. "They've got machine guns pointed at us."

"Yeah, and if you keep throwing rocks, they're going to use them."

Another wave of chlorine passed over them, and everyone started coughing. Sofia was on her knees, gasping for breath, and the man in overalls bent down to help her.

When she caught her breath, she said, "We've got to get everyone back inside. There's going to be bloodshed if we don't."

"We're not going back inside," the man said. "They can't keep us here like this."

Sofia stood and climbed onto the fence to give herself some extra height. The soldiers immediately turned their guns on her. Sofia ignored them and faced the crowd. She raised her voice. "Listen to me. Everybody, listen to me!"

The people in the crowd looked up at her.

"We need to go back inside the hospital and wait this out. We're not safe out here."

"We're not going anywhere," a man shouted.

Sofia's eyes were so irritated by the chlorine that she could hardly see.

Someone shouted, "Look at her. The virus is already taking her."

Sofia tried to tell them it was the chlorine, but too many voices drowned her out.

Then she heard a rumbling in the air. She looked up at the sky.

"What is that?" someone cried.

Sofia turned to the soldiers. They were all looking at the sky.

A moment later, a single Sukhoi SU-34 fighter jet blasted overhead at low altitude. The jet had taken off from Chelyabinsk, two hundred kilometers south of the city, and was traveling at a strike velocity of Mach 1.2. The sound was deafening.

A moment later, a massive explosion knocked everyone to the ground. The people were flung against the gate, almost crushing Sofia. She couldn't hear anything. Her vision went blank. And when she was able to make things out again, she realized she was looking out through the gate at the soldiers. They'd been blown back by the blast too.

She put her hand to her head and touched her ears. Blood was coming from them. She struggled to her feet, using the gate for support, and as the smoke cleared, she realized that the hospital morgue had been completely destroyed.

She shook her head. She didn't know what she was seeing. She couldn't comprehend it.

The people on the ground were beginning to get back to their feet. They were dazed, disoriented, but as soon as they gathered their senses, panic set in. Everyone, at once, wanted out.

The hospital was being bombed.

They took hold of the gate and shook it. Some people began climbing it. It was twelve feet high and wasn't difficult to scale. It had been designed to keep out vehicles, not a crowd. Sofia was trapped, pinned by the mass of people against the gate.

There were loudspeakers on one of the vehicles, and a voice came booming out.

"Get back!" the voice said. "Get back, or we'll open fire!"

The crowd surged forward. More people began to pull themselves up onto the gate. Some had reached the top and were swinging themselves over the spikes.

"This is your last warning," the voice warned.

The crowd continued to pile onto the gate. Two more men climbed over, and one dropped to the ground on the other side.

Soldiers rushed forward and grabbed him. He was followed by another, and another, and the soldiers struggled to arrest them.

"Get off the gate," the loudspeaker said again.

"Get back!" Sofia cried at the people. "Get back! They're going to shoot us!"

She could see it coming. She'd known it since the moment the soldiers first showed.

A man was climbing the fence next to her, and she pulled at his leg. "Get off the gate," she cried. "They're going to open fire!"

He kicked her off, and she began pushing herself through the crowd, away from the gate.

"Get back!" she cried. "They're going to fire!"

And then, the burst of machine-gun fire.

The man she'd pulled at fell from the gate like a felled tree and landed on the crowd right above her. Blood splashed onto her face.

Two more men on the gate were shot down.

The crowd completely lost control. Some people turned around to retreat, but enough surged forward that Sofia was forced back toward the gate.

Another burst of gunfire. And another. Bodies fell to the ground as if mowed down by a scythe.

And then Sofia felt it in her back, the sharp bite of a bullet cutting through flesh.

Lance had bought an apartment in the Watergate while working for the Group. It was empty most of the time but gave him a base close to Langley where he could recuperate between missions.

It was there that the bulk of his relationship with Clarice had taken place, and being there now brought the memories flooding back. Especially what had happened at the end.

The décor was spartan. There were no pictures, no personal effects. The space was cleaned periodically—that was a requirement of the condo agreement—but it hadn't been lived in for over two years, and there was a sterile feel to it, like a hotel room.

The refrigerator was empty. The bookshelves were empty. Lance flicked on the TV but the cable subscription had expired.

In the bedroom, the bed was made, and there were towels and a few basic toiletries in the bathroom. The wardrobes and drawers had some of his clothes in them—

neatly folded stacks of identical white shirts, a jacket, jeans, nothing fancy.

He went through the apartment searching for signs that Clarice had ever been there, that she'd ever existed, and the only thing he found was a paperback spy novel on one of the bedside tables. He picked it up. He didn't remember seeing her read it, but it was on her side of the bed, and he knew it wasn't his. She'd loved reading those books, rolling her eyes mercilessly at the implausible plot twists.

He'd stopped at the grocery store on the way there and picked up a few things, some cereal and milk, some coffee, a toothbrush. He went into the kitchen and put on the coffee. Then he took a hot shower and, after drying off and getting dressed in clean clothes, went back to the kitchen and poured himself a cup of coffee. The TV was still on, a message telling him to call the cable company. He turned it off. Then he flicked open Clarice's novel and read the first few pages.

He was into the third chapter when the knock on the door came.

He went to answer it.

Roth brushed in past him. He was wearing a ball cap and sunglasses.

"You're really spooked," Lance said.

Roth looked at him. "Something's not right," he said.

He took off the hat and glasses, and Lance saw he was tired. It was in his eyes. He'd had a rough night.

"Coffee?"

"Sure."

Lance poured him a cup, and they sat at the counter. "Sorry for your loss," Lance said.

"She wasn't my loss."

"You liked her."

"I cared about her."

Lance nodded. Roth had a reputation for being something of a ladies' man, but Lance wasn't implying that. "There was a pile of takeout menus under the door," Lance said.

"I'm not hungry."

"You look like you could eat."

"No, it's fine," Roth said. "Really."

Lance nodded, and they sipped their coffee. Neither spoke for a few minutes until Roth broke the silence.

"So, if I'm going to read you in on this thing, I need to know you're back," he said.

"All right," Lance said.

"You don't need to think about it?"

"I thought already."

"Because you sure had your doubts back in Montana."

"You want me back or not?"

Roth sighed. He looked old. Losing Laurel had really been a blow.

Lance looked at him. "You want me to sign something?"

"Would you?"

"You serious?"

"Yes, I'm serious."

"A piece of paper?"

"If I had one, would you sign it?"

"If it made you feel better."

"All right," Roth said. He reached into his briefcase and pulled out a tablet computer.

"You're really going to make me sign something?"

"Of course not," Roth said, opening the files.

A picture of Tatyana Aleksandrova came on the screen. She was in a designer dress, expensive shoes, every bit as beautiful as Lance remembered.

"You know this woman, right?"

"*Know* is a strong word."

"What word would you use?"

Lance shrugged. "She was a Widow, an operative sent in to seduce targets. Get dirt on them."

"I know what a Widow is."

Lance smiled. "Of course you do."

Roth remained stern. "Keep going," he said.

"We ran into each other in Syria."

"Was she targeting you?"

"No. She thought I was Delta Force."

"You're sure of that?"

"She wasn't targeting me, Levi."

"You wouldn't know it if she was."

Lance shook his head. "It wasn't like that."

"Then what was it like, Lance?"

"It was something... off the books."

"Off the books?"

"She wasn't part of my operation. I wasn't part of hers. Everyone was in this tiny part of the city. Us, the Russians, NATO, news reporters. All in the same neighborhood. The same handful of hotels."

"So you just happened to be in the same place at the same time?"

"You've been to Damascus. You know how it is."

"A coincidence?" Roth said skeptically.

Lance shrugged.

"Well, ain't that a regular love story."

"Very funny."

"No, really. They could shoot a movie."

"Roth," Lance said, "this isn't what got Laurel killed."

Roth sighed. He got up and poured himself more coffee.

"You knew she was a Widow, and you didn't think that was worth reporting up the chain?"

"It wasn't my job to make sure the generals kept their dicks in their pants."

"You could have come to me with it."

"Oh, come on. You had much bigger worries than one Russian honeytrap. You'd have told me to quit wasting your time."

"Maybe."

"Her mission had nothing to do with ours. We were like two different species in the same jungle. She had her prey. I had mine."

"All right," Roth said.

"We're on the same page, then?"

Roth shrugged.

Lance was conflicted. He'd had contact with this Russian agent, and Laurel might have just paid the price for it. "I get the feeling there's more you want to say," he said.

Roth shook his head.

"If there's something you need to say, then say it," Lance said.

"All right. I'll say it. You're an arrogant prick, Lance."

Lance nodded. He deserved that.

"This Russian's basically a prostitute. She gets on her back whenever some slob in Moscow tells her to, with whoever they tell her to. She asks no questions. Does what she's told. And you're sitting here telling me that in the middle of all that, she was just so attracted to you that she fell right into your arms?"

Lance said nothing.

"And it didn't cross your mind for one second that maybe you were being played? Maybe she was with you for more than the sheer pleasure of your company?"

"I wasn't her target, Levi."

"I don't buy it."

"She couldn't have been playing me. There was nothing to play."

"Nothing to play? What if Clarice found out?"

"This was before Clarice and I were together."

"Then why didn't you tell her about it?"

Lance made to speak, then stopped himself.

"That's right," Roth said.

"I don't think you should be bringing up Clarice," Lance said.

"Or what? You'll shoot me?"

"Maybe."

"I've apologized for what happened," Roth said. "Believe me. No one was more shocked about it than me. Lance, if I'd had any idea, you have to believe me, I would never have made that order."

"You should have spoken to me."

"I didn't know if you were in on it."

"Oh, come on."

"I made a mistake, Lance. I made a mistake that I can never unmake. If that's going to stop us working together, you might as well tell me now."

Lance let out a long sigh. He looked at Roth and asked himself what he felt. It wasn't hatred. It had never been hatred—only pain. "Can we just talk about what we're going to do?" he said. "Laurel's down. Tatyana's down. The least we can do is make sure they didn't die for nothing."

"Fine," Roth said. "Let's move on."

"Fine," Lance said.

"You sure you're ready?"

"Just get on with it."

Roth looked at him. "You had an unreported fling with a

foreign agent, you basically let the Main Directorate into your bedroom, and then this vial shows up with your name on it."

Lance shook his head. "Look. If you want to nail me all day long about this, there's nothing I can do to stop you. But the longer we spend talking about it, the more time we waste."

"So you have no clue why she sent it, to you personally, out of all the people in the world?"

"She needed to get it to someone she trusted."

"And she trusted you?"

"Yes."

"Well, now she's dead, and near as we can tell, so is Laurel."

"Near as you can tell?"

"We'll get to that."

"On the phone, you made it sound like she was dead."

"I said we'd get to that."

"What happened?"

"Well, your Russian *friend*—"

"Don't call her that."

"What should I call her?"

"Come on, Levi."

"The Russian agent," he said. "Is that better?"

"Yes."

"The Russian *agent* gave us the location of a dropbox. Laurel went there to meet her. And something went wrong."

"What went wrong?"

"A lot of things."

"What exactly?"

"We haven't recovered the bodies."

"Either of them?"

"Laurel was shot in the upper torso. We have drone

footage and local witnesses. A man followed the Russian to the meet."

"He's the one who shot them?"

"Laurel and the Russian opened fire on him. Laurel hit him, but he hit her too. Then he followed the Russian. Security footage in the Christopher Street subway station shows her being shot and falling into the path of an oncoming train."

"But you didn't get her body either?"

"We found her blood, but no body. We're still trying to figure out what happened."

"And what about Laurel?"

"She was bleeding out in the street. People came to her assistance. They say she was in critical condition. Blood was coming from her neck, from her mouth. An ambulance was called."

"But?"

"But the man came back before the ambulance got there. He stole a car outside the subway station. He fired his gun in the air. The people helping Laurel dispersed. She was unconscious. He picked her up and put her in the back of the car."

"What a mess," Lance said. "Do we have any idea who this man is?"

Roth pulled up another picture on the tablet. It was from footage the drone had taken, a man in his fifties. "Recognize him?"

Lance shook his head.

"We're running him through the system now. So far, we've got nothing."

"Without the bodies, there's a chance both of them are still alive."

"There's a chance," Roth said, but his tone wasn't optimistic. "If Laurel's alive, you know what they'll do to her."

Lance nodded. He looked at Roth, then down at his coffee. "This is my fault," he said.

Roth said, "There's still something you're not telling me."

"About what?"

"About why this Russian put your name on the vial."

Lance shook his head.

"Tell me, Lance. What are you holding back?"

"Something happened in Damascus."

Roth leaned forward. "I'm all ears."

"The details don't matter."

"What do you mean, the details don't matter?"

"The only thing that's relevant is that she felt I was someone she could trust."

42

A fter the meeting with Roth, Lance went to Laurel's apartment on U Street. The building's ground floor was a furniture store, and he made his way to the back. Next to the steel delivery doors was a set of concrete steps that led to a second door. It was also steel, not the kind of door you could kick in, but above it was a fire escape leading to a metal balcony.

Lance leaped, grabbed the bottom of the fire escape, and pulled himself up to the ladder. He climbed to the balcony and tried the window. It was shut, but a window air conditioning unit meant it couldn't lock. He pulled it open and climbed into the apartment.

Inside was a spacious room with a kitchen at one end and a luxurious four-poster bed at the other. Between them was a sofa, a TV, a few bookshelves, and a coat rack by the door. He noticed a goldfish bowl next to a fancy espresso machine. There were no fish in the bowl.

He'd only spent a few hours with Laurel and knew next to nothing about her. This was his starting point.

From what he could see, she had the same workaholic

personality as everyone else Roth hired. She lived for the job.

Handlers were required to go through a similar onboarding process to the one Assets went through, cutting their relationships with anyone who knew who they were and adopting a new legal identity. From what he could see, Laurel had made sure every clue to her prior life had been erased. There were no photos in the apartment, no personal documents, not even any dirty laundry in the hamper in the closet. She lived like a ghost.

He opened the refrigerator. It was almost empty. There was an unopened stick of unsalted butter, a few bottles of sparkling water, and a pint of strawberries that was beginning to turn. The only thing in the freezer was a bottle of Grey Goose vodka, two-thirds full. There were a few cans of vacuum-packed Italian coffee next to the espresso machine and a box containing packets of sweetener. She wasn't one for cooking, that was clear.

He clicked the TV remote, and the news came on. He clicked it back off.

He sat at the counter and thought about the one thing he knew for certain. If the man who'd attacked her put her in his car, then there was a chance she was still alive. Why go to the trouble of taking someone who was about to die? And if he was the kind of man who could take out two trained agents, he was the kind of man who knew the difference.

There was a chance she was alive.

And that meant he had to find her.

He got up and went to the sofa. There were copies of a few major news magazines on the coffee table. There was a laptop charger plugged in, but no laptop. Next to where the laptop would have been was a notepad.

On the top page was written the address of the Econo-Lodge hotel in Deweyville, and the words "Two Rooms" underlined.

Looking at it made him feel guilty. She'd come, and he'd turned her away.

There was a wastepaper basket next to the table, but it was empty.

He went over to the bed. It was a solid oak antique. It looked expensive. The bedding was Egyptian cotton. The bed was placed halfway between two huge windows that looked out onto the street. Light came in through lace curtains and fell on the bed, making the white sheets glow.

Apart from the espresso machine, the bed was the only sign of luxury in the apartment. That said something about her.

He ran his hand over the sheets. He lifted a pillow and smelled it—freshly laundered with a hint of lavender.

He felt like a voyeur. He wasn't sure what he was looking for.

There was a dress form at the end of the bed with a silk negligee draped over it. He touched the silk.

He stood at the window and looked out at the traffic on the street below.

His phone rang.

"Where are you?" It was Roth's voice.

"At her apartment."

"Anything out of place?"

"Not as far as I can tell."

"Listen, we just got a match on the assailant."

"Who is he?"

"A US citizen with suspected ties to the GRU."

"Where can I find him?"

"I'm sending the file now. He lives in New Jersey, but my bet is this will lead us straight back to Moscow."

"I see," Lance said. He hung up the phone, took one final glance around the apartment, and let himself out through the same window he'd entered by.

43

Tatyana woke with a gasp. Everything was black. For a split second, she wondered if she was still alive.

Then she saw the steam billowing from the ventilation shaft. She was soaking wet and freezing cold, so cold she was in danger of hypothermia.

A gust of steam came from the vent beneath her and warmed her for the briefest second. Then it was gone, and the icy cold returned. The steam kept her just warm enough to stay alive, but it also made her wet. If she left the vent, she'd freeze in a matter of minutes.

Memories of what had happened came rushing back to her.

She remembered getting rid of her electronics. She remembered struggling along the tunnel as far as a steel ladder. She remembered crawling through a ventilation shaft for what felt like an eternity.

Every second had been agony, the bullet wound in her arm burning like fire.

She didn't remember stopping, but if it weren't for the steam, she'd have frozen to death.

She looked at her watch. It was analog, her grandmother's. It said seven.

The ID she had, the credit cards, all of it would lead the GRU right to her. She went through her purse and counted her cash—a couple of hundred dollars. She got rid of anything that would have allowed Igor to track her. She didn't have her gun. She'd thrown it away when she realized the bullets were duds. Goldin must have changed them in the hotel room.

She thought about the gun for a moment. She remembered when she'd gotten it.

She'd been careless. Distracted. She'd let her guard down, rushed to make the meeting with Spector, and that had caused her to make a mistake.

This was the price.

Her tights were tied around the bullet wound under her clothing. She vaguely remembered doing that. It would need proper attention soon.

She stood up and felt faint. She instantly felt the absence of the steam. She was shivering so badly she had to hold onto the wall to steady herself. She looked down at her clothing. She was in black, which would conceal some of the dirt. Her feet were completely bare. There was a bullet hole in the Chanel dress. That hurt almost as much as the wound.

There was a ladder leading to a manhole above her, and she could tell from the ring of light around it that it led to the surface.

She climbed the ladder. The cover at the top was locked, but there was a safety mechanism that allowed it to be opened from the inside. She turned it and pushed. The cover was heavy. It took all her strength to move it, but it opened. She climbed through and found herself in a maintenance shed, light streaming in through some grimy windows in the roof. She sat on the ground for a few seconds, catching her breath, then walked across the shed and tried the door. It opened, and outside she saw the banks of the Hudson River. Across the water, she recognized the Hoboken and Jersey City skylines.

The shed was in a small waterfront park, and she would have to cross West Street to get back to the city. Walking barefoot in the snow hurt. When she reached the street, the morning traffic sped by. She waited for a break in the stream of cars and managed to get herself across.

Then, she stood as straight as she could, pulled her coat around her, and tried to flag down a cab. It took a few minutes for one to stop, and every second she had to wait was frigid torture. Her entire body was shaking by the time she got into the cab.

The driver noticed her distress. She was blue with cold. She was barefoot. There was blood and dirt on her hands and face.

It took all her strength to get any words out.

"Don't get any ideas," she said.

"Lady," the driver said in a thick New York accent, "whatever you been through, it's over now."

"Turn up the heat," she said.

"You report everything to the police," the driver said. "Don't let them get away with anything."

"All right," she said.

The driver nodded. "Where to then?"

"Penn Station."

He brought her to the train station, and when they arrived, she told him she had no money.

"Fair enough," was the extent of his protest.

She got out and ran up the steps of the station and through the main hall. There was a storage locker there she'd set up in advance for situations like this. She had a number of them around the city, and no one, including Igor, knew about them.

Sheldon Goldin was a trained assassin. Igor had set a trap for her. She should have picked up on it when he'd called. He'd acted strangely on the phone. She wondered how he'd found her out.

And Lance. He'd screwed her too. She'd thrown caution to the wind, going to the meet even though she knew she was being tailed. She would never have done that if she'd known Lance wouldn't be there.

And the female agent—Tatyana wondered if she'd survived. She'd seen her go down. She'd done everything right. It was Tatyana's blank bullets that screwed them.

Tatyana hadn't had time to tell her much. If she was dead now, she supposed it didn't really matter.

She reached her locker and spun the combination dial. Inside was a backpack. She grabbed it and went back to the main concourse. There were clothing stores in the station, but none of them were open yet. She'd have to wait for that.

There was a drugstore, and she bought a pair of black socks, some tights, some toiletries, isopropyl, and a first aid kit. Then she went to the washroom, locked herself in one of the stalls, and examined the wound. It was beginning to change color. She doused it in alcohol and wrapped it in a clean bandage.

She cleaned her face and hands at the sink.

There was a hotel nearby that rented rooms by the hour and accepted cash. She went back outside and got another cab. When it let her out at the hotel, she had to pass drug addicts and prostitutes on the steps. Next to them, her tattered clothes and disheveled state stood out less. She went inside to a guy sitting at the counter, and when she spoke, emphasized her Russian accent.

"I need room."

"How long?"

"All day."

"That's three hundred," the man said.

It was the kind of place that didn't ask questions. It let a woman rent a room, leave every hour, and return with a new man. There were some pimps hanging around in the back, but you weren't required to be with them.

She searched in her purse and pulled out most of the cash she had. "I have two-twenty," she said.

"Price is three hundred."

"I'll go across street," she said. There was a similar hotel there.

The man sighed and pulled a key off its hook on the wall behind him. "Fine," he said. "Two-twenty. No shooting up in there."

"I know."

"You shoot up in there, and you'll get the shit knocked right out of you."

"Okay."

"Worse than you already got."

"I heard you," she said, grabbing the key.

44

Lance sat on a commuter train from DC to New York. The train passed endless rows of cookie-cutter houses, warehouses, big-box retail stores. It looked like the world was becoming one big logistics solution.

He stretched out and made himself comfortable. He had four seats to himself, the two he was sprawled across, the two facing, and the small Formica table between them.

A man with a cart came down the aisle, and Lance asked for coffee and a tuna sandwich.

"I don't recommend the tuna," the man said.

"How about the cheese?"

"It's safer."

"Thanks for the tip," Lance said.

The train wasn't an express service. It stopped literally everywhere, but that was fine. It was one of those smaller stations he was headed for.

The file Roth had sent for the gunman had an address in Trenton, New Jersey. A house in a quiet neighborhood called Chambersburg. Lance doubted anyone was home, but he would pay a visit all the same. It was a starting point. He knew Roth was right, that the trail would lead to Moscow, but he wanted to check all the stops along the way first.

The file was surprisingly comprehensive. There was a name—Sheldon Goldin—a photo, the address in Trenton, civilian and military records.

Lance couldn't be sure if the civilian data was original or tied to an identity that was later assumed, but if accurate, Goldin was born in New York, was fifty-eight, and had served in the army. He'd been a lieutenant in the First Infantry Division during Operation Desert Storm. An army medical report said he'd been at Khamisiyah in Iraq when Saddam's chemical weapons stockpiles were discovered.

Lance flipped through the medical report. Complications followed the discovery of the chemical weapons. Goldin's unit was sent in to destroy them with C-4 explosive and wasn't given any kind of protective clothing to do the job. The report contained hand drawings by men in the unit of the markings on the weapons. Lance recognized them as Iraqi military markings for munitions containing Sarin gas.

Goldin's entire unit got sick afterward. They couldn't breathe and suffered uncontrollable muscle spasms. They had to be medevacked to an army hospital in Saudi Arabia and from there to Germany. Some of them died in Germany —it was unclear how many—and there was talk of a lawsuit, but it never materialized.

When the train arrived in Trenton, Lance got a cab to the address on the file. The place looked like a good, working-class neighborhood, no different from a thousand others built in the sixties. The house was modest, but there was an expensive black town car parked in the driveway. Someone was sitting in the driver's seat. He wasn't Goldin.

Lance got out of the cab and knocked on the window of the town car. "You the vehicle owner?"

"Who's asking?"

"Law enforcement."

The driver raised his hands. "Hey, I'm just a driver. I go where I'm told."

"You want to get out of here for a while? This might not be pretty."

The driver didn't need to be told twice. He turned the ignition and pulled out of the driveway.

Lance went to the door of the house and knocked.

A voice from inside called out, "Hang on."

There was some activity inside, and then Goldin appeared in the doorway. He had a five o'clock shadow and was dressed in a ratty robe and slippers. He didn't look like a highly-paid GRU assassin.

Behind him, Lance could see through to the kitchen where an elderly woman, also dressed in a robe and slippers, was sitting at a table.

"I'm sorry," Lance said. "Is this your house?"

"It's my mother's house."

"I didn't mean to interrupt your breakfast."

"Where's my driver?"

There was a newspaper on the step, and Lance bent down and picked it up. He handed it to Goldin. Goldin took it, and Lance noticed his shoulder was bandaged. He moved it tenderly. If they got into a fight, there wouldn't be much to it.

"Well?" Goldin said.

"Can I come in?"

"What for?"

"I want to discuss the Sarin poisonings in Iraq. The legal case."

Goldin tried to shut the door in Lance's face, but Lance stopped it with his foot. "I'm from Veteran's Affairs. We're looking into compensation."

"I'm not interested."

"But you were there when the incident occurred?"

"I ain't talking to no one."

Lance nodded. "All right," he said. "All right."

Goldin tried to shut the door again, and Lance said, "Don't make me do this in front of your mother."

Goldin froze. He looked at Lance again as if seeing him for the first time. "You're not from Veteran's Affairs."

"Don't fight me," Lance said. "She'll only have to watch."

"What are you saying?"

"I'm saying we can do this civilized. What is she? Eighty years old? Watching you die will destroy her."

Goldin's fist was clenched around the door handle. He was thinking about his wounded shoulder—calculating. Lance could see it on his face.

Lance needed information from him. He didn't want him to run, and he didn't want to kill him before he talked. "That incident in the Village," he said. "The woman you shot, the woman you *took*, she's one of ours and we want her back."

"I don't know what you're talking about?"

Lance watched him closely. His temperature was rising, his pulse quickening. He was acting calm, but any second, he could bolt. "The other woman was a GRU operative," he said carefully.

"What is this?" Goldin said, his voice trembling slightly.

The old lady called out from the kitchen. "Who's there?"

Lance looked around Goldin. He saw that she had a boiled egg in front of her and was tapping the shell with a spoon. "How about you invite me in, give me some tea, and tell me what I want to know?"

"You're out of your mind."

"Maybe I am. Maybe we all are. Looks to me like we both have a little in common. You served in the 82nd. I served in the 82nd."

"So what?"

"So we both had reasons to quit Uncle Sam."

"What do you know about it?"

"I know they covered up your unit's Sarin gas exposure."

"Mister, why are you here telling me this?" Goldin said helplessly.

"Because I want you to invite me into your house so I can ask you a few questions. Real civilized."

Goldin shook his head. He looked Lance up and down and knew he meant business. This was no social visit. He stepped aside. It was as if he'd gone limp. Lance could read it on his face. Some men were defeated before you ever got to them.

"I just want you to know," Goldin said, "I never betrayed my country."

"That's fine," Lance said. "I'm not here about that."

"I never targeted Americans. The woman I shot, she wasn't supposed to be there. As far as I knew, I was following a Russian. They opened fire on me first."

Lance entered the house. He hadn't mentioned the cab driver or the innocent bystander who'd also been shot. He wasn't sure Goldin even remembered them.

"Who's this now?" the mother said from the kitchen.

"It's nothing, Ma."

"Why's he coming in?"

Lance took a seat on the sofa in the living room and acted like he hadn't heard her.

"He's from the VA, Ma."

"What do they want?"

"It's work. I'll be back in a minute." He came into the living room and shut the door to the kitchen.

"You always lived with her?" Lance said.

"Not always. Now, what *exactly* did you want to talk about?"

"You shot my colleague."

"Like I said. She fired first. Hit me through the windshield. I had no choice."

"All the same," Lance said.

The man sighed.

"Just so you know," Lance said, "I'm going to have to make that good."

Goldin held out his hands as if to show he had no objection to that idea, vague as it was. "I understand," he said.

"Oh, you do? You understand?"

"I always knew my time would come. You don't get into this line of work thinking it will end with a nice retirement party."

"No, you don't," Lance said.

The man looked toward the kitchen door.

"So, what are we looking at?" Lance said. "Like I said, my people want her back."

"She ain't dead, if that's what you're wondering."

Lance let out a long breath. "Where is she?"

The man looked away again.

"Just tell me."

"I'll tell you what," Goldin said. "I don't want to die here today."

"Well, tell me where she is, and maybe it won't come to that."

"I never killed Americans. That was the one thing I told him. I'd do his dirty work, but I'm no traitor."

"Who did you tell that to?"

"Some creep in Moscow."

"I want a name."

Goldin didn't hesitate. "Timokhin. Fyodor Timokhin."

"Never heard of him."

"Sure you have."

Lance shrugged. "What kind of jobs did he give you?"

"Honestly, it was mostly killing other Russians. They have more leaks than a sieve. He had someone he wanted me to take care of every few months."

"And you did it?"

"It paid. I did it. Sue me."

"What did he tell you about your target the other night?"

"He said she was a Russian agent. She was meeting someone. They wanted me to find out who she was meeting."

"And kill them?"

Goldin shook his head. "I already told you, they opened fire on me first. I had no choice."

"Well," Lance said. "She's dead now. What did Timokhin say about that?"

Goldin shrugged. "She was a Russian agent selling secrets. She knew the rules of the game."

"Rules of the game?" Lance said. "I guess I could say the same thing about you right now."

Goldin shook his head. There was a pack of Pall Malls on the table, and he took one out and lit it.

"What did Timokhin pay for a hit?"

"For this one?"

"In general."

"Thirty. Forty. Fifty. It varied."

Lance looked around the room. The house didn't look like it had seen forty or fifty grand in a while.

"I got my own place in the city," Goldin said. "There's a few strip clubs I go to. I spend it all on the girls."

"Look at you. A regular philanthropist."

Goldin said nothing.

"All right, I'll tell you what I'm proposing."

"Fine," Goldin said. He was still trying to appear calm, but his clenched jaw betrayed him.

"I'm not going to kill you."

Goldin said, "I could tell you were a gentleman by the way you came up to the door."

Lance smiled.

Goldin offered him the pack of cigarettes. Lance took one and lit it. "I need my girl back, though," he said. "If she dies, or if something bad happens to her, I'm coming back for you."

Goldin nodded. "I followed orders. That's all."

"And what were those orders?"

"I put her in the car," he said. "I drugged her. Then I brought her to Teterboro."

Teterboro was a small airport in the New Jersey Meadowlands. It had a strict weight limit that made it mostly used by private jets and charters.

"What happened at Teterboro?"

"There was a jet waiting."

"You ever put someone on a jet before?"

"I delivered some people to some places before. Not to a jet on the tarmac, though. No."

"Where was the jet going?"

"I didn't ask, but I figured Russia. Everyone there seemed Russian."

There was an ashtray on the arm of the sofa, and Lance

stubbed out his cigarette in it. At the same time, the door to the kitchen opened. It was the old lady, and she was holding a Glock 41.

Lance leaped forward, just in time to dodge three bullets. The old lady had good aim. The bullets landed within inches of each other, right where he'd been sitting.

Lance grabbed Goldin by the head and swung himself behind him.

The old lady followed him across the room, firing off bullets, but she stopped short of hitting her son.

Lance didn't hesitate. With one hand on Goldin's chin and the other on his opposite temple, he yanked his head to the side with all his strength. There was a loud crack, and then Goldin went limp.

"You killed him," the woman screamed, then unloaded her weapon at Lance.

45

Igor wasn't sure why he was there. He'd been sitting by the receptionist's desk for twenty minutes. It was humiliating. He was used to being the one who made people wait, the one with flags by the door, and guards, and a receptionist behind a desk.

He looked at the clock.

Thirty minutes.

"Is he going to show?" he said irritably to the receptionist.

"He said to wait," the receptionist said.

"I *know* he said to wait. I've *been* waiting. Now I'm asking how long."

"If you want to leave..." the girl said, indicating the elevator.

Igor scoffed. He'd have enjoyed a chance to teach her some manners. The image of Agniya's face as he strangled her flashed across his mind.

Another thirty minutes passed before the girl finally told him he could go into Timokhin's office. She had remained in her seat.

"He's been in there this entire time?"

The girl shrugged.

"He made me wait on purpose."

She didn't know what to say.

"Well, aren't you at least going to show me to the door?"

"You remember the way," she said.

"No," he said pointedly. "I don't."

She sighed and, with an immense display of effort, got up. When they reached the door, Igor entered without knocking. The guards looked at him, but Timokhin, who was inside the anteroom smoking a cigarette, waved them away.

"Ah, Igor, thank you for making it up," he said, leading them to the inner office.

"You kept me waiting an hour," Igor said.

"You strangled Agniya Bunina to death."

"I did no such thing."

"Come now, Igor," Timokhin said, eyeing the nasty scratch across Igor's face.

"You were using her to spy on me," Igor said.

"It wasn't me who was using her," Timokhin said. "And you'd better hope that whoever it was doesn't take this personally."

"If it wasn't you, who was it?" Igor said.

"You'll find out soon enough, my friend. Right now, we have a more urgent problem."

"What problem?"

"We haven't found a body for your girl."

"Tatyana?"

"No need to sound so pleased."

Igor shook his head. It was no secret he'd been upset at the news she was dead, but this was more worrying. "Anything show up on the radar?"

"Radar?"

"Her phone? Credit cards? Database access?"

"No, and it won't. She's not that stupid."

"You wouldn't tell me, even if it did," Igor said.

"There are people around, Igor, who are beginning to question your loyalty."

"What's that supposed to mean?"

"They're wondering if maybe she was tipped off."

"Tipped off? She walked straight into the trap. A trap I helped lay."

"Still. They wonder."

"Who wonders?"

"The same people who are upset that you killed Agniya."

"What people?" Igor said, and there was a hint of fear in his voice that hadn't been there before.

"You need to stop sticking up for this slut and help us track her down."

"Your assassin can't help with that? He's the one who botched the job."

Timokhin looked agitated.

"What's wrong?" Igor said.

"My assassin is dead, Igor."

"What?"

"Yes. Not an hour ago. Killed in front of his eighty-year-old mother, if you can believe it."

"Those *animals.*"

"You see?" Timokhin said. "That sarcasm is what's going to be your downfall."

"Calm down," Igor said.

"Look at you. Grinning. I haven't seen you this happy in days."

"The only thing that upsets me about this whole situation is that whoever killed your man deprived me of the pleasure."

"Igor, you've really got to stop talking like that. First Agniya. Now this. You have no idea how much danger you're in."

Igor eyed Timokhin carefully. He couldn't tell if he was bluffing or not, and that in itself set alarm bells ringing.

"Tatyana Aleksandrova is damaged goods, Igor. For your sake, I hope she's dead."

"I do too," Igor said, but he couldn't keep the mirth out of his voice.

"You need to forget about her, Igor. Now that she's on the loose, she's going to get you in trouble. Go to a whore house like everyone else. Stop shitting where you eat."

Igor nodded.

"It's unprofessional," Timokhin added.

"Of course."

"In any case," Timokhin said, "I'm going to need a list of all of her known resources. Contacts. Safe houses. Drop boxes."

"I'll have a list sent up just as soon as I get a new secretary."

"Very funny."

"She had it coming."

Timokhin shook his head. "You can't be this stupid, Igor. The people she was working for.... I shouldn't even be saying this to you, but they're not to be treated lightly."

"Who are they?"

"People you do not want to deal with."

"So mysterious."

Timokhin smiled then, and it was his turn to act mirthful. "Let's just say, if I were you, I wouldn't start any long books. I'd hate for you not to find out how the story ended."

46

When Laurel came to, she couldn't see. She couldn't move. It was pitch black, and her feet and arms were pressed against the sides of some sort of sealed box.

She tried to move, and the pain at her clavicle shot through her like a dagger.

She was cold, and there was a loud noise coming from outside the box.

She kicked at the walls, pushing against them with all her strength. She felt the wall with her fingers. It was a wire mesh. As her eyes began to adjust, she realized she wasn't in a box at all but a cage.

It was a transportation cage.

And she was in the hold of an airplane.

She struggled against the walls, but it was no use.

She called out, "Help! Help!"

No one came. Her throat was dry. She needed water. She had no idea how long she'd been unconscious.

She could feel a change in air pressure in her ears. Were they taking off or landing?

She thought back to the incident. She'd shot the man in the cab, but he'd shot her too. She'd lost consciousness then.

What had gone wrong?

The Russian must have been followed to the meet. She'd expected to find Lance at the bar. But she found Laurel instead. And that was when things went wrong.

She felt the plane tilt as if coming in for landing. The air pressure changed, and then the moment of touchdown.

She tried not to think about where she'd been taken or what was in store for her.

The plane taxied and then stopped. Everything was still for a long time. She tried struggling again, but it only caused her pain. There was no way she was going to break out of the cage.

And then she heard some movement above her. A door opened, and she looked up into the blinding beam of a flashlight.

"That's her," someone said in Russian.

Some men in overalls lifted the cage out of the storage compartment and carried her off the plane. They placed the cage on the concrete floor of a hangar and then stood there, looking at her.

"She's wounded," one of them said.

"Where am I?" she said in Russian.

"She speaks!" The men all laughed. From their accents, she guessed they were from Moscow. One of them poked her through the wire mesh like she was some sort of animal. She ignored it.

"Well, looks like that's the only cargo," a man said.

They looked at each other and then began to walk away.

"Wait," Laurel said. "Where are you going? You can't leave me like this."

She watched them leave, hugging herself to conserve as

much body heat as possible. The door of the hangar was wide open, and the wind was ice cold. It was snowing outside. And it was night.

She was still in the clothes she'd been wearing in New York. The gunshot wounds had been bandaged, and thankfully they'd put her back in her coat. The expensive ski coat. It was stylish, with its little logo that looked great when she was in line at her local Starbucks, but as she lay there on the concrete, huddled and shivering, she swore she'd never choose a coat for style again.

The minutes stretched on, and she told herself over and over that no one would have brought her all the way to Moscow just to let her freeze to death on the floor of an aircraft hangar. Nevertheless, she was getting so cold that she felt herself starting to get sleepy. She struggled not to lose consciousness again.

Time stretched on.

Flurries of snow whipped into the hangar.

And eventually, she heard the clack of electrical lights coming on.

That was followed by a door opening.

She had to squint to adjust her eyes, but she gradually made out the figure of a very short, very small man, walking her way with the aid of a cane. He walked with a hunch, taking his time, tapping out each step with the cane like a blind man might.

He was smoking a cigar that he held in his mouth as he walked. The suit looked expensive, the black leather of his shoes gleamed, and as he got closer, she made out fine silver details on the cane.

He got to the cage and stopped, looking at it as if he'd expected to find something else.

For some reason, Laurel avoided looking at his face. She

focused on the cane, the silver lion at the top. The hand that held it had a large, gold ring on every finger. Some of the rings had gems in them.

"You're injured," the man said.

Laurel placed his accent as Saint Petersburg. He spoke like he had something distasteful in his mouth. He made a sucking sound with each word.

"You need medical attention," he said as if it were her fault.

She looked at his face for the first time and immediately wished she hadn't. He looked to be in his seventies. He was not blind. The way he ran his tongue over his lips made her think he was planning to dig into a meal. His face was pocked mercilessly, as if by some childhood illness. He had facial hair, but it was patchy. Mangy was the word she'd have used.

She'd been right in her initial assessment of his size. He was five feet tall at most and probably weighed less than 120 pounds. He looked too frail to be out there alone—the kind of man people offered their seat to on the subway.

He pulled a phone from his jacket pocket and croaked into it. "I need a medical team at hangar two, right away."

He took a long suck from his cigar and then just stood there, leaning on the cane, smacking his lips like he was thinking of eating her.

"A dog cage," he muttered to himself. "How appropriate." Then to her, he said, "Who has the key?"

She said nothing.

He rattled the cage with his cane. "Come now. Don't be rude. I asked a question."

Laurel's Russian was a little rusty but good enough to get by. "I don't know," she said.

"What?" he said, sucking as if he had a candy in his

mouth.

"I don't know who has the key."

He nodded and hit the cage again with the cane. "Do you bite?"

She looked at him. He was grinning, and if she'd thought he couldn't get any uglier, she was wrong.

"Woof, woof!" he said.

She pictured what she'd do to him if she ever got out of that cage. He hit the cage again, harder, as if testing its strength. "You know what we do with bitches in Russia?"

She didn't answer.

"We beat them," he said, grinning again. He pushed the tip of the cane through the wire mesh and poked her with it. He poked her hard, where she was wounded, and she reached for the cane and grabbed it.

She couldn't hold onto it, though.

"Feisty bitch," he said.

She wondered how long this would last. If he was all they'd sent, she wouldn't be getting out of the cold any time soon.

"You're shivering," he said. He bent down to get a closer look at her. They were face to face. "Pretty, pretty," he said, and her blood shivered at the look in his watery eyes.

He blew cigar smoke into her face. "My name is Evgraf Davidov." He said his name clearly, enunciating each syllable as if it was very important that she remember it. "Maybe you've heard of me? Your predecessor certainly did."

Laurel hadn't heard of him but wouldn't have told him if she had. She wondered what he meant about her predecessor. Was he referring to Clarice?

"And you are Laurel Everlane," he continued. "Levi Roth's new favorite."

Laurel was surprised. He seemed to know a lot about her. Had the Group been infiltrated?

"That's right," he said. "Your reputation precedes you. In fact, in the circles I move in, you're quite well known."

She said nothing.

"Don't be shy," he said. "What you did, changing yourself like that...." He leaned in closer to her, so close she could smell his rancid breath. "Look at you! Remarkable." He brought the burning tip of his cigar to the cage. It was so close to her face she could feel the heat of it. "After all that work, it would be a shame if someone were to spoil it."

She tried to back away from the cigar.

"Your dedication set the bar to new heights for my handlers," Davidov said. "But I wonder. Did they reconstruct the pussy too? Or just the face?"

She wanted to spit at him. The cigar was so close.

"If the pussy doesn't match, what good is the face?" he said. He laughed, amused at his own joke.

If they knew who she was, there was no question of what would happen next. They'd torture her mercilessly. They'd torture her to death.

Roth would come for her, she had to believe that, but if she was in Moscow, the chance of her being found in time was virtually nonexistent. The Russians weren't going to take any chances with her.

She was getting colder, and her shivering was beginning to get out of control. She was shaking so much the cage rattled. She knew it wouldn't take long for the cold to become a bigger threat than the gunshot wounds.

"What are you going to do with me?" she said, but as soon as she spoke, she regretted it. It was a sign of her weakness, her desperation.

"I'm sure you can *imagine*."

Laurel grimaced. She was in trouble, and she knew it. The next few days of her life were going to be utter hell. She would be tortured and interrogated in some dungeon built by Stalin, and no one would ever come to save her.

They'd pull her apart, limb from limb, body from soul, and strip her of anything that could possibly be of value to them. And when they were done, and she had nothing useful left to offer, they'd continue anyway, torturing her all the way to the end, prolonging the process, making her suffer as much as possible, until finally, in the end, her life would slip away like a leaf falling from a tree.

She would be one more casualty of war. No one would miss her. The world wouldn't even notice she was gone.

"I'm freezing," she whispered.

Davidov shrugged, like it was something he had no control over. "The nurses will be here any minute," he said. "You can tell them."

He was old, and hunching down was difficult for him. Nevertheless, with some effort, he moved around so that he could get a better look at her face. "Such a pretty thing," he said. "And so much work. I almost feel guilty destroying it."

He brought the cigar to the mesh again and carefully slid it through the gap in the wire. It was scarcely an inch from her eye.

Laurel's hands were pressed against the wire, and it was hard to move them, but she managed to squeeze them up past her chest and knock the cigar away. It fell from Davidov's hand to the ground.

He laughed. His face was so close to hers she almost could have clawed him through the mesh. He was staring at her intently.

"What a perfect face," he said. "I'm glad I got to see it so closely before I destroyed it."

47

R oth gave Lance the address of a hockey rink in Alexandria for their meeting. He told him to use all precautions, and Lance spent two hours getting there, doubling back, covering his tracks, making sure he wasn't being tailed. At the hockey rink, a game was going on between two local teams. The crowd provided plenty of cover.

He waited outside the rink, and when Roth arrived, Lance watched for an extra twenty minutes to make sure no one was following him.

When he got inside, Roth was sipping coffee by the concession stand. Lance ordered one for himself.

"What took you so long?" Roth said. "I was beginning to worry."

"I was making sure you were clean."

Roth nodded.

"Did you bring the passports?" Lance said.

Roth had a black briefcase with him, and he slid it toward Lance. "There are some clean papers in there. Nothing from the Group's files."

"Nothing traceable on your internal system?"

"No," Roth said. He looked dejected. It wasn't a look Lance had seen on him too often.

"How bad is this hack?" Lance said.

Roth shrugged. "There's talk of shutting me down."

"Over this?"

"Yes, over this! I'm supposed to be completely under the radar. That's the whole point of my existence."

"How much did they get?"

Roth shrugged. "My guys are still looking into it. But it's bad."

"How did they get in?"

"How do you think?"

Lance shook his head. "A rat?"

Roth nodded, almost imperceptibly, as if he couldn't believe it himself. "It's beginning to look that way. They've been a step ahead of us for weeks. I thought they were just lucky. I didn't dare think I'd been breached."

"What are we going to do?"

"I don't know," Roth said. "One thing's for certain. Something serious is about to go down."

Lance leaned back in his seat. "Do they know about me?"

Roth leaned back next to him and shrugged. "I don't know. Until I can determine the full extent of the breach, I think we have to assume the worst."

"That they know everything?"

Roth nodded. They both sat in silence for a minute, then Roth said, "How was New Jersey?"

"He gave me a name."

"What was it?"

"Timokhin."

Roth leaned in closer. "Timokhin?" he repeated.

"You know him?"

Roth nodded. "GRU. Top floor."

"Makes sense," Lance said. "If they have a rat in our house, someone on the top floor would be running him."

Roth nodded, but Lance could tell something else was bothering him. "What is it?" he said.

"Nothing."

"Roth!"

Roth sighed. "If I tell you this...."

"Just tell me," Lance said.

Roth looked at him. "Timokhin's not just top floor."

"What do you mean?"

"He's Dead Hand. He answers directly to our old friend, Davidov."

Lance nodded slowly. That was very bad news.

The Dead Hand was the reason the CIA needed people like Roth. It was the reason Assets like Lance were permitted to exist. Groups like the Dead Hand didn't play by the rules. They were the spy equivalent of a dirty bomb—of Mutually Assured Destruction. While they were tightly connected to the Kremlin and answered directly to the Russian President himself, they acted more like a terrorist organization than a member of the Russian intelligence community. They didn't take their orders through ordinary political channels, and they didn't seek normal Russian state objectives. The Dead Hand came into play when a situation called for something more drastic. It was known to pursue terrorist and anarchic outcomes.

It had one objective—to protect the Russian President and ruthlessly pursue his personal interests.

If they were involved, it meant this entire situation had just become a whole lot more serious. Roth had been in a life-and-death struggle with them for years, for decades. He and Lance knew all too well how dangerous of an opponent they were.

"Something very bad is about to happen," Lance said.

Roth nodded. "And we're in disarray."

"We've got to get Laurel back."

"I'm tracking every source I've got," Roth said.

"The guy in New Jersey said he put her on a jet at Teterboro."

"I tracked it. That plane flew directly to Moscow."

"They're going to skin her alive, Levi."

"I know what they're going to do to her."

"I'm going to Moscow. I've got to get her back. It's my fault she was captured. If I'd come when she first asked, this never would have happened."

"Slow down, cowboy. I'll fly the other assets to Moscow too. We're going to need all hands on deck."

"I can't let Davidov get ahead of me a second time," Lance said.

"And he won't. I'll get the other assets to fly in immediately. To get to Davidov, you'll need their help."

"Agreed," Lance said.

"And don't let your personal history with Davidov cloud your judgment," Roth said.

Lance looked at him. "This isn't about personal history. Davidov is the one man I can think of who might actually release an uncontrollable virus. He wouldn't think twice about it if he thought it would increase his power. No matter how many people it killed."

Roth nodded. "Trouble is coming, Lance. I can feel it. Every bone in my body says he's going to make a move. Something devastating."

"What could he be thinking? A bioweapon is going to cause outrage. It will lead to war. How will that help them?"

"They've got an election coming up. The president has reached his constitutional term limits. They've got protests in the streets, students fighting the police."

Lance shook his head. "They'd risk war to win an election?"

Roth looked at him. "They'd do anything to stay in power." He pulled out a tablet and opened some video footage. It was satellite surveillance of a Russian city. "This is Yekaterinburg," Roth said.

"What am I looking at?"

"That's the former Biopreparat Biological Weapons compound. Compound 19, they call it now."

The compound looked like any other utilitarian Russian science facility. Steam billowed from a chimney stack. Cars made their way from the front gate toward one of the buildings.

The camera panned away from the compound to another location in the city.

"What's this?"

"One of the city's main hospitals."

It was a big facility. Multiple buildings. It looked like a group had gathered in the parking lot to protest something.

"What's going on?"

"The hospital was on lockdown. From what we've been able to tell, there was a leak at a bioweapons production facility in the city. People were getting sick."

"Are those corpses?" Lance said, pointing to some tarps in the parking lot.

Roth was about to answer when, bang! A flash of light disrupted the footage.

"What was that?"

"An airstrike."

"Their own?"

Roth nodded.

"They hit their own facility?"

Roth nodded gravely.

Lance said nothing for a moment. Roth didn't have to explain. They both knew that anything that could cause the Russians to bomb their own hospital in broad daylight was serious. "What are you proposing?"

"Flying you to Yekaterinburg."

"So that compound is where the bioweapon was produced?"

Roth pulled up satellite images. "The compound is quite large. They've got a lot of low-security buildings in there. Army administration. A factory producing kevlar vests. Another working on drone technology."

"So a lot of workers?"

"A lot of workers. A lot of traffic."

"Not a lot of security?"

"You won't have any trouble getting into the compound itself. This building here is the Permafrost Pathogen Institute. From what we've been able to gather, that's where the bioweapons research is being conducted."

"Do we have schematics for the building?"

"Yes. They're incomplete, but we were able to get the drawings from when the building was originally constructed in the seventies. It was intended to be a civilian research center. It's been retrofitted, but the layout should be mostly the same."

"All right."

"Your biggest risk won't be getting in. It will be accidentally releasing a pathogen." Roth pulled up some more photos. "This is another facility in the south of the city," he said. "This is where the leak seems to have occurred."

"This is where the sick people are coming from?" Lance

said.

"This building here is a textile factory. The first cases came from there. Then they spread in this direction. This is a school. These are apartments. That's a shopping mall."

"The area is very contained," Lance said.

Roth nodded.

"And we're not seeing cases spread exponentially?"

"No," Roth said. "Not as far as we can tell. They seem to have contained the initial outbreak to this one area."

"How is that possible? From what you and Laurel showed me of the virus...."

Roth shook his head. "That's the thing. We don't think this outbreak is a virus."

"What is it then?"

"It's got to be something else. Something that isn't transmissible. Given the history of the facility, our best guess is that it's some sort of anthrax strain."

"So they're working on more than one bioweapon?"

"They always are."

Lance looked at Roth.

"I know," Roth said. "That's why I want to get you over there as quickly as possible. Destroy this facility. Grind this thing to a halt."

"All right," Lance said. "So they've got a lab and a production facility?"

"Yes. The lab's the real target. The production facility seems to be using pretty ordinary pharmaceutical equipment. These tanks here are the main production vats. There are four of them. This building, we think, is for drying and milling ingredients."

"It doesn't look very high-tech."

"As I said, it's low-value equipment. Given the fact that there was a leak, it doesn't even seem like they've customized it for military use. It's just ordinary industrial-grade stuff. Nowhere near up to the task."

"Why would they develop deadly new pathogens and then cook them up in old vats like these?" Lance said.

"Same reason we shipped sixty M224 mortars to Basra with no four-pound shells. The left hand doesn't know what the right hand is doing."

"If this is how they produce anthrax, we better pray they don't start production of the virus."

Roth nodded. "That's why the main priority has to be the institute. That's where the research is coming from. Destroy the lab, and you destroy the new weapons at their source."

"So just walk in and start blowing shit up?"

"That sounds like a recipe for disaster."

"No kidding," Lance said.

"You're going to need help. The institute is led by this woman." Roth pulled up a photo. "A scientist named Sofia Ivanova. If you could somehow capture her and get her to guide you, it would make your job a lot easier."

"And why do you think she'll help?"

"Because we ran background checks on every scientist in the institute. If they have a weak link, ideologically, it's her."

"But she's head of the institute."

"It looks like they hired her because of what she could achieve in the lab, not because of her party loyalty."

Lance swiped through the other scientists. "What about this guy? You scored him highly."

"Vasily Ustinov. Second in command."

"Dagestan."

"Yeah, but go for Ivanova first. She's his boss."

"Good fighters in Dagestan."

"She's our best bet."

"You're sure of that?"

"Someone got that vial to Tatyana. My bet is it was her."

"I see."

"It beats walking in and blowing shit up, as you put it."

"All right," Lance said. "And you got the schematics there?"

"As much as we could find."

Lance looked at Roth. The old man looked like he was struggling. As far as Lance knew, there had never been a breach of Roth's systems before. Not in all the years the Group had been in operation. There would be repercussions.

"Hey," Lance said. "They can't be thinking of shutting you down. Not with this going on?"

"I don't know what they're thinking," Roth said. "The president spends all his time with Mansfield now, and Mansfield has been trying to eat up our operation for years."

"Yeah, but Mansfield's a blowhard. If he gets the job, the Russians will walk all over us. The president knows that."

"Times have changed. Mansfield's top dog now. And if he gets his way, the CIA will be relegated to a second-tier agency. The Special Operations Group will be the first thing he cuts."

"They can't replace you that easily."

Roth shrugged. "We'll see."

Lance finished his coffee. "I'll go to Yekaterinburg. But you find Laurel. I'm not coming home without her."

"All right."

"I mean it. I don't give a shit about the rest of it. I want her out. She deserves that much from us."

"I'll find her, Lance. And I'll get the other Assets in position to assist. By the time you're done in Yekaterinburg, I'll have a location for you. You have my word. "

48

Tatyana had a fever. She had to clean her wound every few hours. She woke frequently during the night and didn't always know where she was. Twice, she heard footsteps outside her door and reached for her gun. Both times it was just hookers plying their trade.

In the backpack, she had antibiotics, weapons, cash, and clean ID.

When morning finally came, she went into the bathroom and examined the wound. It looked like it would heal, but she needed rest.

There was a kettle in the room, and she made tea. Then she sat on the bed, sipping it and thinking.

This was it, she thought. The time had come. She'd always known that eventually, she'd be on the outside. The things she'd done at the GRU, the men she'd served, the men she'd killed—it wouldn't last forever. She'd been in survival mode her entire life, and she'd known that in the end, either they'd come for her, or she'd come for them.

This was it, her strike against them, her act of defiance against the system that killed her mother.

She didn't care that it might cost her life. At least she'd die fighting.

She finished her tea, packed her things, and went down to the lobby. No one was at the desk. She'd paid for the room in advance, so she walked outside and hailed a cab.

There was no one she could trust now. She knew that. She was alone and would be for the rest of her life.

Igor had turned on her. That meant everything, all the resources she'd carefully put in place, were potentially compromised. She had nothing, and no one, to turn to.

"Where to?" the driver said.

She needed to create distance. The search for her would begin in Manhattan. She needed to get away from the city, buy herself some time to think, and figure out her next move.

The driver looked at her in the rearview, her bare feet and ripped dress. He looked out the window at the seedy hotel.

"I'm not working, Romeo."

He raised his hands in protest. "I didn't say anything."

"I need to get out of here."

"How far do you want to go?"

"Queens. And I need a Walmart."

"There's a Target in Flushing."

"That will do."

She ignored the driver's ramblings as they drove. On their way to the Queensboro Bridge, they passed the entrance to the Four Seasons Hotel. It seemed like a lifetime had passed since she'd checked in there. She would have liked nothing more than to go back up to her room and sleep for three days.

But she couldn't.

Even driving by felt reckless.

In Flushing, the driver dropped her off at the Target. She went inside and bought ordinary clothes and sneakers, some snacks, a cheap phone and laptop, and some more medical supplies. She changed her clothes in the store's fitting room.

From there, she caught a cab to Flushing's Chinatown, where dozens of seedy hotels were ready to rent her a room without ID. She had clean ID and credit cards now, from the locker in Penn Station, but the less she used them, the better. Cash was safer.

She found a place called Lucky Dragon Lodging and went inside. "What's the price?" she said to the woman at the counter.

"Sixty a night."

"I need my own bathroom."

"Those rooms are all taken."

"I'll give you two hundred dollars if you can find me one that's available."

The woman typed on her computer and then took a key from beneath the counter. "Room 404," she said. "Take the stairs."

Tatyana climbed the stairs, opened the door, locked it behind her, and collapsed onto the bed. She fell asleep for a few hours, and when she woke up, the streets outside had come to life. Market stalls, hawkers, hookers, dealers of every type.

She had a lot of work to do, but she was too exhausted. She went into the bathroom and had a shower. Then she dressed her wound and changed into some fresh clothes. It felt good to be clean. She went down to the ground floor and asked the woman at the counter to order her some food.

Then she went back to the room and turned on the television. She sank into the bed and watched some people bid on the contents of a storage locker in California. It was surprisingly engaging.

When the knock on the door came, she took the gun from her backpack and slipped it into the back of her jeans. It was the woman from the counter. She had two brown bags full of Chinese takeout. Tatyana tipped her well.

She sat on the bed and ate three times her normal amount, the food sprawled out on the bed in front of her like a picnic. She watched the TV to see if the guy who'd won the auction on the storage locker made a profit from the contents. It was touch and go, but in the end, he found some collectible baseball cards that saved him.

All the while, she mulled over a single question—who'd found out she was leaking information to the Americans?

And how?

She pulled out the laptop she'd bought and tethered it to the burner cell phone. Then she downloaded the Tor browser and began setting up a VPN.

49

Igor stood by his office window, his forehead resting against the cold glass, and wondered what to do.

He reached into his pocket and felt the crumpled, blood-smeared piece of paper. It was still there. Wishing it away did no good. He pulled it out and looked at it. On it, in Agniya's handwriting, scrawled just before he'd killed her, were her credentials for a top-secret, high-level database.

He thought back to her final moments. He regretted what he'd done. He'd never fully trusted her, but he'd wanted to. There had been moments when he'd thought maybe she was the one person on earth he'd be able to let his guard down for. That was not meant to be.

He could still feel the structure of her throat as it collapsed under the pressure of his thumbs. The memory of it made his stomach turn. He'd been so blinded by rage—by betrayal—that he'd killed her even though she gave him what he wanted.

It all came down to this database. It was the reason she'd been assigned to his desk. She was a spy for the top floor, a mole right beneath his nose. But it hadn't been him she was spying on.

No—it was Tatyana.

They'd been watching her for years. There was some relief in that—that they hadn't been watching him. Whatever Tatyana was messed up in, it didn't appear to have implicated him. And whatever the top floor knew about her, they'd kept from him on purpose. That was the only reason he was still alive.

He was scared of using the credentials. He'd held off on logging in to the database. It would only draw him deeper into a problem he had no desire to be a part of, attract more unwanted attention, but he was out of options. He'd stumbled into this, and he wasn't going to be able to stumble back out. Between Timokhin and the top floor, his best chance of coming through alive was to arm himself with as much information as possible.

He went to the door and opened it. He half expected to see Agniya, sitting at her desk the way she always had, facing him, her computer angled so he couldn't see what was on the screen.

He'd surprised the two guards, and they shuffled themselves to attention. "Leave," he said to them.

He waited for them to shut the door behind them, then sat at Agniya's desk and powered up her computer.

He pulled up the SQL terminal. This was it. There'd be no turning back from this.

He took a deep breath and entered the credentials. The database was encrypted, and he had to wait some time before anything happened. After a few minutes, a black screen appeared with a search box in the center, a cursor blinking inside it.

He hesitated another second, took a deep breath, then entered Tatyana's name.

He hit enter.

Instantly, it found a match.

Identifier: RP_008374

   Name: Tatyana Aleksandrova

   Loyalty: Russia (compromised)

   Agency: Main Directorate

   Lead Agent: Igor Aralov

   Status: Manhunt in progress. Kill on sight.

   Restricted Database

Below the match was a list of entries—literally hundreds of them, going back years. They detailed Tatyana's every movement down to the finest detail—her operational assignments, transcripts of phone calls, location coordinates taken periodically from her phone. Some of the entries had been made by Agniya, sitting at that very desk, but there were many others. Real field surveillance. Agents had been assigned to follow her, to monitor her every moment, both in Russia and abroad. Bugs had been planted in her apartment and hotel rooms. Drones had been requisitioned to watch her movements from the air. There were even transcripts of her meetings with Igor, meetings that had taken place between the two of them in the privacy of his office.

Agniya truly had betrayed him. She'd listened to everything—everything—and dutifully sent it up to the top floor.

There was a specific date he remembered, and he scrolled through the transcripts until he found it. He scanned the entry, looking for the part he was concerned about.

Transcript

Igor Aralov: You know what I want.

Tatyana Aleksandrova: The same thing everyone wants.

Igor Aralov: And you want to give it to me?

Tatyana Aleksandrova: I want to serve my country.

Igor Aralov: Then come closer, my dear. If you want to serve your country, this is the best way.

Tatyana Aleksandrova: [Indistinct].

Igor Aralov: Don't be shy.

Tatyana Aleksandrova: Like this?

Igor Aralov: That's it, my dear. You know how.

Tatyana Aleksandrova: You like that?

Igor Aralov: Yes.

Tatyana Aleksandrova: [Indistinct] Oh, baby. [Indistinct].

Igor Aralov: Oh god, oh god.

Restricted Database

Igor felt his face redden. He'd taken liberties with many of the women under his power, but that was the only time he'd done it with Tatyana. For some reason, he hadn't ever been able to bring himself to repeat it. It brought him too much embarrassment when he looked at her afterward, too much shame.

But he knew that wasn't the encounter that would matter most to the top floor. They'd flagged the ones they were interested in, including Tatyana's most recent trips to Istanbul and New York.

Igor ordered the entries chronologically and opened the very first file that had been flagged.

Identifier: CI_050303
  Target: Tatyana Aleksandrova
  Agency: Main Directorate
  Location: Hotel Europa, Damascus, Syria
  Restricted Database

This was the oldest thing they had on her. He checked the date. It was four days later that the top floor had assigned Agniya to his desk.

This must have been the real reason.

If anything marked the beginning of Tatyana's downfall, the beginning of her being put onto the radar of whatever agency had created this database, it was this incident.

It was a mission Igor had sent her on. Her first overseas mission. He remembered it clearly. It had been a failure. The target was a Syrian military commander, a nasty piece of work named Hammoud Hassan, and Tatyana came back empty-handed, reporting that she hadn't been able to get the man to so much as look at her. That had surprised Igor. He remembered being suspicious. Hassan had a well-documented fondness for prostitutes. Dark features like Tatyana's were his favorite. For her to completely fail to catch his eye didn't add up.

He remembered thinking that maybe Tatyana wasn't cut out for the job. It wasn't unusual in their business for a girl to lose her nerve. Some of them just weren't built for it. Her being so new at the time, with so few successful jobs to her credit, made him question her abilities, her commitment to the cause.

The incident of him taking advantage of her in his office occurred soon after. He recalled that part of the reason for it was to see if she could go through with it.

Now he saw the real reason she'd been unsuccessful in Damascus.

The report was difficult to read. There were so many code words and redacted segments that Igor had to go over it a few times just to make sense of it. But from what he could gather, a secret Russian Agency with the code RA_999 had been following a high-value American target coded as AP_000245.

The high-value target was an assassin for an elite CIA unit, and his arrival in Damascus had been leaked to the GRU by someone on the American side coded as AP_006758. The leaked information included not only the cover the target was traveling under but also the hotel he'd be staying at—the Hotel Europa. They didn't know the room number, but because of the target's priority, the Russian Agency pulled out all the stops, placing microphones and cameras in all ninety rooms of the hotel, as well as the lobby, the bar, and other public areas.

Igor remembered something about that. There had been complications for his own operations at the Hotel Europa during the period.

He needed to refresh his memory.

He opened a new SQL terminal and navigated to the Main Directorate database. He accessed his own file for Tatyana's Hammoud Hassan operation and scanned through it. It was all there. Hammoud Hassan had stayed at the same hotel—the Europa, room 55. Igor had been denied authorization to bug Hassan's room because the top floor had a conflicting surveillance request that took precedence. Igor had to tell Tatyana to take Hassan to her own hotel across the street, the Royal Damascus, as that was the only way he'd be able to get the liaison on film.

Igor flipped back to the other terminal and continued reading. AP_000245 checked into the Europa in room number 57, putting him directly next door to Hassan.

Tatyana came back from Damascus reporting to Igor that she'd never made meaningful contact with Hassan. She said she'd approached him in the hotel lobby and that he'd completely ignored her. She'd tried a second time at the bar the next night and was again unsuccessful.

According to this report, on the second night, Hassan hadn't ignored her at all but bought her a drink at the bar. Igor watched the video footage, which had been recorded by RA_999. There was no audio, but he could see Tatyana doing her job perfectly, drinking with Hassan, flirting with him.

According to the file, when Tatyana left him at the bar to use the washroom, she set up a sound recorder in her purse. Hassan must have told her he wasn't going to go to her hotel, in which case, she was following the correct protocol by capturing audio of the liaison on her own recorder. Audio wasn't nearly as useful, but it was better than nothing. Tatyana was still doing her job exactly to protocol.

While she was in the washroom, Hassan ordered her another drink. When it arrived, he drugged it. Igor watched the footage. He did it right there at the bar, right in front of the bartender. Hassan pulled a small bottle from his pocket and sprinkled it into the drink. Igor rewound the footage and watched it again. The bartender definitely saw him do it.

By the time Hassan and Tatyana left the bar, she was barely able to walk, and Hassan had to practically carry her to the elevator. A hotel employee actually pressed the button on the elevator for them.

Hassan brought Tatyana to his room, room 55, and handcuffed her to the bed.

The top floor's surveillance team watched the whole thing. They weren't there because of Tatyana or Hassan—it was purely coincidence that they'd bugged the entire hotel because of their American target—but because of that, they had a camera in Hassan's room and had eyes on everything that followed.

According to the background research conducted by top floor after the fact, Hassan apparently had a history of violence against prostitutes. He'd tortured over a dozen of them. Four died. One of the survivors was brave enough, or naive enough, to go to the Syrian police about it. Her case was buried. She was later found dead in a public drain outside the city, shot by the same model of handgun that was standard issue for Damascus police. No cop in Syria would ever dare look into a man as powerful as Hammoud Hassan, and that was why Igor had had no knowledge of the report when he sent Tatyana in.

If he'd known, he would have included it in her briefing.

He'd sent her in blind.

And that was why, for her first-ever overseas mission, Igor had inadvertently placed Tatyana into the hands of a man who got his kicks by slowly strangling and reviving prostitutes—sometimes to the point of death.

Igor had to stand up. This was his first time learning any of this, and he needed a breather. He opened the top button on his shirt and loosened his tie. Then he poured himself a stiff drink.

He couldn't believe it. He'd had no idea. All this time. Her first-ever mission. The start of everything.

He read back over the last part of the file, and the thing that really stood out, what really bothered him, was that the RA_999 surveillance team who'd bugged the hotel just sat back and watched the entire thing unfold. They'd watched one of their own, a female GRU agent on her first real mission, get strangled to within a hair's breadth of her life over a period of four hours.

Oh, they'd sought authorization from Moscow to intervene, but when that request was denied, they simply sat on their hands and watched.

RA_999 had said the American target was too valuable to lose for a single GRU prostitute.

Igor couldn't believe what he was reading. It was a wonder Tatyana had ever been able to go back into the field again. It made him feel even more guilty about what had just happened to her in New York. He'd misjudged her— underestimated her. It made him wonder what else had happened? What other things had she suffered in the line of duty that he didn't know about?

The surveillance team watched for hours, certain that Tatyana was going to die. But when death seemed most imminent, as Hassan's cycle of strangulation and revival was coming to its inevitable end, something unexpected happened. Someone intervened.

The footage was all there, and Igor clicked on the file marked 'Room 55'. He was looking at Hassan's room. Tatyana was naked, splayed out on the bed, her wrists cuffed to the bedposts. Hassan was also naked. He was straddling her, both hands on her neck, choking her until the very last moment before she lost consciousness.

She was struggling, writhing on the bed, begging him to

stop, and it went on and on, her movements getting weaker and weaker. It didn't look like she would be able to survive much more of it when a knock came on the door. Hassan turned toward it. He put a rag in Tatyana's mouth and grabbed a handgun from the bedside table. The knock came again. Hassan, still naked, crept toward the door and peered through the peephole.

The second his face touched the door, it burst open and knocked him to the ground. A man entered the room, struck Hassan in the face with his knee, looked at the bed, and saw what was happening to Tatyana.

He ran to the bed and pulled the rag from her mouth. Tatyana gasped for air, and then her eyes widened when she saw what was about to happen. Behind the American, Hassan rose to his feet, holding his gun out in front of him.

The American turned in time to take a bullet to the chest. It didn't stop him.

Hassan pulled the trigger twice more, but the man leaped at him, and the bullets missed. He grabbed Hassan by the waist and brought him to the ground, where he proceeded to slam his head against the floor, over and over and over, until Hassan's body went limp and his skull began to give way.

The man looked down at what he'd done and rose slowly. His hands were covered in blood, and his chest was bleeding where he'd been shot. He wiped his hands on his shirt and went back to the bed.

Tatyana looked at him, her eyes wide with terror. There was a key on the bedside table, and he used it to unlock the cuffs. Then he wrapped her in the bedsheets.

Igor wiped his brow. A note on the file said that the man who'd intervened was the high-value American target that RA_999 had been trying to surveil.

Igor scrolled to the next flagged file and opened it. It was from a camera in room 57 of the hotel—the American's room.

A few hours had passed. Tatyana seemed, at least physically, to have recovered somewhat from her ordeal. She'd showered. Her hair was wet. There were marks on her neck from where Hassan had been gripping her, but it looked like they'd been somewhat concealed with makeup. She was standing at the counter making tea.

The American's gunshot wound had been tended to, and he was sitting in a chair watching Tatyana.

"Thank you," he said to her when she handed him the tea.

"You're welcome," she said, her voice weak.

"You're Russian?" he said.

She looked at him for a moment, sitting on the bed before answering. "Yes."

"What are you doing in Damascus?"

She hesitated again, then said, "Please don't ask me that."

"Why not?"

"Because I don't want to lie to you."

He nodded, and they sipped their tea. "That man was a Syrian military commander," the American said.

Tatyana said nothing.

Then he said, "Don't you work with any support?"

"What do you mean?"

"The team that sent you in. Weren't they watching? Making sure something like this didn't happen to you?"

"What team?"

"The GRU."

"How do you know I'm GRU?"

"Call it a hunch."

She'd finished her tea, and the American got up and poured her some more.

"How's the wound?" she said.

"You're changing the subject."

She looked away.

"How's your neck?" he said.

She reached up and touched it tenderly. "I think I'll live."

"They sent you in alone, didn't they?"

She nodded.

"And what are you supposed to do when something like this happens?"

"Something like this isn't supposed to happen."

He nodded. "Is that what they told you at the academy?"

She looked around the room. Igor recognized what she was doing—scanning for cameras. It didn't look like she'd seen any. "We were supposed to do this in my hotel," she said. "Not this hotel."

"Would that have made you any safer?"

She shrugged. "This was my first operation," she said quietly.

The American got up and went to the window. He sipped his tea, then said, "Well, no offense, but I think you might want to consider a career change."

She shook her head, which he didn't see her do, but he went to the closet and pulled out a bag. He reached inside for something.

"What's that?" Tatyana said.

"They didn't give you a gun, did they?"

"A gun wouldn't have helped me tonight."

He handed her a handgun. Igor saw that it was the old Browning Tatyana brought with her on every mission. It was against regulations—a gun was a potential giveaway—but he hadn't challenged her on it.

"Never go on another job without this," the American said. "It will save your life one day."

She looked at him. "Why are you helping me?"

"What do you mean?"

"You didn't have to come into that room. You got shot over it. Now you're giving me your gun."

"I'm American," he said. "I've got more guns."

She smiled sadly. "What are we going to do about the body?"

"Leave that to me. I'll get rid of it."

"Thank you."

"And don't tell your handler anything about this. Just talking to me would put you on a watch list."

She nodded.

"Just tell your handler the guy wasn't interested. No one's going to think you killed him."

"All right," she said.

"Now, do you have somewhere you can go?"

"I have a room at the Royal."

"Go back there. Act like this never happened. That's very important. If anyone ever finds out you and I met, it will make your life very complicated."

Tatyana got up, but as she was putting on her coat, she stopped. Igor leaned closer to the screen. It looked perhaps like she had started to cry. The American looked at her awkwardly for a few seconds, and when she didn't stop, he said, "Is everything all right?"

Igor shook his head. His face was very close to the screen. He was transfixed, watching the footage as though it were a movie. And one thing was clear—the American was no Clark Gable. Now that Tatyana was crying, he had no idea what to say to her.

She looked at him incredulously. "Is everything *all*

right?"

"Sorry," he said.

"Someone just tried to strangle me."

"Of course."

She finished putting on her coat, but something stopped her from leaving the room.

"Well..." the American said, seemingly eager to bring the encounter to a close.

"I could stay here," she said.

"What?"

"With you." When he didn't respond, she said, "Sorry. Forget it."

"No. I'm sorry."

"I thought you'd want me to stay."

He cleared his throat, then said, "If you're going to survive in this game, you've got to look after yourself. Don't tell your handlers everything. Only tell them what you have to. And always carry a weapon."

"They don't allow weapons. It's a potential giveaway."

"Even hookers carry weapons," he said.

She nodded. "And that's what I am, isn't it?"

"That's not what I meant."

"No," she said. "I understand. You're right."

"I wasn't judging you."

She was embarrassed. She went to the door, then stopped. "You're a soldier, aren't you?"

He nodded.

"What's your name?"

He paused for a moment, then said, "Lance Spector."

She looked at him. "Is that your real name?"

He said nothing.

"If I ever wanted to contact you," she said, "if I needed help, I could use that name?"

"You could try."

"And a message would get to you?"

"If you gave it to the right person."

"And who would the right person be?"

"The military. Delta Force."

She nodded and opened the door, then looked back. "Thank you for the help. If I can ever return the favor, my name is Tatyana Aleksandrova."

The video ended there. Igor could see why Tatyana had been put on a watch list. That American was a priority. She'd formed a connection with him—a real connection.

If RA_999 wanted to get to him, watching her was as good an option as they were going to get. Eventually, she'd contact him, or he'd contact her. They knew enough about human nature to know that was inevitable.

Everyone in the GRU wanted a potential way out—a Plan B. Something they could comfort themselves with when they fell asleep at night.

This American was Tatyana's.

Igor didn't take it personally. It was only natural. The work they did took a toll. She'd just been through a terrible ordeal. This man helped her. Of course she would want to turn to him.

The question Igor needed to answer wasn't why Tatyana wanted Spector. That much, he understood perfectly. What he wanted to know was who'd been watching the Hotel Europa? Who'd placed Agniya?

Who was RA_999?

And how much power did they have?

He closed the file and opened the search terminal. He looked at the blinking cursor for a second, then typed in 'RA_999'.

The hit came back.

Identifier: RA_999
  Agency: Dead Hand
  Lead Agent: Evgraf Davidov
  Restricted Database

Igor's blood went cold.

L ance was passing through the Watergate plaza on his way to the apartment when he sensed something wasn't right. As he approached the elevator, he saw the reflection of two men behind him. Both wore black suits, like a pair of FBI agents in a kids' movie, and he could hear their shoes on the tiled floor behind him.

The elevator dinged, and the doors opened. Lance stepped inside and turned in time to see their faces. One of them hurried forward to grab the door before it closed and then held it for his companion.

"Going up?" Lance said.

The men nodded, and all three of them stood like sentries as the doors closed.

The second it shut, Lance ducked. The man to his right swung for him and missed. Lance grabbed him by the waist and drove him back against the wall.

The other man pulled a knife and stabbed downward at Lance's back. Lance kicked back, hitting him in the groin before the blade made contact. The knife fell from his hand to the floor.

Lance rose up, smacking the man above him on the chin with the back of his head, then immediately pushed his head forward, butting the first guy in the face and smashing his nose.

The man behind drew a gun, but the added length of the silencer made it unwieldy. The extra second of fumbling gave Lance time to swing the other man around as cover. He took three bullets in the back. Lance then pushed him forward, crushing the gunman against the wall.

Letting the dead man fall to the ground, Lance gripped the gunman's wrist and yanked it backward, forcing him to drop the gun. Then he kneed him in the groin. The man doubled over, and Lance finished him with a knee to the face.

The elevator dinged, and the doors opened on Lance's floor. Lance pulled the man who was still alive into the corridor and dragged him to his apartment.

Once inside, he filled a glass with water and poured it on the man's face. As he regained consciousness, Lance said, "If you want to live, tell me who sent you."

The assassin shook his head. "You know I can't do that."

Lance pointed the gun at him. "Talk, or I shoot."

"I'm already dead," he said.

"Then what difference does it make?"

"You don't understand," the man said. "I don't know who I work for."

"Bullshit."

"I take anonymous contracts."

"Cut the crap, buddy," Lance said. "No one takes anonymous contracts. I want to know who sent you, and I want to know why."

He shook his head, and Lance pressed the gun against his knee. He put his finger on the trigger and was about to shoot when the man started to blab. "All right, all right," he said. "I'll talk."

"Who sent you?"

"A Russian."

"What's his name?"

"I don't know."

"How does he contact you?"

"Someone calls my phone. I don't know who they are. I tried tracing the call and couldn't do it. They give me a target, some details, and I make a hit. That's it. After the job is done, I get the number of an offshore account. The pay is already in there."

"What about the guy in the elevator?"

"I hired him. They said this one was going to be dangerous and to bring back up."

"You should have brought more," Lance said.

The man nodded.

"So, you say they phone you with a target?"

"Yes."

"But how did you get started? Someone must have recruited you initially."

"That was years ago."

"How did it happen?"

"There was a woman."

"Of course there was," Lance said.

"A Russian."

"Describe her."

"I don't know. I don't remember."

Lance pressed the gun against the man's inner thigh, dangerously close to his balls.

"All right. All right," the man said.

"Who was she?"

"She was attractive. Very attractive."

"What else?"

"She came up to me in a bar, dressed like a hooker. Got me to go to a hotel room with her."

"Poor you."

"It wasn't like that. She played me."

"Tell me what happened?"

"She said they had dirt on me."

"What dirt?"

"I was a cop back then. They knew some shit I was mixed up in."

"What was it?"

The guy looked around.

"Eyes on me," Lance said. "What was it?"

"Drug dealer shit. I was on the take. They knew more about it than I did. They told me I'd go to jail if I didn't do what they wanted."

"So you agreed to kill for them?"

"I never agreed to anything. They started giving me small jobs. I did them reluctantly, and the money was good. Over the years, the jobs got bigger."

"And the money got better?"

The man nodded.

"And that's how you went from being a dirty cop to an assassin for the Russians."

"It's an easier road than you'd think."

"All right," Lance said. "So they told you to kill me?"

"Yes. I got a call."

"When?"

"A few hours ago."

"What did they say?"

"They said you were CIA. That you were trained. Probably armed."

"What else did they say?"

"I don't know."

"Think."

"They said you were right-handed."

"What else?"

"Nothing else."

"You want me to kill you now?" Lance said.

"What? No!"

"Make it easier for you? Like you said, you're a goner anyway."

"I don't know what I am."

Lance shook his head. "What's this country coming to?"

The assassin didn't know. Lance looked at him. He was about Lance's age. Similar height and weight. Similar features. "This woman who recruited you," he said.

"Who blackmailed me," the man said.

"Did she have any defining features?"

"What do you mean?"

"What did she look like?"

"She had dark hair, dark eyes."

"What else?"

"What do you mean, what else?"

"You know, in bed."

The man thought for a second and said, "She had a birthmark."

"Where?"

"Inner thigh."

"Which thigh."

"I don't remember, I swear."

"How big was it?"

"About the size of a bottle cap."

Lance's phone started to ring. He picked it up, and the man made a move. He leaped to his feet like a panther and dove into Lance's torso. Lance brought an elbow down onto his head as he fell backward onto the bed. The bloodied man was on top of him, and they struggled for position until he managed to get his hands on Lance's throat.

Lance swung his body around and got him in a choke-hold between his thighs. He held him, deadly tight, and felt the assassin get weaker and weaker. After about five minutes, he wasn't struggling anymore.

Lance checked his pulse. He was alive but unconscious.

Lance checked his phone and saw that the call had been from Roth. He called him back. "Someone just tried to kill me," he said.

"What?"

"Two guys. My apartment. They attacked in the elevator."

"How did they find you?"

"I don't know, Roth. I was going to ask you that."

"Listen," Roth said, his voice frail with stress. "We're in free fall. You're on your own."

"What does that mean?"

"Do what we discussed. Go to Russia. Take out these bastards. The Group's been compromised. Don't contact anyone at Langley. Don't trust anyone."

"What do you want me to do with this guy?"

"What guy?"

"One of the assassins is still alive."

"Tie him up. I'll take care of the clean up."

"All right."

"And Lance..." Roth said, hesitating a moment before completing the sentence. "The other Assets—it looks like they're not going to make it after all."

51

I gor felt as if the oxygen had suddenly been sucked from the room. He looked at the screen.

The Dead Hand.

Evgraf Davidov.

He'd suddenly entered very dangerous territory. The Dead Hand was something people in Igor's position knew about but never talked about. It was a part of the Russian intelligence community that even senior GRU officers were afraid to mention. Its existence had never been officially acknowledged.

And the reason was simple. Talking about the Dead Hand, or showing any kind of interest in its activities, was a death sentence.

In normal military parlance, a dead hand was an autonomous defense system, something that activated automatically, even if the people responsible for it had all been killed. The most famous was a Soviet-era system known as Perimeter. The Soviets had always been afraid of an American first strike. They knew they had enough nuclear weapons to destroy every man, woman, and child in the

United States a thousand times over, but under certain scenarios, if the Americans launched first, the Russian early-warning system gave the Kremlin just four minutes to issue a retaliatory strike. If they failed to respond in that time, Moscow would be obliterated while all its nuclear missiles were still in their silos.

To protect against this scenario, they built a system that guaranteed that if Moscow was ever hit, a retaliatory strike would be automatically launched against the United States, even if everyone in the Kremlin was dead.

To achieve this, seismic sensors were installed deep under the Russian capital. In the event of a nuclear attack, the sensors would detect the strike and automatically launch satellites across the Soviet Union. The satellites were preprogrammed with top-level General Staff launch codes, and thirty minutes after reaching orbit, they would transmit those codes to every Soviet nuclear bunker capable of responding.

Unless the satellites were recalled by the Kremlin during those thirty minutes, which would not happen if the Kremlin had been destroyed, there was no way to stop the launch codes from being transmitted.

In effect, it meant that if Moscow was ever destroyed, the rest of the world would go down with it.

After the collapse of the Soviet Union, the Perimeter system was never dismantled. It continued to provide its dead hand guarantee of mutual destruction, and the CIA and the Pentagon were all too aware of that fact.

Inside the GRU, this led to the term 'Dead Hand' being used to describe a specific special group that was secretly authorized to do anything necessary to protect the president and his position. This included maintaining a list of names of senior Russian officials, hundreds long, who would automatically be assassinated if anyone ever struck at the president personally.

It was the main reason there had never been an uprising inside the Kremlin against him. Everyone knew about the group and how ruthlessly it would act if they ever made a move.

The Dead Hand was extremely brutal, operating more like a South American drug cartel than an intelligence service. It ruled by fear, hunting and killing anyone who threatened the regime. Opposition politicians, members of the Russian parliament, even judges of the highest courts in the land had been brutally murdered in their homes, along with their families.

It made examples of its victims. It left them strung up on lamp posts in Red Square with cryptic messages stuffed in their mouths. It beheaded them, dismembered them, tortured them in ways that made even the men of the Lubyanka squirm.

And no one dared question it. To challenge the Dead Hand was to sign your own death warrant.

The President of Russia had been in power for over twenty years, and despite constitutional restraints limiting his tenure to two consecutive six-year terms, no end to his regime was in sight.

No one challenged his rule. No one in Moscow talked about regime change. No one truly expected change to occur so long as he lived.

Igor was used to living his life according to certain rules. He dealt in death every day—but the rules gave the game a modicum of order. They made it possible for him to live a relatively tolerable life, to sleep at night without fear of being shot in his bed, to eat in restaurants without fear of being poisoned, to walk in parks without fear of a sniper picking him off. Like everyone in the Kremlin, he lived within the bounds of a game set up by the Dead Hand, and so long as he remained within those bounds, he was safe.

But the moment he crossed the line, all rules ceased to apply. Nothing was sacred. Like the Perimeter system that would unconditionally destroy the planet if certain conditions were met, the Dead Hand guarded its boundaries ruthlessly.

Igor felt the sweat run down his back.

Killing Agniya, accessing this database, poking his nose where it didn't belong, brought him up against those boundaries.

His heart pounded in his chest as he logged out of the database and shut down the computer.

What he'd stumbled into had the very real potential of being a kiss of death.

52

R oth later called it the Night of the Long Knives. It was a devastating attack—a purge.

The four highest-value assassins in the nation, all with flawless records, attacked simultaneously in four separate operations.

Between them, the Assets had completed dozens of the most complex and dangerous covert actions ever attempted by the CIA. They'd assassinated heads of state, infiltrated the most secure of secure locations, rooted out moles and traitors deep within the military-industrial complex.

And all without leaving a trace.

They were so accustomed to watching their own backs that there were rumors they literally slept with their eyes open. Getting close to them was like trying to pull the tail of a cobra. They struck fast, and their fangs were razor sharp.

And in a single strike, three were gone. Dead. It was the single deadliest loss in Group history.

Roth had known he had a problem ever since the comms went down on the sixth floor. He'd been around the block too many times to believe the tech team when it said there'd been no breach. His instincts told him he was compromised. What he hadn't realized was how badly.

Now, he knew, and he desperately needed to speak to the president. The gloves were off. War was coming. But the president wasn't returning his calls.

He let out a long sigh, stood up from his desk, and went to the window. The evening traffic was thinning out. He paced across the room and opened the door.

His team was working furiously, banging away on their computer keyboards, debating in the conference room with raised voices, gesticulating at maps and images and graphs in an atmosphere that was becoming increasingly frantic.

Thirty-two people worked at Group headquarters— himself, four handlers, and twenty-seven specialists. And they'd just had their asses handed to them.

To make matters exponentially worse, Roth knew that one of them was a rat. That was the only way the Russian cyberattack possibly could have succeeded. It required a physical transmitting device to work. Someone on the inside must have planted it.

A specialist looked up at him from her desk. "Need anything, boss?"

"Get my car," he said.

He shut the door, and his eye went straight to the bar cart. He had a bottle of forty-year-old Islay single malt. It had been a gift from the president. He hadn't opened it—it was a two-thousand-dollar bottle—but he was tempted now.

He shook his head and poured himself yet another cup of coffee. He had a long night ahead of him—a lot of explaining to do. Everyone would be looking at him. No one would say it, but he was fighting for his professional life.

Four briefs had been prepared by his staff—one for each Asset.

Rebel, Camaro, Hornet, Mustang.

There wasn't much to them, a few flimsy pages, but they captured the salient details. He flicked through them. They were his last hope—because one of them had been purposefully falsified.

He read the first.

Rebel: KIA

Hotel Imperial

Ringstraße 16

Vienna, Austria

Assassin rappelled from roof of hotel and entered room through window. Eight shots fired from a suppressed .22 caliber pistol. Asset died from multiple gunshot wounds. Satellite surveillance shows indistinct figure on roof of building prior to attack.

Suspects acquired: None

Special Operations Group Database

The crime scene was in the hands of the Austrian police, and they could be trusted to acquire forensic evidence reliably. The Vienna field office had already been in touch with them. But it would lead nowhere. At best, and even that was a long shot, they would find the assassin. But Roth knew that would be the end of the line. When the Dead Hand hired assassins, and there was little doubt that this had been a Dead Hand strike, the orders always came from an unknown source—a typed note in a mailbox, an anonymous phone call, an encrypted digital message. All payments were untraceable. An assassin knew nothing of what he was doing or why, and he certainly didn't know who he was working for.

Roth opened the second file.

Camaro: KIA

Rand Airport

Johannesburg, South Africa

Asset was on board a Nextant 400XT charter jet taking off from a small aerodrome east of Johannesburg. Flight was bound for Maputo, Mozambique. CIA satellite surveillance shows a lone actor two kilometers from the runway firing a surface-to-air missile at the jet. Local sources confirm the plane was hit by a Russian-made SA-7 Grail shoulder-held, heat-seeking missile. Both pilots and all four passengers were killed in the explosion.

Suspects acquired: None

Special Operations Group Database

The third report was even shorter.

Hornet: KIA

Regent Street

London, United Kingdom

Asset struck and killed crossing Regent Street at Tenison Court. Vehicle was a stolen London TX4 hackney carriage. Metropolitan Police and MI5 in control of scene.

Suspects acquired: None
Special Operations Group Database

He held the fourth in his hand before reading it. It was the one he'd doctored. It was Lance's only chance.

Mustang: KIA

Watergate Plaza

Washington DC

Asset killed in elevator of Watergate Plaza by multiple gunshot wounds. One assailant also killed. Scene in control of DC Metro police.

Suspects acquired: None

Special Operations Group Database

There was a knock on the door. "Yes?"

"Your car is ready, sir."

He put the four files in his briefcase and hurried to the elevator. When he reached the ground floor, he rushed through the lobby and past security.

"The Watergate," he said to his driver when he got to the car.

He stared out the window as they crossed the city. Everything was decked out for Christmas, lights and trees and massive billboards announcing the start dates of various sales.

"You got holiday plans, sir?" the driver said.

Roth didn't answer.

When they arrived at the Watergate, he had the door

open before the car even stopped. "Wait here," he said to the driver before rushing off.

There were four police cars parked outside the building, and when one of the officers stopped him on his way in, he flashed some credentials and kept walking.

In the lobby, the police had congregated around one of the elevators. A dead body was lying on the floor.

They didn't pay any notice to Roth and weren't too interested in the building's security guard either, who was sitting at his desk, sipping coffee from a takeout cup. Roth walked up to him and asked, "Did they ask for the security camera footage yet?"

The guard shook his head.

"I'm going to need to see it."

"It's in the control room," the guard said, pointing down a corridor. "The data is stored remotely, but the equipment is down there."

"What's the name of the security company?" Roth said.

"Let's see," the guard said, heaving himself out of his seat. He picked up a bunch of keys and his coffee. Then he led Roth down a corridor to the control room. Inside, there was a mop and bucket, some cleaning supplies, a furnace, and some communications equipment. One of the servers had a sticker with the name 'Securico' on it.

"Thanks," Roth said.

They went back to the lobby, and Roth approached the elevator. The cops looked up, taking notice of him for the first time. "Who's in command here?" he said.

One of the cops came forward, a lanky guy with a mustache like Tom Selleck. "I am," he said.

Roth showed him the credentials, which were issued by the CIA Local Security Office, and said, "What are we looking at?"

"Looks like three gunshot wounds. We're waiting for homicide to show up and take over."

"Just the one body?" Roth said.

The cop nodded.

Roth pulled a document from his pocket and handed it to the cop. "I'm going to need you to file this for your incident report."

The officer read it, then looked up at Roth. "This says that two bodies were found."

Roth nodded and handed him a card. "Call this number," he said. "They'll walk you through the process." The number was for a specialist who'd been briefed on the situation. She didn't work inside the Group and didn't have sixth-floor security clearance. She couldn't have been Roth's mole.

The officer sighed. "Am I in for a long night?"

"There's some paperwork," Roth said, "but nothing you're not used to. You'll need to get NDA's signed by your colleagues and the security guard. Now, can I use one of these elevators?"

"You'll have to take the stairs," the officer said. "The elevators are all down."

Roth nodded, stole a glance at the body in the elevator, then made his way to the stairs. When he got to Lance's floor, he saw that the carpet was damp. Lance had cleaned it. He went to the apartment door and ran his hand along the top of the doorframe, where Lance had left a key.

He let himself into the apartment and found the would-be assassin in the bathtub, stripped to his underwear, bound and gagged, with a pillowcase over his head. Roth removed the pillowcase and untied the gag.

The assassin coughed, and when he'd regained his breath, said, "What the hell is going on?"

"You're American," Roth said.

"Yes."

"And you know that the man you tried to kill works for the CIA?"

The assassin didn't answer.

"And you work for the Russians," Roth added. "You know what that makes you?"

"What is this?" the assassin said. "A civics lesson?"

"You know what the punishment for treason is?"

The assassin clenched his jaw.

Roth knew the look in his eyes. This man had already given up the fight. It wouldn't be difficult to get him to cooperate. Roth just had to give him a little motivation. "You know where I'm going after I'm done talking to you?"

He didn't answer.

"The White House."

The assassin looked at him.

"That's right," Roth said. "And do you know who I'm going to see when I get there?"

The man said nothing.

Roth smiled. "You guessed it."

"Bullshit."

Roth shrugged. "You believe what you want to believe, but I don't have a lot of time, so I'm going to make this very simple for you. Either you tell me what I need to know, or I'll have you shipped to a CIA black site where you'll never be heard from again."

"I don't believe you."

Roth grabbed the man by the chin and forced him to look at him. "Listen to me very carefully. Either you talk now, or you go to a very dark, very painful place for a very long time. Where I'm going to send you, they have a special place for traitors. "

"I'm not a traitor," the man said.

Roth nodded. "That's good. I'm glad to hear it. Now tell me what I want to know."

"If I talk, they'll kill me."

"If you don't talk, *I'll* kill you."

The man sighed. Roth let the information sink in for a moment, then said, "What were you supposed to do after you killed your target?"

Another silence. Roth drummed his fingers on the side of the tub. Finally, the man said, "They gave me a number to call. An answering machine. I was supposed to leave a message."

"All right," Roth said. "That's what we'll do. We'll make the call and leave a message saying that you were successful."

"What happens after that?"

"I'll send someone to come get you."

"And then?"

"You'll continue to cooperate," Roth said. "My team will debrief you. If you can make yourself valuable enough, maybe you'll be able to cut yourself a deal."

"The Russians will come for me."

Roth lifted the pillowcase that Lance had put over his head. "Your other option is to get used to the idea of wearing a whole lot more of these."

He let the man mull over his options while he went to the kitchen. Lance had left the assassin's phone on the counter, and Roth got it and brought it back to the bathroom. "Ready to make the call?"

The man nodded and gave Roth the number. Roth held the phone up to the man's face while he left the message. He reported that he'd successfully killed his target and that the CIA was moving in to secure the building.

"Very good," Roth said. He would have had someone come from Langley to bring him in, but because of the mole, he couldn't risk a leak. For Lance's sake, this had to stay under wraps. "Sit tight," he said. "Someone will be along."

"Someone will be *along*? What does that mean? Be along for what?"

Roth stuffed the gag back in the man's mouth, ignoring his protests, then checked the restraints.

He stood up and looked down at the man. "Don't struggle. Don't try to escape. Someone will be right along." The last thing he did before leaving was put the pillowcase back over the man's head.

When he got to the corridor, he took out his phone and called the head of the surveillance team that had been watching the mail store in Manhattan the night Laurel was shot.

"This is Roth. I need you to do something."

"Yes, sir. What do you need?"

"This doesn't go through Langley. It doesn't go through the desk."

"Is something wrong?"

"Yes, something's wrong. I've got a rat in my house."

"I see."

"So don't talk to anyone. Don't call in your crew. This stays off the books. Understood?"

"Loud and clear, sir."

"I need you to hack into a company called Securico. You know them?"

"I've heard of them."

"There was an attack on one of my agents at the Watergate tonight. Securico runs the cameras. Will you be able to get into their servers?"

"I think so."

"Find the footage and delete it. All of it."

"Understood, sir."

"After that, I need you to come to the Watergate and do a little babysitting."

"The assailant is still there?"

"That's right. He's tied up for now, but I'd rest easier knowing you were watching him. Make sure he doesn't go anywhere."

"You got it, boss. I'll be there in a few hours."

Roth left the apartment and went back to his car.

"Where to now?" the driver said.

"The White House."

It was scarcely a five-minute drive from the Watergate to the White House security post on 17th Street. The driver took him through the checkpoint and then pulled up to the secure entrance of the Eisenhower Building, which was where Roth and the president usually met when discretion was paramount. It was a large building, with over two miles of corridor and hundreds of rooms, all built to the exacting standards of a French Second Empire palace.

Roth was greeted by an aide at the entrance and taken to the opulent four-story library, where he was to await the president. He sat on a leather sofa, imported from London in 1850, and stared into the log fire that was burning in the hearth. Next to him was a twelve-foot-high globe made of gold and opal. Above him, a hundred-bulb chandelier bathed the room in warm light.

For decades, this palace had been the very epicenter of American power. It had once housed the State Department, the War Department, and the Navy Departments, and it was from its halls that the United States became the greatest military power mankind had ever known.

It was the place where American power was born. It was where American hegemony first found its footing.

And Roth knew only too well that what had been born there could all too easily die there if he didn't step up to this present crisis.

53

L ance flew to Istanbul from Dulles on a Turkish Airlines business class ticket. On the flight, he studied the schematics for the Sverdlovsk Military Compound, as well as the other information Roth had been able to gather. Roth had compiled the brief personally—he was too afraid of leaks to have it prepared by headquarters —and it showed. It comprised sixteen disorganized, hastily typed pages, completely unformatted, and a lot of the data Lance would have expected wasn't there. Given the circumstances, he felt Roth had done pretty well. The brief had the elements—if not the complete form—of a workable plan of attack.

At Istanbul, he had a twelve-hour layover and paid for access to a lounge where he showered and got some sleep. When his second flight landed at Koltsovo Airport outside Yekaterinburg, he was ready for action.

He entered Russia on one of the passports Roth had given him, under cover of being a contractor for a French engineering firm. Lance had been ready at the airport for mishaps—none of the planning was up to the usual stan-

dard—but after a few questions, the border official waved
him through without incident.

At the airport, he rented a Volkswagen sedan from Hertz
and drove into the city on a new highway that followed the
banks of the Iset River. He left the highway at the third exit,
making his way for a weapons cache that, according to
Roth's notes, was located in an apartment building overlooking a large new supermarket. He found the supermarket, parked in the lot, and reread the file. The address was
incomplete. Roth had handwritten in the margin, 'Ninth
Floor, Apartment 93A', but he hadn't identified which building, and there were over a dozen in view.

Lance would have to go through each of them, but
before beginning, he went into the supermarket and bought
a few items that would make lock picking easier. He also
bought some local clothing so he could blend in better.
They included a pair of cheap winter boots and a knock-off
coat with faux fur lining around the hood.

He went back to the car and put them on, then walked to
the nearest apartment building and took the elevator to the
ninth floor. There was no apartment 93A. He left the
building and went to the next, hurrying across a playground
as the wind whipped up from the river. Again, the building
had an apartment 93 but no 93A. The next building only
had seven floors, so he skipped it entirely.

When he reached the fourth building, the elevator
was out.

He began the laborious climb up the stairs, and on the
landing between the third and fourth floors, came across an
old lady with heavy grocery bags.

"Let me help you," he said in Russian.

She gave him the bags, and he accompanied her to the
door of her apartment on the sixth floor—61B.

When he reached the ninth floor, he found 93A and looked up and down the corridor to make sure no one was watching. He knocked on the door. There was no answer, and he knocked a second time, harder than before.

A woman appeared at the door across the hall. "Who are you looking for?" she said. She was in her thirties and had a towel on her hair.

"My aunt," he said.

She eyed him suspiciously. "That apartment's been empty for months."

Lance nodded and made to leave. The woman watched him. He got all the way to the stairwell, and she was still there.

He could have ignored her and kicked in the door, but that would alert local law enforcement unnecessarily. He could have decided to hurt her, but that was also unnecessary. It was easiest to wait her out. He had time to spare—it was before noon, and he didn't want to enter the compound until after dark. Instead, he went back down the stairs he'd just climbed, crossed the lot to the supermarket, and bought a cup of coffee and a pastry at the bakery near the entrance.

He'd spent a lot of time in Russia, but a few years had passed since his last visit, and he felt out of touch. He sat down in the bakery and let the feel of the country come back to him. He'd always felt that the people there shared a certain no-nonsense attitude, a sense that the things people in other countries worried about were pointless—frivolous. He watched the clientele, listened in on their conversations, and finished his coffee and pastry. Then he went back to the apartment, again climbing the nine floors of stairs. When he got to the door, he quietly picked the lock and let himself in.

Inside, the apartment was completely unfurnished. In the center of the living room was a stack of plywood shipping crates. Lance opened the first and found Russian and American cash, as well as some local non-picture ID cards. He took the cash and flipped through the IDs until he found something matching his description.

The next crate contained a Czech CZ 75 semi-auto pistol, along with ammo and a suppressor. The third was larger and contained canvas carryalls and a rifle case.

He took out the heavy rifle case and laid it on the floor. Inside was an M82 sniper rifle, a night vision scope, and a selection of .50 caliber BMG ammo, including silver-tipped M8 armor-piercing incendiary rounds. With its equipment and ammo, it weighed over thirty pounds.

There was another carryall containing eleven-inch bricks of C-4 plastic explosive wrapped in Mylar film. Each brick weighed just over a pound, and together with the detonators and fuses, the bag amounted to another forty pounds.

The remaining crates contained other equipment that could be useful, including flashlights, rope, wire cutters, and a toolkit.

He packed the pistol and silencer, rifle and scope, explosives and fuses, and as much ammo and other equipment as he could carry, then let himself out of the apartment as quietly as possible, setting the latch to lock behind him. As the door shut, it clicked loudly.

Immediately, the door across the hall opened and the woman from earlier re-emerged. "You're back," she said.

Lance wasn't sure what to say. He was done with the apartment. It was a write-off now, as far as being a cache was concerned. It still contained equipment, but nothing that would give away CIA involvement. And in any case, he doubted this woman was the type to call the police.

He adjusted the weight of the straps on his shoulder.

"What's in the bags?" she said.

"I don't think you want to know."

She looked at him a moment and said, "I have a child in here. If trouble's coming this way, I'd like to know."

"No trouble," Lance said. "Just forget you ever saw me."

She nodded and shut the door. Lance looked at it for a few seconds, then went back to hauling the hundred plus pounds of equipment down nine floors of stairs.

When he reached the ground floor, he stopped and made sure she wasn't following him. She wasn't. Her apartment overlooked the supermarket, and as he made his way to the car, he knew she could be watching.

He would have to switch vehicles.

He loaded the equipment into the trunk and drove back to the airport. There, he returned the vehicle to Hertz and went to the desk of another rental company. It was a local company that specialized in premium vehicles. "I need something fast," he said.

"What's your budget?" the girl at the counter said.

"What have you got?"

"The best I can do is a BMW 5 series."

"What color is it?"

"Black."

"That will be perfect," Lance said.

54

"**S**tay down," Sofia hissed.

Olga ducked out of view, just in time to avoid being seen by a passing army jeep.

The two women were hiding out in a convenience store a few blocks from the hospital. They'd been there since the airstrike, having escaped the hospital grounds during the chaos that followed the explosion.

Sofia had been shot, and Olga had to practically carry her to safety. The army had evacuated the entire district prior to spraying the streets with chlorine, and the buildings were, for the most part, empty. Many of the windows had been blown out during the airstrike, and Olga chose the first place to hide that she could find.

As it turned out, a convenience store was actually a good place to hide. It had an entire shelf of vodka, which Olga was able to use to clean Sofia's wound, and she also found a sewing kit, which she sterilized and used to stitch it up.

They spent the first few hours in the front of the store, staying out of sight behind the shelves. They later moved to a storeroom at the back, where Olga had found a small gas heater.

There was a television in the storeroom, and Olga watched it with the volume on low while Sofia slept. The news reporting infuriated her, with government officials coming on to claim that the explosion had been caused by a gas leak at the hospital's morgue. The official line was that the morgue had been operating at overcapacity, and the hospital administrators would be held fully accountable. They were already being rounded up to face the full force of the law. The report also said that the reason for the strain on the morgue, and the reason the hospital was on lockdown in the first place, was an anthrax outbreak in the south of the city. The outbreak had been traced back to a single supermarket distributing contaminated meat. The view switched to a reporter standing in front of the offending supermarket. Olga could see the chimney stacks of the Empress Catherine rising behind it. She shook her head. No one would believe this story. Half the city must have seen the fighter jet.

Sofia continued to sleep, and as night fell and it got increasingly cold, Olga decided to search the building for somewhere warmer than the storeroom. She found an apartment on the top floor and made sure it was empty. Its windows were still intact, and its heat was running normally. She brought Sofia up to it, and they slept together in a double bed, the door to the room locked.

Throughout the night, they were woken by sporadic gunfire. The hospital had been overrun by the military, and they seemed to be clearing the surrounding streets too, gunning down any stragglers unfortunate enough to be caught in the open.

At a certain point, still a few hours before dawn, Olga

gave up trying to sleep. The shooting seemed to have quietened, and, after checking that the curtain was shut as tightly as possible, she lit a single candle.

"How's your shoulder?" she said to Sofia, who was also beginning to stir.

Sofia touched it. "I was lucky. It's just a flesh wound."

Olga nodded. She knew as much, having tended to it. She removed the bandage and replaced it with a strip of the bedsheet that she ripped from the bed.

"It's only a matter of time before they realize we're not among the casualties," Sofia said.

Olga nodded but said nothing, concentrating on the bandage. There was a sudden burst of gunfire in the street directly below. They blew out the candle and went to the window, pulling back the curtain ever so slightly.

Two soldiers were outside brandishing guns, and three bodies lay dead in the street in front of them. The soldiers left, leaving the bodies where they lay.

"What the hell is going on?" Olga stammered, dumbfounded by what she'd just seen.

"They're clearing the district," Sofia said. "They'll start going through the buildings soon too."

"Clearing the district?" Olga repeated quietly. "I don't understand."

Sofia didn't understand either. She'd never seen anything like this.

Her cell phone was dead, but there was a landline in the apartment, and she used it to try Vasily's number.

There was no answer.

There was more gunfire outside, followed by the sound of a woman screaming. "How does any of this make sense?" Olga said.

Sofia clenched her jaw. She wasn't innocent in all of this, and she knew it. She was complicit, and now innocent people were paying the price. "It makes sense to the Kremlin," she said.

"But if they're trying to orchestrate a cover-up, this is the wrong way. They're being too heavy-handed. They'll only draw more attention."

"This is what they do," Sofia said. "They lay down the law. They show us who's in control. They can act with impunity, and they want everyone in this city to know it."

Olga went back to the window and peered out at the street. Aside from the bodies, it was deserted. "It just doesn't make sense," she said again.

Sofia watched her from the bed, her form silhouetted against the light of the moon. She envied her. She was still innocent. Unlike her, Olga hadn't specialized in an area that drew the Kremlin's roving eye. She hadn't published papers on anthrax, and smallpox, and the viability of reanimating ancient pathogens. She'd never been plucked out of civilian life and thrown into the vortex that was Russia's military-industrial machine. She didn't have blood on her hands.

Not that any of that would protect her. The life Olga had known was gone. There would be no going back. The government would want a full accounting of the bodies recovered from the wreckage at the hospital, and as soon as they got it, they would begin compiling a list of names. Then, one by one, they would hunt down everyone who was left—everyone who knew what had happened there. No one who knew the extent of their crime would be left alive.

"The president needs every last citizen of this country to know that they can lose their life by his hand at any moment," Sofia said. "That's how he rules. That's how he maintains order. Any time, any place, it doesn't matter who you are, it doesn't matter what TV cameras are watching, he can kill us with complete impunity, and no one will lift a finger to stop him. Not the Americans. Not the Europeans. Not NATO."

"He's shooting people in the street like dogs," Olga said.

Sofia nodded. That was exactly the point. She got up from the bed and relit the candle. Then she went to the kitchen and put on a pot to make coffee. Olga followed her and took a seat at the table.

"We can't stay here," Sofia said to her.

"But where can we go?"

"I've got to speak to Vasily. He'll have a plan."

"But he's not picking up," Olga said.

"If I can get to the institute—"

"They'll shoot you on the spot," Olga gasped.

"There's no other choice. The longer we wait, the more time we give them to figure out we're not among the dead."

A silence stretched out, then Olga said, "I'm coming with you."

Sofia didn't respond. She finished making the coffee, then poured two cups and joined Olga at the table. "Olga, if we don't make it…."

"I'm coming with you," Olga said again.

Sofia took a sip of her coffee, then said quietly, "Thank you."

Olga nodded. "We should leave soon. Before it gets light."

They went back to the bedroom and searched the closets for civilian clothes. Their doctors' scrubs would be a giveaway.

From the clothing they found, it was clear that an older couple lived in the apartment. The woman was similar in size to both of them, but her style was dramatically more mature.

"You look like one of my old school teachers," Olga said when Sofia presented herself.

"You look like my father's secretary," Sofia said.

As they left the building, the first signs of dawn were just beginning to appear on the horizon. They left through a side exit and avoided the main street. They each had a car in the hospital lot, but going there now was out of the question. They proceeded on foot, sticking to side alleys and cutting a wide berth around any military presence.

Once they got out of the cordoned area, traffic seemed to be relatively normal. They found a bus stop and joined a few other early morning commuters. When the bus arrived, they boarded, feeling very exposed in its bright light. They took a seat at the back, sitting so close to each other they looked like surreptitious lovers.

They got off the bus near the central square, and it was as if they'd entered another world. Walking past the cafés and stores that were getting ready to open for the day, it was hard to believe the atrocities they'd witnessed were just a short bus ride away.

"I feel like we've crossed into a different world," Olga said.

Sofia looked around. This area was affluent, and the people still felt that the government was on their side. The system was working for them, and it had their support. These people didn't want to think about airstrikes and soldiers gunning down their fellow citizens in the streets. They'd voted for the president and would continue to do so. The thing was, Sofia knew that the people at the hospital, and the workers at the Empress Catherine factory, had felt the same way. "We're not safe here," she said.

Olga nodded, and they hailed the first cab they could. They asked the driver to drop them off near the entrance to the compound, but even before they got there, Sofia could see it would be impossible to reach Vasily. There was a heavy security presence in the area, and the military had set up checkpoints approaching the compound.

"This won't work," Sofia said under her breath.

Olga nodded. "We need somewhere to lay low." She gave the driver the address for her apartment, and they got out a few hundred yards from the building. "I don't know if this is safe," she said as they approached the entrance.

"Safer than wandering the streets," Sofia said.

They entered the building and took the elevator to Olga's floor. Olga gave Sofia a worried look, but when the doors opened, the corridor was all clear. They went to Olga's door, and she unlocked it.

The door swung open ominously, and there was no one inside.

"Does everything look normal?" Sofia said as Olga locked the door behind them. "Do you think anyone's been here?"

Olga shook her head. "It looks fine." There was a half-eaten slice of toast on the kitchen counter, and Olga looked at it. "I feel like a year has passed since I was here."

Sofia went to the phone and tried Vasily's number again while Olga packed a bag with some essential belongings, including her passport and whatever cash and jewelry she had at hand.

"Still no answer," Sofia said, hanging up the phone. She stood by the window and watched the street below while Olga finished packing.

"What are we going to do?" Sofia said when Olga came

out of the bedroom, a leather overnight bag slung over her shoulder.

"We need to get as far from here as possible."

"But how far are we going to get? I don't think it's even safe to use our passports."

"We can get a train," Olga said. "We can go to Irkutsk."

Sofia shook her head. She knew it would be one of the first places the government looked for them.

"They're going to find us, aren't they?" Olga said.

Sofia nodded.

"And Vasily—"

"Vasily's... *incommunicado*," Sofia said, refusing to allow herself to think of what might have happened to him.

"So," Olga said, "what now? Do we turn ourselves in? We saw what they were doing to the people in the streets."

"I have one idea," Sofia said hesitantly.

"What is it?" Olga said.

"Something we might be able to trade."

"Trade? With who?"

"I don't know. The West?"

"The Americans?"

Sofia nodded. "If we can get to one of their consulates, I don't know...."

"What did they mix you up in, Sofia?"

There was no judgment in Olga's voice, only sympathy, but the question brought a knot of emotion to Sofia's chest. "They might be watching my apartment," she said. "I work at the institute. I'm higher on the priority list."

Olga nodded. "And we have to go there?"

"I have some files on a hard disk hidden beneath the sink. Things the government wouldn't want to get out."

"Things the Americans would want to see?"

Sofia nodded.

"Then it's our only chance," Olga said.

They left Olga's apartment as cautiously as they'd entered and hailed another cab. When they reached Sofia's building, Olga waited in the cab while Sofia went to the entrance.

"Doctor Ivanova," her doorman said.

"Petr," she said, trying to sound as relaxed as possible, "I didn't expect to see you still here."

"I'm covering for Mikhail," he said. "His wife works at the Empress Catherine, so he couldn't come in."

"I see," Sofia said, feeling another knot of emotion forming in her throat. "And has anyone come calling for me?"

"Not a soul," he said. "Been here all night."

She beckoned Olga to join her, and they hurried through the lobby to the elevator. When the door shut, Olga looked at her. "Are you all right?"

Sofia shook her head. "I'm fine."

"This isn't your fault, Sofia."

"You don't know that," Sofia said. "You don't know the things I've done."

"I know you, though, and I know you wouldn't purposefully hurt people."

Sofia let out an almost inaudible laugh. "*Hurt* people? If only you knew what I gave them—the power, the destructive potential."

"You're not responsible for what they do."

"But I am responsible for this outbreak. These germs were in a place so remote, so far from human settlement, that no one should ever have been within a hundred miles of them."

"You did what you had to do," Olga said. "They gave you no choice."

Sofia suddenly felt it all coming down on her. Now that she was here, in her own building, the gravity of the last few days suddenly hit her like a ton of bricks. She couldn't breathe. She had to get out of the elevator. The second the doors opened, she rushed past Olga into the corridor.

And the instant she stepped out, a man grabbed her by the throat and slammed her against the wall.

55

Igor looked at the clunky phone on his desk for a long time. He was painfully aware that what he was about to do could well end up being the thing that killed him. Maybe not soon, maybe not for years, but when death came, as it surely would, it would trace back directly to this moment.

And yet, it was a call he had to make.

It was the price of admission, the path to power, the key to the kingdom. Whatever his fears, he'd long ago learned that the only way to do this job, to inhabit this world, was to accept that one day it would kill him. Anything less would be a weakness, and men like Davidov could smell weakness a mile away.

He picked up the phone and was about to dial when he stopped himself.

His hand was trembling. He glanced at the cupboard under his desk and, even as he told himself he needed a clear head, reached down and pulled out a bottle.

He poured four ounces of vodka into his teacup, then got up and brought it to the window. He looked out at the massive construction site. The first time he saw that view, he'd thought it was the grandest moment of his life. Before that, he'd spent sixteen years in a windowless office on the second floor, categorizing NATO intercepts.

There'd been times when he thought he was destined to spend his entire life in that second-floor office. It was little more than a closet. There'd been an old clock on the wall above the door, and he was certain he'd spent more of his life looking at its round face than at anything else on earth.

But then, advancing in an organization like the GRU was, above all else, a waiting game. And it was in that closet that Igor learned to wait.

He waited, he watched, and eventually, something happened.

His job had been to read intercepts, to categorize them. Someone else, higher up the chain, would decide what they meant. In sixteen years, he must have read over fifty thousand intercepts. While some related to important developments like troop movements along the frontier, or the location of NATO defensive missile systems in former socialist states, the vast majority were exceedingly mundane. They covered topics like the seating arrangement at a formal function in Paris, or the maintenance records for water heaters at a military housing facility in Berlin, or parking permits for visitors at the American embassy in Madrid.

Igor read them all, and in sixteen years, no one ever asked his opinion on them.

They should have. Because, alone in his closet, Igor was paying attention. The names and codenames gradually became actual people to him. When ambassadors' wives sat next to each other at dinner parties, he pictured them in their gowns and pearls. He imagined what they spoke of. He figured out who was friends with whom, who liked each other, and, most importantly, who hated each other. When someone lost their parking spot at an embassy or gained a corner office at a consulate, Igor noticed.

He had a talent for picking up on patterns, and the intercepts formed a vast tapestry in his mind. The people became more real to him than the people in his own life. Their petty communications took on the status of groundbreaking revelations.

He became a machine for decoding the soap opera of intrigues that played out across thirty nations, from the Atlantic coast of Portugal to the shores of Turkish Anatolia, and from the Finnish Arctic to the North African coast.

He saw NATO for what it was. He saw the players as characters in a tragic play. They were a different species to him—people who loved and laughed and cried and had hopes and dreams. They were people who lived life.

Igor was not a person like that. He was not a participant. Igor was the one who watched.

One day, when a low-level embassy staffer in Vilnius began passing information to a contact she met at a Paris ball, Igor saw it with all the vividness of an opera.

And when a member of the German parliament was assassinated in his Berlin apartment a few days later, Igor felt like he was watching the blade actually slit the man's throat.

Of course, he made the connection. He saw how the two events, a thousand kilometers apart, were connected. He saw the bigger picture.

And more importantly, he saw how to exploit it.

Bringing his findings to his bosses had been a gamble, but within six months, he was on the eighth floor. Two years later, he was in the director's office, with its view and its nubile secretaries and its armed guards in brass-buttoned uniforms.

Now, for the second time in his life, he was going to take a risk.

He'd spent the night reading every single entry in Agniya's restricted database. He'd figured out what the codes stood for, who the players were, and how they related to each other. In a single night, he'd put together in his head the rich tapestry that was the Russian top tier, the Kremlin's elite players, and the Dead Hand organization that safe-guarded their interests.

He knew what they wanted, and what they feared.

As he dialed, he took a sip of the vodka and told himself that fortune favored the bold.

A voice answered, a woman, and to Igor's ear, her accent put her in Krasnogorsk—exactly where he'd expected her. This woman knew who was calling, and that was the point. She provided verification, like an escrow service. When she called Davidov, she would be able to assure him that Igor was who he said he was.

"I need to place a call," Igor said.

"Destination?"

"Evgraf Davidov. Prime Directorate."

"Authorization code?"

Igor gave Agniya's authorization code.

"Stand by. I will call you back at this number in exactly fifteen minutes."

Igor hung up. He lit a cigar to calm his nerves. He waited, smoking and sipping vodka, and almost knocked the phone off the desk when it finally rang.

"This is Aralov," he said.

"Please hold for Director Davidov."

He waited and a moment later heard the connection click. "Director Davidov?" he said nervously.

"Director Aralov," Davidov said.

The two men had never met, and Davidov's voice sounded odd to Igor, like he was sucking a lozenge. He found it faintly nauseating. "Please, sir. Call me Igor."

"Very well," Davidov said without reciprocating the courtesy. "You have some nerve making this call, *Igor*."

"It's not what you think, sir."

"You shouldn't have killed Agniya Bunina. She was under my protection."

"She betrayed me, sir."

"You let your feelings for her cloud your judgment."

"I had no feelings for her."

"You had a camera installed in her bedroom, you creep. You accessed the feed every single night. I know you, Igor Aralov. I've seen your hand pumping your little cock at that desk you sit at now, so don't lie to me."

"Sir!" Igor gasped, his face reddening.

"The only reason you're still alive is because I thought you might be useful. But I was wrong."

"Wrong? Sir, please," Igor said, panic flooding through him. "I can break the American for you. Laurel Everlane. I know her weakness."

"I don't need you to break her."

"I know what you're planning, sir. I know what you need from her."

"I'm not planning anything," Davidov said, his voice betraying his agitation.

"Of course not, sir. But I can break her for you. Torture her for you."

"Timokhin is going to break her, Igor. He's got a knack for that sort of thing."

"Spector then. I can get you Spector."

Davidov laughed. "How do you propose to do that?"

"I'll pick up where Tatyana left off."

"She had a connection with him, Igor. She and the American had a... *thing*."

"I know what they had."

"No offense to you, but I hardly think you're going to have quite the same *appeal*."

"I know how to trap him. If she's still out there, I can pretend to be her. I know everything about her. I can draw him in, make it look like she's still trying to make contact."

"Spector is already dead, Igor."

"What?"

"All of Roth's Assets are dead."

"How is that possible?"

"You don't know as much as you think you know."

"Sir!"

"Don't play coy with me, Igor. I knew the instant you accessed the database. You've been on it all night, brushing up on the answers, getting ready for this call like it's some sort of school exam."

"Director, sir! Please let me explain."

"There's nothing to explain."

"Sir, please! I have *kompromat* on everyone. Thousands of Americans. The NSA. The CIA. Whoever you want."

"You're referring to your collection of sex tapes?"

"They're valuable, sir. Let me prove it."

"How?"

"Roth. I can get you Roth."

"I think that maybe you read too many secrets, Igor."

"I know you want Roth, sir." Igor was begging, pleading for his life. He was desperate, and they both knew it. He'd accessed the Dead Hand's database. That meant either he proved his worth on this call, or he was a dead man. "I'm begging you, sir! Let me go after Roth for you."

"Roth's on the ropes," Davidov said. "I've hacked his network. His Assets are dead."

"Let me finish him off."

"I don't need you to finish him off. The American President is shutting down the Special Operations Group as we speak. Roth is done. He's a spent force. A week from now, he won't even have a Secret Service detail."

"Sir!" Igor gasped. This was it—his last-ditch attempt. It was all or nothing. "I see the big picture."

"Oh, bully for you, Igor."

"I know what you're doing, sir. I'm not just another yes-man like Timokhin. I'm more valuable than him."

"You think so?" Davidov said. Igor could hear the sneer in his voice.

"This pathogen in Yekaterinburg. I understand why you're letting it out."

"Letting it out?"

"Yes, sir."

"We're not letting it out. We're doing everything in our power to contain it."

Igor was reaching. He was acting on a hunch. The database had said nothing about the outbreak, and Igor was sure Davidov himself wasn't totally aware of what was going on up there. But it was a problem, and Igor was going to solve it for him. "You want the Americans to know about this leak."

"That leak has killed over a thousand people, Igor."

"Casualties of war, sir."

"What are you talking about?"

"You know what all master strategists know. I've seen it in your plans. It's genius."

"What is?"

"I know how to read between the lines, sir." He had Davidov's attention. He'd found something Davidov was interested in. Now, all he had to do was close the deal.

"Why don't you enlighten me?" Davidov said.

"Well, sir. What's the point in having a weapon as destructive as this pathogen if no one knows of its existence?"

"Continue."

"It would have no deterrent effect."

"Perhaps we don't intend to use it as a deterrent."

"As a tactical weapon, it has no value. It's like mustard gas. It flows everywhere—kills everyone. It would kill as many of our men as the enemy's."

"Then why did we develop it?"

Igor knew the true answer. It was the same reason they did anything. They developed it because of its immense destructive power, because their scientists had the knowledge to do it, and because they'd been ordered to. In terms of the pain and death it could deliver, it was as powerful as an army—as powerful as a nuke. When God smote Pharoah, he did so with plagues. The president wanted that same power.

The Russian President was a paranoiac. Igor knew that. He'd seen the clinical reports. The man was obsessed with holding onto his power. He grasped for every inch of it like a deranged miser. He was consumed with stamping out every trace of internal dissent. And he was fixated on the wave of forces emanating from the United States that threatened to relegate Russia's superpower status to the dustbin of history.

"You developed it," Igor said, "because you want the Americans to fear we're preparing for war."

"We can't win a war with the Americans," Davidov said.

But Igor already knew he was on the right track. "We don't have to win a war," he said. "We only have to keep the president in power."

"There's no risk to the president's position."

"I know that, sir. Of course there's no risk. The president is as secure as a king. As a god, even."

There was a pause. They both knew that was not true.

Igor filled the silence by saying, "We're simply putting our pieces on the board. Taking up the best positions."

He waited.

Davidov was silent for a moment. Then he said, "Are you a student of history, Igor?"

Igor took a deep breath. He wasn't out of the woods yet. "I am, sir."

"Do you remember what the Germans said before the First World War?"

"They said many things."

"They said, 'better now than later.'"

"They did, sir."

"That was a war they couldn't win," Davidov said.

"And they knew it, sir. That was why they wanted a fight in 1914. Because it was better than a fight in 1915, or 1920."

"Exactly."

"I understand that, sir. And I can help you make others understand it."

Davidov sighed. "Maybe," he said.

Igor knew he'd done it. He could feel it. He'd saved himself. He cleared his throat. "Tatyana Aleksandrova," he said. "I taught her everything she knows. Let me find her for you."

"You don't have the first clue where she is."

"But I know her, sir. I know how she operates. I know how she thinks."

"If you knew her so well, she wouldn't have slipped through your fingers in the first place."

"Sir, Timokhin ran that hit."

"Careful what you say about Timokhin, Igor."

"Give me this one chance, sir. You want her back. I know you do. We can't let her get away with this betrayal."

"I don't trust you to bring her in."

"Of course I'll bring her in."

"You've had a taste, you filthy swine. You're fond of her now."

"On my mother's grave, sir, I'll bring her in."

"Why should I believe that?"

"Because she's a traitor, sir, and my track record speaks for itself. Look what I've done to those who betrayed me. Look at Agniya Bunina. I had a taste there too, but that didn't stop me. If you let me go after Tatyana, I'll cut her throat and rip her heart out through the slit."

56

L aurel was strung up like a slaughtered steer. The rope had rubbed the flesh raw on her wrists, and she could feel blood dripping down her arms. Her bullet wound had been cleaned and bandaged, but it burned in agony.

She was in an ice-cold, pitch-black room, and the pain in her arms had gone from extreme, to absolutely unbearable, to completely and utterly numb.

She had no idea how much time had passed. It could have been hours. It could have been days. She fell in and out of consciousness.

When the lights finally came on, and she saw an enormous bear of a man entering the room, it was almost a relief.

"Laurel Everlane," the man bellowed.

Laurel was blinded by the floodlights that were pointed right at her.

"Tell me about your friend, Levi Roth," he said.

This wasn't the same man she'd seen at the airport hangar. He was a giant, a freak of nature, and in his hand was a long, thin blade. The steel glinted in the light and reminded her of the knives used to scale fish.

He pushed a yellow button, and a crank began to turn, slowly lowering the rope that held her until her feet brushed the ground. As well as the yellow button, she saw that there was also a green one and a red one.

She was too weak to hold herself up, and as the crank continued to lower her, she slowly crumpled into a pile. It was only then that she realized she was naked.

The room had the feel of a cellar. No light came in from outside. The floor was wet. Water was dripping somewhere. The ceiling was about twenty feet above her with a small ventilation shaft above a crossbeam.

Apart from the lights, the man, the rope, and the winch, the room was empty.

The man pushed the green button, and the rope again grew taut, gradually pulling her up—pulling her arms over her head, then forcing her onto her knees, then her feet, before finally lifting her back off the ground toward the beam.

She cried while it happened. She tried not to, but she couldn't help it. When her limbs were forced to take the full weight of her body again, she screamed.

He let it raise her about a foot from the ground and then said again, "Tell me about your old friend, Levi Roth."

She said nothing, but the way he spoke—so jovially, so casually—it made her feel like it wouldn't be such a bad thing if she did. Even if it was just to tell him a little of what he wanted to hear. She could lie to him. What harm would that do?

He pushed the yellow button, and again, she was slowly lowered to the ground, the weight on her feet relieving her arms, her shoulders, her elbows and wrists.

She crumpled back onto the ground, and he came over to her.

"I met him once," he said in heavily accented English. "We were friends then." He looked at her for a reaction. "It's true. He poured me a very fine scotch. A bottle he'd been given by the president, if I remember correctly. You'd never believe it now, of course, it's hard for people your age to imagine, but the CIA and the GRU were the best of friends back then. Gorbachev and Bush were practically golfing buddies. We were all pals, all backslapping and glad-handing—all so full of promises."

Laurel lay on the ground, struggling to breathe, the searing agony burning in her limbs.

"So gullible, you Americans," he continued. "You thought because the Wall was coming down, that you'd won the war." He let out a chuckle. "You used to know better. Wars don't end like that. They don't end on a golf course. Only when your opponent has been brought to his knees, only when he is staring annihilation in the face and has seen the very bottom of the abyss, is war over."

She tried to back away from him but was too weak.

He reached out and touched her cheek. His tone softened. "He likes the ladies, doesn't he, your boss?" His thumb caressed her face, making her skin crawl. "I'll admit, I'm no angel myself, but your boss...." He whistled to emphasize his point. "It really is quite shocking. With all your political correctness, I never thought Americans would tolerate such behavior."

Laurel struggled to focus. The light was so bright she could hardly see.

"He's as bad as any GRU director," the man continued. "I'll grant him that much."

Laurel summoned the strength to push his hand from her cheek.

He smiled and grabbed her hair suddenly, yanking her head back. "It always was blondes with him, too. Yes, always blondes, and always young. So very young. Too young, if you ask me."

Laurel knew what he was doing. At some level, deep in her mind, her brain knew the techniques he was using and the results they were designed to elicit. She knew how they worked. She'd been trained in all of it.

But it was so hard for her brain to make itself heard above all that pain.

"He never had a liking for *you*, did he?" the man said, letting go of her hair. "I mean, I would understand if he did, pretty little thing like you. Young enough to be his granddaughter. I could forgive him even. I mean, look at you."

He took her chin in his hand and forced her to face him. She strained to make out his features.

"But that wouldn't be right, would it?" he said. "He's your boss, after all. It would be an abuse of his position. America is a civilized country. There are rules against that sort of thing. I mean, we all know they're not always obeyed, but still, you pay lip service to them. You *try* to live up to them, am I right?"

He leaned in closer. She could smell the acrid odor of his breath.

"You wouldn't ever let a man like Roth get under your skirt, my dear, would you?"

It took all the strength she had, all of her courage, but she managed to do one thing in response to his question. She spat straight in his face.

He smacked her hard with the back of his hand, then

stood. "Feisty little bitch," he muttered, then went to the wall and pushed the green button.

The rope began hoisting her back up. When she was a foot above the ground, he released the button and she stopped. "It does go higher, you know. All the way to the ceiling."

She said nothing and he put his finger over the red button. He looked up at her and she was certain she'd never seen a face so vile. He sneered, then pushed the red button. Instantly, she dropped. She fell hard against the ground and screamed in agony. When the pain receded enough for her to think, she was sure she'd broken both her legs.

"Oh," he said in a nauseatingly saccharine tone. "I'm so sorry, my dear. Did I push the wrong button? Let me try that again." Again, he pushed the green button, and again, the machine began cranking her upward. He held it until she was not one foot above the ground, but two. "Anything to tell me about your old friend?" he said.

She spat again, and blood came out of her mouth.

"I'll tell you what," he said. "You tell me if he ever fucked you, and in return, I won't push this red button." A smirk crossed his leering face. He wet his lips with his tongue. "I mean, I don't see why you should suffer for a secret like that. Do you? He shouldn't be doing it in the first place. At his age, he should have learned to keep it in his pants. Why keep that secret for him? Why pay in agony to hide his shame?"

There was something about this line of questioning that was getting under her skin. She was ready to take the pain, she was ready to hold out until the end, but there was something she had to get off her chest first.

He put his finger back on the red button and she strained to speak. No words came out.

"What's that?" the man said. "Throat a bit dry, is it?"

She moaned something unintelligible.

"No," he said. "I didn't quite make that out. Maybe another spill will loosen you up."

"He never laid a finger on me," Laurel managed to croak.

"Very good," the man said. "He never laid a finger on you. Good for him. And good for you. What would people say about you around the office if he had?"

He pushed the button.

57

"Get into the apartment," Lance said in Russian.

He was holding one woman in front of him, his CZ 75 pistol pressed against her temple. The other was frozen in terror.

"Go on, get inside," he said again.

The door was unlocked.

The woman he held was beginning to panic. She couldn't breathe. Her friend was about to scream. Lance said, "Don't make a sound, or she dies."

The friend stepped into the apartment, and Lance, still holding the other woman, entered behind them and kicked the door shut.

"Are you armed?" he said to the friend.

She didn't respond. Her eyes were glued to the two dead soldiers on the floor in the middle of the room. Blood pooled around their heads like crimson halos.

A cat mewled insistently from the bedroom. Lance had locked her inside to keep her from the bodies.

"Sit down," he said to the friend.

She sat on the sofa, and he pushed the other woman

down next to her. The two of them stared at him, numb with terror. They were already exhausted—he could see that much. They were close to their limit. He knew who they were, knew they were doctors, and had a likely idea of what they'd been through since the beginning of their ordeal. They were unlikely to be a threat.

He pointed the gun at them and told them to put their hands on their heads. Then he patted them down to check they weren't armed.

The woman he'd grabbed was the scientist Roth had shown him—Sofia Ivanova. "You've been shot," he said to her.

"I'll be okay," she said.

"You're sure?"

"We're *doctors*," the other said.

The cat was so loud it was distracting. Lance went to the bedroom and opened the door. It ran into the room and jumped onto Sofia's lap. Sofia's eyes filled with tears.

"I fed her," Lance said, putting the gun in his belt. "And I know who you are. You're Doctor Sofia Ivanova, director of the Permafrost Pathogen Institute."

Sofia said nothing.

He turned to the other. "And you're Doctor Olga Abramova of the Infectious Disease Center."

Sofia looked from Olga to Lance. "She's got nothing to do with this. She's a colleague, a doctor from the hospital, nothing more."

"I know that."

"Then what are you going to do with me?" Olga demanded.

Lance raised an eyebrow. For someone in her position, she was surprisingly punchy. "Well," he said, "I can't just let you waltz out of here, can I?"

She said nothing.

"Besides, I don't think you'd make it very far."

"You have no idea how far I'd make it."

Lance shrugged.

Olga turned to Sofia. "But I'm not going anywhere without you."

The relief on Sofia's face was palpable. Lance went to the door and made sure it was locked. Then he went to the window and pulled back the curtain a few inches.

"You're American," Sofia said.

"What gave it away?" he said, watching the street below.

"You need to work on your accent."

He turned back to them. "We don't have a lot of time. We should move."

The women looked at the two dead soldiers.

"They were here when I got here," Lance said.

"Like that?" Sofia said.

He shook his head. "No. Not like that."

"Oh," she said, realizing her mistake.

"Did you know they were looking for you?"

"I thought they would take longer to realize I wasn't caught in the blast."

Lance looked at her closely. She wasn't resisting him. She wasn't fighting back. If anything, she seemed relieved he was there. It wouldn't have gone well for her if the soldiers had been alive when she got there, and she knew it.

He decided to roll the dice on Roth's assessment that she'd be willing to help. "As you might have guessed," he said, "I'm not here for a social visit."

"You're here for the research," Sofia said, eyeing Olga as she said it. "The live samples. The models."

"I'm here to destroy the virus and everything that would allow your government to recreate it."

Sofia's face was a mix of emotions. She looked from Olga to Lance. "Thank God," she said quietly.

"You don't object?"

"I'm relieved."

"Then you'll help?"

"How could I? I wouldn't know where to start."

"I can get into the institute," Lance said, "but I need you to show me exactly what needs to be destroyed."

"It will be dangerous," Sofia said, looking at Olga again. "For all of us."

Olga reached out and put her hand on Sofia's. "We have to do this," she said. "There's no other way."

"But this isn't your problem to fix," Sofia said. "It's not your fault. You had nothing to do with any of it."

"Maybe," Olga said, "but then, I was never leaned on by the government. If I'd been put in the position you were in, I have no doubt I'd have made the same decisions you made."

Sofia said nothing, and Lance cleared his throat. "All right," he said. "So we're clear on what needs to be done?"

"I can take you to the live samples," Sofia said. "And I can show you the servers that contain the relevant research."

Lance nodded. "We need to hurry. Like I said before, time's not on our side."

"There are files here too," Sofia said. "Backups of the key findings."

Something about the way she said 'key findings' gave Lance the feeling she wanted to say more. "What do you mean?" he said.

"I made copies. Things that I could trade if things got... *complicated.*"

"Trade?"

"With your government."

"I don't think this is the time to be cutting deals," Lance said.

"This virus is the real thing," Sofia said. "It's... *powerful*. Your government is going to want to see my files. "

"I know what kind of power this virus is."

"It's our ticket," Sofia said. "For both of us. I know how the world works. Without some form of leverage to bargain with, we'll be thrown to the wolves as soon as you no longer have a use for us."

Lance was quiet for a moment, then he said, "You'd trust the American government with a thing like this?"

He saw the doubt in her face. "More than I trust the Kremlin."

"Hmm," he said.

"What's the matter?" she said. "Too much self-interest for your delicate sensibilities?"

"No," he said, "not too much. You should look out for yourselves, by all means."

"I'm still sensing you don't approve."

"I'll tell you what," he said. "How about you destroy your backups too, destroy everything, and I'll make sure you're not left in the cold?"

"Without those files...."

"You'll have no leverage?"

She nodded.

"You need to ask yourself, is that the kind of leverage you want?"

"What's the alternative? Please don't tell me it's trusting you."

He smiled thinly, then gave her a slight shrug.

"Forgive me," she said, "for not feeling very reassured."

"Look," Lance said, "you're between a rock and a hard

place. None of this is ideal. You've got to choose between bargaining with the devil and trusting me."

"The US government is not the devil."

Lance shrugged again, which only seemed to frustrate her further.

"So you'd prefer that I put our lives in your hands? Put all our trust in you and your word?"

"Safer money is on me," Lance said.

"Oh, *really*?"

Olga interjected. "Sofia, I trust him."

Sofia looked at them both for a moment, then got up and went to the desk across the room, where she began deleting files from her computer.

"No funny business," Lance said.

When she was done with the computer, she went into the bedroom and returned with two external hard drives.

"That's everything?" Lance said, taking them from her.

She nodded. He brought the hard drives over to the stove in the kitchen and turned on a gas burner. Then he held each drive over the flame with some tongs until the circuitry melted completely. The apartment quickly filled with the acrid smell of melting plastic.

"What about the soldiers?" Sofia said as she stepped over them.

"They won't be troubling anyone."

"They'll think we killed them," she said.

"I'm sorry, ladies," Lance said, "but that ship has sailed. You're going to be on the run for a lot more than murder for the rest of your lives."

Olga looked scared, but Sofia said, "How do you propose we get inside the institute? There are soldiers all over it."

"Leave that to me," Lance said. "I'll figure something out."

"Why don't you let me make a phone call first?" Sofia said.

"Who are you calling?"

"One of the scientists inside the compound. He'll help us get in."

"Be careful what you say," Lance said. "They might be listening."

Sofia went to the landline and dialed a number. She looked surprised when someone actually picked up. "Vasily! Are you all right?"

Lance went over and pressed the speaker button on the phone.

Vasily was whispering, afraid of being overheard. "Sofia, where are you?"

She hesitated. Lance shook his head. "What's the situation there?" she said, ignoring his question. "What's going on?"

"Don't come here," he said. "Get as far away as possible. Yevchenko and his men are asking everyone if they know where you are."

"What did you tell them?"

"I told them you'd gone to the hospital but it looks like he's gearing up for a manhunt."

"What about you? What are they going to do to you and the others?"

"Honestly..." Vasily said before letting his voice trail off.

"What is it, Vasily?"

"We're the enemy now, Sofia. They've brought in a new team from Moscow. They're handing everything over to them."

"Who are they?"

"They're from the Fifteenth Directorate. They're packing

up our samples, our methodology, everything, and taking it back to Moscow."

"What's going to happen to you, Vasily?"

"There's nothing you can do for me now."

"Vasily—"

"They're going to kill us, Sofia. All of us."

58

Roth was left waiting in the Eisenhower Building's library for over an hour. As he stared into the flames of the log fire, he began to doze. When someone finally arrived, they had to wake him.

"Roth," a tall man with tightly curled red hair said. Then louder, "Levi!"

"Oh," Roth said, rousing himself, "Mansfield. *You're* here?"

Mansfield rubbed a finger on the side of his mouth to indicate Roth had been drooling. Roth wiped his mouth and began rising to his feet.

"Please," Mansfield said, "don't trouble yourself."

Roth, looking up at Mansfield's youthful vigor and dashing good looks, suddenly felt very old and tired. Mansfield was everything Roth was not and never would be, regardless of how hard he tried. Mansfield had attended all the best schools, knew all the right people, and was a member of all the right clubs. At Princeton, there was a library named after his grandfather. At the Annapolis Yacht Club, he had the best mooring, right next to the clubhouse.

And at the Berehaven Country Club, he'd been given an honorary lifetime membership on his seventh birthday.

Roth still remembered the very polite letter he'd received from Berehaven when he applied for membership. That was over forty years ago now, back when he still entertained the possibility of hobnobbing with the elites. The letter said he was ineligible for membership without specifying why. This despite the fact he'd been on a waiting list for three years, was willing to pay the sixty thousand dollar initiation fee, and had been invited by a current member and then-CIA Director, David Connery.

"Isn't it past your bedtime?" Roth said.

Mansfield smiled thinly. "Why don't you straighten yourself up for the president?" he said. "You look like a bum."

There was a crystal water tumbler on the table, and Roth poured himself a glass. He was just taking a sip when the president's foghorn voice preceded him into the room.

"Gentlemen," he bellowed.

Even now, after all these years, his Maine accent still sounded to Roth like someone's cheap impression of a Nantucket whaler.

"I was beginning to worry you didn't want to see me," Roth said.

"Of course I wanted to see you," the president said, butchering the words.

President Montgomery wasn't a tall man, Roth had a good six inches on him, but he was as thick and muscular as a bulldog. Everyone, from *New York Times* cartoonists to the editorial board of the *Economist*, compared him to Winston Churchill. This was because of his physique, his manners, his clothing, and the enormous cigars he perpetually smoked. He'd won some notoriety for himself by lighting them up even in the nation's most hallowed government buildings, in direct contravention of the federal government's zealous public health rules.

He had a cigar now, unlit. Mansfield suddenly had a lighter in his hand and offered it up obsequiously.

"Always ready to help," Roth said.

The president leaned into the lighter and puffed. When the cigar was lit, he said, "How about something to drink?"

"Mr. President, if I can be so blunt as to get to the point?" Roth said.

"By all means," the president said, looking at Mansfield.

"My operation has been the target of a concerted attack."

The president nodded. "Mansfield briefed me."

Roth looked at Mansfield, who was nodding eagerly. "I see," he said. He would have liked to wring Mansfield's neck for him.

"Four strikes. All four Assets out of action," the president said.

"Yes, sir. Simultaneous actions in London, Johannesburg, Vienna, and here in DC. I've never seen anything like it."

The president looked at Mansfield. Mansfield gave him a knowing nod, as if to confirm something they'd already discussed.

"Roth," the president said, "according to my NSA bulletin, your operation has been completely and irredeemably compromised."

"I admit there's been a breach, sir."

"From what Mansfield says, every Russian agent from Saint Petersburg to Yakutsk has been poking around your hard drive."

"I think that's an exaggeration, sir."

"In any case, the Group is in no position to assist in the current situation?"

"Without the Assets, sir, I'm afraid that's true."

"In which case, I'm handing responsibility for containing the bioweapon threat to Mansfield."

Mansfield, still nodding like one of those Elvis car ornaments, looked like he'd just been made hall monitor by the teacher.

Roth hesitated. He wanted to speak to the president alone but didn't know how to tactfully get Mansfield to get lost.

"How about something to drink?" the president said again, stepping toward the drinks cabinet.

"Mansfield," Roth said, "have you got boots on the ground in Yekaterinburg?"

Mansfield looked at the president, and the next thing he said made Roth want to knock his lights out.

"I think, given the compromised status of the Group, that I should keep my operation as compartmentalized as possible."

"What are you implying?" Roth said, jaw clenched.

"Why, Levi! Did I touch a nerve?"

Roth took a step in Mansfield's direction. "Careful, Harry."

Mansfield took a step back.

"There's no need for that," the president said.

Roth took a breath. "Mr. President," he said, "I have some other business to discuss with you."

"I think the current crisis takes precedence, don't you, Levi?"

"This refers to my captured agent."

"Everlane?"

"Yes, sir, and I'd appreciate speaking alone."

Roth and the president had known each other for a very long time. They'd had their run-ins, and they certainly didn't see eye to eye on everything, but they'd steered the country through more than one crisis, and they trusted each other.

The president knew Roth had a closer eye on national security strategy than anyone else in Washington, and despite the arrival of new favorites like Mansfield every once in a while, both men knew they'd still be there, manning their posts, long after men like Mansfield had come and gone.

"Harry," the president said, turning to Mansfield, "you have enough to get started. I want a proposal to put before the Joint Chiefs by dawn."

"But, sir—" Mansfield said.

"That will be all, Harry."

"Yes, sir," Mansfield said, turning to leave.

"Bye, Harry," Roth said as he left.

When he was gone, the president said, "Couldn't you at least try to get along?"

"I'm sorry," Roth said. "He reminds me of the head waiter at the Four Seasons."

"The one who spilled the wine on your tux?"

Roth nodded. "Sir," he said, "I need to tell you something very sensitive."

The president had poured them each a scotch and handed Levi a glass. They sat down by the fire, and the president said, "What's really going on, Levi?"

"I have a rat in my house," Roth said, easing into the subject.

"There are rats in every house," the president said.

"The malware used in this breach was based on technology we know was developed by the Dead Hand," Roth said.

"The Dead Hand?"

"Yes, sir."

"So they're behind this?"

"It gets worse," Roth said.

"What could be worse than that?"

"The breach required direct access to my office."

"What does that mean?"

"It means someone physically placed a device in my office."

"Physically?"

"Sir," Roth said, pulling a small electronic device from his pocket. It was about the size of a matchbox. "Someone walked into my office and hid this under the desk."

The president took the device from Roth and held it up to the light. It was like something you might buy to upgrade your computer. "You're telling me," the president said, "that someone literally walked this into your office?"

"They must have had inside help, sir."

The president drained his scotch. "Mansfield's right. We're going to have to shut you down."

Roth nodded. "Yes, sir, I'm flushing my team now. Setting breadcrumbs to see what filters back. I'll catch my rat, sir. I can assure you of that."

"And that will take time."

"I know, sir. The operation in Langley is shot, but I'm not shut down completely."

"What do you mean?"

"The Russians think they killed all my Assets."

The president's eyes suddenly lit up. "There he is! There's the man I pay the big bucks."

"They only got three of them, sir."

"Who did they miss?"

"They missed Lance Spector."

"Spector? I thought—"

"Spector's in play, sir."

"Spector's in play," the president echoed.

"He's in play, and he's in Russia."

59

L ance, Sofia, and Olga spent the next few hours in Lance's car, getting the lay of the land around the compound while simultaneously killing time until dusk. As the afternoon wore on, the streets got quieter and quieter. The military presence in the area steadily increased, so that by dark, there was very little traffic at all, and any they did see was military.

"Have you ever seen it like this before?" Lance said. He was in the driver's seat, Sofia next to him, and Olga in the back.

"No," Sofia said. "This is different. This is all because of the outbreak."

"We might be pulled over," Lance said. "If we're stopped, you two show your credentials and tell them you've been summoned to the institute."

"What about you?" Sofia said.

"I'm your driver," Lance said.

"Will they buy that?"

"Who knows?" Lance said, squinting to see up ahead.

They were approaching the front gates, and it was clear the compound was under heavy lockdown. Three infantry carriers blocked the entrance, their Pecheneg machineguns pointed out at the street. Overhead, a helicopter provided additional support.

Lance didn't slow down as they approached the gate.

"Turn!" Sofia said. "Turn here."

He kept going straight, below the speed limit, all the way to the main street in front of the compound, before finally turning left. "It would look suspicious to take those alleys," he said.

They were driving along the eastern perimeter of the compound, and Lance examined the rusty chain-link fence as they passed it. It was about twelve feet high, and there was a second, taller fence behind it. The area between the two fences was about twenty feet wide, overgrown with brush, and not well lit.

"What's this building here on the left?" Lance said, slowing down.

"I don't know," Sofia said. "I think it's an office."

They pulled into the parking lot behind the building, and Lance stopped the car. He looked out at the building. It was dark. It seemed empty.

"You two stay here," he said. "I'm going to take a closer look."

"What if someone comes?" Sofia said.

"No one's going to come."

"What if they do?" Olga said.

Lance sighed. He reached into his coat pocket and pulled out the CZ 75 pistol. "Don't use it if you don't have to."

"We're not idiots," Olga said.

Lance attached the silencer to the gun and handed it to Olga. "Don't use it, Olga," he repeated.

He got out of the car and went to the trunk. He grabbed the bag containing the M82 sniper rifle and heaved it onto his shoulder. There was a fire escape overlooking the parking lot, and he was able to use it to get to the roof of the building.

Once there, he set up the rifle on its bipod, attached the night vision scope and suppressor, and loaded it with .50 caliber armor-piercing rounds. He scanned the compound through the scope, identifying each building from the satellite surveillance Roth had shown him. He could see that the soldiers were concentrated at the two entrances—the one they'd just passed and another on the western perimeter. There wasn't a lot of patrolling going on inside the compound. Once they were inside, they'd have a clear path to the institute.

While most of the compound was quiet, the institute itself was a hive of activity. Soldiers and scientists were out front, hard at work dismantling research equipment and loading it into the backs of military transport trucks.

From the data Roth had given him, he knew that only the inner perimeter fence was electrified. There were guard posts stationed periodically along it, each manned by two guards and a pair of attack dogs, but the posts were too far apart to provide adequate coverage.

Lance scanned the inner fence and found what he was looking for—the transformer that served the electrified fence. He took aim at it, adjusted for wind and atmospheric conditions, and pulled the trigger. A clean bang rang out into the night air.

As soon as the shot was fired, he got up, packed the rifle into its bag, and climbed back down the fire escape. When he got to the car, the two doctors were leaning on the hood, smoking cigarettes.

"I'm sorry, ladies," he said. "I'm not disturbing you, am I?"

"What was that sound?" Olga said.

"Come on, let's go," he said.

They stubbed out their cigarettes, and he opened the trunk. He pulled out a canvas carryall and loaded it with plastic explosive, charges, and detonators. He also took the bolt cutters. He put the rifle back in the trunk and shut it.

Throwing the bag over his shoulder, he said, "You two ready?"

They nodded and followed him around the building. They stopped at the street and looked carefully in both directions. Everything was quiet.

"We're going in through the fence?" Sofia said.

Lance nodded.

"It's electrified."

"I'll handle it."

Sofia turned to Olga. "I think you've come far enough."

"What are you talking about?"

"If we go in, there's no guarantee we're coming back out."

"I know that."

"I have to go in, Olga. This is my fault. My responsibility. You can still get away."

"I'm not leaving you alone with this guy," Olga said.

"Olga," Sofia pleaded.

"I've come this far," Olga said.

Sofia sighed but seemed to accept the situation.

"Come on," Lance said, leading them across the street.

Brush had grown up against the fence, and it provided some cover. They crouched in it as Lance cut an opening in the chain-link. He led the way through the opening into the no man's land between the two fences.

There was no sign of the guards or their dogs, and they hurried across the gap to the second fence, where small metal signs showing a stick-man getting electrocuted gave Sofia and Olga pause.

Lance looked at them, then reached out and grabbed the fence.

They gasped. Nothing happened.

Lance grinned.

"Jerk," Olga whispered.

He cut another opening, squeezed through the hole, and held it open for the two women. Then they all ran to the closest clump of trees for cover.

Before them stood several buildings and a long driveway leading to the front of the institute. It was one of the biggest buildings in the compound, and it looked ominously imposing at the end of the road, the old-fashioned street lights illuminating the soldiers and scientists loading the trucks.

"They're wearing protective gear," Lance said.

The scientists were in full hazmat suits, and the soldiers were wearing masks and surgical gloves.

"I know where we can find protective clothing when we get inside," Sofia said.

Lance nodded. "We're going to cut along these trees by the road," he said. "Stay low. There's still more danger from bullets than germs."

They ran through the trees, staying out of sight of the guards who occasionally shone their flashlights across the lawn, and rounded the building so they could approach from the east. Lance had memorized the schematics and knew the east side loading bay was smaller and less accessible than the front. His hope was that it was also less guarded.

When they got to the loading bay, they stopped and scanned the building. The brush had allowed them to get very close without being seen. A number of military transport trucks were in front of the loading bays, but the heavy bay doors were still shut, and apart from a few guards, there didn't appear to be anyone else there.

"Will we find protective clothing if we enter here?" Lance said to Sofia.

She nodded.

"All right," he said. "I think now would be a good time to call your friend."

Using Olga's cell, Sofia dialed Vasily's number and waited. When he answered, she said, "Vasily, can you talk? I'm going to pass you to the American."

Lance heard him say, "Wait," as he took the phone.

"Vasily," Lance said. "Are you on the ground floor?"

"Who is this?"

"A friend of Sofia's. We're outside the east loading bay."

"Why have you brought her here? It's not safe."

"Vasily, I need you to listen to me. Are you and the other scientists being kept on the ground floor?"

"We're in the office, yes."

"Can you slip away?"

"I don't know. They're not watching us closely, but there are soldiers everywhere. If I'm seen in the corridor, there will be trouble."

"The office is in the administrative section?"

"Yes."

"Then there's a service corridor leading from the back of the office straight to the east loading bay. Correct?"

"Yes, but I don't know if I can get to it."

"What if I create a distraction?"

"I don't know," Vasily said.

"There'll be a large explosion outside, Vasily. When you hear it, come let us in."

"Explosion? What are you talking about?"

"The east loading bay," Lance repeated, then hung up.

60

Consciousness flooded back to Laurel's body in an overpowering surge of pain.

She gasped and opened her eyes to the blinding lights. She was still dangling from the rope, and the man was back, yanking a syringe out of her arm.

"There we go," he said, as calmly as if he'd just given her a flu shot. "Now, let's not waste any more time."

He went back to the wall and pushed the green button. The crank raised her three more feet from the ground. "I don't know what happened to your legs earlier," he said. "There's some swelling there. I hope we didn't break anything."

Laurel moved her lips, but no sound came out.

"What's that, my dear?"

It took all her strength to speak. "I said, fuck you."

"Ah, yes, fuck me. How clever you are. I can see why you were always his favorite."

He put his finger on the red button. "This will do some real damage," he said. "Look how high you are."

She looked.

"That's it. Look down. It's quite a drop. And for someone in your condition.... I don't know. Things will start to break. All those tiny bones in your feet. They'll snap like brittle twigs. You'll be walking like a gimp for the rest of your life."

"Fuck you," she said again, her mind too numb to think of anything else.

"I don't know if I introduced myself to you properly the first time we met," he said. "My name is Fyodor Timokhin. Director Fyodor Timokhin, mind you. I'm not so very important here in Moscow, but I know a thing or two about inflicting pain."

He stepped away from the buttons, and Laurel felt a sudden rush of relief. Every atom in her body was bracing for the next fall, dreading it, praying he wouldn't push the button, but knowing he would.

"You know," he continued, "we know so much about Levi Roth and his little Group that I'm having a hard time coming up with questions for you that I don't already know the answer to. Four Assets, all dead. Four handlers, all out of a job now, wouldn't you say? From what I hear, Roth himself's out of a job. Say what you will about the president, but the man's not a complete idiot. What use does he have for a secret agency that's been spread open wider than a virgin's legs on her wedding night?"

He moved closer to the buttons, and Laurel's pulse increased.

"Hmm?" he said. "That's right. None. None at all. All disbanded. All shut down. Roth's rivals will be thrilled. I can tell you, we're certainly thrilled here at the Kremlin. On the top floor, you know what they did? They opened champagne. I tell you all this just by the way, so you know that whatever you tell me, whatever you don't tell me, it really doesn't matter. It makes so little difference to us here in

Moscow. It's all academic now. Roth is finished. The Assets are dead. The game is over."

He reached up and put his finger on the red button. Laurel knew what was coming. The twisting ankles, the snapping shins, the broken knees.

"No!" she cried. Tears came to her eyes, and once they started, she couldn't stop them.

"Hush, child," Timokhin said, approaching again, lumbering over like a walrus. He was so large, so tall, that high as she was, he could almost look her in the face. "There's no need to cry. We're going to be friends, you and I."

She looked into his eyes. "You should know something," she said.

"What's that, my sweet?" he said, smiling at her like he expected a profession of love.

"You're looking," she spat, struggling to speak, "at the person who's going to end your life."

Timokhin looked deadly serious for a second, like he'd just seen a ghost, then just as quickly, his face returned to its smiles.

Laurel shut her eyes in disgust but swore to herself that what she'd just said was the truth. She'd make it the truth.

"You know," Timokhin said, going back to the buttons, "as much fun as this has been, I do have a job to get back to."

Laurel was so tired of this man and his games. She tried to clear her head and focus. What was his objective in all of this? What was he looking for from her? What was he trying to gain? He'd spent all this time wearing her down without giving away a thing. He was skilled.

If he was really good, the whole encounter could end without her ever knowing what it was he'd wanted. She might die in that room, not knowing if there was a purpose to the torture, not even knowing if she was holding out, or giving up everything.

That was all part of the game—the not knowing. She knew the technique as well as anyone.

Most people, if they knew they held some prized piece of information, something specific, would be able to take that information to their graves. The location of an attack, for example. Countless terrorists had died in black sites taking such information with them.

But if the information was more general, more vague, more dispersed, like what you'd been eating, what the weather was like, what clothes you wore, most people wouldn't give up their life to hold onto such secrets. They'd give up that information during torture, and in the process, give away far more than if they'd been asked direct questions.

That was why the interrogator's first goal was always simply to get his subject talking—about anything.

"Let me tell you what's going to happen," Timokhin said. "Our two countries are going to go to war."

Laurel didn't care what he was saying. What he said might be true or might be completely fabricated. It made no difference to her there, strung up, dying.

But she did want to know what he was looking for. If she could figure that out, she could keep it from him.

"If you go to war with us," she said, "we'll pound you into the stone age."

Timokhin kept smiling. He came close to her again, and she was torn between revulsion and relief that his hand was further from the red button. She had to make sure he didn't press that button. As high as she was now, if he dropped her, she'd never be able to escape. Her legs would be worthless.

He looked up at her. "My dear, how can we lose a war?

When Napoleon brought all of Europe to the gates of Moscow, did we lose? When Hitler launched the largest land invasion in history, did we lose?"

"When Hitler invaded, you lost twenty-seven million people," Laurel said.

Timokhin smiled. "Some people say we lost twenty-seven million. Some people say we lost forty."

"What's your point?" Laurel said.

"My point is, when the numbers pass a certain point, when they're so big that even the people tasked with calculating them lose track, do they still matter?"

"Of course they matter."

"Matter to who, my dear? To the dead? Certainly not."

"You're insane," Laurel said.

Timokhin came so close she could feel his breath on her skin. "I heard a very interesting rumor about you," he said.

"What's that?"

"I heard that your face—your lovely, pretty face—I heard that it's not really your face at all."

"Oh, it's mine."

"But it was someone else's first, no?"

"You believe what you want," she said.

Timokhin nodded. "I believe you let Roth give you painful, invasive surgery, I believe you let him give you the face of another woman, just so he could use you to seduce an Asset who was going off the rails. Isn't that true?"

Laurel knew she had to be careful. She was getting emotional. She could make a mistake. "Going off the rails?" she said.

"Didn't you hear? He was a liability. Completely losing it. No one wanted him. Not the CIA. Not the president. Roth thought giving him back the love of his life would soothe his savage soul."

"What are you talking about?"

"And the sad part, the part that must really get under your skin, my dear, is that it didn't work. You went to Spector, looking like you do, exactly like his lost lover, and it didn't work. After all that, he rejected you."

"Fuck you," Laurel said.

"He rejected you, and now he's dead. All that surgery, all that pain, for what?"

Laurel raised her knee suddenly, trying to hit Timokhin's face, but it only made him laugh.

"And now, after they disgrace you like that—after they humiliate you, erase your face, make you into nothing, into no one—you're going to hang here and die to protect them."

She said nothing.

Timokhin nodded. "Anyway," he said, shifting approach, "I think we can all agree the dead do not mourn the dead."

"What does that mean?"

"It means if I kill you, my dear, it would be a tragedy, would it not?"

Laurel didn't imagine there would be many mourners at her funeral but said nothing.

"But if I killed a million, it would cease to be a tragedy. It would simply be a chapter of a history book. If that."

"So you want to kill a million people?"

"Good heavens no," Timokhin said, feigning shock. "Do you take me for a monster? Of course I don't. Only a madman, only a psychopath, would think of doing such a thing."

He was staring intently at her face. "No scars," he said.

She tried to turn away from him.

"I'd have thought, with all those procedures, they'd leave some mark."

She looked up at the ceiling, the machine holding the ropes, the ventilation shaft.

"Remarkable work," he said. "You know, I've seen your before-and-after pictures. Between you and me, I much prefer the original."

Laurel wasn't sure how much more of this blabbering she could take.

"The Great Patriotic War, as we call it," he said, changing tack again, "killed 26.6 million Soviet citizens. That's the best number we've got. That doesn't include two million service personnel who are still officially classed as missing." Timokhin let out a snort. He found that amusing. "*Missing*," he said again. "Can you imagine? Seventy years have passed. There's no way those men are missing. Two million of them? Where are they? If that's not optimism, I don't know what is."

"You can talk and talk," Laurel said, "but it doesn't change the fact you'll never beat us in a war."

He laughed again. "The point I'm making, my dear, is that we don't care whether we beat you in a war. The last war killed 27 million of us. Stalin killed another thirty million all by himself. Needlessly. Just for the hell of it."

Laurel didn't know what to say to that. The numbers were true enough, depending on which historian you asked. But she was starting to see the point that Timokhin was trying to make. Stalin killed more Russians than Hitler.

"Who won that war?" Timokhin said.

Laurel said nothing.

"Come now. You're the expert. You tell me, who won the Second World War?"

"I know what you're saying," Laurel said.

"Hitler died alone in a bunker. Mussolini was executed by firing squad. Winston Churchill was voted out by a landslide. It was one of the biggest election defeats in British history. Think about that. His party lost almost two hundred seats."

Laurel looked at him, the excited walrus of a man with his slimy face.

"Roosevelt died in 1945," Timokhin said.

"I get it," Laurel said. "They were all gone by 1945. All of them but Stalin. Stalin remained in power. He won."

Timokhin nodded. "He won," he said. "Thank you."

Laurel had stopped listening.

"The people I work for," Timokhin went on, "that's how they think. They don't want to win the way Churchill and Roosevelt won. That kind of victory is hollow to them. It's meaningless. It does nothing for them."

Laurel was barely registering the words.

"No," Timokhin said. "The people I work for, they want to win the way Stalin won."

She felt like she was losing her mind. She could focus on only one thing—that ventilation shaft. She kept it in her mind—its location, its shape, everything—so that she would remember when the lights were out.

"She was pregnant, you know?" Timokhin said.

Laurel looked at him. "What did you say?"

"That's how this works," he said. "I tell you things, and you tell me things."

"Who was pregnant?"

Timokhin laughed and turned off the lights. He was gone.

And Laurel was left in her delirium, wondering if she'd heard the words at all or only imagined them.

61

Roth's neighborhood was an expensive enclave of suburban DC reserved mostly for diplomats and senior government officials. Tatyana felt very conspicuous driving around it in her cheap white rental car. Every house had private security, and she expected at any moment to be pulled over.

When she found Roth's address, she thought she must have read it wrong. Even the smallest properties in the area sold for well over a million dollars. This house was a veritable mansion. She double-checked the address to confirm she had the right place.

She did.

As far as she'd been able to tell, Levi Roth, Director of the CIA's Special Operations Group, was sixty-nine years old and had never married. This house was an awful lot of real estate for a bachelor.

There was a car parked at the end of the driveway, a secret service detail, and behind the car was a high iron gate.

She drove past them without slowing down. She

couldn't see the house from the road, but there was a sign for the private security company Roth used. She doubted they would cause her much trouble.

She rounded a corner and looked for someplace to park her car that wouldn't draw attention. There was an entrance to a hiking trail, and she pulled in there. It was night, not a likely time for a hike, but it was better than leaving the car at the side of the street.

She locked the car and followed the trail a few hundred yards until she was at the back of Roth's property. The fence was iron, at least fourteen feet high, but it wasn't electrified. Tatyana walked along it looking for sensors, either on the fence itself or in the trees beyond. She didn't see any.

She found a place where a fallen tree made climbing the fence a little easier, but it was still an ordeal getting over it. Her gunshot wound was healing, but it was tender, and when she leaped down on the other side, it throbbed with pain. She checked to make sure it hadn't reopened. It looked okay.

She walked through a forested area, careful for sensors or cameras, and emerged onto a beautifully manicured lawn, laid out with symmetrical flower beds lined with topiary.

At the end of the lawn was a pool. It was covered for the winter, but she could imagine how inviting it would be in summer.

She'd never met Roth and knew very little about him other than what she'd been able to gather over the past few days. She wondered how it was that he'd become so wealthy. A high-up position in the CIA paid well, but this house was beyond the means of even the highest government salary. Perhaps Levi Roth was on the take, she thought.

She crouched at the end of the pool and examined the

house. She knew Roth wasn't home. There were a few lights on, but she guessed they were on timers. Closer to the house were some motion sensors, but they were only connected to lights. She knew, in a neighborhood like this, there would be far too much wildlife for motion sensors to be taken too seriously by private security firms.

The back porch overlooked the pool, and she walked up to it. Some lights came on, but she ignored them. She sat on one of the wicker chairs by the pool and lit a cigarette. It was a nice night, cool but clear, and she knew she wouldn't have long to wait.

It was Roth's dog that alerted her to his arrival. She heard the barking inside the house and got up. From the porch, she could see through some sliding doors to the kitchen. She waited, watching through the glass. She didn't even put out her cigarette.

The light in the kitchen came on, and Roth entered. Just him and the dog. He didn't see her standing there outside the doors, and went to a cupboard, took out a can, and opened it at the counter. "Good girl," he said, scratching the dog's ears as he put down her bowl.

Then he went to the refrigerator and took out a half-empty bottle of white wine. He poured himself a glass.

Tatyana let him enjoy the first sip before reaching up and tapping lightly on the glass.

Roth froze. The dog started barking and ran to the window.

Tatyana tapped again, and when he looked up at her, she gave him a little wave, like a neighbor who'd come to borrow sugar.

He didn't move. Instinctively, he waited.

He waited to see if she'd pull a gun and blow his brains out.

Then he glanced around the room to see if anyone else was there.

"It's just me," she mouthed through the window.

He stepped toward the dog and pulled her back by the collar. Then he opened the sliding door, and the dog ran to her. Tatyana wasn't much of a dog person but she let her sniff her hands.

"Come on, Rosy," Roth said. The dog went back to her meal, and Roth said, "How did you get past my security?"

Tatyana smiled and stubbed out her cigarette. "You're lucky no one knows who you are," she said. "Getting to you is as easy as climbing a fence."

She brushed her way past him into the kitchen.

"They told me that system was state of the art," he said.

She raised an eyebrow at that.

Roth looked at her. It was like he didn't know where to start. "Tatyana Aleksandrova," he said.

"And you're director Levi Roth of the Special Operations Group."

"I might as well get a billboard announcing the fact," he said.

She nodded.

He stared at her like he couldn't believe she was actually there, in his kitchen. "You sent us the vial," he said.

"And I hope your scientists are working on it," she said, "because it's the real deal."

"I know it is."

Tatyana looked at the wine on the counter.

"How rude of me," he said, getting her a glass and filling it.

He handed it to her and led her into the living room. The room was elegant, classic, everything tastefully selected. She guessed he'd used a decorator.

He flipped a switch, and a gas fireplace came to life. "Please, sit," he said.

She took the couch, and he sat on a leather armchair facing her. "This is a very nice house," she said.

"Thank you."

"You have good taste."

"I like what I like."

She looked around. "It can't have been cheap," she said, running her hand along the leather arm of the sofa.

He smiled. "I know what you're thinking."

"I didn't say anything."

"My father bought this house."

"Fair enough," she said.

Roth looked around. "He always thought a house like this would buy him acceptance."

"And he was wrong?"

Roth nodded. "But enough about that. What about you?"

"What about me?" she said, sipping her wine.

"You took an awfully big risk trying to reach Lance Spector."

"Yes, I did."

"And it cost you dearly."

"Yes, it did."

"It almost cost you your life," he said.

"I'll recover."

"Your own side is after you."

"Yes, they are."

"Why didn't you come to us sooner? We could have helped you."

"Because you, Mr. Roth, have a leak."

Roth looked at her. "That wasn't from our side," he said. "You were followed to the meet with Laurel."

"I'm not talking about the meet with Laurel."

Roth shifted in his seat uncomfortably.

"This isn't a trap, Roth. You know you have a leak. I know you have a leak. Your four dead Assets know you have a leak."

Roth pulled the collar of his shirt from his neck. "How do you know all of this?"

"The question isn't how I know. The question is, how did it happen?"

"And you're going to help me find out?"

"Yes, I am."

"Why?"

"Because your leak almost got me killed too."

Roth nodded. That was true. "We thought you were dead," he said.

Tatyana shrugged.

"You fell in front of a moving train."

"I was lucky," she said.

Roth saw that her glass was empty. He drained his own and stood up. "A refill?"

She nodded, and he went to the kitchen for the bottle. While he was gone, she looked around the room. There was nothing personal about it. No photos. No personal effects. On the walls were some modern paintings. No doubt expensive, but they said nothing to her about the man who'd purchased them. There were books on the shelves, but they seemed to be for show, decorative objects with fine leather covers, the titles embossed in gold leaf.

"I think we need to be frank," Roth said when he returned.

She looked up at him. He had a gun in his hand. "All right," she said.

He came closer, and she saw that it was her gun, the

Browning Lance had given her years earlier in the hotel in Damascus. 'It will save your life one day,' he'd said.

"Can I ask you a question?" Roth said.

She knew what he was going to ask and nodded.

"Why did you ask for Lance Spector?"

She suddenly felt embarrassed. She took a sip of her wine to buy herself a moment. "I met him once," she said.

"Now is not the time to be coy," Roth said. "What happened between you?"

"What does it matter?"

"You mean, now that he's dead?"

She looked at him. Those words were still a shock to her. She barely knew Lance Spector, but he'd been more important to her than he ever would have known. "Yes," she said, "now that he's dead."

"You know," Roth said, "I'm not in the habit of trusting Russian agents."

"I came to you with the vial," she said. "I didn't have to do that."

"You could have been sent."

"I was almost killed by my own side when I tried to meet your agent."

"I know," Roth said. "*Almost* killed. By a speeding train, no less. And yet, miraculously, here you are."

"This isn't a setup."

Roth turned over the gun and showed it to her. "You see that marking?" he said.

She nodded. She'd looked at it a thousand times. She'd wondered about it—a star carved into the base of the grip.

"My father made that mark," Roth said. "In Europe. During the war."

"*Your* father?" Tatyana said, realizing what he was saying.

"He gave me this gun," Roth said. "It saved his life many times. He told me it would save my life too, one day."

"And you gave it to Spector?"

Roth nodded. "I have no sons."

"I see."

"I don't know what the two of you had together," he said, "but I know Lance wouldn't have given you this gun for no reason."

He handed it to her. The moment it was back in her hand, she felt safe.

"It's good for both of us if you trust me," she said.

He sat back down and poured their wine. "And why is that?"

"Because I know how to find your leak."

62

Sofia and Olga crouched in the scrub and watched.

Lance ran up to the enormous transport truck that was being used for the research equipment and took cover. Rounding the truck carefully, he snuck up behind the soldier guarding it. He rose up behind the man like an apparition, then, in a single motion, grabbed him, jerked his head to the side, and lowered him to the ground. Sofia glanced at Olga. Lance had just snapped the man's neck.

"Who is this guy?" Olga said.

"I don't know."

"Then why are we helping him?"

Sofia shook her head. "I have no choice. I created this thing. This is my only chance to make it right."

They watched as Lance rolled under the truck. He was attaching plastic explosive to the undercarriage.

"That's the administrative building," Sofia said, pointing to a gray office block. There were a few lights on in the windows, but most were dark. "It's low security. You could go there. Wait until morning."

"I'm not abandoning you, Sofia," Olga said. "You were there for me when no one else was."

Sofia looked at her friend. "That was different. My life wasn't on the line."

"But mine was," Olga said.

Sofia was about to protest when Lance returned. "All right," he said. "The explosives are ready."

The women looked at each other.

"Once this thing blows," Lance said, "there are going to be soldiers everywhere."

They nodded.

"Someone should go back to the vehicle now," he said. "Make sure it's ready for us to get away."

"Olga will go," Sofia said.

Lance looked at Olga. He reached into his pocket and pulled out the key. "Keep the engine running," he said.

Olga nodded. She still had the CZ 75 and handed it back to him.

"You know the way back?" Sofia said.

"Yes," Olga said, taking the key.

"Wait in the parking lot," Lance said. "If anyone comes, drive away. Don't look back."

They watched her go, and then Lance turned to Sofia. "You ready for this?"

She nodded.

They backed away from the building and found a good place from where to watch. Then Lance took the electronic detonator from his pack and handed it to her. "You do the honors."

She looked at him. Somehow, even now, he managed to make her feel like she might get out of this alive.

She pushed the button, and a moment later, the truck leaped upward from the ground in a massive explosion. It lit up the entire lawn, followed by a cloud of billowing black smoke.

"That will take care of whatever they'd loaded so far," Sofia said.

Lance nodded. "Now, back to the loading bay and pray your friend shows up."

Skirting around the building, they made their way back to the east side loading bay. They had to wait quite a few minutes, and Sofia grew nervous Vasily wouldn't show. There was commotion everywhere—soldiers running to and fro in every direction, no one knowing what was going on.

Another minute passed, and Lance turned to Sofia. "Is there another way in?"

"He'll show," she said. "Just give him another minute."

"This is our only window," Lance said. "It won't be long before they regroup."

But then they heard the sliding metal door of the loading bay as it opened.

Sofia was about to get up, but Lance put his hand on her shoulder. They waited until the door was completely open, and Vasily stepped into view.

"Is that him?" Lance said.

Sofia got up and ran toward him without answering. Lance followed.

"Sofia!" Vasily said.

"What took you so long?"

He shook his head.

Vasily brought them straight to the changing rooms so they could put on protective suits and masks. "What's the plan?" he said as they dressed.

"We're going to burn it all down, Vasily."

"All of it?"

"Every last test tube."

"The servers too?"

Sofia nodded.

"Good," Vasily said.

Sofia looked at him. Something wasn't right. "What's wrong?" she said.

"It's nothing."

"Vasily."

He looked at her. "They killed Anna," he said.

Anna was Vasily's research assistant. Sofia suspected the relationship was more than just professional.

"What?"

"She refused to show them the live samples."

"She was brave," Lance said. "She died fighting."

"She died for nothing," Vasily said. "They just got someone else to show them."

"She didn't die for nothing," Sofia said. "We'll make sure of that."

Vasily nodded. Lance and Sofia finished suiting up, and Vasily said, "We should start with the servers. The lab's crawling with the new team from Moscow."

"Do they know what they're doing?" Sofia said.

"I hope so," Vasily said. "If they fuck up, we're going to have the mother of all outbreaks."

"All right," Lance said. "We'll get the computers first. We can deal with the lab after."

Vasily led the way toward the servers. He knew where the soldiers were most likely to be and how to avoid them. In the midst of the chaos, they managed to reach a back staircase that led straight to the fifth floor.

They climbed the stairs, and on the fifth-floor landing, Vasily stopped. "I don't know what we'll find behind this door," he said.

Lance took the lead, opening the door slowly. It led to a wide corridor with vinyl flooring. On either side of the corridor, observation windows looked in on various laboratories. The floor seemed deserted. "What are these labs?" he whispered.

"They're for isolating strains," Sofia said. "But we don't need to worry about them. The live strains are in the main lab."

"All right," Lance said, entering the corridor.

Sofia and Vasily stayed close behind. "The servers are around the corner on the right," Vasily said.

They crept silently down the corridor, staying low and stopping at each window to check for soldiers. Inside the last lab, they saw the bodies of two researchers on the ground, blood all over their white lab coats.

"Monsters," Sofia said.

"Come on," Lance whispered.

He reached the corner and carefully peered around it. There were two soldiers standing there, not twenty yards away, talking to each other and smoking.

"Wait here," Lance whispered, pulling a knife from a sheath.

With his face concealed inside the hazmat suit, and the knife hidden behind his wrist, he walked briskly toward the soldiers.

"Hey," one of them shouted, raising his hand for Lance to halt.

"There's been a leak on the ground floor," Lance said in Russian, ignoring the gesture. "You need to get suited up." As he reached the first man, he grabbed him, pulled him close, and slid the blade over his throat. The man jerked, letting out a barely audible gasp. The second soldier reached for the gun at his waist but only in time for the knife to spin twice and strike him in the eye.

Lance crouched to one knee and scanned the corridor. Everything remained silent.

"Come on," he whispered, reclaiming his knife from the soldier's eye socket.

They stopped outside the server room and carefully opened the door. It was empty.

"Watch the corridor," Lance said to Vasily.

Lance went inside and placed the explosives. When he came back out, he said, "Is this all the computer data? What about the cloud?"

Sofia shook her head. "All our research is locked down here. The servers are completely isolated. Impossible to hack."

"There's someone coming," Vasily said.

Lance drew his gun. Another two guards were rounding the corner from the direction of the elevator. They saw the bodies on the ground and were about to raise the alarm when a silenced bullet hit each of them in the head.

"What floor is the virus on?" Lance said.

Sofia answered, "Second floor, main lab."

Lance turned to Vasily. "Are any of your team still on that floor?"

"None," he said. "They rounded us up and brought us to the office as soon as they arrived."

"So, what will we find there?"

"All the live strains of the virus," Sofia said. "They're in special isolation pods. We have to destroy them, or all of this is for nothing."

"How can we destroy them? I can't just blow them up."

"No," Sofia gasped. "Each pod is equipped with its own

incinerator. If you can get me to the pods, I can trigger them manually."

Vasily nodded. "The science team from Moscow has been examining the isolation pods since they got here. They're extremely wary of opening them."

"They're better trained than Yevchenko's previous team then," Sofia said.

Vasily nodded. "From what I could gather, they haven't removed any of the live strains yet."

"They're scared," Sofia said.

"What about soldiers?" Lance said. "Are there soldiers on that floor?"

"Oh yes," Vasily said. "Everything they do is being closely watched by soldiers."

"Like *we* always were," Sofia said.

Vasily nodded in agreement.

"Here's what we're going to do," Lance said. "You two are going to go join Olga. I'll trigger the incinerators myself."

"What?" Vasily said. "We can't leave you here."

"We should stay together," Sofia said.

Lance shook his head. "It's not going to be easy to get out of here. Once they realize we're in the lab, it's going to be a shit show."

"We're not leaving," Vasily said. "We stand together."

Lance looked at him. "You ever fired a gun?"

Vasily smiled. He took the silenced pistol from Lance, pointed it at one of the dead soldiers, and pulled the trigger. The bullet hit the man in the chest.

Both men looked at Sofia. She snatched the pistol from Vasily, went over to one of the dead soldiers, put the gun against his forehead, and pulled the trigger.

Lance and Vasily looked at each other. Lance arched an eyebrow. They followed her over to the dead soldiers, and

Lance took the gun back from Sofia. "All right," he said. He searched the bodies and took three sidearms and three AK-12 assault rifles, as well as ammo and a radio.

"Don't use them unless you have to," he said as he passed out the guns. "They'll give us away."

They nodded.

"The plan's simple," Lance said. "We'll use the stairs to get to the second floor. From there, we'll stay low and make our way to the main lab. You two stay behind me. We only have one silencer."

"What if we're seen?" Sofia said.

"I'll take care of it," Lance said. "We stay together, no matter what. Under no circumstances use your guns unless the alarm's already been raised. Right now, they're still running around trying to figure out what happened outside."

"What happens at the lab?" Sofia said.

"When we get there, we can set off the explosives I just laid on the servers. That will create another big diversion. If we're lucky, the chaos will allow us to incinerate the virus strains without being seen."

"And if we're not lucky?" Sofia said.

"If we have to light them up, we light them up. The primary objective is to destroy those live strains. Getting back to the east loading bay is secondary. Understood?"

Vasily looked ready. Sofia looked worried.

"Look," Lance said, "hopefully, it doesn't come to that. They're carrying assault rifles. We do not want a gunfight. If that happens, there's a very slim chance of any of us getting out."

Vasily and Sofia nodded.

"Just stay low and don't get seen," Lance said.

They went back to the stairwell. On the fourth floor, a

soldier was sitting on the steps beneath them, smoking a cigarette. Lance took him out with a silenced pistol shot to the top of his head.

When they reached the second floor, Lance opened the door slightly and peered out. A scientist in protective clothing was walking down the corridor toward the main lab. He was about thirty feet ahead with his back to them. Lance motioned for the other two to follow, and they crept down the corridor behind the scientist, careful to maintain their distance.

When the scientist reached the door to the lab, they saw that it was unlocked and unguarded. There were large viewing windows looking into the lab about two feet from the ground.

They crept along the corridor to the door, keeping below the windows. When they reached the door, Lance drew the pistol.

He made eye contact with Vasily and Sofia before opening the door. "This is it," he said.

He inched the door open. The main lab was huge, occupying almost the entire floor. Some of the equipment had been partially dismantled by the scientists as they tried to figure out how to safely transport the live strains. The space was divided into sections by screens which could be used for cover.

It looked like the scientists were concentrated at the far end of the lab. Lance could also see at least a dozen soldiers watching them work. The soldiers were only wearing masks and gloves.

Vasily said, "They should be fully suited."

"We'll be lucky if they don't cause an outbreak," Sofia said.

Lance looked at her. "Where are the isolation pods?"

"Those glass rooms along the back wall," she said.

"It looks like they haven't started to dismantle them," Lance said.

"At least they're aware of the danger," Sofia said.

Lance nodded. "What about the light switches?"

"Over there," Vasily said, pointing to the nearest corner. There was a panel of light switches on the wall, as well as a fire alarm and a hose.

"All right," Lance said. He took the detonator for the explosives from his pack and handed it to Sofia. "I'm going to go shut out the lights. As soon as they're out, you press that button. Then follow me to the corner. Stay low. It will be dark so just follow the wall."

Sofia looked scared, but she gritted her teeth in determination and nodded.

Lance took a deep breath and entered the lab. He crept to the corner without being seen. He waited a few seconds to make sure no one was looking, then reached up and shut off all the lights. It didn't make the room pitch black—there were emergency lights—but it was a lot darker than it had been.

"Hey," one of the soldiers called out, "what's going on?"

At that very moment, the entire building shook from the force of the explosion on the sixth floor.

Then the fire alarm went off.

Water poured from overhead sprinklers, a bell began clanging, and the emergency light was supplemented by flashing red bulbs in steel cages on the ceiling.

As Sofia and Vasily made their way along the wall to the corner, Lance used the flashing lights of the fire alarm to pick off one, then two, then three of the nearest soldiers with the pistol. In the confusion, none of the other soldiers even noticed it happening.

"Evacuate!" a soldier said, and everyone began rushing for the emergency exits at the far end of the lab.

"Wait!" an officer shouted at his men, but Lance waited for the flash of light to put a bullet in his head too.

As the chaos continued, with scientists and soldiers scrambling for the exits, Lance said to Sofia, "You ready to do this?"

"Yes," she said in a tone that left him in no doubt.

Lance reloaded the pistol and handed it to Vasily. "You need to keep this exit clear. That's our way out."

Vasily nodded.

Lance and Sofia crawled between the desks toward the first isolation pod. In the chaos, they were able to move undetected. They made it to the first pod, and Sofia opened a panel on the wall, entered a pin code on a digital display, and set a five-minute timer.

They made their way methodically to the next five pods and repeated the same steps.

After they'd set the timer on the last pod, they looked up to see a soldier standing right in front of them. He was as shocked as they were, and before he'd even drawn his gun, Lance pulled his knife and stabbed him in the groin. Then he grabbed his head and slit his throat.

They were just getting back to Vasily when a torrent of flames filled each of the sealed isolation pods, destroying everything inside. The flames gave the lab an eerie orange glow, and in the light, Lance saw that Vasily had shot two soldiers who'd tried to enter through the door.

He looked at Vasily and Sofia. "Good work."

They nodded.

"Now, let's get out of here," Sofia said.

63

Laurel knew it was impossible. Her body no longer had the will to fight. Her limbs were so numb that even thinking of moving them made her tremble in fear.

But it was the only way.

The distance was twelve feet. Twelve feet of rope. The same length used to hang a man.

If she could climb that rope, she could get to the ventilation shaft. And if she could get the cover off the shaft, she could possibly climb into it and use it to get out of the building.

It was such a long shot that she had to force herself not to think about it. She knew her chance of escape was next to zero. And even if she did somehow get herself out of the cellar, her chance of finding somewhere safe to hide in the Russian winter without being turned over was minuscule.

She had no idea how long she'd been suspended by the rope and, therefore, no idea how long it would take her body to recover. She couldn't remember being fed, or even being given water, which suggested she hadn't been there as long as she thought.

Laurel decided that if she was going to die, she would rather go out fighting, and it was that thought alone that made her struggle against the rope.

The room was in complete darkness, the kind of darkness that only existed underground, the kind her eyes would never adjust to.

She tried gripping the rope to see if she could even hold onto it. It took an immense effort—her hands barely felt like they belonged to her—but after a few minutes of trying, she managed to get some semblance of a grip.

Then she tried pulling herself up. There was no way she could lift her own weight, not at first, but by pulling against the rope and taking some of the weight onto her arms, she was gradually able to bring them back to life. The blood began to flow, and with it, agony. It was so much pain she was afraid she'd lose consciousness.

Tears poured down her face as she struggled to hold the full weight of her body.

Eventually, after what felt like an eternity, she managed to pull herself up toward her hands as if doing a chin up.

Then she slipped, and in an instant, all her progress, all her strength, was reduced to nothing—to less than nothing. So much pain poured through her that she thought her arms had been ripped off.

She cried and went limp.

She gave up.

She surrendered to the pain—to the despair.

And then, she started over, trying again to regain the strength just to hold onto the rope.

It took hours, and dozens of slips, and an ocean of agony, before she was able to heave herself up about two feet.

She knew she wouldn't be able to maintain that strength for long. She had to do everything she could to get her feet onto the rope too. If she slipped before that happened, she didn't think her arms would recover.

Somehow, she managed to put one hand over the other and keep going. She did it once, and she did it a second time, and before long, she'd done it half a dozen times. She was another foot higher, and the slack rope looped down in front of her as she climbed.

She was exhausted. Every sinew of her body begged her to stop, but by some miracle, she managed to climb another foot, and another, until eventually, she was able to get her feet onto the rope and wrap it around them.

Instantly, she felt the relief as the weight came off her arms. The struggle wasn't over, but little by little, with the use of her legs too, she made it to the top. Once there, she swung her legs over the metal crossbeam and pulled herself onto it.

She lay back on the narrow beam and prayed she didn't fall. When she felt stable enough, she untied the ropes from around her wrists. They'd been so tight that the flesh beneath was completely raw.

She'd memorized the layout of the ceiling while Timokhin had been giving her his history lesson, and the next challenge was to get herself directly underneath the ventilation cover.

Very carefully, with her back on the beam, she pushed herself along it until she was beneath where she thought the vent was. Then she reached up into the darkness and felt for it.

She held her breath, not certain what her fingers would find, but when they felt the wire mesh of the vent cover, about twelve inches from her face, she cried for joy.

The mesh was welded in place, and she began to pull at it. It didn't take long to realize it was securely fastened. She scrawled at it with her fingernails until they bled. She tried to squeeze her fingers into the mesh, but it was too tightly woven. She kept digging at the edge of the mesh, where it was attached to the shaft, and the sharp metal cut her fingers so badly that blood dripped onto her face.

But the mesh didn't budge an inch.

There was no way she would be able to open it, not even with a crowbar. And when she realized that, the tears on her face stopped coming.

She couldn't do it.

She couldn't get out.

64

L ance, Sofia, and Vasily ran down the stairs to the ground floor corridor. Lance ran ahead, and when he saw soldiers, he didn't slow down but kept running, pistol outstretched in front of him.

With four shots, he took down four men at the east loading bay, but not before they managed to return fire. They missed, but Lance heard chatter on the radio about gunshots in the east corridor.

He got to the loading bay before Sofia and Vasily and used his assault rifle to take out three more soldiers outside. "Come on!" he yelled back at Sofia and Vasily.

They ran from the building, but as they crossed the grass toward the brush, two more soldiers appeared behind them. Lance and Vasily sprayed them with bullets and kept running.

The institute was in such chaos that no one followed them.

Lance heard dogs in the distance. He led the way back to the spot in the fence they'd entered through and scanned for guards or dogs.

"All clear," Vasily said.

Lance nodded, and they ran to the fence and scrambled through the opening.

As soon as they were through, Lance saw a guard. He was patrolling the space between the two fences and had dogs.

"Get down," he said to Vasily and Sofia.

They crouched and saw the soldier. He was about four hundred yards away. The gap to the other fence was twenty feet, but the guard was coming their way and would see them as soon as they moved.

"I really hope I don't have to shoot those dogs," Lance said.

"What do we do?" Sofia whispered.

"We've got to go," Lance said. "We can't go back."

"He'll see us," she said.

"Just run for the gap. It's right across from us."

"What about you?"

"I'll be right behind you."

Sofia went first. The instant she moved, the guard saw her and released the dogs. Vasily and Lance were right on her tail. She reached the fence and slid through to the brush on the other side. Vasily went next. Lance watched as the dogs closed the distance. He still had the pistol in his hand.

"Come on, Vasily!" he said.

"I'm stuck."

Vasily's shirt was snagged on the fence, and Lance ripped it free. Vasily got through and began running after Sofia. Lance looked at the dogs one last time before slipping through the fence and sprinting after the others.

Olga had the car waiting for them, engine running, right by the curb. Sofia rounded the car to get in front. Vasily got in the back and held the door open for Lance.

More guards were running down the street toward the car, and Olga started moving very slowly.

Lance ran for all he was worth.

"You, there!" a soldier called out. "Stop, or we'll shoot!"

Then they saw the two dogs on Lance's heels. Lance could feel them nipping at him. They were about to pounce and pull him down, but he reached the car and leaped in. Vasily slammed the door as the dogs smacked up against it.

The soldiers were running for them, but the presence of the dogs stopped them from opening fire.

"Gun it!" Lance yelled.

Olga put her foot down, and the powerful car leaped forward, burning rubber as it skidded around the first corner. "Where am I going?"

"Just drive," Vasily shouted. "Get us out of here."

Olga sped down the street, not stopping for red lights or stop signs. It was the middle of the night, and the streets were deserted, which made it easier to drive fast but also made them easier to follow.

They whizzed through intersections, one after the other, for about twenty blocks without stopping once. At one intersection, a huge tanker jammed on the horn, narrowly missing them as it swerved around them.

Olga pulled onto a highway on-ramp and then really floored it. They drove about five miles to the first exit, and Lance told her to take it before the military figured out what was going on and got their helicopters organized. There was nothing so easy to track from the air as a single vehicle on an empty highway.

They were headed south, and Lance said, "Are we close to the Empress Catherine factory?"

Sofia looked back at him. "We can't," she said. "They'll be waiting for us."

"No, they won't," Lance said.

Sofia turned to Olga. "I know where it is," Olga said.

"We don't have any more explosives," Sofia said.

"We won't need any," Lance said. "Stop here."

There was a gas station up ahead. It was deserted, but the pumps looked like they accepted credit card payment.

Olga pulled over, and Lance got out and swiped a credit card at the first pump. He followed the instructions, and the pump became active.

They didn't have a jerry can, but the gas station sold one-gallon containers of washer fluid. The new containers were locked up for the night, but there was a pile of empties next to them. Lance grabbed five. He filled them with fuel and put them in the trunk of the car. "Drive carefully," he said to Olga as they pulled back onto the road.

"What are you going to do?" Sofia said. "Burn it down?"

Lance nodded.

Olga drove them toward the industrial area, and as they got closer, they saw police cars and a fire truck flashing their lights ahead.

"It's a roadblock," Vasily said.

"Turn here," Lance said.

Taking smaller side streets, they avoided the roadblock and entered the Chkalovskaya industrial district.

"Put your hazmat masks back on," Vasily said.

As they approached the production facility, Sofia and Vasily were shocked that no soldiers were present. "They had no clue what they were doing," Vasily said through his mask. "Cooking up anthrax like it's soup."

"It's criminal," Sofia said. "I tried warning them. I swear it."

"We'll make it right," Lance said.

They stopped at the fence and looked through. There

was nothing stopping them. Even the fence was falling apart.

"This is how they make a deadly bioweapon," Vasily said. "Can you believe that?"

Lance thought back to the satellite surveillance Roth had given him. Four vats for production. He could see them through the fence. "That building's for drying and milling," he said.

"How do you know that?" Vasily said.

"CIA footage," Lance said.

They'd abandoned the bolt cutters at the compound, so Lance hopped the fence and had Vasily pass him the fuel containers. "You two stay with the car," he said to the women.

Vasily hopped the fence as well and went with Lance to the control building. There were hazmat suits and a decontamination shower that was just a hose and pump connected to a tank of industrial disinfectant.

"They were asking for disaster," Vasily said. "That fucking Yevchenko. He should be shot."

The two men poured a gallon of fuel into each production vat, did the same with the grinding equipment, then set it all on fire.

65

Roth sat next to Tatyana in the back of the Escalade. "Nervous?" he said.

"Should I be?"

He'd only just met her but had to admit, he was charmed. She was exactly the type he'd have hired—someone with the *right stuff*. For a split second, he wondered if she'd be good at Laurel's job, then felt a pang of guilt for having had the thought.

"You're a GRU agent," he said, "about to enter the head-quarters of the Central Intelligence Agency. That doesn't make you nervous?"

"To be honest, Levi," she said, and he thought he couldn't imagine a more sexy accent, "I'm more nervous every time I step into our building in Moscow than I am here."

Roth nodded. "I suppose that's one thing the Kremlin will always have on us."

"What's that?"

"No matter how bad things get, no matter how dire the situation, there's really nothing we can threaten Russia with that doesn't pale in comparison to what your own government can do to you."

She nodded. "That's truer than you know."

He looked at her and wondered what it was they'd done to her. He'd get a file opened as soon as he could. He had no doubt it would make for interesting reading.

The driver pulled up in front of the building, and they got out. Roth had called ahead to get a clearance for Tatyana, describing her as a foreign defector who was being debriefed, and a pass was waiting for her in the lobby.

They went through security, and he called his receptionist. She met them as they got out of the elevator, and Roth told her to escort Tatyana to a secure conference room.

"Just wait there," he said to Tatyana. "You'll be locked in, but I'll have some people come to you as soon as possible."

Tatyana went with the receptionist, and Roth shook his head as he watched them leave. He'd just brought an agent of the Main Directorate right into the very heart of his operation. If someone had told him a week earlier that he'd be escorting a Russian agent to the sixth floor, he wouldn't have believed it. But he had nothing to lose now. His entire network had been hacked. If she could help find the source, any risk was worth it.

He went to the tech desk and found his network analysts. They were both young guys, recent MIT graduates, and Roth hadn't spent a lot of time getting to know them. "This is your lucky day, boys," he said.

They looked up from their screens. They'd been working overtime trying to find the source of the breach, and both looked a little worse for wear. "What do you mean?" one of them said.

"Follow me," Roth said. He was painfully aware the rat

was still out there and didn't want to say anything that might be overheard. "Bring your laptops," he added.

He led them to the conference room and opened the door. They were both surprised by what they saw.

"Boys, this is Tatyana Aleksandrova," he said, then turning to Tatyana, "You'll have to forgive their drooling. It appears they've never seen a woman before."

"Sorry," one of them said.

"Tatyana is going to help you trace the breach," Roth said. "She's a trained GRU agent with experience of the method used against us."

The techs nodded.

"None of you leaves this room without my permission," Roth added. "This stays under wraps."

He left them to it and went to his office, where he shut the door and picked up the phone. "Levi Roth for the president," he said into the receiver.

A moment later, he heard the president's voice. "What have you got for me, Levi?"

"Sir, I had a visitor waiting at my house tonight."

"What visitor?"

"The Russian agent we were trying to make contact with."

"The one who gave us the vial?"

"Yes, sir."

"She came to you?"

"She did, sir, and she said she could find out who hacked my network."

"She's working on it now?"

"Yes, sir."

"And you think we can trust her?"

"Yes, I do, sir."

"Well, keep an eye on her, Levi. And keep me updated. I want to know who the leak is the second you find out."

"Very good, sir."

Roth hung up the phone and went back to the conference room. "How's it going?" he said as he opened the door.

The techs looked up from their screens. Tatyana was typing on a keyboard. "This is the real deal," one of the techs said. "It'll take some time, but she knew how to find the back door."

"Will you be able to tell me who planted the device?"

"The device contains timestamps," Tatyana said. "If we find out exactly when it was planted, we'll be able to cross-reference it with location data for your team members."

Roth nodded. The idea that one of his team had been betraying him made his blood boil. Now that they were closing in, his heart pounded faster.

He cleared his throat. "Can I get anyone coffee?"

The techs shook their heads.

"Tatyana?"

"Sure," she said without looking up.

"How do you take it?"

"Black with sweetener."

Roth nodded. It was how Laurel took hers. The thought of her sent him to the situation room, where they'd been working round the clock trying to track down her position.

He opened the door and looked inside. Eight people were working around a large table. A screen at the far end of the table showed a live satellite feed of the greater Moscow area.

Roth looked around the table and wondered if any of them was his leak. He'd know soon enough, and if anything happened to Laurel because of them, there'd be hell to pay.

"What have we got?" Roth said. He knew they'd have

contacted him if they'd found anything major, but he needed an update.

"We got a track on the name you gave us, sir."

"Timokhin?"

"Yes, sir. His vehicle left GRU headquarters some time ago. We've been analyzing traffic cameras all over Moscow to try and find out where it went."

"How long will it take?"

"We already know he headed north."

"Where was he going?"

"We're recreating the trip, sir. There are no exit cameras on the main highway north from the city, but we're pulling in satellite data."

"How long will it take?"

"We think we'll have a destination for you soon, boss."

"I don't need to remind anyone here that Everlane's life is on the line."

"No, sir."

He let them get back to work. He went to the coffee machine, made two cups, and went back to the secure room.

"Sir," one of the techs said as soon as he entered, "you need to sit down."

"What is it?"

"Please, sir. Shut the door."

Roth shut the door. "All right, boys. Spit it out. We've got lives on the line."

"It's not a member of the team, sir."

"What do you mean? That device was found in this building. In my office."

"Sir, did you have a meeting with Mansfield the night of the system glitch?"

"What are you talking about?" Roth said, trying to cast

his mind back to that night. It seemed like a lifetime ago. "I don't think so."

"He was here, sir. That night."

"He's here all the time," Roth said. "What of it?"

They pulled up security camera footage from the night of the glitch. It showed Mansfield entering the building. It showed him passing security on the ground floor. It showed him signing in on the sixth. None of that was suspicious. Mansfield had top-level clearance. He came and went as he pleased.

The tech zoomed in on the guest registry. Mansfield's reason for visiting was given as a meeting with Roth.

"We don't have a meeting with Mansfield on your schedule, sir," the tech said. "The only item you had that night was a meeting with Laurel Everlane in the main conference room."

"Yes," Roth said. "I remember now. Mansfield came by unannounced. I missed the meeting with Laurel because of it."

"As you know, there's no surveillance footage inside your office, sir."

Roth nodded.

The techs turned to Tatyana. "The footage shows you leaving your office with Mansfield before seven," she said.

"That's right. We went to the third floor," Roth said. "There was an emergency meeting regarding Ukraine. We went together. I was there when the glitch hit."

"And was Mansfield still with you?"

Roth looked at her. "I have no idea. Half the leadership was there. I don't remember if Mansfield was there or not."

They pulled up more footage, showing Mansfield leaving the briefing on the third floor and going back to the sixth.

"What's he saying there?" Roth said as Mansfield passed the receptionist.

The tech pulled in the audio. He had to isolate the other sounds in the office. He cleaned it and hit play. "Forgot my keys," Mansfield said as he passed the receptionist.

"That son of a bitch," Roth said.

"The timestamp on the device, Levi. It's 7:24 p.m. It was planted exactly when Mansfield came back for his keys. The glitch occurred immediately afterward, at 7:25 p.m. That was because of an error on Mansfield's part. He probably hadn't been trained properly with the device."

"Mansfield's the leak?" Roth said.

"Yes," Tatyana said.

Roth looked down at the two cups of coffee that were still in his hands. "Mansfield's leading our bioweapon response," he said. "He's the president's most trusted security advisor."

Tatyana looked at him. "Levi, we've got to do something. Now."

66

L ance, Sofia, Olga, and Vasily went to the only safe place they could think of—the train station.

They needed to get out of the city urgently, and Lance knew Moscow was the most likely place Laurel had been taken. Given that it was over a thousand miles away, he needed to start moving west sooner rather than later.

The airport was too dangerous. There was no way the four of them would slip through security undetected, especially since Olga, Sofia, and Vasily didn't have fake credentials.

At the train station, they split up so as to be less conspicuous and bought their tickets to Moscow separately. Once on the train, they would regroup.

"Keep your eyes on the ground. Don't make eye contact with anyone. Don't look at police," Lance said. "Don't look at each other. Keep to yourself and get on the train as quietly as possible."

Lance bought his ticket last and then went to the platform. It was fairly busy. The Trans-Siberian to Moscow was an overnight service and an important connection.

He scanned the crowd and found Sofia first. She was sitting on a bench in an outfit that Lance now had time to think was strangely old-fashioned for a woman like her. She had the collar up on her coat and was keeping her head down like he'd told her.

In the other direction, he found Olga, similarly dressed, also keeping her head down and avoiding eye contact.

Vasily should have been the easiest to spot with his large frame and mane of black hair, but Lance didn't see him on the platform. He looked at his watch. It was five minutes until the train arrived. He walked up and down the platform.

Vasily wasn't there.

He checked the station's clock. Just two minutes now, and the display said the train was running on schedule. People were beginning to get up from their seats in anticipation of its arrival.

Something wasn't right. Vasily should have been there.

Lance checked his gun and looked at the clock one last time. One minute until the train arrived.

He took the steps down from the platform to the tunnel that passed beneath. He was at the last platform and looked down the length of the tunnel back in the direction of the concourse. It was completely empty.

He started running along the tunnel, checking each set of steps as he passed. Most were empty. In one, he saw a couple making out. In another, a woman struggled to get a heavy suitcase up the stairs.

In the next, he saw three men. Two were police officers, and they were arguing with the third, who was Vasily.

"Hey," Lance said.

As the first cop turned, Lance caught him in the groin with his knee, then knocked him out with a blow to the back of the head. Vasily got the second cop with a punch to the face, then finished him with his knee.

"What are you doing?" Lance said. "You're going to miss the train."

"I'm not getting on the train."

"What?"

"I've got some unfinished business here."

"What unfinished business?"

"I watched how this happened," Vasily said. "I saw how they backed Sofia into a corner. It was all Yevchenko. And I'm not going to let him get away with it."

"You want to go back for him?"

"A thousand people died in this city because of what he did."

Lance thought for a second. "Who am I to stop you?" he said.

Vasily looked at him. "Thank you."

"Take this," Lance said, handing him the CZ 75 and silencer.

"You'll need that," Vasily said. "I know where I can get a gun."

"It's not going to be easy, what you've decided to do."

"I can handle myself," Vasily said.

Lance shook his hand. "Well, good luck, Vasily Ustinov."

Vasily nodded. "Good luck to you, Lance Spector."

They heard the noise of the Trans-Siberian pulling into the station. "That's your train," Vasily said.

Lance turned and hurried back to the platform. The train was already pulling away, and he had to run after it and jump onto the steps on the last carriage.

Once onboard, he found Olga and Sofia. They were sitting in the dining car, sipping hot tea.

"Where's Vasily?" Sofia said.

"He's not coming."

"What do you mean?"

"He wanted to go back for Yevchenko."

"And you let him?"

"It was his choice."

"It's suicide," Sofia said.

Lance didn't know what to say. It was dangerous, but Vasily was his own man. It was his decision to make.

Lance sat down, but the two women didn't speak to him. They were angry. He stood up again.

"Where are you going?" Olga said.

"To see the conductor. I'm going to upgrade our tickets to a sleeper."

"Let me go," Sofia said. "I don't want your accent giving us away."

"I'll come with you," Olga said.

They both left, and Lance sat there for ten minutes before realizing they weren't coming back. He went to the sleeper section and knocked on the first door. It opened, and he saw a family getting ready for the night. The next door was answered by a priest.

He knocked on the third, and Sofia opened it.

"Can I come in?" he said.

She sighed and let him in. The sleeper was a small, self-contained cabin with two sets of bunk beds facing each other and a foldout table by the window. The two women sat on one of the beds, leaving the other for Lance.

They stared at him for a minute before Sofia broke the silence. "I can't believe you let him go back."

Lance said nothing, and a few more minutes passed.

"I don't think I can sleep now," Sofia said.

"Why don't I go to the bar car and get us something?" Lance said.

She nodded, and he left. At the bar he bought a small bottle of vodka and some Coke. When he got back to the sleeper, the lights were out, and the women were lying in their beds, their blankets pulled up over them.

Lance left the vodka and coke on the foldout table and went back to the bar, where he ordered a beer. He sat and watched the last lights of Yekaterinburg go by. Before long, there was nothing outside the window but blackness.

It was the first chance he'd had to stop and think, and all he could think of was Laurel. He knew the kind of place they'd have taken her. He also knew the things they would do to her. It wasn't pretty. If he could have willed the train to go faster, he would have.

He was finishing his beer when the train started to slow down for its first stop. It was the city of Pervouralsk, not far from Yekaterinburg. The conductor said they would be there for fifteen minutes, so Lance got off the train and found a payphone on the platform. He called Levi's secure line and prayed he wasn't redirected.

"Lance?" Levi said.

"I never thought I'd be so happy to hear that voice," Lance said.

"What have you got for me?"

"The lab's destroyed. Whatever samples they had have been incinerated."

"That's good work," Levi said.

"What about Laurel? What have you got?"

"We think we have something. We tracked Timokhin. He's been visiting a secluded shed in the middle of a forest north of Moscow."

"Okay," Lance said. "Listen. I'm on the train. We just left Yekaterinburg. It won't be in Moscow until tomorrow night."

"I don't think she has that long," Roth said.

"Neither do I," Lance said.

"You're going to have to risk the airport."

"What do we know about the shed?" Lance said. "Do we have confirmation Laurel's in there?"

"No. We only know that Timokhin's traveled there. It looks consistent with the type of place they'd hold someone, though."

"Can you give me the coordinates?"

Roth read out the coordinates, and Lance memorized them.

"Are there any flights from Pervouralsk to Moscow tonight?" Lance said.

"I'm checking. Yes. There's one. But you'll have to be fast. It leaves in ninety minutes. If you catch that, you'll be in Moscow before morning."

Lance hung up and got back on the train. He went to the sleeper and began writing a note on some scrap paper. Sofia turned on the light. "What are you doing?" she said.

"I have to go."

"What are you talking about?"

He wrote down the name of a hotel in Moscow. "I'll meet you at this hotel."

"You can't leave us here," she said.

"You'll be all right. Just stay on the train until Moscow and then go to this hotel. Get a room. I'll find you there."

They both stared at him like he was out of his mind.

The conductor blew the whistle.

"I have to go," Lance said.

67

T he Dead Hand had a reputation for playing the long game—for watching and for waiting. When you feared no one and could kill anyone, why rush? Why panic?

Which was why Timokhin found it all the more alarming that Davidov was putting so much pressure on him.

He'd been fielding Davidov's calls pretty much hourly since Laurel had been handed over to him.

"I'll break her," Timokhin said into the phone. "I just need a little more time. You know what will happen if I rush."

He was in the back seat of his car, his driver in front, and they were parked outside a small shed, deep in a forest near the Vostochny District. Laurel was such a high-value prize that Davidov hadn't wanted her taken to an official GRU site. His family kept a dacha near these woods, and he'd told Davidov of this location, a ramshackle wooden shed with a reinforced concrete bunker hidden beneath. That was where Laurel was now.

Timokhin took a cigarette from the case on the armrest next to him. The driver passed him back a lighter.

"You've given me nothing, Timokhin," Davidov said. "Not one single thing."

"It's not easy, sir. She's been trained well. It will take time to break her."

"I don't care if she was trained by Roth himself."

"She *was* trained by Roth himself," Timokhin said. "And he put extra care into her."

"I don't need to remind you what's at stake, do I?"

"Of course not."

"There's been an attack in Yekaterinburg. The lab is gone. The virus strains are gone. The research is gone."

"How is that possible?"

"You tell me how it's possible, you worm. Ask the girl."

"I am asking her, sir."

"Roth's down, but he's not out. Not yet. The lab's gone, that slut is still on the loose in New York, and now I've got Igor begging me for a seat at the table."

Timokhin's eyes widened. "What?" he said.

"You heard me."

"What does that weasel want?"

"What do you think he wants?"

"You're not considering giving it to him, are you?"

"Maybe I need someone with his touch. He specifically expressed an interest in interrogating Everlane. I told him you were on it, but maybe I made a mistake."

"You did not make a mistake, sir. I am on it, and I will get you the information you want."

"As far as I can tell, Igor's never had a problem getting these sluts to spread their legs."

"It was his agent who created this mess."

"And maybe he's the man to clean it up."

"This happened on his watch, sir. Don't listen to anything he says."

"Look at it from my perspective, Fyodor. Igor got the decryption key from Agniya. He knew exactly what to make of the database. He contacted me and made overtures. He's sending all the right signals."

"Give me two more hours with her. To hell with it. I'll drop her from the ceiling if I have to."

"Don't let her die, Timokhin."

"I won't. But she'll never walk again, that's for sure."

"Just get me something I can use. I want Roth's balls in a vise. This shit show in Yekaterinburg is making me look bad."

Davidov hung up. Timokhin's heart was pounding in his chest. "What are you looking at?" he spat at the driver.

He got out of the car and threw his cigarette on the ground. Reaching into his pockets, he took out his leather gloves and put them on. Things were about to get messy.

He crossed the muddy driveway to the building and used a key card to deactivate the time lock. A minute later, the door buzzed open. The building looked like a forestry barn from the outside, forestry equipment was scattered around, and it had been purposely allowed to deteriorate, but beneath the surface, its security systems were top of the line.

He entered the barn and used a pin pad to lock the door behind him. Then, using a metal key, he unlocked a heavy iron trapdoor in the ground. He descended some concrete stairs and unlocked the final door, leading to the underground cell Laurel was being held in.

He entered and turned on the lights. It took a second for

his eyes to adjust, and when they did, he saw something that wasn't possible.

Laurel was gone.

68

L aurel didn't wait for her eyes to adjust. She knew where the door was and simply leaped. If she hit the ground, she would die.

But she didn't hit the ground.

She landed on Timokhin, his massive hulk giving her a bit more margin for error.

She was naked, she had no idea if her muscles would function, but there was no other choice.

She wrapped her legs around Timokhin's neck and clenched her thighs as tightly as she could. Timokhin didn't know what hit him and flailed wildly, knocking over the lights, which smashed, leaving the room in darkness again.

Laurel had been in darkness for so long it barely made a difference to her. She moved rapidly. If Timokhin got his bearings, he had the strength in his enormous body to fling her around the room like a rag doll.

She wrapped the rope around his neck once, twice, then looped it back inside itself and released his neck from her thighs. She reached for the wall, searching for the green button. She knew it was there.

Her fingers found a steel box that was used to house each button, but from behind, Timokhin's bearlike body pressed against her, crushing her against the wall. He heaved himself at her, thrusting forward and grabbing her by the throat with two massive hands.

As his grip tightened on her neck, she struggled wildly. She couldn't breathe. She tried to break free, but he was too powerful. She tried to claw at his eyes but couldn't reach.

He pushed her forward, knocking her head against the wall, and began shaking her. Her hands searched desperately for the buttons. Her fingers were so ravaged she barely knew what she was feeling. Her head hit the wall over and over, and then, by some miracle, her fingers found the buttons again.

The green button was the topmost of the three, and she pressed it. Immediately, the rope began to retract.

Timokhin's massive hands continued to crush her neck, but she kept her finger on the button, and the rope continued to retract. When it became taut, it began to pull Timokhin away from her, and it was only then that he realized what was happening.

He let go of her, reaching for his neck desperately as he realized what was happening. It was too late.

Laurel broke free of him and kept her finger on the button. The rope continued to retract. Timokhin was forced to walk backward. He almost tripped but managed to stay on his feet. It only bought him an extra few seconds before the rope pulled him off his feet. He struggled wildly, kicking and grasping at his throat while the rope slowly heaved his enormous bulk from the ground.

Laurel let go of the button to turn on the overhead lights.

Timokhin's eyes almost popped out of his head when he

saw her. She looked at him for a moment, his toes still reaching the ground and preventing the full weight of his body from crushing his neck, then jammed her finger on the button.

She was going to let him hang, but just as his toes were leaving the ground, the crank pulling the rope jammed.

He was too heavy for it.

He clawed at his throat as his feet kicked wildly, struggling to find the floor and keep as much weight as possible from his neck.

She looked at him as he struggled like a fish on the end of a hook—his face purple, his eyes popping, his fingers digging so deep into his throat they were drawing blood. He was in for a very slow strangulation. It was a cruel fate. It would have been kinder if the crank had lifted him.

Laurel knew if anyone deserved an agonizing death like that, it was Timokhin. But she also knew that if she inflicted it, if she watched it, if she took pleasure in it, she would be one step closer to becoming him.

She walked behind him and took his gun from his belt. Then she went back around to face him.

"Any last words?" she said.

He clawed at her desperately, gasping and gurgling, but his hands kept returning to his neck.

"You don't deserve this," she said, then she pointed the gun at his forehead and pulled the trigger. His head flew backward, blood spraying onto the wall behind it, and the enormous body went limp.

She was still naked, and she removed his enormous jacket and put it on. It was more like a tent than a garment. She checked the pockets. As well as the gun, there was a wallet, some keys, and an electronic keycard.

It was a struggle for her to walk, her legs were so weak,

and every step sent shards of pain up her spine. She pushed through the agony and left the cell, climbing the staircase to a room that looked like the inside of a work shed. It was built from corrugated steel and had a concrete floor. It was cold inside, and light came from a small window next to the door.

She glanced out the window and saw she was in a forest. There was snow on the ground. There was a car parked outside, and a man in a driver's uniform was leaning on it, smoking a cigarette, his back to the shed.

She went to the door and tried to open it. It was locked. There was an electronic pad next to it, and she tried the key card she'd taken from Timokhin. The lock beeped, and a green light flashed.

She drew the gun and checked that it was loaded. Then she crept out the door and ran for the nearest trees. The snow hurt her feet. She reached the treeline and crept slowly toward the car, careful not to make a sound.

When she was about twenty feet from the driver, she rose up and pointed the gun at him. "Hands up!" she said, approaching the car.

She expected him to offer no resistance, but instead, he moved like a trained agent, diving for cover behind the vehicle and pulling a gun of his own.

Laurel leaped onto the hood of the car, slid across it, and collided with the man. Before he could overpower her, she jammed her gun into his ribs and pulled the trigger three times.

69

Tatyana got off the train in New York and called Roth. "I'm in the city," she said as she crossed the terminal.

"All right," Roth said. "I just got the location."

"Where is the bastard?"

"The Four Seasons."

Tatyana stopped in her tracks. "What?"

"I know," Roth said. "It's where you were staying the night you were attacked."

"The GRU practically owns that place," she said. "Going back will be very risky."

"Tatyana, you don't have to do this. We can call it in. It will take some time, but we've got more than enough proof to persuade the president."

"No," Tatyana said, "we can't wait for that."

She hung up and caught a cab outside the station. She told the driver to let her out a block from the hotel. As she walked toward the entrance, the events of the past few days came flooding back to her, and she felt an overwhelming rage at what had happened. She'd had no time to process it, but now that she was back, the depravity of what they'd done made her skin crawl.

They'd ordered her to seduce her own assassin, to let him have his way with her, to let him do whatever he wanted, knowing that later that night, he would kill her.

She knew Spector had already killed the man, but she still felt a burning rage for the GRU men who'd set it up.

She'd always known her job was dangerous. She'd accepted that fact a long time ago. And she knew she'd put herself in extra danger by leaking the vial to the Americans. She'd betrayed her country. There was a price that had to be paid for that.

But the way Igor and Timokhin had played her, getting her to seduce her own killer, that went beyond all decency. It added insult to injury. No man would ever have to die that way.

She had the Browning in her coat and ran her fingers over its cold steel.

As she entered the hotel, everything she'd done in her years at the GRU came back to her. She'd slept with targets. She'd slit their throats. She'd furthered the interests of the power-hungry men who controlled her.

But worst of all, she'd broken her own code.

"Men will do many things to you in your life," her grandmother had told her. "They'll do things you'll think will destroy you. They'll have their way with you. They'll hurt you. They'll violate you. But only you can ever truly let them fuck you, Taniusha. You decide. You."

In all her years at the GRU, Tatyana had thought she was living by that advice. She'd thought she was in control. Even when she let them sleep with her, she thought she was holding them back, protecting herself, preserving the part of her soul that mattered.

But she was wrong.

She'd been fucked, and not because she'd allowed it.

As she walked through the lobby of the hotel, she felt as if she was tempting fate. The place was *GRU Central*. Any active agents in the city were likely staying there. They could be in the bar right now, sipping expensive cocktails as she'd done. If there was any place in the world where she was likely to be recognized outside Moscow, this was it.

She went to reception and told the concierge she'd lost her room key.

"What room?"

"707."

"You have your ID?"

She showed him the ID she'd checked in under, and he created a new key for her. That meant the clock was ticking. Someone, somewhere in the GRU, was being notified at that very moment that there'd been activity on her hotel account.

She didn't care. If she was going to go out, she would go out in style. She wanted to send Igor a message—a message in the only language he understood. She wanted him to know she was coming for him.

She walked past the Chanel boutique where she'd bought the dress a few days earlier. She looked through the window as she passed. The girl who'd served her saw her and waved. Tatyana waved back.

Those days were over.

As much as she hated to admit it, that hurt too. She'd liked those expensive things. They'd symbolized something to her. They were her armor, her sign to herself that she'd defeated something, some monster under her bed that no one but her knew existed.

And then she thought of Spector.

An Asset, the Americans had called him. That was before all four of them had been wiped out.

It was because of him that she was there, because of him that she'd betrayed her country, lost everything she'd ever valued, and almost lost her life.

And it was because of him that she'd finally stood up for herself, finally said enough to the men who'd been fucking her for as far back as she could remember. It was because of him that she'd dared to challenge the men, and the system, that had taken her mother from her, and her father, and her grandmother, and almost her own soul.

She'd been a GRU agent, fighting for the most powerful men in Russia, and the only man who ever stood up for her was an American.

She sat at the bar and ordered a martini. Across from her, right there, barely thirty feet away, was Harry Mansfield, Director of the NSA—the traitor who'd caused Lance Spector's death.

The bar was busy, and she made sure he didn't see her, not yet. But she watched him.

He was drinking a beer, relaxed. He looked at his watch every few minutes. He was waiting for someone.

This was Roth's mole. The leak. He was the reason the Assets were dead. He was the reason Igor found out she'd leaked the vial. It all came back to him.

And here he was, sipping a beer like he didn't have a care in the world.

She'd change that. She couldn't wait to see his brains splattered across the mirrored glass of the bar.

The bartender brought her drink, and she took it with her as she rounded the bar. On her way, she caught Mansfield's eye, and when he saw her, she thought for a second that a look of recognition flashed across his face. Maybe he knew her. Maybe his GRU contacts had shown him pictures.

This was it. She had her hand on the gun and was ready to pull it out and put a bullet in his smug face. But then he smiled.

He didn't recognize her, or if he did, he'd mistaken her. "You must be Diamond," he said.

Tatyana smiled. She let go of the gun. In her sweetest voice, without hiding her accent, she said, "They never told me you were so handsome."

He offered her the seat next to him, but she shook her head. "I've got a room," she said. "And I've got a friend already up there, warming the bed for us."

"A friend?" Mansfield said. "What are you talking about?"

"And a message," she said, caressing his hand and pulling him off his seat.

"Wait a minute," he said.

She brought his hand to her mouth and sucked seductively on his thumb.

"Holy shit," he said, taking some cash from his pocket and leaving it on the bar.

Tatyana smiled and led him to the elevator, letting him hold her around the waist.

"What's the message?" he said, stepping into the elevator with her.

She waited for the doors to close, then leaned in and put her lips to his ear. "From Moscow, with love," she said.

Then she jammed the barrel of the gun into his groin. His eyes widened as he realized his mistake. "What is this?"

"Don't move, or I'll blow it off," she said.

The elevator dinged, and she pushed him forward through the doors. They walked down the corridor, and she opened the door to her old room, pushing him inside. She brought him to the center of the room, where she knew Igor's cameras had the best view. She wanted to make sure he got this message loud and clear.

"Hello, Igor," she said in Russian.

Mansfield was confused. "What is this?" he said again, his face breaking into a panic.

"This is checkmate," Tatyana said.

"You don't have to do this. I'm with you guys. I work for you."

"What are you talking about?"

"You're Russian, right?"

"Yes," she said, "and you're the director of the NSA. My orders are to kill you."

"Kill me? No. Those can't be your orders."

"My orders come straight from the Main Directorate."

"The Main Directorate? Who in the Main Directorate?"

"What difference does it make to you?"

"You're making a huge mistake. Listen to me. Who gave you your orders?"

"Igor Aralov."

"No. Listen to me. Tell him to call the Prime Directorate right now."

"He can't call the Prime Directorate."

"Yes, he can. Please. He's making a huge mistake. He needs to speak to Davidov. Evgraf Davidov."

"Evgraf Davidov?"

"In the Prime Directorate. Just make the call. This goes straight to the Kremlin. I swear, your boss will thank you. "

Tatyana was about to pull the trigger when the door burst open. She grabbed Mansfield and swung him around, using him as a human shield as bullets flew at her. Two men dressed entirely in black were standing in the hallway, and as their bullets continued to strike Mansfield's body, she raised her gun and put a bullet in each of their foreheads.

She let Mansfield's corpse slump to the ground.

Then, looking in the mirror above the vanity, one of Igor's favorite locations for placing a camera, she said, "Igor, I'm coming for you next, you son of a bitch."

70

Vasily Ustinov had killed a man before. It was years ago—a local politician from his hometown of Izerbash in Dagestan. The man had been using his position to swindle Vasily's grandfather out of his farm. When the police refused to get involved, Vasily took the law into his own hands. He was fifteen years old at the time.

He hadn't meant to kill the man, but things got out of hand, they got into a fight, and the man's head hit the ground. Vasily tried to revive him afterward, but it was no good. The man was dead, and there wasn't a thing he could do about it.

Vasily was wracked by guilt. He thought of that day as the day his own life ended too. He felt cursed and was sure nothing he ever did would atone for the blood on his hands. In the years that had passed, that feeling never went away.

And that was why he was willing now to kill this general. In his mind, he had nothing to lose. Yevchenko had caused the deaths of hundreds of people, he deserved to die, and if Vasily lost his own life in the process, it was a cheap price to pay.

After leaving the train station, he got a cab back to his apartment in the city, where his grandfather's old Nagant seven-shot revolver was hidden beneath the floorboards. He loaded the gun with its distinctive Type-R cartridges and put it in his coat pocket.

Then he drove his own car back to the compound. When he got to the front gate, security was in disarray. There were soldiers and military vehicles coming and going, as well as ambulances and fire trucks.

The soldier at the gate couldn't have been older than eighteen, and Vasily showed him his credentials.

"There's been an explosion at the institute," a soldier said. "We've been instructed not to let anyone pass."

"I know there's been an explosion," Vasily said. "I'm here on the orders of Major General Yevchenko."

"Yevchenko?" the soldier said, recognizing the name.

"Go speak to your commanding officer. Tell him Yevchenko's science liaison is here."

The soldier left and came back a moment later with the officer.

"I don't have time for this," Vasily said. "Yevchenko will have all our heads if I don't report pronto."

"Who are you?"

"Vasily Ustinov. Assistant to the director. I'm here to replace the science team that just got taken out." Vasily saw the uncertainty on the officer's face and added, "There's going to be hell to pay if I don't get to him soon."

"All right," the officer said, "let him pass."

As Vasily drove toward the institute, he saw that the fire had been put out, and dozens of soldiers, firefighters, and paramedics were gathered around the building.

The science team from Moscow was still there, but there wasn't much they could do now that the samples had been destroyed. Vasily shielded his face from anyone who might recognize him and parked right in front of the main entrance. He knew that in situations like this, appearing to have authority was what counted. There was a group of soldiers guarding the building, and he said, "Hey," as he stepped out of the car, "where do I report to the Major General?"

"He's still inside," one of the soldiers said.

"Watch my car," Vasily said as he breezed past them.

From the first floor lobby, he saw that the office was empty. His colleagues, who'd been kept there with him since the beginning of the outbreak, were gone.

There were more soldiers by the elevators, and Vasily said, "You men, where are the scientists who were here?"

The soldiers looked at each other. "Who are you?" one of them said.

"I'm the Major General's science liaison," Vasily said. "Who are you?"

The soldier looked to his comrades uncertainly. Vasily had his hand on the gun in his pocket and was ready to pull it out, but another soldier said, "The Major General had them taken to Novouralsk."

Vasily was relieved. Taking them to Novouralsk wasn't ideal, but it meant the government still had a use for them. They would be used in some new project. They wouldn't have much of a say in the matter, but it was better than being locked up in a prison cell, or worse.

"Is the Major General still on the second floor?" Vasily said, guessing that was where he'd be.

"Yes," the soldier said and then hesitated before adding, "sir."

"Have the elevators been restored?"

"Yes, sir."

Vasily brushed past them into the elevator. He pushed the button for the second floor and waited for the doors to shut. Then he drew his gun, checked it, and concealed it in the sleeve of his coat.

When the doors opened, Vasily was surprised to see Yevchenko standing right in front of him. He was with another soldier, and the two were arguing about what had to be done now that the samples had been incinerated. They barely looked at Vasily as they entered the elevator.

"Going up?" Vasily said as the doors shut.

Yevchenko looked up, but it was already too late. "You!" he gasped.

Vasily had the revolver by his waist like an old western sheriff, and he pulled the trigger twice, once at Yevchenko, once at the soldier. Both men fell to the ground. Vasily put an extra bullet in Yevchenko's head for good measure.

The elevator stopped at the top floor, and Vasily pulled them out and dragged them to the nearest office. Then he went back to the elevator, rode it to the ground floor, and walked out of the building as briskly as he'd entered.

71

L aurel jammed the car into gear and slammed
down her foot. She was speeding along a muddy
forest track in Timokhin's Mercedes, running on
pure adrenaline. She had no idea where she was going or
what her plan was.

All she knew, the thought blaring through her skull like
a fire alarm, was that she had no time.

The Russians would realize very quickly that Timokhin
wasn't answering his phone. She also knew there was a
tracker built into the vehicles of all high-ranking officials.
And there was little doubt that additional security services
were stationed close by.

All of which combined to mean there was virtually zero
chance she was getting out of that forest alive.

She felt like she was going to start hyperventilating. The
car careened down the track, swerving madly around each
curve. She didn't even have proper clothing. She'd taken the
driver's shirt and pants, and his gun and ammo too, but
none of that would get her very far.

Her only chance was to get to the city as quickly as

possible and disappear. But how was she to get there? She didn't even know where she was. And she couldn't keep this car. Just looking at the fancy navigation screen reminded her that every move she made was being tracked.

She had Timokhin's wallet. It contained enough cash to keep her off the grid for a few days, but she was getting ahead of herself. Her mind was running at a million miles an hour, and she had to shut her eyes to clear her thoughts. The image of Timokhin's head being blown open flashed through her mind.

The car swerved wildly, and she jammed on the brake, sending it into a spin. "No!" she cried as the car skidded off the track and crashed into the brush. It came to a sudden halt against a large tree, glass shattering, and airbags filling the vehicle on all sides.

She was jolted violently against the front airbag, and it took her a few minutes just to realize what had happened.

The airbags deflated, and she looked around. The car was a write-off. It wasn't going anywhere.

She let that fact sink in for a moment. That and the thought of being brought back to the cellar and strung up again on the rope. She pounded her fists on the steering wheel and screamed as loud as she could for as long as the air in her lungs allowed.

Then she forced herself to get a grip. She could still run. She'd be on foot, but it was better than waiting to be picked up.

All she could see was forest and snow in every direction. She had no shoes. No supplies. No idea where she was. And the GRU was on its way. But she knew she'd rather die naked in the forest, being hunted by dogs, than taken back to that cellar.

Out of desperation, she tried starting the car, but it made only the feeblest attempt to fire up.

She sat there, frantically trying to come up with a plan as her body grew colder. That was another thing she needed to worry about. The cold. Very quickly, it would start clouding her judgment.

Then she saw a vehicle approaching along the track. They'd been even faster than she expected. She still had the gun, and she checked that it was ready.

She would go out in a hail of bullets. Better to die fighting than surrender.

The car came to a halt fifty yards down the track, and a man in a black coat stepped out. She trained her gun on him and waited to see if anyone else followed. No one did. It was just him. One man. She could kill him and take his car.

She aimed at his head. If she spared his clothing, she could take those too. She wouldn't make the mistake of leaving the shoes a second time.

She put her finger on the trigger and was about to pull it when a sudden realization flashed through her mind.

She didn't believe it at first—she thought her mind was playing tricks on her, but she kept looking, and there was no denying it. The man she was looking at was *him*. That was *his* face. There was no way this wasn't real.

It was Lance Spector.

She dropped the gun, opened the door, and ran to him. By the time she reached him, she was crying so hard she could barely see.

She'd thought she was going to embrace him, but when she got to him, all she could do was pound her fists on his chest. She hit him over and over, so hard he had to put up his hands to block her from hitting his face.

"Easy," he said. "It's over now. It's all over."

She let him hold her, and then she screamed, long and hard, into the collar of his coat.

When she was finally done, she took a deep breath and let herself look at him. She still couldn't believe it. She wondered if it was a trick, a trap, but when she touched his face, she knew it was him. "What the hell took you so long?" she cried. "Where were you? Where were you?"

"Laurel, there's no time to talk. We've got to get out of here."

She wasn't listening. She struggled to get free of his arms, pounding him with her fists again as he kept hold of her.

"You need to calm down," he said, loosening his grip.

She was out of breath, still crying. When he let her go, she slumped to the ground. He picked her up, carried her to the car, and put her in the backseat.

He drove out of the forest, and only when they got to the highway, headed toward the city, did she calm down enough to think.

"I'm sorry," he said.

"Where were you?"

"I didn't get your location until a few hours ago. I came right here. I didn't waste a second."

"How did you find me?"

"Roth found you. I don't know how. I was in Yekaterinburg, and I came immediately. I swear to you."

"You should have been in New York," she said.

They were entering the city, and Lance got off the highway and stopped at a shopping mall. He turned to face her. "I know," he said. "I should have been there. I should have been with you. I should have listened when you came. I should never have sent you away."

"If you'd been there...."

"I know, Laurel. I'm sorry. I know I should have been there."

She looked at him and was just so grateful he was there that she started to cry again.

"Are you hurt?" he said.

"I'll recover."

"I'm going to go into this mall and get you some clothes. Then we'll go to a hotel."

She began crying again, and he had to calm her down all over before leaving her alone in the car.

When he left, she lay on the back seat, covered in Timokhin's enormous coat. She shut her eyes. When he got back, he tapped lightly on the window. He'd brought her clothes and waited outside while she got dressed. His taste wasn't quite to her standard, but the fit was close enough.

"Not bad," he said when he got back into the car.

"Not bad? I look like I'm about to enroll in a convent."

"It suits you," he said.

She shook her head. "What now?"

"We need to get you to a hotel. Your body is exhausted. You need sleep."

They got back on the highway and made their way into the city. On the way, Lance pulled out a cell and handed it to her. "You should call Roth," he said.

72

Roth entered the Oval Office and took a seat. He'd been told the president would be along shortly and poured himself a scotch from the bottle on the bar cart. It was a liberty, giving himself a drink before the president arrived, but he felt a celebration was in order.

Laurel was alive. He'd just gotten off the phone with her. She was recovering at a hotel in Moscow, was operational, and she and Lance would soon be ready for their next mission.

Roth took a sip of his scotch and went to the window.

"I see you've made yourself at home," the president said, entering the room.

Roth turned to face him. "Oh," he said, embarrassed, "I thought you wouldn't mind."

"Not at all. I heard you had some good news."

"And about time we got some, if you ask me."

"The Russian lab has been destroyed?"

"Yes, sir. And we recovered my captured agent."

"So, you have a clean house now?"

"Yes, sir."

"Ready for action."

"I hope so, Mr. President."

The president nodded. "Always at the ready," he said.

Roth looked at him.

"I feel I owe you an apology, Levi."

"Not at all, sir."

"I was the one who forced Mansfield down your throat."

Roth looked at him.

The president poured himself a scotch and held up the bottle. "A top-up?"

Roth nodded, and the president topped up his glass. They sat on the sofas in the middle of the room, and the president let out a long sigh.

"This was not your fault, sir," Roth said. "Mansfield was a traitor, pure and simple."

"I can't believe I let him get so deep."

"It's happened before. And it will happen again."

"It's my job to make sure it doesn't happen."

"They'll keep hitting us, sir. The only thing we can do is hit back."

The president sipped his scotch. There was a small coffee table between them, and he put his feet on it. "However hard they hit us," he said, "we'll hit them back harder. Every time."

"Correct, sir."

"Like two kangaroos in a ring."

Roth smiled sadly and nodded.

"It's a senseless game we play," the president said, "isn't it, Roth?"

"Sir," Roth said, "it was senseless long before we got here, and it will be senseless long after we're gone."

"Those are some pessimistic words."

"Yes, they are, sir."

"But I suppose no one put us in power to pick daisies with the Russians and wish things weren't the way they are."

"No, they did not, sir."

The president leaned back and let out a long sigh. There was a humidor on the table, and he opened it. "You want one?" he said.

Roth shook his head.

"You sure? They're Nicaraguan. Very dark."

"All right," Roth said, taking one of the cigars.

They took a moment to light them, and the president said, "I don't suppose you brought the footage from the hotel room?"

"Sir, I don't think that's anything you want to see."

"Do you have it, Roth?"

Roth took a tablet from his briefcase and opened the file. The president watched it all, shaking his head, and when it was finished, he watched it again. "That filthy traitor," he said. "He deserves everything he got."

Roth nodded.

"And the girl? Tatyana? Still no sign of her?"

"Not a peep," Roth said. "She disappeared after the hit. I've got a team searching for her, but my guess is, unless she wants to be found, we'll never set eyes on her again."

"Is that something we can live with?"

"It's not ideal, sir. We like to be the ones calling the shots."

"But we've got bigger fish to fry."

"Yes, we do, sir, and I think it's fair to say she's as sympathetic to our cause as anyone from her background could be. She helped us when she had the chance to hurt us."

"She brought us the vial in the first place."

"Yes, she did."

"I hoped maybe we'd find a spot for her on our team," the president said.

Roth nodded. "I did too, sir. Believe me."

The president looked at Roth. "I bet you had an office picked out for her and everything."

Roth smiled. "Maybe we'll see her again."

The president nodded. He puffed on the cigar, filling the room with a blue cloud of smoke. "Anyway," he said, "she managed to get us some very valuable information before she disappeared."

"Absolutely," Roth said. "One last gift. The great Evgraf Davidov himself."

"We knew the Dead Hand was involved."

"We did, sir. But we had no idea how high it went."

"Davidov is one of the president's closest advisors."

"They grew up together, sir. They're practically brothers. His being involved raises the stakes significantly."

"If we needed any more confirmation that the Russians were preparing for war, this is it."

"It absolutely is, sir. I think it's fair to say, war with Russia is closer now than at any time since the end of the Cold War."

"End of the Cold War?" the president said. "What a farce. That war never ended. The whole song and dance about openness and political reform in the nineties was nothing more than a sideshow, something to distract us while the KGB built a police state as totalitarian as anything Stalin ever dreamed of."

"Everything they fed us was a crock of shit," Roth agreed. "The Kremlin needs this war."

"Yes, they do, Roth. They're up against term limits. If they don't get the constitution ripped up soon, the president will have to step down."

"And there's no way that's going to happen."

"A war with us is far preferable," the president said.

"It's the biggest distraction there is."

The president stood up and went to the window. Through it, he could see the lights of downtown Washington, the capital city of the most powerful nation ever to put its flag on the map. Economically, it was unstoppable. Technologically, unsurpassed. Its military was more powerful than anything ever fielded by any nation or empire in any era in human history. Absolute supremacy, absolute power, could be brought down on any spot on the planet.

But watching him, the way his shoulders sagged, the way his head hung, Roth knew he felt anything but powerful at that moment.

The president turned to Roth. "Let us not forget the significant interests in our own country that want this war."

Roth nodded. "Mansfield made that abundantly clear."

"That little slimeball," the president said.

"And who was paying him?"

"Vultures, the lot of them," the president said.

"Trillions of dollars are at stake, sir. The military contracts alone would be enough to change the economic landscape of the entire nation for generations."

"They're always after the same thing," the president said. "No matter how much things change, they always stay the same."

"But who are *they*, sir?"

"Who are *they*? Why Roth, they're the men who run this country."

Roth thought about that. He thought about the networks of global interests that reached into Washington that even he, at the highest level of the CIA, couldn't begin to infiltrate. He thought about the flood of foreign money that poured into congressional and senatorial election campaigns that no oversight committee could ever hope to stop. And he thought about Mansfield's golf club, just a few miles away, that hadn't wanted him as a member.

The president looked at him. "This war will create a whole new generation of American oligarchs, Roth. You think we live in a shitshow now? Wait until you see what our democracy looks like after this."

"It will massively concentrate power," Roth said.

"Oh, those bastards will tighten their fists like a vise-grip. They'll move in on the banks, on the capital markets, on the voting system, and you better believe they'll move in on the military."

"The contracts."

"The average American won't know what hit him, Roth. And the crazy thing is, I'm the president, and there's not a thing I can do to stop it."

"You mean if there's war?" Roth said.

"Oh, they'll be untouchable for generations to come."

"If this virus hits, sir... frankly, it will cut through us like a scythe in a cornfield. It will ravage us. There won't be a person in the country who isn't touched by it."

"And even the most peace-loving doves will be chomping at the bit for war."

"If they release this virus, sir, God himself couldn't hold it back."

The president nodded. "A virus this powerful? It will wipe out entire swaths of the population. But would Davidov really use it?"

"All I can say," Roth said, "is that he ordered it to be harvested. He sent someone up there to dig it out of the ground. It didn't crawl out of the permafrost on its own. He sent them looking for it."

"And when they found it...."

"When they found it, they brought it to a lab and weaponized it. Tatyana said that when she was at the lab, they had at least two vials. One of them was given to her."

"The one she passed on to us?"

"Yes, sir."

"And the other?"

"Was for Davidov," Roth said.

"Every strand of this leads back to him," the president said. "He's the one man in the Kremlin with the mandate to do anything, literally anything, to keep the president in power. Even if it means unleashing Armageddon."

"Sir, they'd release a thousand Armageddons if it kept them in power."

The president nodded. He looked at Roth and said, "And the four horsemen of the Apocalypse."

73

L ance had to go to a number of Roth's safe houses around Moscow to get everything he needed. He might have been going overboard, but this was one job he wasn't taking any chances on.

The word Kremlin came from the word for 'fortress,' and the complex in central Moscow was one of the most formidable on earth. Its two miles of defensive walls were over sixty feet high and twenty feet thick.

The walls enclosed four cathedrals, five palaces, museums, gardens, and the president's senate building, which housed the Dead Hand.

The precise location of the senate building was a triangular-shaped area between the former presidium site, the arsenal, and the Kremlin wall behind Red Square. It was widely regarded as one of the most securely protected and difficult to infiltrate patches of land on earth.

Breaking in had been compared in complexity to breaking into the Pope's private office in the Vatican or the section of the Louvre that housed the Mona Lisa.

That wasn't to say it couldn't be done.

It could, and had. The Mongols did it. Four hundred years later, the Poles did it. And in 1812, Napoleon did it.

Napoleon actually ordered the entire fortress demolished on his retreat. The explosives were laid, the charges were set, and for days, the site was ravaged. But the vast complex proved impervious to Napoleon's efforts, and any damage was quickly repaired.

All those infiltrations had one thing in common—they'd been performed before the Soviet Union's security upgrade program turned the Kremlin into a technological, as well as a physical, fortress.

The senate building, in particular, was regarded as a difficult target. Lenin had made it his official residence in 1918. After his death, Stalin occupied it from 1924 until his own death in 1953.

While it was still the official seat of presidential and executive power in Russia, the current president didn't actually live there, preferring to make his residence at the Novo-Ogaryovo estate west of the city.

And that was the one thing Lance and Laurel had going for them. Since the president's move to the estate, the senate building's electronic security system had fallen down the list of upgrade priorities. It meant Lance and Laurel, from their hotel room overlooking Red Square, and with the aid of a plethora of highly advanced communications and infiltration equipment, were able to hack the senate building's secure network and disable most of the sensors.

Lance was examining the Kremlin walls through the lace curtains of the hotel room window.

"A sniper rifle, Lance? Come on."

"This scope is some real space-age shit."

"What if someone sees you?"

Through the multispectral scope, he could see the roof

of the senate behind the walls. Slight variations in the surface temperature of the roof showed him where power lines ran and where cameras and other motion sensors were set up. From what he could see through the scope, he was able to figure out exactly which electronic controls needed to be disabled.

Laurel was sitting on the bed. She'd set up a satellite link with the Pentagon, and they were waiting for the connection to be activated.

He put down the rifle and said, "How do you feel?"

She looked at him. "Better."

He'd examined her wounds and patched her up as best he could. She'd been badly hurt—the swelling in her feet and legs had been particularly concerning. When he found her in the forest, he'd been scared the damage would be permanent. That didn't seem to be the case, and the swelling had gone down, but he was still worried about her mental state. She hadn't told him the details of what had been done to her in the cellar, but he had no doubt she'd been through hell and back. That was something he wouldn't forgive himself for. It was his fault. If he'd gone to New York when she asked, she never would have been taken. "I'm going to tell you something that you might not like," he said.

She'd gotten up to make coffee and was standing at the machine. "Okay," she said.

"The plan, whatever Roth and the Langley guys say, it's got to be me going in alone."

"I've got all the training for this," Laurel said.

"I know you do," he said. "And believe me, I'm not trying to put you in a box."

"But you're telling me to sit this one out?"

"After everything that's happened, I just think...."

"I know what you think."

"What's that?"

"You think I'm a helpless little girl."

"That's not it."

"What is it then?"

"You were tortured, Laurel. They could have killed you."

"That's the game we play, Lance."

"But, I can't... I mean...."

"*You* can't?" Laurel said. "*You* can't what?"

"I can't stand the thought of losing you again."

"*Again*?"

"You know what I mean."

"You're thinking of Clarice!"

"I thought you were dead," he said, his voice rising.

"I can't believe this," she cried, shaking her head. "You're looking at me, but you're seeing her."

"No, I'm not."

"You lost her once. Now you're going to lose a girl who looks just like her."

"You need to calm down."

"*I* need to calm down?"

He took a step toward her and stopped. She was right. What he'd said, it was a mistake. He didn't know what he'd meant. "Laurel—"

"No, Lance. I'm doing this. I'm coming. There's nothing you can say that's going to stop me."

"I can't accept that."

"I don't care what you can accept. This isn't your call. It's mine. I'm not Clarice. I'm not your girlfriend."

"But you're my handler."

"No, I'm not. I could have been. I wanted to be. But you sent me away."

He shook his head. She poured two cups of coffee and

held one out to him. The memory of Sam throwing hot coffee in his face came back to him.

"Take it," she said.

He took the cup from her.

"Look," she said. "I don't know what you and Clarice had, and I don't want to know. I look like her, but I'm not her. I'm not your girl. I never have been, and I never will be."

The satellite connection had been accepted. A call was coming through from the Pentagon. Lance stared at the laptop, but he wasn't ready to take the call.

Laurel looked at him. "Aren't you going to pick up?"

He made to speak, but his voice caught in his throat.

"What is it?" she said. "What's wrong?"

He looked away from her.

"Lance, what is it?" she said again, her voice getting nervous.

"You looking like Clarice—it's not just a coincidence, is it?"

She shook her head. "Can we not talk about that now?"

He took another step toward her, and she stepped back. He reached out and took her chin in his hand. "*He* did this to you, didn't he?"

"Lance," she said, pushing his hand away.

"You let him do it."

She shook her head again. It was all she could do. "We need to answer this call," she said, looking at the computer.

"You let him give you plastic surgery?"

"Lance, we need to answer." She accepted the call.

"Laurel," Roth said, a screen opening up to show a situation room in the Pentagon containing not just the president and Roth, but the Joint Chiefs, the CIA director, and a number of Pentagon specialists.

"Mr. President," Laurel said, "Group Director Roth, Generals."

"Laurel," the president said, "I'm glad to see you safe and sound."

"Thank you, sir."

"Now, I'm afraid there are some cold feet around here," he continued. "There are also doubts that breaking into the Kremlin is even viable."

"Oh, it's viable," Laurel said.

"There are also doubts, politically, about the wisdom of attempting it."

"Politically, sir?"

"If there's a war coming—and we believe there is," the president said, "then breaching the Kremlin might make it look like we were the ones who started it."

"Well," Laurel said, turning to Lance for support, "there are a number of scenarios we've drawn up, sir."

"Maybe you could walk us through some of those."

"As you know, sir, Davidov spends most of his time with the president."

"At the presidential compound at Novo-Ogaryovo," the president said.

"Yes, sir. It's one of the few places in Russia that's even more secure than the senate building."

"Significantly more secure, I hear."

"That's correct, sir."

"And what about when he's traveling between the Kremlin and Novo-Ogaryovo. Is he vulnerable then?"

Lance listened to them, and he couldn't stand it. This shit with Roth, the plastic surgery, the manipulation, was precisely the kind of thing that caused him to leave the agency in the first place. Now they were letting political considerations complicate the decision to go after Davidov.

It was always the same song and dance, and he'd had about as much of it as he could stomach.

He got in front of the screen. "Mr. President," he said, "it's like this. We thought about taking Davidov while he traveled between locations. He normally moves by armored cavalcade. It's heavily guarded, but there are certain spots, such as along Tverskaya, where it's vulnerable to attack."

"But that plan's changed?"

"The Russians are spooked, sir. Laurel killed Timokhin. Tatyana killed Mansfield. They're feeling the heat, and Davidov's taken to traveling strictly by helicopter. He flies directly from Novo-Ogaryovo to the Kremlin and back. We can't shoot him down. There's too high a likelihood he'd be killed, and we want to talk to him if possible. So either we grab him at Novo-Ogaryovo, or we grab him at the Kremlin."

"And you prefer the Kremlin?"

"If you're worried about optics, and political fallout, then maybe taking him at Novo-Ogaryovo is preferable. But operationally, given the security upgrades that have been performed on that compound over the last decade, taking him at the Kremlin is the preferred route."

"I see," the president said.

"We'll be in and out in a matter of minutes," Lance said. "And sir, if I may be frank, regardless of what happens during this mission, I highly doubt the Russians will ever admit that we'd successfully broken into the Kremlin."

"You think they'd be afraid of losing face."

"Wouldn't you, sir? That fortress has symbolized their military power for the best part of a millennium."

The president looked at some of the generals and advisors who were seated around him. "Gentlemen, ladies," he said, "what do you make of this?"

"This Davidov," one of the generals said, "he has the last remaining sample of the virus?"

Roth answered. "That we know of, general. The lab that isolated the virus in Yekaterinburg has been destroyed. The lead researcher from the institute has confirmed that all experimental strains were destroyed in that attack. Other than those, we know of only two vials that ever left the institute. One was given to Tatyana Aleksandrova."

"Which she gave to us," the president said.

"Yes, sir," Roth said, "and which we sent to Ramstein Air Base before destroying it. That leaves only one other vial. The one given to Major General Anton Yevchenko, who we believe passed it on to Davidov."

"So we take Davidov, and we take the last of the virus?"

"That's the hope, general," Roth said.

The general nodded. Roth looked at the president, who seemed satisfied also. Everyone in the Pentagon turned to face Lance and Laurel. Roth cleared his throat. "You're good to go."

"God speed," the president added.

74

L aurel stood next to Lance, but neither of them said a word. They were in Moscow's largest department store, the State Department store as it was known, which was located directly across Red Square from the Lenin Mausoleum. Behind the mausoleum was the sheer, red wall of the Kremlin's outer perimeter.

The walls were equipped with underground sensors to prevent tunneling, motion sensors along the outer face to prevent climbing, and infrared cameras along their length to detect any attempted entrance.

Laurel had disabled all those sensors, which wasn't particularly complicated, but also tricked the security system into thinking they were still active, which was significantly more difficult.

Lance could see why Roth held her in such high regard. She was certainly more than just a pretty face.

It was dark outside, and the department store was beginning to shut down for the night.

"You want a cigarette?" Lance said.

Laurel shook her head.

"Take one," he said. "You'll blend in better."

She took a cigarette from the pack and leaned in to let him light it. "You're mad at Roth, aren't you?" she said.

Lance nodded.

"He had his reasons for what he did," she said.

"Don't talk to me about Roth's reasons. I could tell you things about that man that would make your blood boil."

"Like what?"

He looked at her, then away again, saying nothing.

"He was trying to protect you," she said.

"I don't want to talk about it."

"He cares about you."

He turned to her. "I don't see how you're not more upset. He made you get cosmetic surgery. Think about that—how twisted it is. It's worse than twisted—it's inhuman. What did he think? That I'd take one look at you and forget all the things he'd done?"

"What things?"

"You know, I almost killed him once. I was this close." He held up his thumb and forefinger to show her the inch between them.

"It worked, though, didn't it?" she said.

"What worked?"

"Me. My face."

"It didn't work."

"You're here."

Lance shook his head. He took the pack from his back and let it fall to the ground.

"What are you doing?" Laurel said.

"I swore a long time ago I'd had enough of Roth's shit."

"You can't walk away."

"Why not?"

"Lance!"

He began walking across the square.

"Lance!" she cried.

He looked over his shoulder at her, hurrying after him, her pack on one shoulder and his on the other.

"I'm not letting you go," she said.

"It's not your choice to make."

"You can't let your anger at Roth stop you from doing what you know you have to."

"I don't have to do anything."

"It wasn't his idea," she said.

Lance stopped. He looked back at her. "What wasn't his idea?"

She caught up to him and handed him his pack. "You know what."

"What are you talking about?"

"I was the one who suggested it. I saw the pictures of Clarice, and I saw it immediately—the resemblance. I was the one who suggested it."

"You suggested surgery?"

"Yes, Lance."

He looked into her eyes and slowly shook his head. "What were you thinking?"

She looked back at him, but her lips didn't move. He could see in her eyes that she didn't know what to say. She'd made a mistake, and she knew it. "I thought it would bring you back."

"Bring me back? You'd never met me. What was I to you?"

"They said they needed you. They said that without you, they had no use for me. They were going to get rid of me."

"And you wanted to stay so desperately...." His words trailed off.

Her eyes filled with tears. "I wanted to serve my country."

"That isn't how you serve your country, Laurel."

"They shot my father in the back," she said, the tears running over her cheeks.

He shook his head. "You won't ever be able to make that right."

She was about to say something but stopped herself. Then she said, "I know."

Lance sucked his cigarette and threw the butt on the ground.

She looked at her watch. "It's almost time."

Lance let out a long sigh and adjusted the weight of his pack. They were dressed in black, carrying black backpacks, and wearing earpieces for communication.

"Lance, it's now or never."

He nodded.

"We're clear on the plan?" she said.

He nodded again, then said, "You want to know the worst thing about it?"

"We're done talking. It's go time."

"The worst thing," he said, "is that you still don't know what you've done."

"What are you talking about?"

"I told you before, Laurel. Things are never what they appear with Roth."

"What does that mean?"

"I wasn't in love with Clarice. You went and got the surgery, recreated her face over your own, and I didn't even love her."

"Of course you loved her."

"Why? Because Roth told you?"

"Because you went off the deep end when she died."

"I didn't go off the deep end."

"Lance, it's in the file."

"Roth was the one who ordered her killed. Was that in the file?"

"What?"

"She was a traitor. She was the reason the Dead Hand even knows we exist. Everything that's happened—Mansfield getting inside, our network being breached, the other Assets being killed— it all traces back to her."

"That doesn't make any sense."

"Sure it does."

"Why would Roth let me go ahead with the surgery if she was a traitor?"

"Because he thought it might work anyway."

"Might work?" she said, shaking her head. "I don't understand."

He looked straight at her. He wanted to tell her. He wanted to feel the relief of someone else knowing what it was he was holding in. But instead, he said, "It doesn't matter."

He started walking across the square toward the mausoleum.

"Why would it work anyway?" she said. "If he knew you weren't in love with her?"

He didn't stop, and she had to run after him again.

"Lance!" she said. "Lance, wait!"

75

They made their way across the square toward Lenin's Mausoleum, which rose up from the ground like an ancient ziggurat. Lance strode toward it purposefully, and Laurel struggled to keep up.

The square was dark and mostly empty, and the two guards stationed in front of the mausoleum watched them approach.

Lance didn't think—he didn't hesitate. He drew a silenced handgun and shot both guards in the head from fifty feet away. They crumpled into two piles on the ground.

He hurried up the steps and pulled them into the mausoleum's recessed entrance. Laurel pulled their large overcoats up over their faces.

"Come on," Lance said. "They're not sleeping."

"And this isn't the plan we discussed," she hissed.

He looked at her, then jumped and grabbed the ledge above his head, pulling himself onto the first step of the mausoleum's stepped structure. He reached down to help her, but she refused, jumping and grabbing the ledge for herself.

The mausoleum walls were smooth marble, but they were able to climb it one step at a time. When they got to the top, they were forty feet above the square. They crouched and looked at the Kremlin walls in front of them, twenty feet higher still. Directly beneath them, inside the mausoleum, the embalmed body of Vladimir Lenin lay on a stone altar, as it had for generations.

"The sensors are disabled?" Lance said.

Laurel nodded.

"You're sure?"

"Are you going to second-guess everything I've done?"

He took a rope and grappling hook from his backpack and began swinging it. Laurel followed his lead and did the same.

"You sure you're up for this?" he said.

She gritted her teeth and ignored the question.

"Your shoulders were hurt during the interrogation."

"I'm not going back now."

"You're acting on emotion," he said.

She was about to reply but instead swung her hook three times and let go, sending it in a high arc over the parapets of the *Senatskaya Tower* above them.

"See you on the other side," she said and leaped.

She arced through the air, flying over a thin stretch of trees and shrubs, and landed solidly against the Kremlin's outer wall, stopping herself with her feet. Then she began climbing the rope toward the top of the tower.

Lance swung his rope over the parapet next to hers and followed.

She waited for him on top of the turret, and when he was close enough, she reached down to help him. He looked up at her.

"Too proud to accept a hand?"

He grabbed her arm and let her pull him up.

"You all right?" she said.

"I'm fine."

"You want some help with the next jump?"

"I think I'll manage."

"I wouldn't want anything to happen to you."

"All right, Laurel."

"I mean, I'm only looking out for you because I care."

"I get it, Laurel."

They pulled up their ropes and rounded the turret. From its height, they could see out across the *Ivanovskaya Square* toward the Dormition Cathedral and the Patriarch's Palace. Soldiers from the elite Presidential Regiment were on patrol, but it was clear from their bearing that the alarm hadn't been triggered.

"All clear," Laurel said.

Lance nodded and flung his rope across the gap separating the tower from the senate building. The hook caught on the eave of the dome, and he tested it before making the leap. He swung across the gap, sixty feet above the courtyard, but as soon as he reached the wall, the hook lost purchase and slipped before catching on a lower ledge. He dropped about ten feet and had to catch on to the railing of a lower balcony to avoid falling further. The hook lost purchase again and fell past him to the stone ground, where it clanged loudly.

He looked up at Laurel, who was still on the turret. She gave him a thin smile then flung her hook higher onto the dome, where there was a more substantial ledge to grab onto. She swung across the gap and climbed safely to the domed roof. Then she brought her rope over to Lance's balcony and let him use it to join her.

"You all right, buddy?"

He said nothing.

"You really got to make sure those hooks find their spot."

"Thanks for the advice," he said, then pulled up the rope and wrapped it around his arm.

"It doesn't look like they heard your racket," she said, looking down at his hook on the ground below.

"Thankfully," he said.

The senate building was shaped like an elongated triangle, about three hundred feet in length along the longer sides leading to the dome. Beneath the dome was the grand Catherine Hall, over eighty feet in diameter. In the center of the building was a triangular courtyard, crossed by two raised walkways. Beneath the walkways were triumphal arches which broke the courtyard into sections. Lance and Laurel were on the roof of the dome, directly above the Catherine Hall.

Using Laurel's rope, they attached the hook firmly to the roof and rappelled down the inner wall to the central courtyard. They descended the three floors and left the rope hanging where it was. If everything went according to plan, they would be climbing back up it in a few minutes.

There were no soldiers in the courtyard, but they could see them in the corridors inside, standing at attention in their ornate uniforms. They were officially an elite unit but were more ceremonial than anything, armed with World War II-era SKS semi-automatic carbines, complete with foldable bayonets. The guns looked nice and had an illustrious history in Soviet service before their replacement by the AK-47, but it certainly made Lance breathe easier knowing that was what they were up against.

"You know how to find the office, right?" Lance said.

"Do I look like an idiot?"

As well as disabling the sensors, Laurel had been

responsible for memorizing the internal schematics of the building, and she led the way across the courtyard and through one of the triumphal arches.

The glass doors of the building were not locked and led to a grand hallway, complete with wood-paneling and polished marble floors. One side of the corridor was lined with windows looking out on the courtyard. The other was lined with stone statues, interspersed with flags bearing the presidential seal.

There were two guards at the end of the hall, and Lance shot them both with a silenced pistol. He ran up to them and dragged the bodies behind a statue. Then he looked around the corner and saw two more guards at the top of a grand, curved staircase.

They had their backs to him, and he was about to take them out when Laurel tapped his arm.

"We're going this way," she said, leading him past the staircase and further down the corridor.

She counted four sets of doors, and they stopped at the fifth. "This is it," she whispered.

"What's behind these doors?"

"An anteroom, and then Davidov's office."

"Are there guards in there?"

"Gee, Lance, they didn't have little pictures of soldiers on the schematics."

"There's no need for sarcasm."

He grabbed the handle and very slowly pulled the door open an inch. He smelled cigarette smoke and opened the door the rest of the way in a single motion. Before it was fully open, he'd fired two bullets, and two more guards were dead.

There were two more men in the room, and Lance rushed in before they could get a shot fired. He tackled the first around the waist, knocking him back against a table and smashing a Bohemian crystal vase on the floor. The second pulled his sidearm and was about to fire when Laurel put a bullet in the back of his head.

Lance turned to the soldier he'd tackled. "Don't make a sound," he said in Russian.

The guard nodded.

"Where's Davidov?"

The guard looked like he was going to answer but then reached for a knife in a holster at his waist. Lance put his forearm on the man's neck and pressed down, crushing it.

"Ugh," Laurel said.

"I bet someone heard that vase," Lance said.

She nodded. Across the anteroom was another set of doors, and they burst through them.

They were presented with the sight of a frail old man in his seventies, five-foot-tall at most, with a face that looked like it had been through a meat grinder. He waved an ornately decorated cane at them, a silver blade on its end.

Lance grabbed the cane and pulled it from the man's hand.

"What is the meaning of this?" the man yelled.

"Remember me?" Laurel said. "Or would it help if I were in a little cage?"

The man's eyes widened.

"You two know each other?" Lance said.

"We met at the airport," Laurel said.

"You looked better on your knees," Davidov spat.

Lance and Laurel had their guns trained on him, but he didn't seem the slightest bit perturbed by the fact. "Woof, woof," Davidov said, taunting Laurel.

Lance stepped forward and smacked him across the face. The old man flew sideways and hit the wall.

"Lance!" Laurel gasped.

Lance looked at her, then back at Davidov. "You say another word to her, I'll rip your heart out of your chest, old man. I swear to god."

Davidov stared at him and said, "Don't tell me you're still sore over what happened last time."

"I mean it, Davidov. You shut the fuck up, or I'll make you beg for mercy. I'll pluck your eyeballs out of your skull and feed them to you."

"Lance," Laurel said again, "he's stalling for time."

"She's right," Davidov said, grinning, "but really, you're already too late."

"What does that mean?"

"Did you think I'd be stupid enough to simply wait here for you?"

"Where's the vial?" Lance said. "You tell us where it is, or I'll—"

"You'll what?" Davidov said. "Pluck my eyeballs out? You already said that."

"I'll do it," Lance said.

"Go ahead."

"We don't have time for this," Laurel said.

"Listen to the bitch," Davidov said.

Lance leaned forward and smacked him across the mouth with the gun. "You're going to tell me where that vial is right now." They heard voices out in the corridor, and Lance shoved the barrel of the gun into Davidov's mouth to stop him from calling out. "Go watch the hallway," he said to Laurel.

She went back to the anteroom, and Lance turned to Davidov, jamming the gun so far down his throat that he began to gag. "Tell me where the vial is, or I'm going to take you with us."

"You'll never get me out of here alive," Davidov said.

"Then I'll take your corpse."

Davidov smiled at him. "Anything happens to me, and that virus will be all over the planet."

"What are you talking about?"

"It will be all over the globe within twenty-four hours. A Pandora's box you'll never be able to control."

Laurel appeared at the door. "We've got to get out of here."

Lance pressed the gun against Davidov's forehead. "You better start talking, right now."

"There's nothing you can do," Davidov said.

Lance knew he was out of time. "If you don't tell me, you die."

Davidov just kept giving him that same evil grin. "I die," he said, "and everyone dies. That's what a dead hand is."

"Well, let's put that to the test," Lance said, putting his gun to Davidov's head.

"Go ahead," Davidov said, "but you pull that trigger, and the virus is everywhere. Global. You're smart enough to know what that means."

"Lance," Laurel said, "we've got company."

"We're not leaving without this asshole," Lance said.

"Anything happens to me," Davidov said again, "and you'll have unleashed a plague of biblical proportions."

76

Lance dragged Davidov to his feet, slammed him against the wall, and pulled him into the anteroom.

"How do we look, Laurel?"

"Six soldiers," she said. "They're calling for backup. They'll be surrounding the building."

"All right, let's go."

"Out there?"

"We've got this prick as a shield."

"What?" Davidov said.

"Not so smug now, are you?"

"Where do you think you're taking me?"

"You're our ticket out of here, asshole."

"You're crazy. You take me out of here and they'll shoot me."

"I can live with that," Lance said.

"But I already told you, if anything happens to me, the virus goes global."

"Well then, I guess we'd better hope your men understand that."

Lance pushed Davidov toward the door, then, holding him very tightly, his gun pressed against Davidov's temple, they walked into the corridor.

"Stop right there!" a soldier yelled. "Stop, or we shoot!"

Lance held Davidov in front of him as a shield. "Tell your men to put down their weapons."

"What?"

"Do it, or you're a dead man." Davidov hesitated. The soldiers had their carbines trained on them, bayonets extended. "Tell them to drop their guns," Lance said again.

"Lower your weapons, men," Davidov said. "Do it!"

The soldiers looked to their commanding officer.

"On the authority of the President of the Russian Federation," Davidov said, "lower your weapons."

The officer was the first to put down his gun. The others followed.

"Now," Lance said, "where's your helicopter?"

"What helicopter?"

Lance twisted his arm behind his back, and Davidov said, "*Ivanovskaya*, right outside. The square in front of the building."

"Which way?"

Davidov resisted again, and this time Lance lost his patience. He twisted Davidov's arm back so far his wrist snapped like a branch. Davidov screamed in pain and said, "Behind us! Behind us!"

Lance beckoned for Laurel to come out to the corridor. "Check the route," he said to her.

She came out and checked the path to the exit.

"Tell those men to stay put," Lance said to Davidov.

The men didn't need to be told. They stood their ground and watched as Lance and Laurel backed down the corridor.

When they reached the door, Lance pushed Davidov through it first.

Davidov waved his uninjured arm wildly in the air, desperately signaling to any soldiers out there not to fire.

Lance held him by the door and peered out. The chopper was where he'd said it would be, out on the cobbled square between the senate and the Patriarch's Palace.

He turned to Laurel. "You go first. Tell the pilot to get ready for takeoff."

"What about you?"

"We'll follow when you're on board."

Laurel ran the hundred yards to the chopper and got inside.

Across the square was the enormous Tsar Cannon, a forty-ton bronze behemoth capable of firing one-ton projectiles. Soldiers were taking up position behind it but had been ordered to hold back. It wouldn't be long before they got presidential authorization to open fire, regardless of Davidov's safety.

"Get those men to stay back," Lance said.

Davidov yelled at them, but his voice was lost under the noise of the chopper as it fired up.

Behind him in the corridor, Lance could see the six soldiers approaching cautiously.

"Come on," he said, pushing Davidov ahead of him. They began to cross the cobbled square, Lance eyeing the assembled soldiers on the far side, their guns pointed out in front of them like a firing squad.

He knew the elite Kremlin security force was on its way. With their ultra-modern weaponry and tactics, they would alter the situation dramatically. And then there was the sniper threat. He could already see soldiers filing along the walkway atop the perimeter wall. Once in position, they'd have a clear line of sight across the square.

"Come on," he said to Davidov, hurrying him forward.

Behind them, the soldiers inside had reached the door, where they had a clear view of his back. He fired some shots back at the door, shattering the glass and keeping them at bay for a few extra seconds.

"They're never going to let me get on that chopper alive," Davidov said. "I'm too valuable."

Lance knew it was true. Any second, a sniper would be given the green light to take the shot. He also saw that the elite force, dressed in Kevlar armor and armed with modified AK-12 assault rifles, was beginning to arrive, taking up position behind the cannon, their red-dot lasers dancing all over the square.

"This is it," Lance said. "They're going to open fire any second."

"You'll be killed with me," Davidov said.

"Do the right thing, Davidov."

"You can't believe I'm simply going to give it to you."

"You're a dead man anyway. Do this and prevent a war. Prevent a plague, for god's sake."

"What do I care about a plague?"

"Do it because it's the right thing to do. Because millions of lives will be lost if you don't." His time was up. "Please, Davidov," he said, giving it one last shot, "tell me where to find the vial."

The elite force was beginning to advance toward the chopper. The order had come through. Davidov's value as a shield was finished.

"Tell them to get back," Lance said.

"Get back!" Davidov yelled at them desperately, but they kept approaching.

"This is it," Lance said. "Are you really going to take this to your grave?"

"That's the whole point," Davidov said. "What do you think a dead hand is?"

Lance knew there was no way he was going to change his mind. Davidov had spent his life building systems that would guarantee annihilation to anyone who struck at him first. This was exactly what he'd prepared for.

"Davidov," Lance said, one final, desperate time, "this is it. Last chance."

Davidov turned to him. For a brief second, Lance thought he was going to tell him where it was. He leaned in closer to hear.

And then, Davidov spat in his face.

Time was up. Lance could see it on the approaching soldiers' faces. He looked back at the building and saw the soldiers behind him streaming out. Laurel was in the chopper, holding a gun to the pilot's head.

"Take off," he said into his mouthpiece.

That was it. The chopper's liftoff was the signal the snipers had been waiting for.

Lance felt the impact before he heard it. A high-powered sniper bullet struck Davidov's head from the direction of the palace. Lance held up Davidov's dead body and fired his pistol at the elite force. They scattered, but the men behind him opened fire with their carbines.

Lance held Davidov for cover and fired at the tactical team as he ran the final steps to the chopper. Sniper bullets continued to pelt Davidov.

When he was six feet from the chopper, he dropped Davidov's corpse and leaped.

Laurel was firing at the elite force, keeping them at bay,

and Lance landed in the back of the chopper as a hail of carbine bullets clanged all around him.

The chopper jerked upward violently, gaining altitude as the pilot pulled back on the controls, realizing he would be the next target for the snipers.

"Get down!" Lance yelled to Laurel.

They both lay on the chopper floor as the snipers continued to take shots at them. The chopper's windshield shattered. It was a military craft and had been reinforced, but it wouldn't stand up to much more of this punishment.

When one of the snipers damaged the tail rotor, the chopper veered dangerously to the right, and Laurel had to hang on so as not to be thrown out the side.

More bullets rained on them.

"The pilot's been hit," Laurel yelled.

Lance pushed him out of the craft and took his seat. He pulled against the controls, struggling to get the chopper under control. He managed to stabilize the altitude, but as more bullets struck the tail and undercarriage, they began to veer again. They were dangerously close to going into a spin.

"I'm losing control," Lance said.

They'd drifted over the Moskva River and were finally out of range of the snipers, but as they continued to careen wildly, Lance knew there was nothing he could do. He turned to Laurel. "You're not going to like this."

"Like what?"

"We're above the river," he said.

She looked at him and realized what he was saying. She looked down. They were dizzyingly high. The Moskva looked so cold and dark beneath them, with large shards of ice floating in the black water. She pictured herself landing on the rooftop of one of the buildings by the shore. "You want me to jump?"

The chopper veered to the side again, and it took everything Lance had to get it stabilized.

Laurel looked at him. "This is it, Lance. If I jump, we may never see each other again."

He nodded.

"Did Davidov say anything?" she said.

He shook his head. At that moment, none of it mattered —not the virus, not Roth, not the Russians. Not even a plague and a war.

"Laurel," he said as she stepped out onto the landing skid of the chopper. She looked back at him. "There's something I never told you," he said.

She was about to speak when the chopper jerked, and she almost fell. She caught hold of the door as he brought them back over the river.

"Jump now," he said, focused on the controls. "We're in position, but we're going to go into a spin any second."

She looked down again and said, "Can't you get any lower?"

He shook his head.

She looked at him a final time. Their eyes locked, and then she was gone.

A moment later, the chopper fell into a terminal tailspin. Lance fought the controls but they were unresponsive. He was going down, and there wasn't a thing he could do about it.

77

Tatyana felt very strange, passing through customs at Moscow's Sheremetyevo airport with a false passport Roth had given her. It was surreal to be back. She kept expecting one of the soldiers to grab her by the arm and lead her forcefully to an interrogation room. She'd seen it happen enough times.

"Purpose of your visit?" the guard said to her at passport control.

"Visiting an old friend," she said, speaking Russian like a foreigner.

The guard looked at her. She'd altered her appearance —Roth had known exactly what was needed to trick the Russian facial recognition system—and her pulse sped as the guard leaned closer.

"Male or female?" the guard said.

"Excuse me?"

"Your friend."

"Oh," she said. "Male."

"If you don't mind me saying, he's a very lucky man."

Tatyana shrugged. "Not so lucky," she said as he waved her through.

The airport wasn't far from the city, and she rented a sleek Mercedes from one of the desks in the arrival hall. In Moscow, it never hurt to have a car that made you look important.

From the airport, she drove directly to an address Roth had given her. It was for a cheap hotel north of the city center. She parked outside, went through the lobby straight to the room number he'd given her, and knocked on the door.

78

Sofia sat by the window of the hotel room and gazed out. Mist gathered around the streetlights and gave the night a dull, oppressive air. A wine-red Mercedes pulled up beneath one of the lights, and an elegant woman with an Audrey Hepburn-style silk scarf in her hair stepped out.

The hotel was in a poor neighborhood, an area for bootleggers and black marketeers. If you wanted a fake Gucci purse or DVDs of old Sylvester Stallone movies, this was the place.

The room itself was functional, clean enough, with two twin beds and a bathroom with a shower, but Sofia and Olga were beginning to get restless.

"What are you looking for?" Olga said. "He's abandoned us. He's not coming back."

"He'll come back," Sofia said.

"He might not even be alive."

"Of course he's alive."

"You saw the news," Olga said. "The gunfire at the Kremlin. The helicopter crash."

"He's alive, Olga," Sofia said, getting more emotional than she had intended. "I have to believe that."

Olga sighed. She came over and put her hand on Sofia's shoulder. "You don't even know this man," she said softly.

Sofia looked at her. "What's that got to do with anything?"

"You're looking out that window like a sailor's wife staring out to sea."

"No, I am not."

"Look at yourself," Olga said.

Sofia pulled herself away from the window and sat on the bed. "I'm just worried," she said.

"I'm worried too," Olga said. "How are we going to get ourselves out of this mess? We only have enough cash for a few more nights. Then what do we do? They're looking for us everywhere."

There had been pictures of them on the news—two women on the run, supposedly for murdering their husbands. It was preposterous, neither of them was even married, but it was only a matter of time before someone recognized them.

"That's why I know he'll come back," Sofia said. "Because he has to."

They were scared of leaving the room and only did so when necessary. The room had a microwave, and they'd been living off ramen and canned soup, but their little stash was running low.

"One of us needs to go to the store," Olga said. "Do you want to, or should I?"

Sofia shook her head. She didn't know what she wanted. She turned on the television and flicked to the local news station. Everything was about the shooting at the Kremlin. According to the latest update, a soldier with psychiatric issues had gone off the deep end and tried to steal a helicopter. There'd been shots fired, but no one was hurt other than the soldier himself, who'd crashed the chopper in Gorky Park and died in the process.

Olga looked at her.

"What?" Sofia said.

"That was him."

"They're lying, Olga."

"Then who died in that crash? You tell me." Olga was putting on her coat. "I'm going to the store. Do you want anything?"

Sofia shook her head, and Olga reached for the door. She was about to open it when they heard a sharp knock on it. Olga's hand froze in midair. She looked back at Sofia. "What do I do?" she whispered.

Sofia's heart leaped in her chest. Was this it? The end of the road?

"Doctor Sofia Ivanova," a voice said from outside the door. "Doctor Olga Abramova."

"We're screwed," Olga whispered.

The voice was female, Russian.

"Who is it?" Sofia said.

"A friend."

"We don't have any friends."

"Yes, you do, Sofia. It's Tatyana."

Sofia didn't believe her ears. She shook her head as her eyes filled with tears of relief.

Olga put her hand on the door handle and looked at her. Sofia nodded, the door opened, and there she was—Agent Tatyana Alexandrova of the Main Directorate of the GRU. "Tatyana! What are you doing here?"

"I'm here for you."

"How is this even—"

"I'm with the Americans. There's an extraction point outside the city. There'll be a plane there waiting for us."

"How did you know where to find us?"

"Spector called it in."

"Spector?"

"You didn't think he forgot about you, did you?"

Sofia looked at Olga then back at Tatyana. "When's the plane going to be there?"

"Soon. You don't have much time."

"What about you?"

"I'll have to meet you there," Tatyana said. "I have some unfinished business to take care of first."

79

Laurel let the Moskva's current take her about a quarter of a mile downriver before she couldn't take the cold any longer. The water was close to freezing, and it took all her strength to pull herself out onto the paved walkway along the river's edge.

She lay there, shivering uncontrollably in the darkness. When she shut her eyes, all she heard was Timokhin's voice, taunting her in the darkness of that cell.

She needed to get her body temperature up. She was going to die if she stayed there. She struggled to get to her feet, but her body was too weak.

"Hey," someone called out.

She reached to her waist for her gun, but it was gone.

"You all right?"

She squinted in the darkness. The voice was coming from a man in his twenties wearing jogging clothes. "I was in the water," she said.

On the street above, they heard a flood of police cars and other emergency vehicles speeding by, sirens blaring.

The man looked at her more closely.

"Please," Laurel said.

"There's been an accident in the park," the man said. "An explosion. There are police everywhere."

"You have to help me," Laurel said. "If you don't, I'm going to die."

The man looked around. No one was watching. "I'm going to regret this," he said.

"Maybe," she said, "but sometimes you have to do things you might regret."

He said nothing for a moment, then helped her to her feet. With her weight on him, she was just about able to walk. "You're cold as ice," he said.

"Yes," she said.

"Your lips are blue."

She nodded.

"I have a car, not far," he said.

Holding her up, he helped her to a parking lot further downriver. She climbed into the back seat and collapsed. The man turned on the engine and put the heat on full. He had a coat and lay it on top of her. "It will take some time for the heat to get going."

"Drive," Laurel said.

"What?"

"We can't stay here. We're too close to the park. You need to drive."

He pulled out of the parking lot and began driving down the street, away from the emergency vehicles. Laurel pulled the coat up over her body and began taking off some of her wet clothes.

"Where do you live?" she said.

"Not far from here. I have an apartment."

"Do you live alone?"

"Yes."

"Take me to your apartment."

The man looked back at her, then turned onto a bridge and crossed the river. Soon, they were in a residential neighborhood lined with three-story apartment blocks. The buildings were Scandinavian in style, with wooden balconies overlooking the road. They parked behind one of them, and she pulled the coat tightly around herself before leaving the car.

He helped her to the entrance and unlocked the door. When he turned on the lights in the entryway, they saw each other properly for the first time. They hurried up the steps to his apartment, and when they were inside, he locked the door behind him.

"I need you to run me a bath," Laurel said, her teeth chattering so hard she could barely speak.

He brought her to the bathroom. There was only a shower. "Will this do?"

She nodded.

"Are you able to get undressed?"

"I'll be all right," she said.

He left, and she stripped. She got into the shower and let the hot water bring her flesh back to life. At first, her skin was numb, but very quickly, it started to feel like the water was scalding her. She knew it was a reaction to the cold and forced herself to bear it. Then she began to swell up, starting with her feet and hands. It was so bad that she couldn't close her fingers.

She got out of the shower and held herself up by leaning on the sink. As she reached for the towel, her arm gave way, and she fell. She hit the tiled ground hard and knocked over a mirror, sending shards of glass flying.

The man came back and saw her lying on the ground.

He pulled a towel over her and began rubbing her muscles vigorously.

"I do a lot of winter running," he said.

She nodded. He continued rubbing her through the towel, and she felt the life coming back to her muscles. Within a few minutes, she felt strong enough to stand. He swept the floor and helped her to her feet.

"Did you make any phone calls while I was in the shower?" she said.

He looked at her. "Of course not."

"Are you sure?"

"I wouldn't. I'd be in as much trouble as you are."

"Not quite that much trouble," she said, "but thank you."

He nodded.

"Do you have any clothes you could give me?" she said.

"I brought your clothes from the car. They're in the dryer now."

She looked at him. "What's your name?"

"Piotr."

"Piotr, is there a payphone nearby?"

He nodded.

"If I asked you to do me one more favor, would you?"

"What is it?"

"I need you to drive me to the phone."

"I have a phone here."

She shook her head. "We can't use your phone." He looked at her closely, and she tried to smile. "I'm not a bad person," she said. "I'm in trouble, but I'm not a bad person."

He nodded, and they went back to the car. He took her to a nearby strip mall and she got out. "Don't leave me here," she said.

"I won't."

"I need some money for the phone."

He pulled out his wallet and gave her a card.

"It's got to be cash," she said.

He gave her what he had, and she crossed the lot to the payphone. She watched Piotr as she dialed. It would be so easy for him to drive off and leave her. And so much safer for him.

But he didn't.

"Laurel Everlane," she said into the phone when it was answered. "I need the location of the extraction point."

80

L ance lay in the brush, wavering between consciousness and oblivion. The only reason he even knew he was alive was the pain. He looked at his leg. His pants were torn, and blood gushed from an open wound in his thigh in terrifying spurts. At that rate of blood loss, he wouldn't last long.

A hundred yards beyond the brush, the flames of the chopper billowed toward the sky. A thick column of smoke rose from the flames like a beacon, leading every cop car in the city to his location.

Seconds after Laurel jumped, the chopper went into a wild spin. Lance managed to bail, but by that time, the centrifugal force was such that it flung him from the craft like a slingshot. He flew sixty feet through the air before hitting a clump of trees. They saved his life while simultaneously seeming to be custom-designed to shred him to pieces as he passed through the branches.

He didn't have time to think about that now. Nor did he have time to check the damage to his leg. He could tell it wasn't good. He tore the sleeve off his shirt and tied it tightly around his upper thigh as a tourniquet. Then, gritting his teeth through the pain, he forced himself to his feet and began hobbling toward the fence at the edge of the park.

Ahead of him on the lawn, a man in a long black coat stood frozen, staring at the flaming wreckage of the chopper as if trying to make sense of it. In one hand, he held a leash, and at the end of the leash was a stout Rottweiler. Lance wondered for a second if he would release the dog and set it on him, but he did not.

"Hey," Lance called out as he approached. The man was so transfixed by the flames he didn't even turn his head. "Hey," Lance said again, "I need to buy your coat."

The man looked at him—the tattered clothing, the blood, the soot on his face—and put the pieces together. "I saw you fall," he said, a sense of wonderment in his voice.

"The coat," Lance said. "Take it off."

"You should be dead."

"And maybe I soon will be," Lance said. He was wary of the dog. He reached into his vest, pulled out a wad of blood-stained cash, and held it out. "Come on. Throw the coat."

The man looked at the money and, almost absently, took off the coat and threw it.

Lance put it on, then handed him the money, keeping one eye on the dog the entire time. The man said nothing, and Lance left him still staring at the flames. He hurried toward the edge of the park, which was surrounded by a ten-foot-high fence, and when he reached it, he saw just how difficult it was going to be to climb. His leg burned with agony, and he was losing so much blood that his muscles were weakening by the second. He grabbed the wrought iron fence posts and somehow, through bouts of dizziness that almost pulled him from consciousness, managed to get himself to the top. By that time, he was so exhausted that he simply leaned forward and let himself fall to the pavement on the other side. He hit the ground with a thud and gasped in pain.

The fall shocked him, and it took a moment for his mind to clear enough to get his bearings. When he looked around, he saw that he was on Leninskiy Prospekt. To his left, the street led straight back to the Kremlin, and to his right, it went south to the ring road. He got to his feet and shielded his face with his collar as two police cars sped by, sirens blazing.

He waited for them to round a corner, then crossed the street, half walking, half stumbling to the sidewalk on the other side. He passed an apartment building, a bank, and a drug store, before reaching a construction site. Its fence was not as high as the one around the park, and he managed to climb it with slightly less difficulty.

The construction site was dark, and he waited a minute to get an idea of where the police were congregating. His leg was so bad that he was scared to look at it. He tightened the tourniquet but knew he was still losing too much blood. He had to keep moving. He crossed the construction site, kicked open the gate on the far side, and kept going. He passed more stores, mostly closed, and when he felt his leg could no longer sustain his weight, boarded a passing streetcar toward Shabolovska Street.

The streetcar was brightly lit, and the overhead bulbs bathed him in a fluorescent blue hue. Every person on board stared at the sight he presented. He even stared at himself, his bloody, sooty face reflected in the window. "Go!" he said to the driver without bothering to draw his gun.

The driver obeyed, and they went as far as the Lenin Monument before Lance told him to stop. There were enough people in the square in front of the monument to offer at least a semblance of cover.

He stepped off the streetcar and did his best not to draw attention, hiding his limp as much as possible. He hoped the struggled gait and long coat made him look like a drunk stumbling home for the evening.

He walked away from the monument, past the Aeroflot building, and continued along a side street, looking back over his shoulder frequently. He was losing so much blood that it was leaving a trail on the sidewalk. It was difficult to see it in the darkness, but if the police brought out hounds, they'd track him down like a wounded fox.

He turned south at the end of the block, crossed a parking lot, and began to slow down. He couldn't keep going, and he'd created a reasonable distance from the crash site. The police sirens were growing faint in the distance, and it would take time before their search radius extended this far.

He entered a small park and found a bench in a dimly lit area beneath a tree. He desperately needed to examine the jagged gash that stretched across his left thigh before it became critical. He sat down heavily on the bench and glanced around. He didn't think he was visible from the street.

He winced as he tore open what remained of the pant leg, revealing the wound. The sight confirmed his fears. The gash cut from knee to hip and was deep. He'd lost so much blood that if he didn't do something about it fast, it would be game over.

Across the park, he could make out the green neon glow of what appeared to be a twenty-four-hour pharmacy. He sat, staring at it for a few minutes as he gathered his strength, then, with an immense effort, got back on his feet. As he inched his way across the park, he saw two customers enter the pharmacy. He also noticed an armed guard standing near the entrance, as well as multiple security cameras.

He'd have to get in and out quickly. Once he showed his face, the police wouldn't be long in following. He'd also need a car to get away. There was a reasonable amount of traffic on the street outside, but he wasn't at all confident of his ability to drive.

It wasn't much of a plan—someone was likely to get hurt, not least himself—but he gritted his teeth and kept moving. He had no choice. He could feel the initial burst of adrenaline from the accident wearing off. If he waited much longer, he'd have no fight left in him.

He stumbled into the pharmacy, pistol drawn, and had to use one of the plastic shopping carts to support himself. Blood dripped in a pool around his feet, and he made a frightful sight as he waved the gun wildly, yelling at the guard to drop his gun.

"Throw it on the ground," he yelled, "or I start shooting, and you're not going to like the mess."

The customers and cashiers were terrified, and Lance saw the hesitation in the guard's eyes. He limped over to him and grabbed the gun from its holster at his waist. "What's the police response time," he said to the guard.

The guard looked like he'd never heard of the concept and merely shook his head. Lance glanced at the clock above the dispensing counter and figured he had about ten minutes—maybe less. He was in no state for a shootout. He had to get what he needed as quickly as possible, then get out of there before the police showed.

He looked around the store. Everyone was staring at him

—cashiers, customers, pharmacists, their eyes wide with shock.

"All right," he said. "Everyone stay calm. I need some help, and then I'm gone." He pointed to one of the cashiers. "You," he said.

The cashier froze in fear.

"I need medical supplies," Lance said. "Bandages, gauze, alcohol, disinfectant. And a needle and thread."

She stared at him blankly.

"Go!" he snapped. "Now!"

She ran to the aisle and began filling a basket haphazardly. He hoped that in her confusion she would manage to get at least some of what he needed. He pointed at the next cashier. "You! Give me the cash from the till. Big bills. Everything. Hurry up."

She passed him the cash, and he snatched it and stuffed it in his vest, keeping an eye on the guard.

Then he turned to the pharmacist at the dispensing counter, a woman in her twenties with a white coat and glasses, and said, "You, come here."

She didn't move.

Lance pulled open his shredded pants, showing her the mess of blood and mangled flesh. "I need you to give me something fast. Antibiotics. Painkillers. The strongest you have." She seemed calm and began gathering the items he needed.

He looked at the clock—three minutes had passed. The first cashier came back with a shopping basket full of supplies. "Toothpaste?" he said to her.

She was too terrified to function. There was a sewing kit among the items she'd gathered, as well as disinfectant, and he put them in his pocket. Then he put the basket on the ground and limped toward the dispensing counter. The pharmacist had gone into a secure room at the back and he leaned over the counter to see her. She came rushing toward him with a bunch of medications, rounding the counter and handing him some pills and a plastic cup of water. He knocked back the pills while she jabbed a long syringe into a brown glass bottle and sucked up the contents.

"What's that?" Lance said.

"It will help."

He had no choice but to trust her.

She handed him the needle and said, "It needs to go in the leg."

"You do it," he said, looking at the clock again.

She jammed the syringe into his calf, and he instantly felt its effect. His body grew very heavy, and he began to slump slowly toward the ground. It had gone straight to his muscles, and it wouldn't be long before the fog closed in on his mind too.

Outside, he could already hear the police sirens getting closer.

"Alcohol," he said to the pharmacist.

"To drink?"

"No. Not to drink."

She grabbed a bottle of surgical alcohol and poured it liberally on his leg, sending an inferno of pain through every synapse in his body. He gripped her arm in reflex. Her eyes locked on him. He was holding her so tight he was hurting her.

He let go. "I need you to wrap it," he said.

She nodded and pulled away his torn pants. His vision blurred, and then, for the briefest moment, he blacked out completely. The sound of his gun hitting the tiled floor brought him back. He grabbed the pistol and waved it around. No one had moved an inch. He looked at the clock —seven minutes had passed since his arrival. Time was up.

The pharmacist wrapped his leg tightly in fresh gauze, and it immediately began to turn red with blood. The sirens were growing louder by the second.

Lance pulled himself to his feet and said, "Thank you," to the pharmacist as he dragged himself out of the store, knocking products from the shelves as he went.

He staggered into the middle of the street and pointed his pistol at the first car to come his way. The driver jammed the brakes, and his head slammed against the steering wheel as the car skidded to a halt, mere inches in front of Lance.

Lance motioned with the gun for him to get out of the car. "Come on! Leave the keys. Hurry."

The man got out and backed away from the car as the police sirens grew closer and closer. As Lance got into the driver's seat, he saw the lights of the first police car in his rearview mirror. He put his foot down, gunned the engine, and the car lurched forward with a screech of burning rubber. He picked up speed and tore around the first corner onto a side street, smashing the side of the car against a dumpster. He accelerated again and blew past a stop sign, losing a wing mirror on its metal pole.

He was dizzy from the drug and blood loss, barely able to lift his foot from the gas pedal to the brake, and careened wildly around corners and along narrow alleyways until he reached a ramp onto the Garden Ring. There, he swerved into the faster-moving traffic as horns blared and a large transport truck narrowly avoided ramming into his rear.

In the sky above, the red and blue lights of a police helicopter were already closing in.

81

Tatyana sat in the Mercedes and watched the entrance to Igor's building. Her fingers drummed a staccato rhythm on the steering wheel. She was growing impatient. Maybe he wouldn't show. Maybe he'd already gone to ground.

He had to know she was coming for him.

She looked at her watch. More than an hour had passed. Sofia and Olga would be getting to the extraction point soon. The plane would arrive shortly too. If she didn't leave in the next few minutes, she'd miss the flight.

The plan was for her to be on the plane, but there was no way she was leaving without Igor. His number was up, and she was going to be the one to deliver the *coup de grâce*, no matter what it took.

It wasn't just the mission. It was personal.

Looking back at her life, at her time in the GRU, on some subconscious level, she'd always known this was how it had to end. There was no other way. It all came back to that thirty-eight-cent dose of streptomycin—and to those days, as a four-year-old child, she'd spent trapped in a two-room apartment in Saint Petersburg with her mother's corpse.

The men who'd recruited her, who'd trained her, who'd prostituted her in service of the Motherland, were the same men who'd condemned her mother to that lonely, painful death—the same ones who'd failed to maintain the freon pipe on her father's submarine.

They weren't her compatriots, they weren't on her side, they were her enemy, and the time for reckoning had come.

She'd known it the moment Sofia handed her the vial.

The two women never discussed it. They never explicitly agreed on what they were going to do. It was somehow just understood, communicated invisibly between them, that they had to resist—they had to fight back.

They knew that if they didn't get that virus out of the hands of the men who controlled them, no one else would.

There'd been two vials that night at the institute. Sofia gave one of them to Tatyana. That was the act of resistance, and Tatyana, without any prior coordination or planning, left that vial outside the US consulate in Istanbul with nothing more than the name of a soldier she'd once met written on the front of the envelope.

The reason she was outside Igor's apartment now, apart from the revenge she was intent on taking, was that the second vial was still missing. It was the sole loose end. The lab in Yekaterinburg was gone. The live strains had been incinerated. The research had all been destroyed.

But what of that second vial?

Tatyana lit a cigarette and cracked open the window. She knew Sofia had turned it over to Yevchenko and that Yevchenko had passed it up the chain to Moscow. But where had it ended up? Roth had found no mention of it in his intercepts, but Tatyana had a hunch.

Her cell began to ring, and she looked at the screen. It was Roth's operator. She wondered if it was worth the risk to answer it. The comms ran on US military satellites, and she'd been assured they were secure, but she'd seen enough to know nothing was ever completely secure, especially when you were sitting in a car outside Igor Aralov's apartment in Central Moscow.

She looked again at the building. Still no sign of life. Maybe the call related to Igor—to his location.

She answered, and a computerized voice said, "Please hold for local connection."

That was strange. Who could be calling her locally? A man's voice, hoarse and breathless, gasped at her. "Tatyana Aleksandrova?"

She recognized it instantly. It was a voice she hadn't heard since that fateful day in Damascus, but she remembered it as clearly as if she'd heard it yesterday.

"Lance Spector," she said.

"I was told you're in Moscow."

"You sound hurt."

"I need your help," he said.

"Of course."

"I haven't completed the mission," he said, his voice very weak. "The vial, it's still out there."

"I'm at Igor's apartment building now," she said.

"Is he there?"

"Not yet." She looked at her watch. "You should get to the extraction point. You could still make it."

"I'm not going anywhere," he said, breathing so heavily she could barely make out the words.

"Lance, what's happened? Where are you?"

His voice was getting weaker by the second. "I'm hurt, Tatyana. I won't be making it to the extraction point."

"You sound drugged. What did you take?"

"My leg is a mess. I sewed it with a needle and thread but...."

"Where are you?"

"It doesn't matter."

"Of course it matters. I'll come for you."

"You have to finish the mission," he said, gasping for breath. "You have to get the last vial."

"I'll try," she said, "but when it's done, I'm coming for you."

"No. That will take too much time. You have to get to the airfield."

"I'm not going without you."

"You have to."

"You saved my life once," she said. "I'm not leaving you behind."

He laughed, a wheezy, gasping laugh. "This is no time for grand gestures, Tatyana. The GRU will find you if you stay."

"Tell me where you are."

"Tatyana," he said, slurring the word badly. Then he went silent, and she wondered if the connection had been dropped.

"Lance? Lance! Are you there?"

"I'm here."

"You're losing consciousness."

"No, I'm okay. It's just...."

"Just what?"

"I've lost a lot of blood." There was another long pause, then he said, "Did you find our friends?"

"The doctors? Yes. They were at the address you called in. They're on their way to the extraction point now."

"That's good," he said.

She could hear it in his voice. He was giving up. He wasn't going to make it. She looked at her watch again. She had to get him to tell her his location.

"Tell Roth..." he muttered, the words fading to nothing.

"Lance!" she cried. "Where are you?"

The drug had kicked in completely. He wasn't hearing her anymore.

"Please, Lance, tell me where you are."

"What about Laurel?" he said.

"Lance. Stay with me. Do you hear me?"

She heard coughing.

"Lance? Remember what you did for me in Damascus?"

"Damascus?" he said. "There was something I was going to tell you on the chopper."

The chopper? She'd never been with him on a chopper. He was losing it.

"Clarice was pregnant," he said. "When Roth ordered her death, she was pregnant."

"I'm sorry, Lance, but you need to tell me where you are."

"Get Igor. That's the only thing that matters now."

Tatyana's mind ran back over everything she knew of Lance, what she'd seen and what she'd heard, and realized there was only one way—that there had only ever been one way—of getting his attention. "Lance," she said. "I need your help."

There was a pause, then he said, "You need my help?"

"I'm hurt, Lance. Bad. I need you to save me."

"Where are you?"

"No. I'll come to you. Tell me where you are, and I'll come to you."

"You'll come to me?"

"I'll come to you, Lance, and you can save me."

He was silent for a moment, then he said, "It was my baby."

She thought maybe he was crying. "Lance," she cried. "You have to save me. Where are you?"

"I'm off the Garden Ring. Do you know Krasnye Vorota?"

"Yes."

"I'm in the park by the metro. At the payphones."

"You can't stay there, Lance. They'll find you."

"I have a car."

"All right. Listen to me. Go to your car and wait there. I'll find you." She needed to get there soon, or he was done for. "Go wait in the car, Lance," she said again. "I'll come. I promise."

"No," he said. "Don't come here. Go to the airfield."

"Watch for me, Lance. I'll come, and you can save me."

The line went dead.

"Lance?" she cried. "Lance!"

82

"Don't speed," Laurel said.

She was sitting next to Piotr as they drove north from the city toward the airfield. She kept her eyes on the rearview mirror, terrified that at any moment, the flashing lights of a police car would show up behind them.

But none did, and as they got further from the city, she felt the tension lift from her body. They were following the directions to the extraction point she'd received from the phone operator, and there wasn't much further to go.

"Thank you for doing this," she said to Piotr as he turned off the highway onto a forest road.

"You know," he said, turning to look at her, "I thought you were dead when I saw you."

She nodded.

He looked back to the road. He seemed tense, driving deliberately—checking his indicators over and over like a pilot before takeoff. "You were so still," he continued, "lying there, blue with cold."

She nodded.

"The water on your skin was beginning to freeze—to crystalize. It made you sparkle."

She wondered where he was going with this.

"I thought you were some sort of ghost."

"I see."

"And then you moved, and I swear my heart almost stopped."

"I'm sorry," she said.

"No, no," he said, "don't apologize. I'm just saying...."

"I'm sure I made a strange sight."

He nodded.

"You can't ever tell anyone about it," she said. "That you found me. That you helped me. Not even that you were there."

"I know."

"Your life would be at stake."

He nodded again, and they drove on, following the road through increasingly dense forest. After a few minutes, he said, "My sister drowned in that river."

Laurel turned to look at him but said nothing.

"Not far from where I found you," he said.

"When was that?"

"A long time ago. We were children. That's why I thought you were dead."

"I'm sorry, Piotr."

"You were... otherworldly."

"I see."

"I thought you were her."

Laurel put a hand on his shoulder.

They drove on in silence. The road got narrower and windier. After a few more miles, there was a turnoff onto a narrow, unpaved track. It hadn't been plowed, but there were tire tracks in the snow.

"This is it," Laurel said.

Piotr stopped the car and kept the engine running. "I don't think I can get up there," he said.

According to the directions, the airfield was less than a mile up the track. "You've done enough," Laurel said. "I can walk from here."

"I'll come with you."

"No," Laurel said, putting her hand on his shoulder again. "You've come far enough."

"I can't leave you here," he said, looking around at the bleak scene.

"Yes, you can."

"What if—"

"You saved my life," she said. "Now get back to the city and never breathe a word of this to anyone."

Before she left, he took off his thick jacket and gave it to her.

"Thank you," she said.

"She looked like you," Piotr said. "Your eyes."

Laurel nodded, then turned toward the path. The snow was deep, and it took an effort to trudge through it. She made her way slowly, and the car remained where it was until she was out of sight.

The moon was out, and the sky was clear. Laurel thought she'd never seen stars so bright. She kept going until she heard the sound of an engine. It came from a clearing up ahead, and she crouched to survey the scene without making herself visible. A rudimentary airstrip, a few hundred yards long and no wider than an ordinary road, had been cut through the trees. She couldn't see if it was paved or not, but at the far end was a small twin-engine turboprop aircraft. The plane's lights lit up the runway, and a man in a black peacoat was inspecting the snow.

Laurel got closer to him, and he looked up.

"Everlane?" he said.

"Yes."

"Your friends are in the plane."

"Friends?"

"Two women. Civilian. Russian."

Laurel went to the plane and looked inside. Two women were sitting in the passenger cabin, huddled together under a blanket, trying to keep warm. When they saw Laurel, one of them raised a gun.

"Whoa!" Laurel said. "We don't want that going off when we're in the air."

"Who are you?" the woman said in Russian.

"My name is Laurel Everlane."

"You're with the CIA?"

"Yes, I am."

The woman lowered the gun.

"And you are?" Laurel said.

"My name is Sofia Ivanova," she said. "This is my friend, Olga Abramova."

"You sent us the vial," Laurel said.

Sofia nodded. "What about Lance?" she said.

Laurel made to speak but stopped. She shook her head.

"What is it?" Sofia said. "What happened?"

Laurel felt a knot in her throat.

"He was supposed to meet us," Sofia said. "We can't leave without him."

"I saw—" Laurel said, but the knot in her throat stopped her.

"You saw *what*?"

"I saw him go down. No one's walking away from that."

Sofia went quiet. Laurel turned back to the pilot. "Are we good to go?" she said. "Can we take off?"

"I'm ready when you are," the pilot said, looking at his watch. "We have room for two more, but our window is narrow enough as it is."

Sofia spoke again. "What about Tatyana Aleksandrova? She was supposed to be here too."

"I'm sorry," Laurel said. "I don't know anything about that."

"She said she'd meet us. We can't leave without them."

"We can't wait," Laurel said again, then to the pilot, "All right. Let's go. Get us out of here."

She knew how the safety window for their takeoff was created—an experimental CIA jamming algorithm that would mask them from Russian radar. Even under the most ideal circumstances, their chances of making the entire flight without being spotted were slim, and these were definitely not ideal circumstances. The Russians would detect them sooner or later, and when that happened, the humble civilian turboprop would be as easy to shoot from the sky as a fattened turkey.

Langley was prepared for their detection and would be coordinating with the pilot to plant a false flight path in the Russian central flight tracker as soon as they were spotted, but that system was far from perfect. There would be a *flicker* in the Russian aviation control system, a moment when their plane, as well as its authorization codes and telemetry, essentially appeared from nowhere. In the vastness of the Russian airspace, such a blip would usually go unnoticed, especially if they were far from any sensitive targets, but after what had happened in the Kremlin that night, the Russians would be on heightened alert. If anyone, anywhere in Russian civilian or military flight control grew suspicious, or suspected for a second that they were part of a CIA rendition operation, then there was nothing Langley could do to help them.

"I can't believe you're leaving them behind," Sofia said as the pilot powered up the engines.

Laurel only shook her head, then turned to the pilot and, with more strain in her voice than she wanted, said, "Come on! If we're going, let's go."

The pilot brought the engines to full power, and the plane began to roll slowly forward. "Buckle up," he said. "This might be a little hairy." He opened the throttle, and the plane accelerated rapidly. The line of trees at the end of the runway rushed toward them, and at the last second, the plane broke contact with the ground and pitched upward, its wheels brushing the tops of the trees and sending a shudder through the craft that threatened to destabilize them before they ever got going.

"Hold on!" the pilot shouted, gripping the controls. The three women held onto their seats as the plane yawed left and right violently. Then it leveled, and the pilot said, "All right. We're airborne."

They took off facing an eastward direction and then turned northward, away from the city. They kept going north toward Arkhangelsk for almost two hours, and when they were detected by Russian radar, they immediately banked westward in a dramatic maneuver that terrified Olga and Sofia.

"Did it work?" Laurel said when they were on the new course and seemed to be flying smoothly again.

"We'll find out," the pilot said. "We're clear of the Saint Petersburg Air Defense District."

"Which is a good thing?" Olga said.

The pilot nodded, but the look on his face did not suggest that they were out of the woods yet.

Laurel leaned back in her seat and shut her eyes. They were all tense, painfully aware that they were fully visible to Russian systems and that at any second, they could be shot out of the sky without warning. They flew like that for two hours, no one saying so much as a word, until the pilot finally announced that they'd entered Finnish airspace.

83

Tatyana recognized Igor's silhouette from all the way down the street. His lumbering gait had been etched into her mind so deeply she'd have known it a mile away. He was alone, and as he shuffled toward the building, he kept checking compulsively over his shoulder that he wasn't being followed.

He lived in Tverskaya, an upscale neighborhood with more than its share of bars and restaurants, and there was a fair amount of bustle on the street despite the hour. Igor approached the entrance, nodding to the doorman as he passed. Perhaps he said something to him—it was difficult to tell.

The building was desirable enough in that utilitarian Stalinist way that seemed to attract GRU officials above a certain paygrade. The doorman's uniform was vaguely military—a double-breasted blazer with brass details—and in the lobby, two armed guards sat behind an imposing desk.

Tatyana threw her cigarette out the window and checked her gun.

She could have barged through the lobby, guns blazing,

but she preferred not to. Igor lived with his wife of forty years, and there was no reason, as far as Tatyana was concerned, to get blood all over the woman's carpets. She'd suffered enough for her husband's sins.

Tatyana had met her once. They even spoke. It was at one of the Main Directorate's painfully awkward social events, and Tatyana had spent most of the night purposefully trying to avoid her. She felt guilty for what had happened between herself and Igor, not that she'd had any control over it, but if his wife suspected anything, she didn't let on. She knew her role as well as everyone else at that party, and she played it to a tee.

Tatyana had been in the restroom, reapplying her lipstick, when Igor's wife came in. Tatyana pretended not to notice her, she did everything possible to avoid eye contact, but the woman sidled up next to her at the vanity and said, "You needn't be afraid of me."

"What makes you say that?" Tatyana said.

"You've been avoiding me."

"I have not."

The woman leaned toward the mirror and looked at herself closely, touching up her makeup from a compact. "It's awkward," she said. "I get it."

"There's nothing—"

"I know how it goes," she said, holding Tatyana's eye. "I was you once, and not so very long ago."

Tatyana looked at her more closely. "I didn't know."

"I've been in your shoes, and you'll be in mine sooner than you think. We're in the same boat, you and I."

Someone else entered then, and Igor's wife got up and left, but the conversation stayed with Tatyana. It gave her something to think about—perhaps it had even pushed her toward this current path.

She lit another cigarette and looked at her watch again. Five minutes had passed since Igor went up. He would come back down, she told herself. She was certain of it. There was no way he had gone up for the night. The GRU was in disarray. The Kremlin was on red alert. She knew how Igor was. He'd be terrified, impulsive—he'd make mistakes. He would come back down in a matter of minutes, and when he did, if she was very lucky, he just might be carrying the thing she'd come for.

She was holding the gun Lance had given her. She looked at it—at the Star of David that Roth's father had carved into the handle. Lance gave it to her on her first real mission. Now she was going to use it to end her last.

She looked at her watch again—it had been ten minutes. She considered going up to the apartment and was about to step out of the car when she saw Igor's distinctive hunched posture appear in the doorway. He was carrying a briefcase.

Tatyana felt a rush of adrenaline. This was it—the moment she'd been waiting for.

And then she saw that he wasn't alone. His wife was with him, struggling to keep up in high heels and an elegant white coat that reached almost to her ankles. Behind her, she pulled a small suitcase on wheels that, combined with the coat, made her look like an air hostess hurrying through an airport terminal. Igor waited for her at the bottom of the steps, then grabbed her by the arm and yanked her with him, back down the street in the direction he'd arrived from.

It was strange that there was no car waiting for them. There was always a car—always a driver. He wasn't just on the run from the CIA, Tatyana realized. He was on the run from his own side too.

She pulled the car out of its spot and began driving slowly down the street after them, matching their speed, maintaining a distance of about a hundred yards. When they reached the park, and the street lights on the sidewalk grew a little dimmer, she pulled up next to them and said through the open window, "Good evening, Mr. Director."

Igor turned and, when he saw her face, stopped dead. "You!" he gasped.

"Didn't expect to see me?" she said, pointing her gun squarely between his eyes.

"I thought—"he stammered.

"You thought what?"

"I can give you anything you want."

"And you will, Igor," she said. "You will."

He glanced around desperately, searching for a route of escape. There was none. Tatyana knew he was armed, but there was no way he'd be able to draw his gun fast enough. She turned her attention to the wife. "Mrs. Aralov," she said, "remember me?"

The wife looked surprisingly calm, given the circumstances. "Tatyana Aleksandrova," she said. "I remember you."

"Can I ask you something personal?" Tatyana said.

The wife nodded. Tatyana had noticed before that she was an elegant woman, but this was the first time she appreciated just how beautiful she was. She wondered what Igor must have done to land a woman like her. Nothing good, she imagined. "Do you love your husband?" she said.

The woman didn't miss a beat. "What do you think?"

"I think not."

"Why, you ungrateful whore!" Igor spat.

"Go," Tatyana said to her. "Go home and stay there. I think you can see how this is going to end."

The woman didn't need to be told twice. She turned and

walked back toward the apartment, the little suitcase rumbling along on the pavement behind her.

Igor watched her leave, then turned to Tatyana. "Well, what are you waiting for? You know what you're going to do."

"I do," Tatyana said.

"I won't beg, if that's what you're hoping."

"I'm not hoping that."

"That's the difference between you and me," he continued. "You were always so willing to get on your knees."

She smiled thinly. "I'm glad you remember," she said, "because this," and she raised the gun a little higher, "is for that day." She pulled the trigger.

His head jerked backward, and his feet left the ground as the bullet entered his skull. He landed flat on his back, three feet from where he'd been standing.

Some people across the street saw what happened and scattered. Tatyana let them run.

She got out of the car, the cigarette still in her mouth, and threw it on Igor's chest. Then she stepped on it, crushing it beneath her Italian leather shoe.

She reached down and touched his neck, confirming he was dead, then picked up the metal briefcase he'd been carrying and put it on the hood of the car. She expected it to be locked, but when she clicked the two latches on the sides, it opened. Inside, it had a protective foam lining, and at the center of the lining was a cutout segment securing a small titanium case. It was identical to the one Sofia had given her at the institute in Yekaterinburg.

She shut the case and got back in the car. Before pulling away, she looked at Igor one final time. She'd imagined this moment before—what she'd say to him before she shot him, how she'd feel when she pulled the trigger—but now that it was done, she didn't feel anything.

He'd always occupied such an outsized position in her imagination, like a monster from the murky depths of the sea. He'd been a mystery, an unknown. But now, he was nothing more than a corpse washed ashore, and she felt that she was finally seeing him for what he truly was. She was seeing all of them—those men who ruled the expanse of Russia—for what they truly were. Theirs was a domain that stretched over six thousand miles, a quarter of the way around the globe, and they truly were monsters.

But not the monsters she'd imagined. They were not ferocious. They were not lions. They were frail, cowardly, skulking things, afraid of their own shadows, terrified of losing what treasure they'd managed to eke out for themselves, guarding it with such jealousy that it warped every fiber of their being.

And yet, beneath their thumb was the button that could destroy the world. Theirs was the power to erase everything, to wipe it all away, to unmake what only a god could make. It made them demigods, after a fashion.

And yet, for all that, when they died, they went out the same way as everyone else, not with a bang but a whimper.

She pulled the car into the street and drove north onto the Garden Ring, then east toward Krasnye Vorota, where Lance had called her from.

The area was quiet when she got there. There were some police sirens in the distance but nothing too close. She got out of the car, taking the briefcase with her, and saw the payphones in the park. They were deserted now, eerily silent in the blue glow of a streetlamp.

She walked along the street, checking every car to see if anyone was inside. She stopped when she saw blood on the door handle of a gray Škoda. She drew her gun and looked around, then approached it slowly. The driver's seat was empty, but looking through the window, she could see that the seat was covered in blood. On the passenger seat were the signs of a hastily executed first aid job—a sewing kit, gauze, and a bottle of surgical alcohol. She glanced around again, but no one was there.

And then she heard it—a phone ringing. It was one of the payphones in the park, the analog ringer clanging so loudly it startled her. She scanned the street, then crossed it, entered the park, and approached the phone. It kept ringing. She picked up the receiver and said, "This is Tatyana."

"Do you see the hotel across the park? The one next to the dome?"

"Lance!"

"I'm in room 402."

"I'll be right there."

She crossed the park and entered the hotel, a modest place with a single old-style caged elevator at the far end of the lobby.

"Can I help you?" the concierge said from behind the desk.

She looked at him closely, tried to get a read on him, then said, "I'm expected by one of your guests."

He nodded, and she took the elevator to the fourth floor. She found Lance's door and rapped lightly. "It's me, Tatyana."

There was no answer. She waited a few seconds and knocked again. Then the door opened. Lance stood in front of her, leaning heavily against the door, his pant leg in tatters. There was blood on his hands and face, and behind him on the white bedsheets was a large, crimson stain.

"We can't stay here," he said. "The concierge saw the

state I was in. He'll make the call."

"Lance!" Tatyana said, her mind racing through the memories she had of him—the moment they'd met, the hotel room, her offer to stay there with him. What she remembered most vividly, what she'd never forget for as long as she lived, was that he'd saved her life. Were it not for him, she'd have perished on that very first mission.

He looked at her for a second, his eyes flicking left and right between her eyes, then he collapsed to the ground.

She bent down, grabbed him under the arms, and pulled him into the room, then shut the door and locked it. They wouldn't stay long—just a few minutes. It was clear he'd taken something. A few minutes' sleep would clear his mind, then she would revive him and get him somewhere safe. She took the blanket off the bed and put it over him, then sat down and watched him.

She lit a cigarette. The room was not dissimilar to the one she'd met him in, and as she tapped her ash onto the carpet, a feeling came over her that everything that had happened in the intervening years—all the violence, and degradation, and deceit—was being washed away. It was like she was being transported directly from that room in Damascus to this one now, and nothing in between mattered.

The moment passed, and she stood up, went to the window, and pulled back the lace curtain. The street below was as deserted as before. She could see the phones in the park beneath the lamp.

She turned and looked again at Lance, then went over and tapped him lightly on the cheek. "Lance," she said, "it's me. It's Tatyana."

He opened his eyes slowly.

"Time to go," she said.

AUTHOR'S NOTE

First off, I want to thank you for reading my book. As a reader, you might not realize how important a person like you is to a person like me.

I've been a writer for fifty years, and despite the upheavals life brings, the ups and downs, the highs and lows, one thing remains constant.

You. The reader.

And I'd like to take a moment to acknowledge that fact and to thank you. Not just on my own behalf, but on behalf of all fiction writers. Because without you, these books simply would not exist. You're the reason they're written, your support is what makes them possible, and your reviews and recommendations are what spread the word.

So, thank you. I really do mean it.

Writing about politics is not easy, and I hope none of my personal thoughts and opinions managed to find their way into this story. I never intend to make political arguments in my writing, and I never intend to take a stand. I'm one of those guys who stays out of political arguments, and I would hate to think that any political ideas raised in the book hampered your ability to enjoy the story or relate to the characters.

I write about people who work for the federal government. The nature of their work brings them up against issues of national security and politics, but apart from that, I truly do try to keep any views I might have to myself.

Because really, this is your story. These characters are your characters. When you read the book, no one knows what the characters look like, what they sound like, what they truly think and feel, but you. The experience is created in your mind as you flip the pages. It belongs to you, not me.

So please, don't let any of my words offend you, and if you spot anything in my writing that you feel is unfair or biased or off-color in any way, feel free to let me know. I do make edits based on reader suggestions.

My email address is below, and if you send a message, while I might not get back to you immediately, I will receive it, and I will read it.

saulherzog@authorcontact.com

Likewise, if you spot simpler errors, like typos and misspellings, let me know about those too. We writers have a saying: To err is human. To edit, divine. And we live by it.

I'm going to talk a little about some of the true facts that this book is based on, but before I do, I'd like to ask for a favor.

I know you're a busy person, I know you just finished this book and are eager to get on to whatever is next, but if you could find it in your heart to leave me a review, I would be truly humbled.

There's really nothing I can offer you in return for the kindness—but a kindness it is, and I rely on it.

If you leave me a review, it will help my career. It will help my series to flourish and find new readers. It will make a difference to one guy, one stranger, you've never met and likely never will. That's got to count for something.

Okay, now that those formalities are out of the way, let's talk about mammoths.

Strange creatures from the past really do turn up in the Siberian steppe all the time. The ground there thaws and freezes. Land that might have been permafrost for thousands of years melts. And bones get moved around.

In 1901, herders in the town of Srednekolymsk in the far north of Yakutia found a fully intact woolly mammoth on a riverbank. Prehistoric animals have been turning up ever since. Not just mammoths, but ancient dogs, steppe ponies, woolly rhinos, and wolves.

There are so many that some hunters in the region have traded in their rifles and traps for spades. A mammoth tusk on the Chinese market can fetch upwards of sixteen thousand dollars. Searching for such remains is illegal, and one of the reasons is because of how well-preserved the carcasses are. They were frozen so completely that they still contain their teeth, their hair, and in some cases, liquid blood. Their DNA is in such good condition that some scientists have suggested they could clone the animals and bring them back from extinction.

But what scares the authorities is the germs. Diseases are found in the ice all the time: anthrax, smallpox, the bubonic plague. Researchers believe it's only a matter of time before something even more lethal, some ancient pathogen that has not been seen since the beginning of the last Ice Age, comes to light. And the fear is that when it does, the Russian military will be waiting.

It won't be the first time they've taken pathogens from the permafrost and weaponized them. Starting in the 1970s, the Soviet Union began scouring hospitals, labs, history books, and ancient carcasses, searching for pathogens that could be turned into biological super-weapons. Eventually, a vast network of secret laboratories spread across the country, employing thirty thousand researchers and manufacturing enough germs to kill every person on the planet a thousand times over.

The pathogens they worked on included: smallpox, bubonic plague, anthrax, Venezuelan equine encephalitis, tularemia, influenza, brucellosis, marburg virus, machupo virus, veepox, and ebolapox. The entire program contravened the 1972 Biological Weapons Convention, and while the CIA suspected it was happening, they had no idea how far the Russians took it.

It wasn't until 1979, when a major outbreak of pulmonary anthrax poisoned hundreds of people close to the Biopreparat facility in Sverdlovsk, now Yekaterinburg, that the West realized what was going on. The Kremlin immediately initiated a cover-up, blaming the outbreak on tainted meat, but the German newspaper, *Bild Zeitung,* published a story claiming the deaths were the result of weaponized pathogens. While the Biopreparat facility was suspected of being a weapons program from then on, it was not until a Soviet defector named Vladimir Pasechnik exposed the vast scale of the operation that the West began putting pressure on the Soviets. Following a now-famous episode of the news program *Frontline* in 1998, the US and UK insisted on inspections.

These inspections were resisted by the Russians, and inspectors repeatedly turned up at facilities that had been hastily torn down and sterilized prior to inspection. While eighteen massive laboratories, including the Stepnogorsk Scientific and Technical Institute in Kazakhstan, the Institute of Ultra Pure Biochemical Preparations in Leningrad,

Printed in the USA
CPSIA information can be obtained
at www.ICGtesting.com
LVHW04055425012Z4
769840LV00022B/131

and the Vector State Research Center in Koltsovo were eventually discovered, the true scale of the Russian bioweapons program remains a closely guarded Kremlin secret.

There are a number of books on the subject, and I personally recommend *The Dead Hand: The Untold Story of the Cold War Arms Race and Its Dangerous Legacy* by David Hoffman. The book is available on Kindle and Audible and makes for some fascinating reading. If you do read it, you'll see how it influenced many of the plotlines in this book.

Finally, I'd be remiss if I did not tell you that Book Two in the Lance Spector series, *The Russian*, is now available. The second book begins just hours after the events in the first wrap up. Lance and Tatyana are still in Moscow, and an assassin is *en route*.

So grab your copy now. I promise, if you enjoyed the first, you're only going to be drawn into these characters more deeply!

God bless and happy reading,
Saul Herzog